Curse by Rich Hayden

2016 Rich Hayden

ISBN# 978-0-9963969-3-6

Chapter 1 - Overture: The Exploits of Insignificant Lives

Part 1. Fog Lake

Time is eternal. Or, at the very least, it will endure beyond the expiration of everything else. The final force of the universe, to, at last, surrender to the command of sleep. The conquest of time is unrelenting and the path it cuts bores on with yield to none. In its wake, discovery and revelation arrive, carrying with them technology, advancement, and opportunity. The surge of these forces, however, do not run stride for stride along with time. No, they take a much more mercurial and meandering tumble down the hourglass.

In the modern developed world, certain pleasurable aspects of everyday life are expected, if not entirely taken for granted. This truth rings nowhere with more volume and vigor than in America. But strife and the unrefined still linger in dark, forgotten corners and deep in the backwoods of the Home of the Brave. Many who occupy the cities and suburbs can scarcely imagine a life of even marginal inconvenience. Those who reside in more rural settings are equally deficient in the total comprehension of actual struggle, as they tend fields and raise livestock while lending attention to smart phones. But the rugged past, ill-fitted with all its hardships, lives on quietly.

In order to discover such a woeful place, a traveler would need more than a map and an automobile. A sense of adventure and the willingness to absorb despondency are the tools necessary to complete such a curious journey. This is a road rarely traversed, as no one elects to vacation to surroundings more miserable than their own. The only souls that can testify to the condition of the spaces that time's companions have forgotten are those that call such environs home.

There is a shriveled mass of land which appears to hang meekly from the western portion of Virginia before dying off into the embrace of Kentucky. Across this land, crushed under the weight of the Appalachian Mountains, runs Route 460. Flanked by an abundance of chicory and the dark blue flowers that it produces, a drive down 460 can be quite beautiful, especially as the autumn warns of the winter scourge to come. Near the state line of the Old Dominion rests the remains of Fog Lake. Route 460 can deliver a visitor to the small town, but not a single sign or exit marker cares to point the way. Along that stretch of rural highway, not even faded glints from the past cast a remembrance to lost little Fog Lake.

Like a ghost enwreathed in shadow, Fog Lake's absorption into obscurity is near completion. This is not an entirely unfortunate twist of events, as all things must reach their end. After all, even milk, with all its life-giving properties, must at times be cast aside once all that was once sustenance has gone rotten. The town is inhabited only by those who have never left, and outsiders are most unwelcome within this living museum of disadvantage. The air that occupies the empty spaces of Fog Lake is warmed only by humidity. The seldom observed yeti of laughter, which echoes though the broken streets, is nothing more than a joy imposter. A fraud of authentic sensation conjured up by the likes of Pruno and homemade drugs.

Every morning, the lethargic sun rises over Fog Lake. A dense haze descends from the peaks above and suffocates the whole of the village. For a moment, this ephemeral blanket feels like a blessing, as it shields from vision all the collapsing barns and untended fields. It buries the decay of the town and hides the slow drowning of scattered trailer homes that are giving in to the unsettled will of the earth. The fog obscures the weathered face of Fog Lake High School and the crumbling foundation upon which it sits. It hides the overabundance of bars and all the despair that they bring, and the great, thick cloud momentarily dulls the image of all the businesses fallen into dereliction.

But the fog is merely a cloak. For every day it lifts, and returns to view the dirt paths and crooked streets fitted with rusted lampposts and faded signs. It brings back to a half-life all the misery of a typical day in Fog Lake. As the swirl rises from the stagnant pool from which the town receives its name, it reveals a damp bed that plays perpetual host to a mosquito orgy. As the humid cloud ushers in the day, it rises with the grace of a fat, arthritic hag as she lifts her heft from a misplaced and beleaguered porch sofa. Toothless, and bent by a life of ill-value, she stares sideways at the girls who push strollers with their teenaged hands. She watches the men as they stagger to work, still sickened by the previous night's boozing. She hears the backfiring of pickup trucks and the obnoxious squeal of fan belts and chokes on the exhaust exhaled from outdated engines. In disgust, she turns away and dissipates into the sky, leaving Fog Lake to rot under the condemning glare of the sun.

As time has cruelly scrubbed its eraser over the town, only paltry value remains. It feels as though Fog Lake is nothing more than a forgotten postcard of Americana from yesteryear. Most of the rail lines, once roaring proud, have been shut down. The few that have managed to cling to existence do so only with the merits of outdated and faulty equipment. A small collection of mines are still operational, but there is more money to be found in crime than from coal. Merchant shops have been turned into seedy strip clubs, and construction equipment rots at the very site of the last job when the money ran out. These mechanized behemoths dot the land like industrial headstones, lost in the shadows of buildings unfinished and over roads never to be completed.

It was within this dying testament to a bitter way of life that Amil Young was born. His father ran into the woods one winter's night, never to return to the world of man. Absorbed into blowing snow and sharpened ice, he ran, nearly naked and wild eyed. His flight from the earth was blamed on madness, but such an affliction fails to explain the absence of a body. After the presumed death of his father, Amil's mother suffered a failure of the mind. Her mental discord sprang from a much less mysterious well, as methamphetamine sunk its hooks into her. Disinterested in childcare, she gave her only son over to his grandparents at three years of age. If thoughts of reconciliation were buried somewhere deep inside of Amil's mother, the drugs paid no mind, as death entertained no detour en route to claim the savaged remains of Raylene Young. In the end, it all made little difference to the orphaned boy.

He never truly knew his parents, and once he was old enough to craft a shaky understanding of them, his feelings were without affection. A blind man gazing upon blank paper, the child was bereft of the arousal of sympathy for his departed creators. Any compassion that he might come to find was eroded away by the name with which he had been branded. At times, he was reminded that the name once belonged to an ancestor of his who fought bravely in the Civil War. Amil was unimpressed. He tired of the stories early on, as his uncommon name earned him taunts from classmates.

Like most youths born into a small and moribund village, Amil landed himself into trouble as a boy. He smoked his first cigarette at nine and drank regularly by the age of sixteen. Amil was on a first name basis with the small police force, for all the wrong reasons, before he squirmed his way through the eighth grade. Thanks to his sharp tongue and the boldness that testosterone brings, he was quick to court a situation that could earn him a black eye. He wrecked three cars before he earned his license and managed to impregnate a girl just barely fifteen, but already a mother. The damned girl, overwhelmed by the needs of her own equally foredoomed child, suffered a miscarriage.

Amil couldn't summon much interest for school, as the routines and formalities grated against his restless mind. The lack of resources made keeping his attention a near impossible task for the strained faculty, whose own interest in education was pitiably thin. After long years of watching children drop out and spiral into oblivion, apathy became the lesson of the day. But Amil did manage to earn his diploma, a feat relatively uncommon in Fog Lake. He may have been something of a malcontent, bred into him from genetics and branded onto him from environment, but brighter than most. The tests he took were aced without the benefit of study, and he regularly received an impressive GPA. The boy, however, found no value in his achievements, as his intelligence was a jagged instrument.

An iron chisel employed to disfigure the materials set before it. More weapon than tool, his mind was unfit for the regulations of higher learning.

Born trash, shackled to a bleak existence during his formative years, the crafty youth used his smarts to get by and avoid the biggest of troubles. Like most teens, he overindulged when it came to alcohol, but the days of headaches and vomiting that followed would serve to end this poisonous relationship. He was a bit perplexed by those that consumed drugs. Amil would enjoy the occasional puff from a stale joint here and there, but he knew the end game of narcotics. His earliest memories gave to him the intolerable rendering of his mother as walking death. To emulate her miserable existence would be tantamount to tribute for the woman who made him an orphan. A witness to the decay and premature decline of his friends and neighbors, he found no use for pills and pipes. But a young man needs money, and so he wasn't above the peddling of such substances when the task could earn him a few dollars. After his close call with parenthood, Amil proceeded with more caution when pursuing the harlots of his hamlet, but it would take a rather nasty introduction to gonorrhea before he embraced the magic of cheap condoms.

He was still a boy by most evaluations, a child forced to grow up quick and mature, lest he sink under the same quicksand as his parents. He knew his opportunities would be few and fleeting, and this reality was made no more poignant than one night in late spring, which, initially, felt much the same as any other.

Around the age of sixteen, he was spending time at the home of a schoolmate, Maggie Dufrane. Her name rang in his ears with comedic irony. Dufrane sounded French to him, and it conjured up images of Paris. The majestic city seemed so exotic and refined, mysterious and gilded with adventure. Plain Maggie, with her acne and gapped teeth, represented to Amil all that Fog Lake could do to things magnificent and elegant.

It was a school night and the clock had spun past one in the morning as Amil sat slumped in the basement with Maggie and a few others. Those that populated the dank room weren't really friends. They were more or less a collection of people who shared a mutual tolerance. Maggie's mother was asleep upstairs. Twitching in her bed, she had been beaten into unconsciousness by sleeping pills. With her interference impossible, the teens blithely sat around passing cheap whiskey and old cigarettes.

The scene was the same as the night before and the one that had preceded it. The day to come would see a tired reprise of this stale act. Amil knew that all too well. As he sat in discomfort inside the grip of a lawn chair with algae clinging to the bands, he leaned his head against the dull paneling upon the wall, and studied the room.

Amil didn't know the kid in the Confederate flag t-shirt who was making out with a girl. She had the soft face of a child, and appeared mildly high. Robbie was there, the token twenty-something creep who hangs out with teenagers. He was entertaining two fat sluts, ripe fruit dangling from the crooked tree of adolescence. John Meyers was there, too. He was failing to play some country-trash ballad on a guitar with four strings. Finally, there was lonely Maggie. She was mired in her usual desperation. Her agony rose as the hours wound on, and became visible once two other boys left the hazy basement. As Amil viewed, and was then disgusted by the pathetic lot,

9

he felt like a prisoner. He could leave the basement, but there was no more freedom to be found outside. Not in the middle of the night, anyway. Unchained, free to roam, only to find the bars of disadvantage set to all sides. But he knew that parole would arrive one day, and until then, he would find his solace on the baseball diamond.

Like many American boys, Amil fell in love with baseball early on in life. He was then introduced to the cruelty of reality and became distracted. He warmed to cold girls and discovered the allure of poor behavior, but the siren call of the game always tugged at him. For lack of other things to do, and for want of no more nights spent in Maggie's basement of sorrows, he decided to try out for the school's floundering team.

Scrawny and aged beyond his years from the toll taken by hard country, he was downright anemic with the stick. However, he more than made up for this lack of batting prowess on the pitcher's mound. He had a knack for something complex that could conjure up jealously in nearly anyone: Amil excelled at tossing a baseball. He quickly became the star of his school's motley varsity team, and, with that recognition, the insults that his name garnered slowly dwindled away.

He tortured opposing hitters and frustrated the coaches of rival programs. Fog Lake was viewed as something of a welcome mat for other schools. They were nothing more than inbred practice dummies, crude stones used by others to sharpen their knives. When Amil pitched, something anomalous took place: they all became something more. For all his efforts, the team never really went anywhere, as they usually lost the games that their ace pitcher didn't start. It wasn't all that strange for the Fog

Lake Badgers to lose on the days that he did pitch. After all, the defense behind him had an annoying habit of lobbing the ball all over the yard.

It didn't matter. Fog Lake had never won a regional championship before, so missing the playoffs wasn't too big a deal. What did matter, what was important, was that someone from Fog Lake could eclipse the performances of anyone else around. The air still stunk, the mosquitoes continued to bite, and the home field still resembled a wasteland, but during the games in which Amil played, the stands were a little fuller, the bars a little emptier, and life, faded and scarred as it may have been, was just a tiny bit brighter.

Rival schools attempted to seduce Amil to pitch for them by the time he reached the 11th grade, but, ever stubborn, he would hear none of it. Drab and virulent as it was, he would rather pitch for his hometown Badgers and win five games a year than play for the schools that painted his whole village as a bunch of incorrigible drunks. For the most part, this disparaging sentiment was correct, Amil knew that much, but he wouldn't give those other folks the satisfaction. Maybe it was the hick in him, the absence of a proper role model, or the poverty that stalked him like a shadow. Whatever the causes, a selfish streak was harbored within him, with a deep desire to prove others wrong by doing things the hard way. After all, he was one of them, an anonymous lowlife from Fog Lake. At least, for a little while longer.

Part 2. A way out

It wasn't often that an outsider would trip across the

border into Fog Lake. There was no earthly reason to visit such a place, and few knew of its existence. But on a warm spring day, Fog Lake is where Ron Jacks found himself. His ancient grandmother had recently passed away, and it was Ron who was burdened with the task of sorting out all the garbage she disguised as possessions. He wasn't the only family Emilia Jacks had left, he was simply the only one who cared enough to go back and see that she received a proper burial.

It was an odd experience. He knew his roots were sunk in Appalachia, but he never would have guessed that the soil they grew among could have been so bitten. As he walked down Center Street toward the dilapidated wreck of his grandmother's home, Ron felt as though he were traveling back in time to some forgotten era of ignorance and lawlessness. It wasn't a Wild-West feel that he sensed. A rough yet romantic image of life lived in harder times. This was something far different, something truly sad that spoke of devolution and illness. Fog Lake, it seemed, was the cradle of misery.

The morning air was peppered with country music that sailed out from the open garage of an old body shop. It was a sharp and discordant crackle, as a stereo long past its expiration purged itself of the tunes. During his journey, Ron's nose was treated to a bouquet of exhaust, and that foul odor given off by the overgrowth of damp weeds. He looked up from the crippled sidewalk that challenged his step and set his eyes on the peaks which towered in the distance. It was a strange vision. The mountains appeared so majestic and strong, and yet at their feet lay their ill-begotten child. Gangly and suffering unspeakable torments of disease, this tortured offspring seemed to beg for the mercy of euthanasia.

At thirty-five, Ron had always been a jovial fellow, his sense of humor proportionate to his ample waist-line. But his senses cautioned him not to engage the locals. He wasn't one of them, and every black-eyed citizen of Fog Lake could smell his foreign stench. The glances they gave him were of suspicion and impatience, so Ron figured it better to keep to himself and handle his business with a quiet urgency.

The late afternoon sun began to hide behind the mountains as Ron set out to leave after a long day of tedium. He couldn't wait to hear the hum of asphalt under his wheels, as a day spent with Fog Lake's lone funeral director had given him a chill that wiggled into the marrow of his bones. The walls of the funeral home were lime green, and most of the windows were glazed by the touch of nicotine. The furniture creaked and the makeup job done on his grandmother was downright deplorable, but for all this, nothing disturbed Ron more than Morton, *The Mortician,* Ansell himself. He was a portly creep with a sweaty bald head and a gut that peaked out from the bottom of his shirt if he raised his arms too high. He smiled a lot, but never laughed, even as he made wildly inappropriate remarks about his young niece, who moped around and masqueraded as an employee.

The cemetery, which would forever hold the earthly remains of Emilia, was unkempt. The soil was loose, and barren earth peaked through the grass, while in other places, shoots and weeds raged on unchecked. Most every stone inside the grip of the small cemetery was placed crooked and washed clean by weather. Even her marker, chiseled days before, already looked aged. Once Ron laid an ordinary collection of flowers over her grave and suffered the strange glances cast by the few others that attended the burial of his grandmother, he quietly stepped away. Ron made his way down the undulating terrain and through the rusted gate of the church yard. As the outsider approached his car, he sighed to himself as an uneasy feeling of observation crept over him.

Across the broken road, he spied a couple of teenagers who studied him like an exotic animal caged in a zoo. The pair couldn't have been more than fifteen, but childhood innocence was a trait that neither possessed. The boy, a crooked, rusted rail of a man, already had crude tattoos on his arms and an equally crude hunting knife slid into his belt. He stared at Ron though narrow eyes and only diverted his gaze to spit tobacco juice. The girl, possibly the young man's sister, or just his dirty plaything, was thinner and similarly weathered. Her bony legs were shrink-wrapped inside a pair of dirty jeans. Her top was pulled up and tied into a knot above her stomach. Her ribs showed through the skin, and her spindly fingers brought a cigarette up to her sloppily painted lips. She brushed a hand through her frazzled hair and turned her head to whisper something to her companion. His mouth bent into a murderer's grin. The crooked wound that split his face exposed yellow teeth. The burning sun reflected off the boy's knife blade, and shot its rays from the metal. It seemed to float in the air like a spectral warning, a promise of violence. It was then that Ron slid his key into the door and welcomed the relative safety that his car offered.

As Ron drove away from the site of the paltry service, he tried his best to forget the stares that had been cast his way. But to remove the patina smeared over him

from Morton was a task that would require advanced
scrubbing. Fortunately, Ron would have the time. A long
drive awaited him, the task coming to his raw nerves like a
blessing. He was to head back to sunny Sarasota, Florida,
and what a welcome sight it would be. He made his home
there and was on the staff of the Single-A baseball club in
town. He also doubled as a scout for the lower level
affiliates of the Cincinnati Meteors. An expansion team to
Major League Baseball, the Meteors filled the void left
years before by the dissolving of the storied Reds. The team
had adopted the moniker as tribute to Cincinnati being
widely regarded as the birthplace of American astronomy.
The upstart Meteors, however, were anything but
magnificent. The rough edges of the young franchise suited
Ron though, as he found it difficult to remain employed
with the more established clubs.

It was never his intention to stay a minute longer in
Fog Lake than was necessary, as he was eager to leave and
get back to the work that awaited him at home. But Ron
always found it difficult to prioritize. With his advanced
knowledge of baseball, he should have been the manager of
a big league club. Such things never happened to break his
way. His ideas of what was important and valuable differed
too much from those in the front offices, and so he got left
behind in the trenches. On his way out of town, Ron drove
past a sun-scorched baseball field, and as though pulled by
forces unseen, he found himself parking his car. This was
the sort of whimsical behavior that always got him into
trouble. He was obsessed with finding that elusive diamond
in the rough. A pursuit that usually amounted to nothing
more than wasted time and gasoline.

There really wasn't a parking lot. A savaged piece

of grass spilled over from the proper field beyond, and so Ron found it as good a place as any to rest his car. Like the ocean at night, the automobile glittered as it sat between rotted trucks and other broken relics of a time passed by. A game was about to start, and, although this experience likely promised to be pathetic and jejune, he slid himself onto the highest portion of a wooden bleacher. It was dry and split. Any slide too aggressive and the wood would surely deliver a generous number of splinters into Ron's ass, but still, for reasons unknown, he sat.

It was an adult recreation league, and, to little surprise, nearly all of the players were beer-gutted men in their thirties. Each one of them fancied themselves a cross between the physical skills of Mark McGwire and the intellect of Tommy Lasorda, but, assuredly, most of them knew far more about Budweiser than baseball. The play was sloppy, hilarious at times, but Ron dared not to laugh. In fact, he didn't do much of anything. Anonymity was a shield, and he felt cautioned to hide behind it.

The top of the 1st inning felt as if it took an eternity, but, finally, it came to a painful end as the second baseman took a spiked shoe to the shin as he miraculously applied the tag for the third out. The runner argued loudly with the umpire, and a fist-fight nearly ensued. The crowd seemed to enjoy this. Small bits of trash were hurled onto the playing surface and obscenities mingled among the air. Children wetted the soil with spit and offered their own chorus of vulgarities to the din. So far, things had gone worse than Ron would have guessed, but he silently vowed to at least suffer through one complete inning.

Up 2-0, Amil Young's team took to the field for the bottom of the 1st inning. The first couple of batters were taken apart with such fluidic ease that Ron nearly missed the pitching clinic that was suddenly on display. He watched as the third batter went down on three pitches, two straight fastballs, which had to approach 90mph, and a brutal sinker that died right over the heart of the plate.

Intrigued by the scrap of a sample that he was given, Ron decided to watch a little more. During the top of the 2nd inning, he studied the young man. The pitcher sat quietly on a bench that ran along the left side of the field. As he sat apart from the rest of his team, Amil looked thin, not just from genetics, but also thanks to a lack of nourishment. His young skin was already browned and lined from a life spent outdoors. His face held a patchy beard that most dirty, twenty-year-old men are apt to wear, and, from under a batting helmet, a shrub of wild hair poked out. Aggravated by the humidity, it was long overdue for a trim.

Ron was attuned to the body language of a ballplayer. He could tell exactly what they were thinking, or so he liked to boast. He could watch men sit as still as stones and practically read their thoughts. He could observe as an on-deck batter overanalyzed his last plate appearance, or a pitcher as he agonized over how to strike out a power hitter. But Amil didn't appear to do anything as he sat. To Ron, it didn't seem as though Amil was thinking about baseball.

Once in the batter's box to face the opposing pitcher, he grounded out, meekly, to 1st base. That was the third out, and so he kept walking to the pitcher's mound among mild applause. He plucked his tattered glove from the dirt and set to work. Like a machine bent on an unattainable perfection, Amil dispatched the next three batters in order. He didn't celebrate this accomplishment or acknowledge the sparse audience. He didn't seem to notice that anything of note had happened at all.

As he sat quietly on the bench again, Ron could sense as a true love of baseball swirled within Amil. The lack of competition couldn't nurture that love, and with opportunity never placed among the spectators, disinterest dominated. But he knew that behind those pale blue eyes a desire for something much greater lingered. Baseball wasn't just a game that Amil enjoyed, it was his only sanctuary. A frayed rope that kept him from the bottom of all that life in Fog Lake threatened to deliver. It was then that Ron reevaluated the object of his rapt interest. Yes, this young man did indeed harbor a love for the game, but it was desperation that radiated from him above all things. Amil was frantic to be more than Fog Lake would allow. He was desperate to leave the only home he had ever known.

After the first batter of the 3rd inning was retired, Amil became bored. He picked a splinter from his hand and stared off into the distance once more. He looked beyond the mountains and the brilliant, orange penumbra that lined them. He remained that way for the duration of the inning, looking past the decay of his town into the enormity of the world beyond.

Ron was struck, for he discovered that this wasn't a simple yokel, peering ignorantly into nothingness. Amil was something more. Ron was convinced he could feel as the young man's mind drifted into other areas of thought, as he gazed the horizon and pondered the mysteries of the world beyond the stagnant waters of Fog Lake. Amil had a thinker's sensibilities. This shone through, as his eyes were in constant observation of something. It would certainly be an unforgivable shame to allow any measure of a mind to waste away in a place such as this. Almost on cue, the prince rose from his trance and assumed his throne back on the pitcher's mound. Night fell, and the small collection of lights that still functioned burst to life. Ron watched in awe as a suppressed artist painted the same magnificent picture seven more times over. As Ron sat under the stars, he was enslaved before this theater of athletic supremacy, and he forgot completely about his long drive back to Sarasota. The display set before him had dominated his mind, and when the game came to a predictable end in the bottom of the 9th inning, Ron nearly lost Amil as he quickly exited the darkened field.

Beside a concession stand, which went extinct sometime around the death of Disco, was where Ron caught up to the enigmatic ballplayer and offered him the deal. Amil leaned against the disintegrating structure and picked flakes of paint from the dry wood as he listened to the pitch. The sky above was black and the stars beyond elaborately decorated the mountain tops as Ron continued to sell the greatness of Single-A ball. It was an overwrought exercise in redundancy. In fact, during the latter part of their conversation, Amil began to wonder why the sell was being pressed so hard. Did Ron actually believe that satisfaction could be found wasting away on the shabby rosters of post high school rec leagues?

The deal to join the Sarasota Suns, long winded and beset with an inessential number of incentives, was sealed with a handshake. Ron and his newest prospect walked back to the punished grass that bore the weight of Ron's late model Chevy Impala, shook hands again, and then parted. As Amil watched the silver Impala disappear into the blackness of a Fog Lake night, he finally felt what it meant to have a future.

Over the next week, Amil quit his job at the Fast Fill Gas Station and packed a few necessary items. He got drunk at a local tavern and made out with Sherry Wilson. Sherry was the rough-and-tumble type, and Amil endured a rowdy bit of teasing over his intimacy with the bruiser. All the same, a few laughs were shared with his reject friends before he staggered back home to the trailer that he shared with his cousin, Bump.

The next day, Amil kicked off his last hurrah as a resident of Fog Lake by attending the local fair. He made himself sick on corn-dogs, and lost twenty dollars playing the money wheel. With his gut twisted and his wallet bereft of cash, he took a seat on the hitch of a rickety pop-out trailer. He watched old Lightning Mike as he ran the Ferris wheel and nodded off periodically from the woes of narcolepsy. Amil ducked his head to avoid interactions with those he knew, and was made uncomfortable as he noticed Colleen Adkins working the kissing booth. She was thirteen and a little dim. With Amil's boots stuck in the muddy ground, he listened to the twang of old banjos as it mixed with the hypnotic rhythms produced by carnival attractions. He rose from the rusted steel of his seat, zigzagging around stray dogs and wandering chickens. He made for home.

Amil threw together a suitcase, and, aside from his grandmother, he told no one of his destination. It didn't feel necessary to relay this news. Fog Lake and all its trappings were better left alone and ignorant. That night, Amil was uncharacteristically quiet, even by his standards. He was in the kitchen, which was placed uncomfortably close to his tiny bathroom, nibbling on the remains of some grilled cheese that Bump had made. His cousin stumbled out of a bedroom, burning through the wreckage of a small joint, when he asked Amil if he wanted to go grab a beer.

"No man, I'm just gonna hang back," he muttered.

"What?" Bump questioned with a drawl, a look of confusion smeared across his face.

"I said I don't wanna go."

"Why not? Sherry and her friends are gonna be there. You know how them girls get when they're all coked up. And I have it on good authority that they're gonna be blowing the good shit tonight," Bump said through a grin of decaying teeth, as he tapped his pockct.

"Not interested, dude," snapped Amil.

Bump shrugged his shoulders. "Your loss, Cuz."

Once he heard Bump pull away on the blasted Honda that he fancied a Harley, Amil stepped outside. He glanced down the road at Miller's Hardware. It had closed up some years before, after Mr. Miller had died of a massive heart attack. Right there at the counter, too. The old bastard had fallen forward into a candy dish and off to the nevermore. The sign outside the store was almost too weather-beaten to read, and the front door hung crooked from its hinges, as some kids pried it open a while back. Amil turned his vision to the house across the street. It belonged to Anden Dixon, a rather violent prick whose body was aged well beyond its forty years. Five years earlier, Anden's wife, Nancy, had been found dangling from a belt in the barn out back. As it turned out, she couldn't bear one more beating.

There wasn't much else to look at from the vantage of Amil's front yard, or rather the mud mush that Bump plowed through with a weed-eater from time to time. He thought about his first cigarette. It was smoked at a friend's house, two streets over. His first beer was sampled there as well, and his first sexual encounter took place in the bathroom of the old junior high school that stood a half mile away. He could practically spit on the cemetery that housed his mother's earthly remains, and the notion seemed rather tempting. Amil had never had much use for the church that stood adjacent to the graves, although he did rob the collection plate once as a boy.

As the sticky air greased him in its film, he felt gnawed to pieces by the reality that the whole of his existence had been lived within about a five-mile radius. But had he really lived at all? Life was supposed to be a journey. It was supposed to be interesting. Some boldly suggested that the adventure offered was meant to be fun. Amil wasn't so sure about that, but he knew one thing for certain: he was done suffering the nothingness that Fog Lake offered. He felt around in his pocket and dug out his keys. After returning inside to grab a Sony Discman that should have died with the 1990s, he bid his tin-can home adieu and sped west. Spinning the second Days of the New album as loud as he could in an effort to drown out the scream of his 1979 Ford pickup, Amil put the pedal down until he crossed over into Kentucky.

Once in Ashland, it didn't take him long to locate the Greyhound Station. Amil parked his vintage POS, which he had no intention of ever returning to claim, and purchased a ticket to Florida. The haul to Sarasota would be long, but it mattered not. The longer it took, the farther he would be from Fog Lake. Such a proposition sounded as close to paradise as a trouble-stirring boy from Virginia could hope to find.

The sun raged hot over the tobacco fields of the Carolinas, but Amil saw nothing except the insides of his own eyelids during this time. It wasn't until they crossed into Georgia that the escapee from Fog Lake arose and again joined his semi-conscious companions. There wasn't much to see out his window. The massive southern state looked pretty much the way he envisioned it would. The only peculiarity that did catch his eye was the utter lack of anything that resembled a hill. The land was unbelievably flat. It was as though the world could stretch on forever.

The landscape of Florida however, was something far different. With the hum of the tires playing soundtrack to his vision, Amil was captivated by the wetland's cypress trees and the grip of the Spanish moss that seemed determined to strangle everything that it could. Nearly every road, cut straighter than the most perfect of lines, was bordered by tall trees. They were horribly thin, and bereft of branches, save for small clusters placed near the top. As they pressed deeper south into the slim state, the foreign geography continued to fascinate the vagabond, only then, he was treated to a discomforting feeling. It was only May, but already the oppression of the Florida sun baked its way through the windows of the bus.

Amil shuffled in his seat, a failed attempt at dodging the boiling spears sent down from the sun. He pulled his headphones off and glanced around the bus. Until this point, he hadn't bothered to examine another soul that was along for the ride to Florida, and this realization struck him. He was truly in his own world of one. A cell only he could see, a box built to shield him from the ugliness of common circumstance. Charlie Manson could

23

have been seated across the aisle, and Amil would have remained ignorant to the fact. He hadn't noticed the young mother of two brats as she sat stone-faced and exhausted. He could have sworn that the black chick in the halter top hadn't been there at all before. Seated behind her was an old man who incessantly scratched his crotch. Hopefully that was all he was doing, but who would be foolish enough to assume such innocence? The hammers of geriatrics might have robbed the old man of proper function, but a predator still shifted behind his cloudy stare. Amil slid back into the sticky embrace of his seat and shut his eyes.

Are we there yet? he thought to himself without the slightest hint of humor.

Stepping out of the station in Sarasota was akin to being greeted by a punch in the face. This was a heat that would have made hell embarrassed to call itself hot. Fortunately, Ron quickly met up with Amil, and the pair headed for the sanctuary of a small café. A place to rest his ass other than a cramped bus seat was welcome and lunch was a nice bonus, but the mammoth glass of cold sweet tea placed before him promised to be the highlight of the day.

Over their meal, the men discussed the days to come. The next day, Ron would show him around the facility, and hopefully he could meet a few of his new teammates. They talked about how he would be used in the rotation and the current status of the Sarasota Suns in the standings. Ron went to great lengths to detail how he convinced the brass to take on a no name twenty-year-old without any formal baseball training.

Amil remained rather unamused with the tale. Sure, he was glad that Ron believed in his abilities, but if Ron was sniffing around for a pat on the back, Amil wasn't the type to oblige. After all, the fact remained he had never asked this leather-encased sausage of a man for a thing. He was given an opportunity, and planned on making the most of it. That's really all the situation amounted to, in Amil's estimation. As he picked at his fries, he silently extended appreciation to Ron's grandmother for having the decency to die during baseball season.

Let's get on with this, thought Amil as he sipped his tea.

Part 3. The rise of Amil Young

Amil finished out the season in a Sarasota Suns uniform. He posted a record of 10-2 with a few no-decisions thrown in for good measure. His ERA was a spectacular 0.82. His walks per start averaged just over one, while his strikeouts per start flirted with a healthy eight. It was certainly a fantastic season, but with a pedigree of sludge, there remained skepticism over Amil's ability to shut down hitters at the higher levels.

At the start of the next year, he was transplanted to North Carolina to play for the Double-A affiliate, the Carolina Bullheads. Here, with the help of a pitching coach to refine his delivery, the dominance of Amil Young continued without so much as a wild pitch to taint his stellar statistics. Playing a full year for Carolina, he polished his fastball and pushed its velocity into the realm of the high 90s. He also refined his sinker and added a fierce curveball to his repertoire.

By the season's end, Amil boasted an impressive record of 17-1. His ERA climbed a bit, but was still a paltry 1.61. He was finally earning a modest wage, which provided a lifestyle he would have thought impossible not long ago. When the season wilted under the command of winter, Amil spent most of his time within the walls of a small apartment he had rented.

He kept to himself and refrained from making any true friendships, as he was destined to move again the next year to the Triple-A club in Kentucky. Amil kept busy by reading through a stack of overdue library books and entertaining local women who like to be seen with ballplayers of any variety. He rarely left the immediate radius around his neighborhood, although he did manage to find a few quiet bars, even as his taste for alcohol had ebbed away. There was a strip club that demanded his patronage. It sat in the middle of an otherwise abandoned alley. The narrow road stunk of piss, while the air inside possessed odors equally opposed to the concept of fragrance. He frequented a rerun movie theater and bathed his nerves in caffeine at a local coffee shop, but for the most part, Amil preferred to spend his time alone.

At twenty-three, Amil Young had his name on the roster sheet of a Triple-A club, the Louisville Fireworks. It was a strange twist of fortune, being back in Kentucky. The last time he had spent a brief moment of significance there, a stable future was a far-flung and elusive beast. And yet there he was, a few tremendous months removed from a possible career in Major League Baseball.

The night before the first game of the season, Amil drove eastbound on Interstate 64, hopped on 77, and rode it to the Virginia border. On the graveled shoulder, he parked his truck, a shiny upgrade from the old '79 he had left to rot in Ashland, and stepped out into the empty night. He stared into the land he left behind, and, as his feet brushed the invisible line that divided the states, thoughts of Fog Lake crawled through his mind.

From the enveloping Southern blackness, a dog wailed in the distance, and its cry told of a wound recently suffered. A tractor-trailer thundered past, and the vibration of the rig caused the concrete below the pickup to shiver. Dust was cast into the muggy air, but for all these uncomfortable stimuli, Amil made not a motion as he continued to gaze into a complete lack of color. He was still, and dared not to step over that unseen barrier that crossed before his boots, lest it suck him back in. Although a part of him felt an odd pull coming from Virginia. Sometimes home is better off relegated to memory, but for all its indigents and strife, Fog Lake would always be the home of Amil Young. Ill-pleased by such an irrefutable truth, he turned away and climbed back into his truck.

Like a man dually possessed by madness and charmed by the grace of the divine, Amil's meteoric rise continued. He stormed through the first two months of the season and made a mockery of the hitters who opposed him. By mid-June, his ERA ticked over two for the first time, but after another couple of starts, it sunk into almost impossible figures once again.

Amil achieved a rock-star status in Louisville, but he kept a rigid focus on baseball. His concentration could not be cracked, and the obsessive-compulsive fervor that he lent to his craft branded him with a prickly reputation. He rarely gave interviews, and the ones he did mostly consisted of one-word answers accompanied by impatient grumbles. To sight him anywhere besides the diamond was akin to spotting a ghost beset with a crippling shyness. The opportunity of a lifetime lay agonizingly close. He was not about to let its fleeting affections slip away on the scales of distraction.

The day that Amil had dreamed about, but figured would never actually arrive, came during the first week of August. Like a fantasy made flesh, he was called up to pitch in the Major Leagues. The expansion Cincinnati Meteors were squirming uneasily in 5th place in the division. Being well out of the playoff race, they decided to test their pitching phenom on the big stage of the Major Leagues. It would be a trial run. Amil would be given seven or eight starts before the winter to prime him for the season to come and all the demands that tether themselves to a career in professional sports.

The August issue of Sports Illustrated was dominated by Amil's face, half obscured behind the curve of a dirty baseball. The headline asked, *Who Is Amil Young, And Why Is He The Future Of Pitching?* It was bold and eye catching, but as he paced the floor of the Meteors' clubhouse before his Major League debut against the visiting Milwaukee Brewers, his gaze avoided the magazine as though it wielded the curse of Medusa.

The time for the future had come, and, as Amil took to the mound for the top of the 1st inning, he received a standing ovation from a mass of people, most of whom had never seen him throw a pitch. He looked into the stadium as it sprawled out. It was barbequed under the might of an August sun and half empty, as many fans of the beloved Reds were hesitant to latch onto the bumbling Meteors. Amil looked to the ball in his hand and checked his signals with the catcher. Amil stared at the batter who stood to the left of home plate. As he had done so many times before, he tossed the baseball from his grip as if he hated its very

28

existence.

A single was lined up the right field line and, moments later, the next challenge crawled to the plate. This hitter wore disinterest on his face, and had slumped himself into a .220 average. All the same, Amil tightened his focus, but walked the batter with nary a pitch touching the strike-zone. There were no outs, two Brewers on base, and Amil stood perilously close to a disastrous first start. A deep breath caused his chest to shiver, and he began to sweat profusely. As he felt the mild prick of a headache developing behind his eyes, his gaze floated to the ball in his hands. It was slicked by sweat and boasted a sparse arrangement of lightly colored soil. He closed his pained eyes and thought of that rancid field in Fog Lake. Just like back home, Amil resolved that he could not be beaten, and, with that arrogant and grandiose notion, he unleashed his deceptive sinker.

Fortunately for the budding star, the next batter grounded into a double play, and Amil was soon relieved of the inning altogether by way of a strikeout. Every man that came before him after that was retired in order. The Meteors offered their pitcher little help, eking out only two runs, but with thirteen strikeouts to his credit and supreme command of his arsenal, little assistance was needed. All told, once the game faded into a fresh history, the record-setting line read: Win - CG, 1 H, 0 ER, 1 BB, 13 K.

The week which followed saw Amil swept up in a whirlwind of activity and attention that would have eclipsed the sum of all the adulation he garnered previously. There were interviews and profiles on ESPN, appearances at a few Cincinnati sports memorabilia shops, and throngs of people eager to score an autograph before his stature rose to the level of untouchable superstar.

On the road to begin a series with the Pittsburgh Pirates, Amil rejoiced, as a portion of the attention that was cast his way would remain behind in Ohio. He was actually grateful that his second start would take place away from Cincinnati. Truth be told, the pressure to succeed was palpable as it bore down over him. As the home fans cheered him on, and as the local sportscasters dissected every one of his pitches, the weight of his occupation mounted. This glut of interest that had begun to follow behind was a strange animal, and he was having a difficult time acclimating himself to its mercurial behavior. After all, stardom in Fog Lake amounted to nothing more than three or more people taking notice of the actions of another resident. At least on the road, most of the Pirates' fans didn't recognize him. Some of the more casual fans had never even heard his name.

Due to scheduling oversights, the second game of the series, which commenced just after noon, was bookended by two 7:30 evening starts. That second game, the Meteors thumped the Pirates to the tune of a 12-2 final count. As a reward, the team was given the rest of the day off.

As he walked out of PNC Park, Amil had nothing to do, but he did feel an itch to wander. Crossing the street and into a parking lot, he noticed a pair of teenage boys. They looked to be transplants from the mid-90s grunge-rock era as they stepped out of an abused 1999 Chevy Malibu. He flagged them down, and, as luck would have it, the kid with an unkempt beard and a faded Mudhoney T-shirt recognized him immediately. Unexpectedly, this actually came as a stroke of good fortune. After a bit of banter, an autograph, and a payment of one hundred bucks, Amil had procured himself a vehicle for the day.

As he promised to return this turd to its dumping ground later that day, Amil bid the boys adieu, and surveyed the inside of his new ride. A dusting of ashes washed over everything, while a few extinguished cigarette butts offered a bit of color to the otherwise barren floor. The driver's seat was torn and the backseat played host to all manner of trash, fast-food wrappers, and a mammoth CD booklet. He rifled through the volume until he came upon a disc which appeared painfully misplaced. Rolling down both windows to relieve himself of the stagnant air, and forcing the tired Malibu into gear, Amil allowed *Bone Machine* to play as he sped off to parts unknown.

Unbeknownst to Amil, he avoided most of the labyrinthine sections of Pittsburgh by drifting onto Route 28 North rather quickly. He drove the neglected 4-lane highway for a few miles before taking a random exit. He chose it for no other reason than because the exit ramp was on the left. It seemed interesting, the path less traveled. The aging, working-class neighborhood he found possessed a subtle charm, but boredom set in rather quickly. As his mind wandered, the hick from Fog Lake did a wonderful job of getting lost. Not that it mattered. He had all night to find his way back.

In a creative pattern that surely would have resembled a crop circle if traced, Amil found himself on Main Street as it cut its way through Sharpsburg. He plodded along uninspired, but, as the disc neared its end, Amil crossed into Pittsburgh's Aspinwall neighborhood. No turns were necessary, but as Main Street morphed into Freeport Road, so too did the scenery around him undergo its own evolution. This charming little place looked fresh and sophisticated. Aspinwall certainly didn't resemble a withered limb of a former industrial giant. The neighborhood vibrated with progress, and all its subtleties fascinated the boy from Fog Lake.

To his right flowed the mighty Allegheny River, which ran parallel to a set of train tracks. But to Amil's left there sprung a quiet village that looked to be ripped from a postcard. It was almost as though the road itself married the old to the new, the raw to the refined. There was a produce stand, a fur shop, delis, and rows of beautiful homes that rested comfortably over cobblestone roads. Standing guard upon a manicured lawn was a large sculpture of a dinosaur that had been accented by stained glass. The sight gave Amil a chuckle. An extinct and fearsome beast made whimsical by the mind of man.

The avenues that broke off from Freeport were lined with trees that offered shade, and they also hosted wide sidewalks, which usually saw a steady stream of foot traffic. Turning down the aptly named Brilliant Avenue, Amil parked his borrowed car and set out to explore this land that promised to be the antithesis of Fog Lake.

He walked around the busy square and among a heavy concentration of dog-walkers, business types, and those utterly unconcerned with the flow of time. It was an elegant space. The streetlights were ornately detailed and the shop signs were made of wood and metal, not the usual cheap collaboration of neon and plastic. The buildings were old but perfectly preserved. The sidewalks were clean and even.

Amil turned and ventured down the narrow confines of Commercial Avenue in a search for nothing at all. The skinny street was walled in by old buildings that had been squeezed tightly up against one another, an arrangement which left the street in perpetual shade. The alley made him think of England. His knowledge of Europe was paltry, but this look of yesteryear was how he pictured the busy streets of London. Narrow and ancient, with structures of heavy stone, the roads of wavy brick making up the paths that supported the rear entrances of pubs and other tiny businesses. This, at least, was how the movies Amil had seen always portrayed the capital of the United Kingdom to be.

He enjoyed his stroll, and, with no thought of destination, Amil sauntered deeper into the embrace of the neighborhood. Under the chromatic umbrella of turning leaves, the direction chosen took him back toward Brilliant and the busy square. There were all sorts of intriguing shops to be found. Tucked among the might of brick and thick mortar, Amil passed pizza shops, salons, a few doctor's offices, bric-a-brac, and hobby stores. He also found some art galleries, and the smell of coffee was ever-present in the air as it wafted out of the many cafés.

Near the conclusion of this gem of a street, Amil stepped off the cobblestone and turned into a diner that looked to have opened its doors for the first time mere moments before. He sat at the counter and ordered a cup of coffee from a waitress who looked eerily familiar. As he sipped his cream-swirled brew and attempted to conquer the omelet he ordered, his curious mind struggled to unravel the mystery as to who the girl truly was.

Tall, at five-foot-ten inches, she had a mound of brown hair tangled up behind her head. A pair of square-framed glasses sat upon her nose and looked to be a pair of tiny televisions, the only programming, a constant exposé that told of the most enchanting blue eyes. Her nails were painted green, and their hue matched her eye shadow perfectly. Her lips were plump and they regularly delighted in the engulfing of the end of a blessed cigarette. Other than a little chub around the waist, this girl was on the slender side, which made her best assets all the more noticeable. Amil couldn't help but assume that the ample set of breasts she sported were purchased, rather than bestowed from genetics.

As Amil studied her unnatural rack, he noticed the name on her tag, Ali. It was then that this clue was put together with her most noticeable and unfortunate of features. A deep scar drove down all the way from the center of her forehead. It skipped over her left eye and continued through the edge of her lower lip before it disappeared along her jaw line. It was a silent, dried out canal. The former path dug out from a river of violence. Like a ghost that can't shed the mad echoes of the past, it immediately gave away her identity. This was Ali Jett.

Amil felt some sympathy for the quiet waitress, as he recalled the story of a Pittsburgh-born fashion model nearly beaten to death by an ex-boyfriend. She must have been forced home from the glamour of the fashion world by the tortured skin that decorated her young face. It was a thought that made Amil shudder, for he was certain that after Ali landed her first contract, she could have never imagined that her future would be serving coffee in Aspinwall.

As he drained his cup, Amil thought of how unpredictable and coldly unfair life can be. Here he sat, on the verge of his dreams, while Ali had nothing but a mangled reminder of hers.

"I know you," he offered to Ali in a friendly tone.

"No, you don't."

"Well not in real life, I mean, I know who you are."

"And?" replied Ali, with no intention of being pleasant.

"Nothing, I guess. Just wanted to talk."

"Well I don't."

"That's fine. I'm generally kinda quiet too. You just don't have to be a bitch about it."

Soured by the rude comment, she didn't reply. She glared into Amil and he stared back. Her piercing eyes and lack of words did little to make him uncomfortable. After all, Ali had already said she didn't feel like talking.

"You want more coffee?" she asked with a bitter tongue.

Part 4. The sordid young life of Ali Jett

Growing up in the predominately white and prestigious Pittsburgh neighborhood of Fox Chapel, young Ali was afforded a wealth of opportunities. Her parents had a stable marriage and both managed to bring home incomes in the six figures. Well liked and intelligent, she could rake in a GPA above 3.00 with minimal effort, and regularly made the honor-roll. Her parents envisioned sending Ali off to a college whose name would look quite impressive on a résumé, but she had different ideas.

While doing some modeling her junior year in high school, it didn't take long before the striking brunette was offered contracts from some of the most coveted brands. Reluctantly, her father stood behind her as Ali pursued a career with the Rypt Jeans clothing line. At 18, she relocated to Chicago. Within the time span of one month, her image could be seen on billboards all around the country. She was viewed as a link to supermodels of the past, and her popularity was predicted to exceed that of Anna Nicole Smith's during her reign as a Guess? girl. However, Ali's defiant streak, paired with the sense of entitlement she harbored from a life of leisure, had lured her into the old traps that had swallowed so many young girls before.

In middle school, raucous and rebellious Ali had developed a taste for heavy metal, weed, and boys. Although rather conservative, her parents took it easy on their daughter, hoping that her indiscretions were just youthful follies. They very well may have been, but by 19, Ali showed no signs of maturity. She went to parties every night, drank heavily, and discovered a fondness for cocaine. The pairing of her wild nature and disregard for responsibility did little to derail her career initially. With the fuel of youth and drugs, Ali made rounds on the nightclub circuit and was photographed with some heavy-hitters in the business. She formed contacts and exchanged numbers with girls who seemed poised to make the leap from cover girl to midrange movie star. She was living the life, basking in glamour and relishing the feeling of moving too fast, but, like a freight train into a Volvo, her career was smashed to pieces.

It was another rowdy night out in the chilly Chicago air, and just another club filled with the stimuli of homegrown house music, flashing lights, and a plethora of mixed drinks. In an act that she had perfected, Ali drank more than her skinny frame should have been able to take as she wiggled through the beats of the music in bizarre clothing. The predictable evening of excess and eventual exhaustion took a fateful detour as Ali and another girl snuck their way into a backroom normally kept inaccessible to the general public.

She followed her friend down the rabbit hole to indulge the only common element they shared: narcotics. Ali's accomplice, a trampy blonde who certainly had set her best days behind her, melted into the arms of a man seated on a circular couch. Once the two women had snorted a few lines off the surface of the drink table, it wasn't long before the blonde slid her clothing off. As she straddled the stranger, this glorified prostitute coerced Ali into a sloppy make-out session. Before the next thump of a new song could be properly established, the cocktail of youthful defiance and the drugs in Ali's blood sent her full throttle into a backroom threesome on the sticky surface of the carpet.

Dirt tends to follow dirt, and, unbeknownst to Ali, her scandalous tryst was captured by the unblinking eye of a cell phone's camera. The sordid contents were sold to the highest bidder, and once the grainy sex video made its rounds on the internet, Ali's contract with Rypt evaporated.

Too embarrassed to come home, she stayed in Chicago with her boyfriend Max, a common thug who fancied himself as the next great amateur porn producer. The cost of their luxury apartment stayed the same, but Ali's income had dried up, and her addiction to drugs continued to swell. As the floor of their place supported an array of collection notices along with the usual smatterings of drug paraphernalia and porn, Ali grew desperate. As she watched the random traffic of hookers and junkies flow in and out of her apartment, and the money that stuck to their trail, it didn't take much convincing before Ali agreed to star in one of Max's handheld features. Locked in a constant haze of hard drugs and alcohol, she was displayed at her filthy worst. This too, was viewed by millions from their home computers. With the graphic content, and with the lust for shame that she seemed to harbor, her image was forever smeared. For her imprudence, Ali was left completely bereft of hope for another fashion contract.

Determined not to have a daughter who starred in pornography, Ali's father disowned her. Hundreds of miles from home, the news didn't exactly shake her, although she did express distress to Max over the seedy film. In a moment of rare sobriety, she was stung by the tastelessness of the film, and was furious that it had been posted online. She had no one to turn to, and, although her own eviction would surely follow quickly behind, Ali announced that she was leaving Max. Forcefully, she attempted to throw him out of the place that her work had bought. With her eyeliner smeared, and the symphonic odor of fast food and cigarettes wafting from between her teeth, Ali unloaded on Max.

Armored in nothing more than a bra and the pumps which she woke up wearing, Ali shoved him toward the door and laced him with obscenities. Ali pitched a bottle at her monstrous excuse for a boyfriend, and watched as it sailed through the glass of a flat-screen TV. Max's delight with this little tantrum only served to further incense the disgraced model. He leered at her like a hungry jackal, and like any proper scavenger, he was only there to pick whatever could be torn from her bones. She flung anything that was within clutching distance at the beast across the room. Her frustration swelled with every result of her flawed aim. But then, Ali saw her opportunity to make her point felt. Max turned away, feeling that her rage had been exhausted. After all, he had seen this show before. It was then that Ali's cell phone crashed into the side of his head, and rained down upon the carpet in an explosion of plastic and buttons. It was that act, Ali's fleeting moment of satisfaction and triumph that served to launch Max into fury.

"You stupid junkie bitch!" he screamed, rubbing his afflicted temple.

"What? Fuck you," she snarled, drawing out the words like an impatient child.

"I should beat you to death," he said with an eerie calm.

"You won't do shit, faggot. You never do shit. You ain't shit. Get the fuck out." After flicking a lit cigarette over to Max, Ali turned away.

With his fists, and without any notion to do otherwise, he beat Ali relentlessly, and knocked her unconscious. Her left arm was quickly broken, and five cracked ribs rose and fell in a splintered palpitation with every heave of her chest. Countless bruises littered her body, and two black eyes would emerge to darken the surface on her face. Max left her crumpled upon the floor, but the assault was far from over. He knelt over her unconscious body and pulled a knife from his jeans. Using a rough and serrated blade, he cut a massive wound down her face. The hot blood spurted out and leaked across his fingers as he cut. Further enraged by this soiling, Ali's ogre brought down a punch that loosened her teeth and sent ribbons of blood onto the wall beside her. With a permanent disfigurement to her once glamorous look, he left her to die on the stained carpet among a collection of drug residue, stains, and porn magazines.

Two days later, Ali woke up in the hospital. Under the influence of more drugs, she was hooked up to monitors and machines like a sci-fi experiment gone wrong. Her eyes were cracked half open and her jaw was wired shut. She slurred fractured speech to the nurse who had come to check on the wounded girl. Her questions were ill-formed and usually forgotten before the answers could come, but when Ali was told that Max had been arrested for attempted murder, she fell back into unconsciousness.

Once stabilized, she became aware that her family had gathered around her, but Ali's father was noticeably absent. At the urging of his wife, he would take back his estranged child. But all of the torments that cuddled up to Ali, he believed to be self-inflicted, and so he elected to not make the trip to Chicago to be by his daughter's side. With her broken teeth clenched by metal and wire, she felt as sadness wove itself into her bed sheets.

Once back home in Pittsburgh, Ali had kicked her dependency on drugs, and her body recovered. She was just 20 years old, and her family hoped that finally she would enroll in school. Ever rebellious, she decided to again try her hand at modeling. The distant relationship between Ali and her father was further strained by this news, but with promises of change, he again provided the monetary support she needed.

With financial aid from her parents, and with what little money she had left after all the drugging, Ali bought a considerably large set of breast implants. She dyed her hair black and had an elaborate tribal tattoo drilled into her lower back. The vicious scar on her face fit with the fierce nature of a local fetish magazine, Brutality X. With caffeine and nicotine as her only crutches, Ali agreed to work for the publication.

She was determined to make it as a professional, clean and sober, all stereotypes be damned. She wanted to prove her father wrong and show the world that she was much more than a vapid cliché. She hated the crowd of TMZ pseudo-celebrities that her name was often associated with, and desired desperately to change her image. Ali envisioned herself redefining the modeling industry and shaking up the ideas of what it meant to be classy, beautiful, and cutting-edge at the same time. She imagined herself rising clean from the wreckage of filth and danger, but, alas, her hopes vanished as raindrops into the sea.

She did a few spreads and some endorsement shoots, but a criminal element ran deep in Brutality X, and her lofty aspirations were soon left to decay. It turned out that it wasn't much of a magazine, more like a loose association of burnouts that liked to take pictures. With no one that resembled a decent human being, and with all of her old demons tagging along, Ali became entrapped in a situation that served to bring her shame.

While strung up in a hard bondage pose, Ali was left helpless to watch as the photographer paused to shoot heroin. Sobbing mildly, but glad to be restrained from a fresh, narcotic temptation, the scarred model was struck by the emptiness of her life. Eventually, she was untied by another woman, who had track marks on her arms. Rubbing her irritated flesh, Ali was left with welts on her skin and a prophetic look into her future if she stayed with Brutality X. After two months of on-and-off work, and a growing list of derelicts in her address book, she was stalked by depression. She knew how this would all end, and she saw the fanciful nature of her dreams. Reality clutched at her stronger than the drugs ever had, and, reluctantly, Ali gave up on modeling.

Incensed that his only daughter had been a junkie, done porn, and voluntarily posed for bondage shoots, Ali's father again severed all ties of kinship. The relationship maintained with her mother was strained, and with every visit being more awkward than the last, their meetings became fewer and fewer. She continued to feel disconnected from her family, and at some point, was made to feel useless. Her existence was a ruse, a cheap imitation of life, as it depended solely on her mother's credit card limit. Removing the cushion of plastic was a scary proposition, but to be free of the barbs that her parents cast her way, Ali knew it was time to go.

In a bold but necessary move, Ali walked away from the wealth of her family and took to the laborious task of making an honest life on the wage of an ordinary working slob. She didn't stray far, but with the industrial look of Sharpsburg, Ali felt worlds apart from the life she once knew when she first ventured off completely on her own.

Her 21st birthday was spent alone, in a tiny apartment in Sharpsburg, as the evening came to resemble the multitude of nights which had preceded it. It was all the better though, for the next day she had to open the diner in Aspinwall. She had worked at the diner for close to a month, and with the last of her Brutality X cash, her possessions and a new kitten had been moved into a ground-level dwelling on Middle Street. Life wasn't where she hoped it would be, and it was clear that it might never be, but finally, Ali was clean and independent. It was almost as though, at twenty-one years of age, she could start living.

She flipped on her TV, and, thanks to a bond she still held with two of her three brothers, Ali had developed a fondness for sports. It passed the time, and all the stats gave her something she could use to occupy her often-troubled mind. As the fall and the playoffs neared, a genuine interest in baseball sprouted within her. The Pirates were in second place in the division, with an outside shot to qualify for a wild card spot. Although they were drubbed the day before, this series with the Meteors was a way to pick up cheap wins. Hopefully, with the series finale, Ali's Bucs would emerge victorious. And so, with a jar of peanuts and a cat in her lap, she settled in for a night she would never forget, at least for the remainder of her natural life.

Part 5. Fate

An evening fitted with an unseasonably brisk chill formed the ambiance which would conclude a rather mundane baseball series and play host to the second start of Amil Young's Major League career. A sizeable portion of tickets had been sold, but with dewy rain peppering the night sky, only a smattering of fans had arrived at the park. It was 7:35, and the first pitch of the night had been hurled across the plate for a strike. As Amil sat in the dugout, he looked beyond the confines of the stadium and stared into an ever-darkening azure sky. His mind loitered in the distance, much the same as it had back upon the rusted diamonds of Fog Lake's fields when he used to gaze into the might of mountains. With a tinge of silent guilt, he hoped that the top of the 1st inning would conclude rather quickly, for he was anxious to take the mound.

Once upon the mound, Amil was relieved of all his hesitations. The troubles brought about from his inglorious background, they faded from his mind. This hump of pampered dirt was where he truly belonged, and upon its cool surface, he reveled in the devotion that this throne commanded, as all his efforts were focused and clear.

During the first four innings, Amil crafted a weapon destined to fillet the record books. He was no-hitting the opposition and had already tallied 7 strikeouts. But history is stubborn, and it cares not to be altered. Furthermore, destiny has never concerned itself with the whims and wishes of man, and so, with intangible forces conspiring against him, Amil's niche place in history was cemented. Robbed of a brilliant future by a failure of the body, this undoing of a man was broadcast over the airwaves for all to witness.

Steve: "Welcome back folks, nothing-nothing ball game, bottom of the 5th inning here at PNC Park, where Meteors pitcher Amil Young is having his way with Pirate batters. Coming off a start where he one-hit the Brewers, Amil has showed no signs of fatigue or jitters."
Greg: "Steady as a stone, no doubt about that. It's really impressive what this young man has accomplished. Even a fan of the home team has to be impressed."
Steve: "All the best to Virginia's finest, let's just hope our Bucs can squeeze a run or two across."
Greg: "The first offering from Amil, and what do ya know?

Strike one. Pitch two, now, and it's fouled off and out of play. Amil's in command now, up 0-2 on Jose Myers. Pitch three, strike three, just like that."

Steve: "Ya can't hit it if you don't swing."

Greg: "Jose wouldn't have hit that if he had an oar, that ball was blistered across the plate. Mikey Hoffman at the plate now. Amil shakes off a few signs from the catcher...and he lobs his splitter over the plate for strike one."

Steve: "That was a bad swing, just an awful swing. Mikey's gonna be embarrassed when he watches this at-bat later on. Come on, Mike, don't let him get in your head."

Greg: "Too late for that. And Hoffman grounds out to short for out number two."

Steve: "The Pirates need more patience at the plate if they want any hope of winning this game. Gotta get that pitch count up, make him earn those outs."

Greg: "Certainly, Amil's looking to make this his quickest inning yet. Opposing pitcher, James Valentine up now for the Bucs. Amil's first offering, and yes, folks, he is human, as it's ball one in the dirt."

Steve: "You don't see that from him very often. That ball just got away from him. He's gonna be gunning right for Valentine. You watch, no fancy stuff here, just heat."

Greg: "Pitch two now, and oh no! Oh no! That ball sailed way wide and it's no mystery why. Amil's throwing arm bent in one of the most unnatural positions I've ever seen as he released that ball."

Steve: "A lot of unraveling just took place around that elbow, and Amil's down on his knees in the dirt."

Greg: "As the trainers come out, Amil's on his side in the fetal position. The pain he must be experiencing has to be

45

overwhelming."

Steve: "That really didn't look good. As a former ballplayer, it sickens me to watch this."

Greg: "To watch his forearm dangle like that, you can't help but feel a great amount of doubt for the future of this young man in the game of baseball. Baseball has too many what-if and almost stories, we don't need another. Come on, Amil, heal up that arm."

As Amil writhed in the dirt with a film of rain on his face, he saw his future with all the clarity of a fortune teller. Its grim image told of surgeries to come and all the failures and complications that would accompany their damned efforts. He witnessed all the rehabilitation and physical therapy, which in the end would only come to amount to a vast squandering of time. He watched helplessly as his dreams decayed. The big contracts evaporated, the adulation disappeared, and endorsements, no matter how small, all vanished into the cool Pennsylvania air. Amil held his love, his passion, and his sense of self, but for as tight or desperate as his grasp may have been, he could do nothing but watch them die. As he lay in the dirt with his future shattered all about him, his mind drifted to the remembrance of the scarred Ali Jett.

Part 6. A common bond

In a predictable and dull fashion, the next year of Amil's life was spent almost entirely with doctors and physical therapists. Unwilling to face the wretched truth of their situation without a fight, the team pumped a generous amount of time and dollars into the mending of their rising star. But alas, no quantity of money, effort or sorcery could put his shredded arm back together. Sure, he could lead a normal life, and under most circumstances, his arm would offer him little discomfort, but a career in sports had become as dead and distant a dream as the muck that shifts on the floor of the great swamp in Fog Lake.

Admitting defeat, the Meteors released their shattered treasure into an uncertain future. Flung from the embrace of certainty, Amil was again left without direction. His bank account was padded by a few game checks and from money he was able to stash during his stint in Triple-A. Some guaranteed cash from defunct endorsement deals would keep him afloat for the time being, but the fact remained, sooner or later, Amil Young would be broke and unqualified to do a damn thing.

For reasons he did not fully understand, Amil jumped in his truck one night and drove out of Cincinnati as a road map of Pittsburgh lay crinkled on the passenger seat next to him. Due to some poor navigation skills, he was well into his fifth hour of driving before he crossed into the limits of the Steel City. It didn't much matter. He had nothing else to do, and nowhere else to go. He felt like the eternal traveler. Pushing on, from habit, away from the world he knew, never to reach a destination.

In a maddening exercise that sent him down a myriad of one-way streets and over bridges whose destinations seemed to be only toward a more fierce set of asphalt puzzles, Amil struggled to find his way around the dark city. But as determined a soul as there had ever been, his goal was fixed on the neighborhood of Aspinwall, and he would indulge no rest until he set his eyes upon that diner on 1st Street.

Parking his truck in the square which played host to the ephemeral activities of wind and moonlight, Amil glanced into the LED eyes of his stereo. The clock read 4:45am. Totally bereft of human company, he stepped outside and sucked in the chill of the early morning air. It was November, and a light dusting of snow had speckled the town as it slept. He crossed the street and peered into the blackness of the diner. It wouldn't open until six. Among the blue glow of the moon as it reflects off snow, Amil rubbed his eyes and retreated back to the warmth of his truck. He stared out the fogged window and hoped that the spin of the earth would increase and deliver 6 o'clock just a bit sooner, but, like most uttered prayers, his plea went unnoticed. With the mild vibration of the V8 as it idled, he was lulled to sleep with his face pressed to the tinted glass of the driver's window.

The sun of a new day cracked the sky, and, as the sounds of activity and life filled the streets, Amil was jarred from his nap. He rubbed the sleep from his eyes and then greeted the cold arrival of the morning. With the sharp air hastening his return to consciousness, Amil pushed his fingers through his hair and did his best to stretch the wrinkles from his clothes. His untied boots pushed their way through another couple inches of fallen snow as he lazily drifted his way to the entrance of the diner.

He sat himself at the counter, as he had a little more than a year before, and ordered a cup of coffee from a rotund man who appeared quite silently from the kitchen. Dropping lumps of sugar into the minute abyss held within his cup, Amil surveyed his environment. The younger patrons were getting their morning beverages to go, with maybe a scone or muffin as company, while the few older men that were there took to immersing themselves in the day's paper. Anxiety tumbled Amil's insides. He felt abandoned by the faculty of focus. A nervous hunger sent tremors to work on his limbs. A trembling hand stirred his coffee to froth, and his appetite betrayed the groans of his stomach, as he ordered nothing more than toast.

As he nibbled the scorched bread, Amil began to wonder if he had the rotten luck of having popped in on Ali's day off. The more he thought of it, she probably didn't work there anymore. He downed four more cups of the burnt blend, ate half a muffin, and felt about as pathetic as any living creature has the capacity to feel.

As he was about to leave, Amil noticed as someone had sat down beside him. He didn't bother to look. The small counter was almost full, and there was most likely nowhere else to sit. He pined for the indifferent grip of loneliness, as a disconnecting from the sensibilities of others rooted itself within him. With his eyes fixated on the tan liquid that lay still in his cup, he hoped in desperation that whoever occupied the space next to him wasn't a chatter. He had no desire for banter, to converse lightly about trivial things destined to be forgotten. The only action left to take was to leave.

"I know you."

To his amazement, Ali had been sitting next to him for at least the last five minutes. He cared so little for the image beside him, before her voice rang out, Amil could only have guessed at the gender of the smear of colors and flesh that occupied the space next to his.

"So, you do move. I thought you'd never look up," said Ali in a flat tone.

"Just a little tired, that's all."

"I've read about you."

"Yeah? What did ya hear?" asked Amil.

"A lot...I watched that game. Ya know, the one where you hurt your elbow."

"Oh yeah, that game. Almost forgot about that one." For the better part of a year, Amil had been haunted by thoughts of Ali, and, as she sat next to him, he could do nothing but act like a prick.

"Why are you here?" Ali asked impatiently.

"Came back for the coffee."

"No you didn't. It sucks anyway. Really, why are you here?"

"I don't really know, to be honest," Amil quietly said as he turned and faced Ali for the first time. "I guess I just wanted to talk to someone that I could relate to."

"Meaning what? You don't know me. Shit, you're practically a stalker."

"I've only come here twice, just once on purpose. I'd have to bother you a bit more before I earn stalker status."

Ali remained unamused.

"Sorry. I just thought we might have something in common. I mean, we've both had our dreams taken away from us, and in public, too." The sentence repeated in Amil's mind. It echoed with the accompaniment of scorn and judgmental laughter. "I drove all night and slept in my truck just for the chance to talk to you, and now that I'm here, I don't know what to say."

"Me neither."

"Fuck it, never mind. Have a nice day," he grumbled out, and turned away.

As the diner door closed at his back, Amil stared

into the falling snow and felt completely lost. There was plenty in Pittsburgh for a visitor to enjoy, but in that moment, all he wanted to do was to disappear. Oblivion promised to be lonely, but perhaps it wasn't as cold. As he slid the key into the icy door of his vehicle, a familiar and bitter voice called his name.

"Hey, that's not what I meant. I wanna talk, too. I don't have the words either. Look, I'm about to start my shift. Gimme a call after 6, okay?"Ali slipped him a folded napkin that contained her phone number. Without a smile, she turned away and hurried back to the diner.

Amil slid into his truck, and the cab held an air of annoyance, a suffocating ambiance of frustration. "What the fuck am I gonna do until 6?" he wondered aloud.

Born into a speck of a village, Amil was afraid to lose himself in a foreign city, and so he didn't wander far from the diner. He drove away, and, upon finding a movie theater, he decided to take in a flick. It was an exercise designed only to waste time, and what a waste of minutes it proved to be. The feature was a rather uneventful and clichéd action film. The world was about to end, government conspiracies were abundant, and terrorist groups ruled the day. Enter the conquering hero, unwilling and unwittingly thrown into the fragile plot, only to discover an uncanny knack for saving the day. Bombs went off, cars were chased, and impossible physical stunts were performed. Boredom and stupidity spread their stains over the screen, and Amil left before the credits rolled. He couldn't sit still, as the flow of time had ground to a halt.

Finally, after the longest afternoon in the history of the measured day concluded, Amil dialed the numbers that he had since memorized. The third conversation shared

51

between he and Ali went along as awkwardly as the two
that had preceded it, but at the end of this massacred
version of verbal exchange, they agreed to meet. He picked
her up outside the diner and Ali directed the way to her
apartment.

Ali usually walked to work, but as the days were
growing colder and night fell early, she savored the chance
to have a warm ride home. Once they slipped into her
apartment, Amil sat in her cluttered living room and
solemnly flipped through The Sporting News as Ali got
changed. He had started to read six different stories when
she grabbed her coat and motioned for them to leave. It was
for the best. Amil had no intention of finishing any of the
articles, for their conclusions were assuredly too warm for
his jaded heart to take.

Ali did her makeup in the visor mirror of the truck,
and all the while directed Amil to a destination unknown to
him. They wove past beautiful homes and discarded houses,
all in a period of time that felt impossibly small. After
about fifteen quiet minutes had elapsed away, Ali pulled a
pink knit cap over her head and slipped on a pair of gloves.
She instructed him to park the truck, and soon, he realized
why his date had dressed so warmly.

They got out of the truck and left it to sleep along
the street under the shadow of a modest castle. The edifice
fascinated Amil, as it stood curiously misplaced in such an
urban environment. The pair walked up the quiet and wide
promenade which ran through the trendy and eccentric
neighborhood of Lawrenceville. Among the chill and the
wrap of darkness, Amil still couldn't unravel his
companion's plan, as not a bar or other such establishment
suited to a casual date was within sight.

"Here, quick, follow me," instructed Ali, as she started to climb an iron fence that ran the length of the sidewalk.

"What are you doing?" asked Amil.

"Just come on, don't be a fag. Hurry up, before someone sees."

Amil took her command, and, as the pair dropped down over the other side of the black bars, they found themselves in Allegheny Cemetery.

"You took me to a graveyard?" questioned Amil, a bit amused at Ali's choice of scenery.

"Is this creepy? It's a little creepy, isn't it?"

"No, not really. It is weird, though. Mostly cold as shit, but a little weird," he said.

"Toughen up, southern boy," Ali said through a laugh.

"It gets cold in Virginia."

"Well it gets colder here, so quit your bitching," commanded Ali playfully.

"You could have warned me, ya know."

"That would have just spoiled the fun."

"So why are we here anyway?" asked Amil.

"Where else were we gonna go? I have chemical dependency issues, so going to a bar is out. You just saw a shitty movie, so screw that, and I work with food all day. Sorry...I hope you ate already."

"I haven't had much of an appetite today, but now that you mention it."

"Here, eat this," offered Ali, as she pulled a Snickers bar from her purse.

"So, back to my original question, why are we here?" asked Amil again, through a filter of peanuts and nougat.

"Because if you go to Pittsburgh, Allegheny Cemetery is one of the places you have to visit."

"We have dead people in Virginia, too."

"Don't be a smartass. This is one of the largest cemeteries in the state. Josh Gibson is buried here, Steven Foster, too," said Ali.

"Who's he?"

"He was a musician...never mind, he's dead. Who cares?"

Amil laughed at Ali's comment and the general circumstances of the situation. They continued to talk, a bit more leisurely, as they paced slowly under the starlit sky. Snowflakes drifted down upon them, and the glow of moonlight bounced off the graves. They must have walked for miles, passing sophisticated mausoleums, unique tombs, and graves so insignificant and small they were barely noticeable. As they started to retrace their route and the ghosts of the footprints left before, Amil softly took Ali by her gloved hand.

"Is it safe here?" he asked, a little intimidated by the urban setting that towered beyond the gates.

"You scared?"

"No, I was just asking."

"Well, I suppose it can be a little dangerous, but I don't usually come down here after dark."

"You talk funny," stated Amil, as he found her accent endearing.

"Me?" questioned Ali, equally amused.

"Yeah, okay," he conceded.

"So, you come here a lot. What for?" he continued.

"I like to be alone. I don't have many friends, and

even when I did, I just did a bunch of drugs and a lot of other shit I'm not proud of. I'm able to think here. You don't get bothered, and even when someone else passes by, they never say anything."

"Then why did you agree to hang out with me?" he asked.

"Because of what you said this morning. We don't really know each other, but I feel like you can understand me. Besides, every time you looked at me today, not once did you look at my scar. Most people don't do that."

"I was happy when you showed up this morning, scars and all," he said.

"You wanna go back to my place?" Ali asked, and then hesitated. "Don't get excited, nothing's gonna happen."

"Okay," Amil said, with a laugh. Coming from anyone else, the comment would have made him uncomfortable, but from Ali, it just sounded natural. Then again, she had taken him to an outdoor party in mid-November with 150,000 of her closest friends.

Back at her apartment, Ali made some grilled cheese sandwiches and brewed a pot of coffee, of all things. The pair sat closely on the couch and watched infomercials for some of the most bizarre garbage ever conceived. Her cat slept in her lap, but was often disturbed as Ali and Amil giggled wearily at the ridiculous contraptions being pitched by the television. As the sun was soon to rise, it became clear that their time together had reached its end.

"What happens now?" questioned Ali as Amil rounded up his things.

"I don't know. I haven't thought of *next* very often over the past year."

"Well, do you wanna see me again?" she asked.

"Yeah, of course I do. I had a lot of fun tonight. It's just gonna be hard because of the distance."

"Don't take this the wrong way, but I'm kinda relieved that we live far apart. I don't know if I'm cut out to handle anything more substantial than a long-distance thing."

"I guess we'll find out. See ya around," said Amil quietly, as he left the apartment.

Over the course of the next few months, Amil and Ali developed something which came to resemble a genuine relationship. Every weekend he would make the long trip to Pittsburgh to be with her, and the couple came to enjoy each other's company more and more with each visit. They had a bona fide first date, and did things that most couples do in the early stages of any relationship. They visited some of the local museums, checked out a few movies, and walked around an art gallery or two. They went to an exhibit on Greco-Roman technology at the Carnegie Science Center, blew some money at the casino, and ate at countless restaurants of every description. Ali scored a couple of outrageously priced Steelers tickets, and as they sat in the crowded, frozen confines of Heinz Field, Amil desperately strained to understand the joy of attending an outdoor football game in January.

It seemed as though the young couple had managed to do a great many things during a relatively short period of time, considering that they usually only saw each other for two days out of every week. In fact, about the only activity they had failed to do was to have sex. They made out and pawed at one another. It was common for Ali to fall asleep on the couch with her head in Amil's lap as they snuggled in front of the TV. They would always sleep together in Ali's bed, but a twitchy repose brought on by strange dreams was the rowdiest activity that the mattress hosted.

"Are we ever gonna have sex, Ali?" questioned Amil on a frigid morning in February.

"Maybe. Yeah, probably one day I figure that'll happen," Ali answered easily.

"I'm serious."

"Is it a problem?"

"Well, no, I guess. I just wanna know where we're at. I wanna know where this is going," he said.

"Let me tell ya something about me."

"Here goes..." Amil joked.

"Since the time I was 15, I fucked about every boy I ever dated within the first week. Shit, some nights I'd just get drunk and bang a random dude. And, oh yeah, the last boyfriend I had made me do porn...wow, you've probably even seen it, haven't you?" questioned Ali, as she began to chew her nails.

"Ali...I'm not like those other guys," whispered Amil.

"Yeah, I know, dumbass, that's why I'm still with you. The point is that every relationship I've had has been based on sex. It holds a lot of bad memories for me. I mean, for fuck's sake, my Dad doesn't even acknowledge I exist 'cause I've been such a slut. So maybe you can dig why I'm a little apprehensive?"

"It just doesn't have to be a bad thing."

"I know. I just don't want you to be another guy on my list that I don't speak to anymore...I love you, Amil. And you better feel lucky for it, 'cause that's not something I've said very often," she instructed curtly, with a sniffle.

"I love you too, Ali. I'll never hurt you," he said as he wrapped her up in his arms.

"Promise?"

"Yeah, I promise."

"Good, because if I don't get laid soon, I'm gonna end up in the nuthouse," said Ali.

Spring arrived. The last heaps of dirtied snow melted away, and the white hue of pulverized salt finally disappeared from the surface of the roads. Amil left Cincinnati behind for good, and, in doing so, he closed the book on his career in professional sports. He and Ali moved a few addresses down to a slightly more spacious apartment on Middle Street. With the last of the cash left over from his impossibly short stint as a Major League pitcher, Amil made the space they shared quite cozy with a full set of new furnishings. He bought Ali a car. It wasn't new, but it beat the hell out of riding the bus every day or walking through the mercurial Pittsburgh weather.

Amil scored a job driving a forklift for a local paper plant. He enjoyed the work, and the pay was better than he had anticipated. The modest wage would never compare to the game checks he was once destined to cash, but it would get him and Ali by. He got on well with his coworkers, as most of the guys liked to talk baseball with him like he was Nolan Ryan. But most of all, the rugged Southerner liked the fact that he could wear jeans to work and keep the shaggy beard that obscured his chin.

As he returned home from an ordinary day at the plant in the late afternoon under the burn of a July sun, Amil found Ali on the porch. Encased in red, weathered brick, solid as a castle's fortification, the porch was shielded on all sides by a brown and moderately tattered awning. Suspended above the cool, concrete surface was Ali, as she hid in the shade within the cradle of a canvas swing. Wearing a tank top, a pair of fuzzy boots, and short-shorts, she lay easily on the fabric, chatting away on the phone. A cigarette hung from her fingers and an ashtray that had long since been conquered by exhausted Newports sat upon the ground. Casting the butt into the mass grave of its fallen brethren, she smiled and gave a girly wave of her fingers to Amil. Before he could exit this vision, Amil smiled too, but not back at Ali, necessarily. The joyful feeling he felt was born from the very condition of their situation. Perhaps leaving his elbow out there on the surface of PNC Park wasn't such a bad offering to fate after all. It then occurred to him that normal life was the treasure he had needed most all along.

There they stayed on Middle Street for the next handful of years, and life for the young couple played out in a predictable, but pleasing, fashion. The little apartment played host to a lot of parties. Beer was drank, cops were called, and every once in a while, a streaker would be traced back to their home. They stayed up late, played music much too loud for the taste of the elderly woman who lived upstairs, and developed a regular sexual routine.

But more went on between the walls on their apartment than the rowdy exploits of twenty-somethings. Ali and Amil had a future plan. Some detours were taken, and the distractions of maladroit spending were a bit too strong to resist at times, but eventually, their dreams began to take a tangible shape.

Part 7. The days of farewell

Two weeks before Amil's 31st birthday, he and Ali purchased a house on Delafield Avenue in Aspinwall. It was large, a full three stories, each of which demanded a great amount of care and attention. But for all its shortcomings, the new owners could see the future, and longed for the day when the building would realize its full potential. Smack in the middle of the street, the house rose from the light color of the brick road and was shaded under the watch of a large maple tree. A set of cement steps grew from the sidewalk, and they ascended to a brick-enclosed porch that bore a striking resemblance to the one at the old place on Middle Street. The difference here, though, was that this charming area had not been savaged by a life spent accommodating the likes of youthful renters. The wood trim that framed it boasted a fresh application of blue paint, and a variety of hanging baskets, which overflowed with life, were left to sway with the breeze. A set of chimes dangled from the ceiling, and a brand new welcome mat graced the threshold.

With all the money the pair could scrape together, and with many of youth's whims sacrificed on the altar of adulthood, the house quickly became a place that Ali and Amil loved to call home. They refinished the hardwood floors, updated the tacky light fixtures that grew from the walls like tumors, and tried their hands at the adventurous art of plumbing. They paid to have a new roof installed after a late-summer storm decorated the yard with shingles, and discovered that wiring is best left to electricians.

Finally, after three years and nary a penny spent on anything else but the house, Amil and Ali had the first floor renovated. The entrance level had been outfitted for a business, while the couple made their home on the upper floors. With nothing more than a few loans and a shared passion for the printed word, the couple, who had never bothered with the formality of marriage, opened a used bookstore.

They stocked their shelves with hard-to-find and eclectic titles, hoping that the outré vibe they chose would attract customers. They plundered garage sales and flea markets, and ordered any volume that was both bizarre and affordable. A sizeable portion of their library was comprised of books with faded covers and tattered corners. This influence of use added to the character of the traveled volumes, and set their little shop apart from the glossy sheen of chain stores. They didn't have a set theme. Ali and Amil preferred it this way. As they collected books on subjects that ranged from the occult to cooking and everything in-between, the couple was flush with excitement.

Like most ventures, this plunge into entrepreneurship started slow, and the utter dearth of business had Ali terrified that she and Amil had cast themselves into an inescapable pit of debt. But time rewarded their commitment and all the sweat put into the raising of the store. Soon, a small but loyal clientele kept The Back Shelf Bookstore afloat, and, once word began to spread, things began to look truly promising.

They both had to keep full-time jobs, and the bookstore was still just an elaborate hobby, but the verdict was in on Amil and Ali's little venture. Write-ups in the local papers, and public endorsements from the alt element of Pittsburgh's indie scene, made their shop a hip place to visit. The bookstore gained the recognition and status usually reserved for shops in the trendy neighborhoods of

Oakland and Shadyside. It gained appeal across a broad spectrum of people. Uncommon it was not to view a greyed and seasoned college professor standing shoulder to shoulder with a punky goth chick as they both set their fingers in the pursuit of strange tomes.

A boom of business was soon the result of the couple's endeavor, and although it was welcome, the unforeseen rise of popularity caught Ali and Amil a bit unprepared. It was a constant grind, as they were forever engaged in the search for unique and affordable titles. The research required to maintain such a high standard became an interminable, albeit rewarding, journey for the new entrepreneurs. In these whirlwind days of nurturing a fresh business, the couple slept less than during the more energetic times of their twenties. But for all the untold challenges that were unearthed, the experience only served to bring Ali and Amil closer together. Although their love was always genuine, it was fused by tragedy and a common pain. At long last, after years with one another, they were finally bonded by positivity.

As money came in on a more regular basis, Ali was able to take a breath. She quit waiting tables and devoted all her attention to The Back Shelf. With this uninterrupted commitment, she slowly transformed the miniature library into a cozy sanctuary for her guests. Thanks to thrift stores, an unconventional collection of furniture, descriptions of which ranged from the elegant to the wickedly strange, made themselves comfortably at home among the shelves. Framed artwork, both bought and graciously donated by customers, was hung from the walls, as were the replications of obscure quotes. A surround sound music system that whispered sonatas was installed, and the ambient air was lusciously fragrant with the aroma of scented oils.

As time wore on, the dedicated couple took out another loan and rolled the dice again as they introduced a small coffee bar to the busy interior of the first floor. An array of sweets and frothy drinks found their place at The Back Shelf. This new addition brought with it more demands, but it also generated a rather steady flow of revenue, with most of the credit going to the seemingly irresistible taste of the blueberry muffins.

All throughout the end of a gentle spring and on into the depths of summer, The Back Shelf swelled with activity. It was a trying feat to keep the bare minimum of necessary materials behind the counter and upon the shelves. It seemed as though their tiny business was destined to become a must-visit hot spot for book enthusiasts of all walks. All this adulation filled Amil with a sense of pride. He never would have dared to imagine such success after enduring the setbacks of his upbringing. Coming from a place such as Fog Lake, and having his dreams of a baseball career evaporate, this life that he and Ali led felt impossibly good. The pace was hectic, but all the activity and buzz kept Amil moving and upbeat. But Ali didn't fully share her mate's sentiment, at least not anymore.

The past few months of their feverish vocation left Ali overwhelmed and exhausted. She felt a pride as deep as Amil's, but to her, being busy felt like being cornered. She started to have minor panic attacks, and withdrew from life spent away from the duties of business. She hadn't told Amil how difficult a time she was having. Ali couldn't find the heart, as she knew how much he loved to watch the shop develop and expand. In pained secrecy, she had hoped that he would pick up on her distance and reach out to her. His focus torn from her, it was as if he had become completely absorbed in their business and the desire to fuel its already substantial growth.

With him still working full time at the paper plant, Ali felt like she was losing Amil. They rarely fought, and a common love went with them to sleep each night, but a space of nothingness was spreading between them all the same. As she lay awake at night, Ali watched the chasm yawn. It was then that she realized far more had been bitten off than she could chew. The last year and a half passed by as if flashed away on a bolt of lightning. And during that seemingly compressed portion of time, The Back Shelf had turned on her and became a burden. There was too much activity, too much responsibility, just too much of everything. Ali felt guilty. She felt like a failure, but she couldn't go on like this. She wanted Amil back, and the small life they once had.

Late on a Friday night when the store would have usually been closed, the doors remained open and allowed the warmth of a late summer's night to drift inside. About twice a month, and to the silent chagrin of Ali, another new element introduced itself to the bookstore. Local bands added color to the air as they performed before small audiences. The flavor was a bit mild for Ali's metallic taste, but Amil found affection for the introspective nature of many of the singer-songwriters. The personal retelling of hardship and the enriched layers with which the yarns were woven spoke to his sensibilities. He could relate to the loneliness and alienation that was spoken of as he was made to remember the limitations of his beginnings in Fog

Lake.

      As they held longer hours on these nights, Ali and Amil employed the help of a neighborhood girl. She was barely old enough to drive, but she could handle a cash register and watch the store while the bands kept most of the customers occupied. Tonight, her assistance felt angelic as Ali sat outside on the bottom step and smoked what had to be the day's thirty-seventh cigarette. She tapped her feet stridently upon the rigid surface of the sidewalk, a march of defiance over the soft chords of the music being played, as she witnessed Amil parking his truck some distance down the street. As he approached with a Taco Bell bag in his hands, Ali flicked the butt into the street and rubbed a hand across her face.

      "What did ya bring me?" she questioned.

      "Who says I got ya anything?" he joked in return.

      "If you wanna have any teeth left to chew that taco, you're gonna produce a burrito from that bag."

      "I got soft tacos."

      Ali laughed. She unwrapped her meat log, and poked Amil in the ribs as he took a seat next to her.

      "Ya know..." she started, with a mouthful of processed food. "That was the most you've said to me all day."

      "What are you talking about? I've been with you almost all day," he said truthfully, ignorant as to the source of her statement.

      "Work doesn't count. I mean, that's the first time today that you've talked to me like I'm still your girlfriend. I think this is getting to be too much. I'm tired, Amil."

      "I'm tired, too. No one ever said this would be easy."

"No, I'm fucking exhausted."

"I thought you loved this place. It's ours. It's something we've made-"

"I do love the shop, but I love you more. And now it seems like we only see each other on the first floor of our own home. We barely talk about anything but what goes on in there. It sounds kinda sick, but I sort of miss life the way it used to be."

"You mean when you used to work for other people?" asked Amil, a little sour.

"Yeah...I do love what we've made, but I've also realized something. You can be in love and be miserable at the same time."

"You're just having a bad day. You were like this when we first opened the shop too," Amil reminded her.

"Some chick came in today and bought a book on '50s pinups. She wants to be a model. She said she's gonna resurrect the classic pinup and sounded real confident about it too. Like I give a fuck. Look at my face, Amil!"

"It's alright. She probably just didn't know," he said softly, hoping to calm Ali quickly, as the volume of her voice was getting quite loud.

"Inconsiderate little bitch," Ali whispered, tears in her eyes.

"They'll be done in there soon. Let's just chill out with a movie, we'll clean up in the morning," offered Amil, as he kissed the side of her head.

"Yeah," responded Ali with a thin breath, as she pulled another smoke from her depleted pack.

Winter arrived, and it was busy business as usual at The Back Shelf. Ali always wore a smile before her customers and lightly chatted with the regulars, but underneath, she was deeply unhappy. The source of her emotional disfigurement was something she could not pin down. Her misery seemed to have been born from a myriad of troubles. The heightened responsibility she took on with the bookstore felt overwhelming at times, and the demands of home ownership wore her down. Her distant moods served to crack the solid relationship between her and Amil, and, as she grew older, Ali began to look back on her youth through the lens of regret.

Once in her thirties, the lines of age coursed their way around her mouth, and her thin thighs of yesterday revealed themselves to be unattainable relics of the past. Ali lost her tolerance for high heels, and her nails, which once changed their shade almost daily, rarely were given any attention.

With Amil out running errands, Ali sat all alone on the couch in a pair of sweats. The Monday Night Football game was on, but she paid little notice to the TV. As she stroked her aged cat, her mind recalled all the mistakes she had made. She had ruined a lucrative career, cut her family out of nearly every aspect of her life, and behaved in a reprehensible manner for years. She and Amil had achieved quite a bit, and they carved out a nice life for themselves, but these thoughts did little to assuage Ali's discomfort. If anything, it only made her mood worse. She should be happy and content, but she wasn't. There was something inside her that was unsettled, something that yearned for a life more spectacular. But that was a life that thirty-something Ali would have to accept as a fantasy never to be. Like a teenager who's furious about being normal as opposed to being a rock star, she felt resentment creep into her.

As she sat slumped over, feeling sorry for herself, Ali envisioned all she could have been. Up against an invincible foe, she couldn't stop the carousel of memories of all the sordid sexual acts she once performed as it spun around her head. They made her feel disgusting, but above all things, they made her think of drugs.

Ali pulled a small bottle from behind the couch and shook up the pills inside. Unknown to Amil, she had obtained a prescription for depression some time ago. She took a few here and there, but nothing seemed to help. While on the medicine, Ali felt like a zombie, staggering on slowly while trapped inside a wheel. She popped the lid open and clicked it shut. Snap, click, snap, click. She hungered for something with a bit more of a bite. After a few minutes had been spent inside the darkest places of her mind, she walked into the kitchen and flung the pills down the throat of the garbage disposal.

Into the cold night, Ali sped off for the nearest bar. Although a sip of alcohol found her lips on occasion, going to a bar alone was something that she hadn't done in over a decade. A tight, knee-length leather skirt hugged her legs, which were adorned with a pair of black stockings and matching set of go-go boots. Her hair tumbled down her shoulders, and the deeply split top she wore attracted more than a few looks as she stepped into a local tavern. She took a seat at the end of the bar and ordered a gin and tonic. Curls of smoke swam among her locks, and smeared recreations of her lips appeared on her glass and on the ends of one cigarette after the next. She stared at the TV in front of her, but, as she anxiously bounced one leg over the other, her seductive vulnerability cried out to the sharks. Although the pub wasn't very crowded, it didn't take long before a caveman in a polo shirt decided to try his luck on the lonely chick already halfway through her fourth drink.

With the brutal concoction of depression and the buzz of booze, Ali's muddled mood enjoyed the attention that was being paid to her. She flirted with the man clearly ten years older than she and managed to score another couple of free drinks. The man, who introduced himself as Larry, stroked Ali's leather-clad leg, and his eyes lingered upon the vision of her breasts. It was an obvious look, and one easily noticed even in an inebriated state, but she didn't mind. It felt good, all of it, the alcohol in her blood, the hug of her revealing top, the touch of a strange man.

"Hey," she whispered to Larry with a stripper's disingenuous smile wedged in the corner of her mouth. "You got any coke?"

He smiled back, like any proper cretin might do. "Nope, but I got these."

"What are they?" asked Ali, as a few pills swam around in a plastic bag that Larry allowed to poke from his pocket.

"They'll do the trick."

"Good enough for me," Ali stated, as she swiped the bag.

As she rose to a rickety stance from her stool, Ali giggled. She smacked Larry on the ass as she made her way to the bathroom. She set the pills out over the porcelain sink and crushed them into a powder. She sucked the line up her nose and felt the backs of her eyes burn with the touch of something toxic. As she washed her hands under the condemning light of a fluorescent bulb, Ali stared into the streaked mirror. Tears welled in her eyes, and as they fell, they carved canals through the thick layer of makeup that she wore. She stood there, bracing herself on the porcelain, and crying endlessly into the sink. When she stepped out, Ali cast a set of daggers over to Larry and shot him her middle finger with its red painted tip.

"What the fuck are you looking at?" she snarled to no one in particular as she emerged out into the chill of winter.

Ali shuffled into her car and fumbled for the ignition. She made her way out of the parking lot and onto the main road before she thought to turn on the headlights. Every light was piercing, and all the other cars whirled by as though moving at the speed of sound, but not Ali's. To her, it felt as though it would require an eternity of driving to make the short trip back home. After a couple of swerves over the center line, she managed to find the cobblestone of her street. She left her car with a crooked placement and cracked the door off a signpost as she exited the vehicle. Over the slick sidewalk, she practically resorted to a crawl as she made her way to the front door.

As Ali staggered up the stairs from the darkened space of the bookstore, she realized Amil was already home. The sight he was treated to was upsetting. Looking beaten, like a convicted criminal, Ali leaned up against the inside of the door and stared at Amil through bleary eyes. Her sexy look was wrinkled, her makeup was smeared, and her body stunk of a mix of smoke, gin and perfume. Her eyes were half open, and a neglected cigarette dangled from her mouth. She tossed her purse in the corner of the room and made her way back to where this forgettable evening had started.

"You wanna tell me what this is all about?" he questioned.

"Try being sensitive, Amil," Ali sniveled, as she sat on the couch.

"Should I be? I don't know what you've done."

"I fucked up, that's what I did. I'm a goddamn drug addict and I'm drunk," she said.

"Is that all you did?"

"Is that how it is? Are you just gonna think of yourself? Do you wanna know if I fucked another guy? Huh? Maybe if you'd fuck me once in a while."

"Jesus Christ, Ali."

"I didn't, okay! I got hammered, hit on some dude, blew a couple of pills up my nose and then I thought of you, so would you please sit next to me?" begged Ali. Although she deeply loved him, Ali wished that Amil would make an effort to be a bit more compassionate. Especially in moments such as this, when the temptation to hurl something in his direction was near irresistible.

"Alright," agreed Amil. He never quite knew the right things to say, but in this instance, he wasn't exactly searching for the words. He felt as though Ali was hiding her behavior behind old excuses, as he struggled to understand the intangible affliction of depression that crept up on her from time to time.

"I'm sorry. Sometimes I just get down on myself. Today was bad...I don't know."

"Maybe you need to see a doctor," said Amil.

Ali laughed in frustration. "They're gonna give me more drugs. I'm not taking drugs."

"It's medicine. There's a difference."

"Not to me. Why can't you understand that?"

"Okay, okay. Then we'll figure this out. Look, if we have to scale things back, we will."

"What about money? We need that," said Ali.

"I'd rather have you happy. Hey, we'll manage, we always have."

With snow still caked onto the bottoms of her boots, Ali curled up on the couch and rested her head on Amil's lap. She closed her eyes, and, within seconds, she passed out. Amil flicked on the TV. There was a rerun of SportsCenter, and the topic being discussed was some possible rule changes that might take place during this year's upcoming baseball season. This came as a cruel coincidence. His exile from baseball usually didn't bother him much, but this certainly wasn't the time. In a way, this felt like their first meeting in the diner all those years ago. Two damaged people set before each other with nothing to say. Amil turned the TV back off and joined Ali in forgetting about the day.

As the invincible hammers of time beat the nails of the past into memory, the space between the couple became an abyss. Amil could feel as the gap widened with every day that crept by, but there was something that he dwelled upon that made healing a difficult process. He was shocked at how blind he had been to her escalating battle with depression. It became so clear to him. Ali hadn't been happy for months, maybe more than a year's time, and he had done nothing to help her.

A swamp of guilt swelled in him, but a retrospective mind keep him from moving forward. Instead, he agonized over all the little things, and the silent cries for help that he had passed off as mood swings or nothing of consequence at all. They had been together a long time, and, as quiet nights found them with more frequency, Amil had ignored the obvious, as he cast the muted evenings into the realm of nothing left to say.

They had done less, laughed less, made love less and, still, Amil had chalked up this lethargy as a symptom of age and routine. But there was more to it than that, something deeper, something darker, which had served to drive them apart. Amil came to see the frost as it settled over their relationship. He hated the apathy that they bounced off each other the way they once used to exchange energy and love.

A dark winter was finally lifting, but it did not go alone. With its passing, the season robbed hope from the couple and replaced it with tribulation and anguish. A string of bad investments, an unexpected dip in business, and a rotten run of luck had left the pair desperate for money. The Back Shelf Bookstore cut its hours, and the coffee bar operated on weekends only. This loosening of responsibilities could have been a boon for Ali, but instead, she was forced back to a waitress's work and the thin hope of a more steady pay. They saw less of each other, but when they shared company, the time was usually spent sleeping, bickering, or mired in a pained absence of speech.

As spring rose from the earth, Amil drove as slowly as he could on his way home from work. His hours had been slashed, and he dreaded having to relay this news to Ali. It wasn't the money, or the fact that they would be forced to again sacrifice barely necessary amenities, he just didn't feel up to the challenge of combating another breakdown. She'd had three pretty wicked meltdowns recently. Amil was counting, and he was reaching his breaking point. The fact that he entertained the thought of leaving Ali in her greatest time of need made Amil hate himself. But the truth remained that, in over a decades' time, he had never felt further away from her than he did right then.

Amil walked through the kitchen and threw his keys upon the counter. He poured himself a glass of juice and stared into the cup in his hand. He gulped down the tart liquid, rubbed his face, and ascended the stairs up toward their bedroom. He found Ali there. She was still in front of the mirror, adding the final touches to her makeup.

"They cut my hours," he blurted out, not knowing how else to start this awful conversation.

"Remember when, no matter how bad your day was, you would give me a kiss as soon as you came home?" asked Ali. "I miss that."

"I miss a lot of stuff."

"What the hell happened?" she wondered aloud as she plunked herself down next to him on the bed.

"Life."

"This ain't life, Amil. Everything happens too fast now. It seems like just yesterday that everything was great. Now everything sucks."

"What are we gonna do?"

"I don't know, I really don't know. We're barely getting by as it is. I just wish things were simpler, like they used to be."

"What do you mean?" questioned Amil.

"Like when we lived on Middle Street. Sure that place was a dump and we were poor, but I've never been happier in my whole life. It was like it was just me and you, and nothing else mattered."

"We can get there again, happy, I mean. This is just gonna be hard."

"Fuck, you always say shit like that," she

74

whispered.

"Like what?"

"You never actually offer a solution. You just say *things are gonna get better, or we'll be okay,* but you can't just wish away all this crap. It doesn't go away just because you ignore it."

"I know. But I don't know what to do. I'm doing all I can just to keep us afloat. You're not making it any easier, ya know?" he said.

"What's that supposed to mean?"

"It's just hard to get motivated to change with you moping around all the time."

"I can't believe you would say that to me. Do you think I enjoy feeling like this every day?" she snapped at him.

"Maybe you do, Ali, maybe you do. Because if you didn't, you might actually get help."

"You'll never understand. I'm going to work."

"Come on, I'll drive you," Amil offered in a hushed tone, as he tried to make amends.

"Don't fucking touch me!" screamed Ali, as she shook his hand loose from her arm and continued down the stairs and further away from him.

Suffering mutual disintegration, they navigated their way through another month of muck and misery with nary a word mixed in with all the waste. The guilt that Amil once felt for failing to recognize Ali's somberness for a legitimate disease quickly faded, and was replaced with anger. He quietly blamed her for the decline of the bookstore. He harbored resentment for her, for this was the second time in his life that a passion he had nurtured was torn away. Ali, meanwhile, sunk into her depression with a lugubrious fervor and sniped at Amil for the way in which he chewed his food and a horde of other even more trivial transgressions. It was as though all love between them had vanished, and all that remained was a couple who had stayed together for years past the expiration date of their union.

"Aren't you even gonna say hi?" she taunted as Amil returned home from work.

"Don't fucking start with me, Ali."

"Just leave."

"This is my house, too. So why don't you pack your shit and get out?" he asked with an impatient gesture of his hand.

"I will, if that's what it takes. I'm leaving you, Amil," she stated.

"I'm surprised you have the ambition to do anything with all the sitting around on your fat ass that you do. Isn't leaving me gonna interrupt all the time you set aside to feel helpless and sorry for yourself?"

His remark shot Ali from the couch like lightning through the fattened underbelly of a cloud and planted her mere inches from his face.

"I can't believe I used to love you," she growled.

"I can't believe I still love you. I just can't stand the sight of you anymore."

Ali shoved him. She indulged old habits of throwing items at the target of her ire, and raked her nails across Amil's face. In the grip of rage, Amil did something that he could have never fathomed he would ever do. With all the vigor he once used to hurl a baseball, Amil smashed his fist across Ali's face. She fell to the floor and started to cry as visions of Max descended over her. Her bottom lip

76

was split, and the fissure leaked a stream of blood onto the carpet. She could feel with her tongue that his punishment had cracked the denture she had worn since recovering from Max's assault. She brought a hand up to her face and twitched as a warm rush of blood ran over her fingers. As she gazed into her reddened hand, Ali experienced the mightiest sensation of betrayal and loss that she had ever felt.

She raised her eyes to Amil. They were polished with a glaze of tears. The old scar upon her face was speckled in new blood. As he looked into her face, a face that he had rendered damaged and pained, Amil knew that he would never escape the condemning glare of her blue gems. What he did was more than a punch, more than a brutal affliction applied in a moment of rage. What he did, no, what he had become, was everything that Ali feared and despised. He was once her source of solace and safety. Now he had joined the ranks of her nightmares and mistakes.

Amil had never before prayed to God, but in that terrible moment, he prayed for any god that might hear him to strike him down and commit his eternal soul to everlasting torture. Even such damnation didn't sound harsh enough. He could never take back what he had done. He could never atone for this most heinous and regrettable of acts.

Amid a crushing silence, Amil turned away from Ali. She lay on the floor, her mouth glistening with blood and her eyes wetted with tears as they stared into him, but he could not bear to stay. He left Ali alone on the floor, and walked out of the house like a corpse tugged on by strings. The door didn't close behind him. As Amil stepped away, the image left behind was as clear as the landscape before his wide eyes. With a haunted clarity, he could see Ali crumpled on her side, legs draped over one another and her arms folded up against her chest. He could see the pain as it distorted her face and the beads of sweat as they matted her hair. Amil couldn't shake the vision of the blood as it ran a twisted course around her chin before dropping to the rug in rivulets of betrayal.

What happened next must have happened to someone else, because Amil's mind retained no memory of his actions. He didn't recall getting into his truck or putting it in gear. He had no recollection of which direction he chose, or whether or not the radio was left to play. He didn't know how long of a drive he took. He had no knowledge of how fast he drove, or if he was mired in a traffic jam. His brain stored no image of the bus he cut off, and he remembered nothing of the accident that totaled his truck and sunk him into a coma for two weeks.

When he awoke, Amil was informed that he had suffered a punctured lung, an assortment of cracked ribs, and a broken collarbone. His left arm had been flayed to bits by an onslaught of glass and steel, and the back of his skull was marked by a fresh fracture. The bones contained within the skin of his right leg were turned to dust, and his foot had been bent in a direction that would have made a blind man wince. He lost a significant measure of vision in one eye, and the left side of his face became a gulag for scars.

As he lay dazed in a hospital room filled with the sounds of monitors, he looked to Ali as she sat by his side. In his weakened state, he couldn't do much other than stare, but the condition of his skinny, grey, and hairless form conveyed his emotions perfectly. Apparently, she had been there the whole time, holding Amil's hand and gently stroking his shaved head. Whatever damage he had done to her had faded from her face, but the solemn look in her eyes told of the ugliness that filled that fateful day. But for all the misery the two had worked so doggedly to craft, it had taken a series of devastating events to remind them of the true force of love.

Amil tried to speak, but Ali delicately shushed his attempt and begged him to save his strength. She ran her fingers across his forehead and whispered something to him before placing her hand in his. He squeezed her thin fingers and watched as she turned away. Ali peered out the window as the invincible urge to cry twisted her face. She was illuminated by bars of light as the sun shone through the slats of the blinds, and, as Amil saw her striped in amber, he felt what it meant to hate.

A feverish animosity for himself and all the ruin he had wrought was born within Amil. He knew Ali had been with him for most every second of his newfound shiftless state, and he was stung by her loyalty and devotion. He wouldn't have blamed her if she so much had neglected to send flowers, but to stay with him and to endure this torture seemed cruelly unfair. It was he who had brought this down upon them, and, through his actions, Ali was again made to suffer. Though he still lacked the capacity to express himself, Amil wished for Ali to leave him. He desired for her to at last be free of their acidic relationship and emancipate herself from the burden that he had become.

As he lay within the stale air of his dimly lit room, Amil recalled all the fractures of their union and his laziness as he had stepped over them. The vision of Ali on the floor with blood upon her lips never left his mind. In fact, it seemed to be all that he could remember. It was a movie with no buildup or climax. It coldly looped that one tragic scene, and its repetition forged Amil onto a guilt so heavy it could have dragged the whole world down to hell.

Though he remembered none of the efforts that were applied in the salvaging of his life, Amil felt like a machine that had been rebuilt with inferior parts. His bald head supported a patchwork of scars, and his leg was rebuilt using a cold collaboration of steel bars and screws. His shredded arm had healed into an unsightly mass of lumpy skin and differently hued scars, while his insides felt like they only operated on a primal and crude basis.

During the months that followed, Ali found strength that she never knew existed as she accompanied Amil to all the physical therapy and doctors' appointments that filled their calendar. She took on the responsibilities of a medical staff, and sleep became a shy and irregular friend, but Ali was as strong with devotion as Amil was physically weak. She became ever patient, and gave him a lifetime's worth of encouragement and motherly affection. She helped him to shower when his legs felt frail, and she stayed up long past his retiring to the land of dreams in order to tend to the laundry and other housework that had gone neglected. She smiled anytime Amil properly pronounced a word, as his speech therapy was a slow go, and slowed her own pace in order to adjust to his struggles with simple conversation.

The Back Shelf Bookstore closed its doors during this time, and the rest of the books were sold off at cut-rate prices. Ali reduced her hours, and the couple scraped by on her meager wages and Amil's insurance and disability payouts. It was odd that after so much had been sacrificed and lost, Ali and her ailing mate were brought closer together. She committed herself fully to him, and, in turn, Amil developed a love for her that bordered on frenzy. He was overcome by her limitless compassion, and clung to her as though she were the only living force on planet earth. It was a shame that such a tragedy was required to make the couple recall the extent of their former love and to heal the wounds carved into their relationship. But in Amil, these feelings also came shackled with a constant reminder of his shame, and it entwined itself through his every cell like a cancerous agent.

"I'm...so sorry, Ali," he slurred out one night as he sat across from her at the dinner table.

"We're both to blame," she whispered.

"I love...you and only...you in this world. Be...be...because nothing else in this world is as beautiful as...you are right now," Amil said.

"I'll always take care of you," she reassured.

"...you shouldn't have to. One d...d...day, I'll make this up to...you. I swear...that one d...d...day...you'll have the life...you deserve."

"I have you," she squeaked through a choked up smile.

Amil finished the daunting task of coercing all of his peas onto his fork and drank the last of his water. He rose from the table, and, using the solid top of the mahogany for support, he shuffled his way over to Ali.

"Amil, you won't be able to get back up," she cautioned as he attempted to kneel by her side.

"As long as I'm by...you, I don't care if I ever get up...again."

As they embraced, Ali felt as a few tears warmed her cheek. She tried to stay strong, but as Amil crumbled within her arms, she allowed a river of grief to spill from her tired eyes.

By St. Patrick's Day, Amil's speech was still a bit off, but he had at least attained some command over language again. He walked with a cane, something that was unlikely to ever change, but he was able to get around on his own and without too much pain. He was able to return to work and relieve Ali of a small fraction of her burden. His sense of humor made a slight return, and, for the first time in months, the couple had sex without the interruption of pain or malfunction. Arduously slow, life wound closer to as normal as it was ever going to be, and as the days passed by, smiles found their way to Ali's lips more often.

But every light eventually yields to blackness, and as such, they were forced to sell the house. A pit of medical debt left them broke, and, although they fought tooth and nail to avoid it, the couple at last gave in to the safety net of bankruptcy. They again found themselves in a small apartment, sharing one beat-up car and dining on cheap ready-made meals. Life was as hard as it had ever been, but Ali persevered. The unconditional love Amil gave to her was all she really needed. He never lost his temper. He never complained or questioned anything she did. All his pure affections served to fill so many of the voids that had long festered inside Ali, but Amil could not shed the anguish he carried, as he felt responsible for robbing her of an independent life.

As Ali lay passed out on the couch, Amil watched her as she slept. She looked so peaceful, so young and beautiful. As he observed her slumber, Amil thought of how she should be out dining with friends, gleefully chasing a small child around the house, or unwinding while on vacation far away from the dreary Northeast. She could be tending to a new garden on Delafield Avenue, cheering wildly at a Steelers game or, jogging around the lake at North Park. But she was never going to do any of those things. Every day would be the same for Ali. She was going to tend to Amil's every need, prepare meals for him, drive him here and there, and stick close to home for fear of his rickety gait sending him down the stairs. And every single night of her life, for the rest of her life, Ali was going to pass out in front of a 21" color TV with basic cable.

In a labored process that almost brought Amil to screams, he knelt by her side, kissed her forehead, and again rose to his feet. He stepped outside and breathed in the clean air of a quiet night. He looked to the moon above and felt a kinship with the deadened orb. It did nothing but circle around the brilliant sun every day to suck away whatever light that it could. It had nothing to give in return, and even if it strived to show affection to its celestial mate, the love it had to offer was paltry. It was a shell, a cold and silent remnant of a life gone away and of a future never to come.

My dearest Ali, you have given me the greatest life a man could ever wish for or dream of. All of my fondest memories involve you there by my side. You are truly the most beautiful person I have ever met, and every day of my life with you has been a blessing. I have tried to give you the wonderful life that you deserve, but I have failed. I should have cherished you more, and I should have never taken you for granted. You are truly an angel, my angel, who has rescued and watched over me time and time again. But I know an angel never gives up, so sometimes, that burden needs to be lifted for you. I've caused you to suffer for too long, you've sacrificed for me long enough. I'll set you free of me, Ali. You deserve this second chance that I know you would never give yourself. You're still young, live your life and find a love that appreciates all the amazing things about you that I could not. I will never hurt you again, and I promise to always watch over you. Just please, remember me the way I used to be. Remember all the good times we had and all the love we shared. I am eternally sorry, my beautiful love. I will understand if you can't forgive me, but I will love you forever.

- Amil

The note dropped from Ali's fingers as she stood in paralyzing disbelief over what she had read. Her eyes shook and a deluge of tears began to wash down her face. She screamed for Amil as she frantically scanned every room for his presence, but she was all alone within the small apartment. She ran out into the street and continued to scream for the man that she loved. It was a hopeless waste of breath, for Ali had no knowledge of Amil's whereabouts, but this realization only fueled the desperate wailing which poured from her throat.

She fell to her knees on the pavement and hugged the rusted shaft of a lamppost. Her head leaned against the weathered metal, which was treated to the salty taste of her tears. She could feel the sunlight on her back and she could hear the sounds of traffic as cars whizzed by. She knew eyes were upon her breakdown, and Ali could sense the confusion that her actions had stirred, but all concern for the world around her had evaporated. As she stared at the cracked concrete at her knees, she could only think of Amil, and prayed for a miracle.

Blown by breeze, her hair clung to the rounded steel and a pool of mucus bubbled up in her throat. Her nose ran slowly, and the ruptured dams that doubled as her eyes were rimmed in red. Crackled squeaks left her mouth, and her entire body suffered tremors as her skin grew clammy and irritated. A busy day may have unfolded around her, but to Ali, the skinny road which supported their ancient apartment building was the sight of the end of the world.

After all the tragedy and misfortune that had found Ali in the past, she finally felt what it meant to have a broken heart. They were poor. Life was hard, but after so much time, she at last had someone who loved her wholly. Amil would never be the healthy, vibrant man he once was, but that was never what Ali truly desired. All she ever wanted, all she ever needed, was his unfiltered love, and, thanks to a grisly car accident, that's exactly what she had. In an instant, it all stood in peril of being ripped away. Once she had cried herself into near dehydration with her arms flung around that metal pole, Ali felt as the biggest part of her dropped out of her being and died upon the dirty surface of the sidewalk.

"Don't leave me, Amil. Please don't leave me. I love you so much," she cried into the thin air.

Far from the loudest scream, Amil continued his march through the woods. Dressed in his favorite pair of jeans and a silk button-down shirt that he had probably only worn once before, Amil slowly stepped into the heart of this land unscathed by man. At the mercy of his disabilities, the daunting task of walking through town and hiking into the seclusion of nature felt difficult enough a chore to rob him of life. Perhaps it would, then, and this laborious jaunt would spare the gun in his pocket from its intended purpose.

But amid muscle aches and heavy breathing, Amil lived. Once he came to a place where he was sure that no one would wander into, he threw his cane aside and dropped to the soft earth below. He sat under the shade of the woods and rested his back against a tree stump, hollowed out and rotten. He looked around, and was touched by the purity of the natural world. There was color, sunlight and shadow, and the air was full of sound. Insects chirped, leaves rattled in the wind, and the commotion caused by a small animal too quick to sight could be heard.

Amil took a handful of dirt and held it in his palm. As he spread his fingers, he watched as the soil fell back down and blended in with the rest of the earth. It was there, and then it was gone. His act was insignificant, and the world would continue on, completely unaware of this mild disturbance to its face. It made Amil think of his own life. He was like the dirt, and soon, he would be the dirt.

That was where he belonged, there among the worms and the decay, that's how Amil saw it. It was time. Time to finish the job that the bus had started, and time to finally lay down the shame that hung so heavy around his neck. It was time to free Ali of her obligation to look after an abusive cripple, and it was time to spare the world another day in the useless life of Amil Young. With a pure-hearted prayer to Ali calmly uttered from his lips, Amil stuck the gun in his mouth and pulled the trigger.

Chapter 2 - The end has only just begun

Part 1. Taken away

Although it had rained for the better part of two weeks, the day was bright and the sky held white smears of clouds amongst its brilliant blue body. Small puddles spotted the ground and the whole of the woods glistened due to the cooperation of sun and water. The abundance of spring brought color back to the earth and new blossoms hung from the trees. But something was amiss. Something terrible, flung beyond the most tortured corners of creation, brought its influence to the woods that held Amil's corpse.

Not a noise could be heard, and not a motion was made. The insects froze their chatter, and small mammals, which normally drench the woods in a bouquet of sound, had all hidden themselves away. The wind died off, and as water droplets fell from the leaves above, the splashes they made were muted. The trees stared straight ahead and their roots tensed with unease as they lay under the soil. All life held its collective breath as death paid a visit to the fen.

Wrapped in an evening dress as black as the most moonless night, a gorgeous woman trod over to where Amil Young's body lay, drained and still. She had a complexion of the whitest shade of gray, and her hair, long and curled at its tips, was the color of snow. As she walked barefoot upon the soil, the grass below her step uprooted itself and died in dry piles of burnt yellow fibers. The water that touched her skin turned acidic and black. Every tiny organism held within the shallow pools blinked out of existence. She ran her thin fingers through a patch of shrubs as she continued on, and behind the trail of her hand, the stems shed their leaves and turned to ash before falling to the ground below.

She knelt by Amil's side, and, as her knees pressed into the wetted earth, the soil screamed under the weight of her affliction. She cradled him in her arms and swept her gaze over the latest victim soon to be woven into her tapestry of oblivion. After this brief observance, and without a moment's thought to the life this body once held, she withdrew a small blade from between her breasts.

She lifted the chain from off her neck and brought the insidious charm that it held to the skin of Amil's forehead. As it hovered above him, the blade shimmered with a silver gleam, but its body was ephemeral and shifted within the rigid stillness of the air. With a call near indiscernible to the ears of any living being, the weapon seemed to howl with the voices of all those who had previously felt its touch. As with any well-kept blade, it gleamed like a mirror, but what it shot back was not the resemblance of its master. Instead, the shine of the dagger appeared to house the afflicted faces of the innumerable dead. Once the tip had touched Amil's skin, however, the knife solidified, and it cut though bone and muscle as though they possessed a constitution no stronger than that of oxygen.

Once he had been slit from face to groin, the abyssic creature slid her fingers between the narrow slice and tore Amil open at the chest. The usual and expected contents spilled forth from her carving. A pair of empty lungs, a liver, a couple of kidneys, an entanglement of intestines, and a deadened heart, but she had not come for the likes of bloodied entrails. She reached her hands deep into the human cavity, but also into another, more mysterious, plane of existence, and pulled forth the intangible prize which she sought to collect. From within himself, a spectral rendition of Amil was dragged forth and into the light of day. This paranormal duplicate lay as motionless as its twin, but unlike the cooling body of its inspiration, this creation would be granted no rest or reprieve from the savagery of existence.

Still upon her knees, the macabre female solemnly looked to the sky above. Once the sun felt the bitter accusation of her glare, it darted behind a patch of clouds and left the scene in absolute shade. She growled at the vastness of the heavens above, and then slid the fingers of her left hand through the damp soil. Her long nails scraped the aether of the underworld and returned with a corroded and tangled length of chain. She fastened the rusted links around the neck of her ghoulish catch like a choker, and pulled the slack tight by means of a violent twist of her forearm.

She rose to her feet, and with her free hand, she slashed at the empty air. Her nails cut a jagged slice into the nothingness, and caused an impossible fissure to appear. As reality lay cleaved, each side of the cut flapped with the rage of hurricane wind as the diseased air of all things dead and decayed exhaled forth. She stepped into this swirled, grayish haze of death, and dragged Amil across the boundary that had been carved. The chasm closed, and all trace of the hellish vision and her prey vanished completely. As the world was again freed of her oppression, the sounds of life returned to the woods. All that was left behind was a dead body, with nothing more than a bullet wound through the back of the skull.

Rich Hayden

Part 2. A land forsaken

Amil awoke, unaware of his whereabouts or of the actions of his last day on earth. He was face down in a dusty field that lay barren and cold under the watch of a darkened sky filled with fattened and bruised clouds. He rolled onto his side and glimpsed this foreign land. It was of the bleakest condition. The ground was cracked and the soil was brittle from a total absence of water. Not a tree grew, nor did any plant, hedgerow, or weed. An immaculate nothingness spread itself out to the horizon of evermore, as all opportunities for life had been starved to extinction long ago.

As he brought himself to his feet, Amil felt around the back of his head and touched the opening that the bullet had so crudely crafted. It was then that he remembered his own suicide. With disbelief, and a fright never before experienced, he turned his vision around this strange setting. Everything remained unchanged, no matter the direction to which he cast his eyes. This jejune pasture looked as though it could stretch on until the end of all time. And that's when it occurred to Amil that perhaps, indeed, he had found himself placed at the end of time itself.

He stood tiny and seemingly forgotten among the silent abandonment. The dark air was cold as it surrounded him, and, with nothing to do but take the first step into a decayed eternity, he began to walk. Direction and destination had lost all meaning. Amil simply continued to place one foot before the other upon this repetitive world of disintegration. The color of the sky never changed, and there was no dawn or dusk to be found. The landscape was

90

gripped by ruin, locked in an interminable circle of despair.

Fatigue never found Amil, yet he felt pain. His muscles begged for mercy, but his legs still carried him. He could feel as sweat left his skin, but to his own touch, the body was dry. He wanted to rest. He felt as though he should, but, like a marionette, he was strung along to a place unknown. He walked for what felt like days, although that measure of time failed to serve any purpose in this place of perpetual extinction. He could have put hundreds of miles behind him, or perhaps the same route was lapped over and over again upon a tiny sphere of uniform decay.

As he cried out into the indifferent sky for his legs to drop him and allow for a moment's rest, Amil pondered the condition of his new-found existence. It then occurred to him that maybe this was his punishment for the failures of the past. To wander the same bleak area with nothing to keep him warm but the memories of all his earthly regrets. Like the raising of a feckless shield before an enemy too mighty to deflect, he closed his eyes for want of something different to look at, and for a respite from the sorrowful land around him. It was just for a moment, an exaggerated blink, but in that instant, everything changed. When his lids ascended, a structure of menacing proportions stood before him in an advanced state of dereliction.

An imposing iron fence stretched the breadth of the land. As it spread, the barrier undulated in a formation that offered spiked rods and other ornamental works of steel to the bellies of the clouds above. A deadened weave of ivy crawled around every bar and post in a brown, flaky webbing of rot. The harsh touch of unsettled weather, long since gone, seemed to have rounded the finer points of the metal creation. All of the bars, once so obviously ornate and meticulously decorated with the most elaborate of details, ran tightly together in a bent collection of rust. This made the many posts appear to be a massive set of teeth. Crooked and smashed into the ground, smeared in a reddish plaque.

At the center of the crafted steel arrangement, an enormous wound lay exposed. The entrance gate, which once mightily served to unite the fence, had collapsed, dissolved into a forgotten obscurity eons before. As he continued to walk toward the mammoth barrier, it only seemed to grow larger and more decrepit. Once he had reached the threshold, Amil stopped. Or, rather, he was permitted to stop by forces far greater than he. He stared into the territory that was shielded behind the fence and contemplated the necessity of cordoning off such a place. It was cruelly besieged by misery in equal measure to the land that lay at his back.

A road of splintered brick, as wide as life was long, appeared under his feet and flowed into the dismal horizon. The stones were jagged, lifted, and disturbed by the unease of the soil as it had shifted with time. Every crack in every rock, like an entanglement of varicose veins upon the skin of an aged giant, was the home to rank soil and a low and brown-shaded grass.

The footing was difficult, and given the limitations of crippled legs, he struggled to navigate the shipwrecked condition of the stone. As he carried on, Amil finally lost his balance and fell to the ground. Bereft of the assistance of his cane, he wallowed amongst this menagerie of brittle rock with only the sounds of his own weeping for company. Consumed by physical agony, and suffering a deeper pain within his mind, Amil rose again. He ventured forth, but still, he was without the slightest idea as to why, and, quite specifically, he was also without the will to do so. It was as though he was being dragged along the road and toward the only thing left in this decayed perversion of reality.

A silhouette of a tremendous mansion loomed on the horizon and conquered Amil's vision. The structure was so massive, it appeared to have no end, as it stretched from one side of the world to the other, and rose deep into the dark envelopment of the sky. Too far away to gain any details of this object, it looked to be nothing more than a swathe of emptiness, a black mass that lay over the land. Or was it simply a hole, a rip in the fabric of eternity into which every description of life is sucked away and devoured? This felt entirely possible, as the realm continued to be as lifeless and desolate as it had been out in the field.

Not far from where he stood, a fountain rose from the exhausted road and finally offered Amil a landmark to help him set his bearings. It looked to have been built from granite, but even this magnificent stone lay weathered and scraped. Cracks wove their way around the robust creation, and water surely hadn't sprung from the top in what had to have been centuries. There was, however, a collection of fluid that filled the fountain's reservoir. It was of a midnight hue, and it supported a layer of filth that floated upon the surface like the dead sent adrift from an island swallowed up by the sea.

As he staggered forward, Amil discovered that he was not alone. A woman, wrapped in a dress as black as the opaque skin of the mansion, sat beside the diseased pool and ran her fingers through the stagnant liquid. She had her back to him, the mane of her white hair obscuring her face.

Fear forced him to slow his walk, but still, he drew near to the figure, even as he felt a great desire to flee from her. Amil knew that he could not run. He could not escape. After all, not even the finality of suicide could spare him from the memories that haunted him still.

He stood on the other side of the spring, but the ominous woman made not a motion. She knew he was there, Amil was sure of that. As sure as he felt the exit wound in the back of his head, he knew she was fully aware of his presence. As his damaged legs were spent, he slunk to his knees and braced himself up on the bench that encircled the fountain. Momentarily halted by hesitation, but without much care for a life that he was certain was no longer his, he dipped his fingers into the water.

The fluid was thick and it burned the flesh of his hand as it crawled up his fingers to the third knuckle. A powerful sensation of nausea filled his gut, and his mind felt like it was split in two by the most violent onslaught of a migraine headache. He cracked his head off the hard ground as he was forced from the bench by the pain that filled his skull. A temporary blindness swept over his sight, and with a feeling that he could not describe, Amil felt precisely the power of death. He was absorbed into its emptiness, only to be spat back out into this shattered rendition of existence. Tremors shook him and then ebbed away. After the shudders withdrew, and with this paradox of a sensation lifting from him, Amil again pulled himself to his feet. He rubbed his eyes and tried in vain to massage the spears out of his temples. The affliction he suffered bored deep within and wound its laces around his nerves, as if to pledge certainty to the lingering effects of the discomforts to come.

"Wh...wh...where am I?" asked Amil to the still figure, with speech more labored than usual due to the bullet hole through the roof of his mouth.

As she turned to him, her face was devoid of eyes. Her sockets were empty chasms that revealed only blackness. Her jaw line was sharp, and her cheekbones were set high. Her lips were full, although heavily cracked, and lines of age slept near the corners of her mouth. He retained no memory of the moment when she plucked his spirit from his body, but as she looked at him beyond the arch of her white locks, Amil knew that she was the one responsible for his current and hollow condition.

"Please...just tell me...wh...where is...is this Hell?"

"There is no Hell," she calmly whispered. "And there is no Heaven, either."

"Then...wh...what is this place?"

"This is just the next step."

"Are you...Death?" he questioned.

"I was called Aphelianna, but that was a long time ago."

"But...you took me from the earth...didn't...you? I don't understand."

"Nor should you," her response was whispered, but agitation coated her words.

"Wh...what am I...supposed to do here," he asked meekly, in irritation and fright.

"Make your way to the mansion. There you will find your place."

"Is that...wh...where we all go...wh...when we die?" asked Amil.

"Your concept of death is inaccurate, but it is indeed where most of those who have passed from the earth

95

now dwell."

"Wh..what do you mean...most of us?"

"Enough questions!" she snapped at him. "I have work to do."

Amil witnessed as her empty vision swept beyond his form and set itself upon the field outside the gate. He, too, looked toward that barren expanse, and what he saw filled his face with dread and forced him onto his knees in morbid appreciation for the magnitude of ruin that was displayed. He was the only soul upon the plain a short while ago, or so it seemed, but it returned to his vision utterly polluted with thousands, perhaps millions, of the dead.

They stood tightly alongside one another in a lethargic mass that seemed to float somewhere between an abyssic sleep and a fragile daydream of torturous proportions. A common groan filled the air, and they inched closer with every twitch of their awkward movements. Many of them appeared quite old, but there was a great collection of young ones too. There were throngs of the disabled and the dismembered. There were infants, and soldiers still dressed in maimed battle gear. There were people bald and thinned from cancer, and there were those who carried the undeniable signs of drug addiction and disease. Some had common wounds, while the tales of battles lost to various maladies stitched themselves across the mass like a cruel puzzle. Among all the horror and torment, Amil viewed those who appeared healthy and somewhat vibrant, even under the dim glare of the sky. He shivered as it became stridently clear that the condition in which the body left the earth was one and the same with the composition of the spirit in this unlife.

"Have...you brought them all here?" he wondered aloud, not really to Aphelianna.

"Yes. While we were speaking."

Aphelianna then walked over to Amil and wrapped her fingers around the back of his neck. Her touch was colder than the most ferocious of winter winds. His skin cracked and twisted as it suffered the distressing effects of immediate frostbite. She lowered her face to his, and as her locks cascaded over his cheek like an avalanche, they rubbed his skin with the grace of a corroded file.

"Forget what you know of time and leave me be, for more of your disgusting kind need my guidance," she whispered into his ear. The vibrations that left her tongue were so sharp, it cost Amil the hearing on the left side of his head.

Aphelianna was not like him. Not human. He came to realize that she was not of human beings either, and probably had little in common with anything in his understanding of the ethereal, as well. He sensed as a fierce disdain for human life bled from her, but still, he resisted her decree, and took not a step toward the mansion.

"...wh...what...will...you do...with them?"

"You may think that you have died, but believe me, you cannot fathom the horror of what it means to die in this place," she warned. "Now go, through the orchard and to the mansion, but do not stray off the path, lest the Spirit Ripper add you to his collection."

Being as though he had already died, Amil had felt no fear of the ordinary concept of death, or of death as he understood it. But as Aphelianna threatened a new demise, Amil was practically crippled with hesitation, and dreaded to learn what a spirit ripper truly was. He watched as she

97

walked away from him and toward the gate, no doubt to harvest another soul from the bitten soil of the field. As difficult as it was to do much of anything, he turned his back to Aphelianna. His curiosity for her was smothered by the fear her presence commanded, and so, with only the trepidation for things to come by his side, Amil continued down the road toward the twisted orchard in the distance.

Part 3. The crucifixion orchard

Perhaps in another time, in another rendition of existence, this orchard was once beautiful, and swollen with fruit and all the colors of life. If such tranquility ever did indeed grace the orchard, all its favors seemed to have died off an eternity before. Ruin was all that remained. As Amil approached the entrance to the orchard, he looked to the trees and how they made a natural border around the grove. They were sewn together by unchecked growth, and the branches spread themselves out, naked and thin. They looked like talons that surely had their hollows flooded with poison, and, as they swayed in the air, they seemed primed to ensnare the weary. The crumbling road beneath his feet fully dissolved, leaving an assortment of narrow pathways that crawled on into the darkness. The trails were muddy, and caked with dank heaps of decomposition, as the breath of wind had conceivably not carried through the trees since the inception of eternity.

As he gave himself to the orchard, Amil saw that every tree was black, and not one of the sickened branches held a single leaf. The trunks were rotted and split, as though they once bore entire hordes of abominations. Their roots rippled the ground as they popped up from the soil,

98

starved to fragility by a lack of nutrients. Entwined with one another and sharing a common decay, they seemed to be minions of the Spirit Ripper.

Amil trod carefully and tried not to make a sound. He attempted to peer through the lines of tress and into the shadows that they held, but the scenery was much too dark. As he walked in silence past each twisted tree, his faulty gaze swept from left to right in pursuit of something that he could not even describe. During his passage down the crowded rows, he was snagged time and again by skinny branches that hung low and extended their withered fingers out toward him. Their touch felt sinister, and, in one particular instance, their malevolent caress caused him to gasp. In was only a mild effusion of air, but his startled exhalation called down a calamity which murdered the quiet and filled the orchard with a din.

Launched from the tops of every tree like an explosion, a murder of crows took to the sky. Their wings beat the air and their cries alerted the master of the grove to the intruder, and the location of his delicate trespass. At first, this frenzied flight obscured what little light there was to be found, but once they had dispersed into the sky, the land around Amil began to brighten. He had been unaware of them as they sat still, but once the birds had taken off, it was clear that their collective mass had been chiefly responsible for the near blackness that hung over the orchard. A new light descended from the sky, a pale and dim resonance. It illuminated a vile perversion of existence and the repulsive condition of the Spirit Ripper's hobby.

Nearly every tree within the interminable grove was decorated by human corpses. Most were women, fastened high off the ground to the prickly bark by all manner of restraint. Some were bound by wrappings of chain, others by wire and tattered cloth. There were those who were tethered by the twisted branches themselves, while smatterings of others were held in place by the knotted entwinement of their own hair. More yet were spiked into the wood with rusted nails, whose placement was as cruel as it was numerous. Some of the women were wrapped in rags and the frayed remnants of the clothing they were captured in, while many hung naked, vulnerable, and bearing the scars of the crows' affections.

Amil glanced around in a stunned absence of speech. He wished to be free of this vision, but his eyes remained wide with dread as they absorbed the despaired description of every sorrowed face. As in the fields, there were old women no younger than his grandmother, and there were girls on the boundary of their teenage years. With no fight left in him, Amil fell to his knees under the weight of the collective sadness that swirled among the trees. He grew unconcerned for the whereabouts of the Spirit Ripper. The realization that such an abominable place could actually exist robbed his mind of all thought beyond that of absolute disdain for the world he now knew.

"He won't hurt you, he only collects women," a thin voice offered.

Although the words were carried upon the same stale air that he sucked into his lungs, the sound of another human voice smashed into Amil with the force of a freight train. The soft utterance threw him backwards, and into mud that pooled near the stump of a forgotten tree. He scurried backwards like a trapped animal. He shook, as one does, while under the affliction of a great fever, although he knew better than to assume that his blood was still warm, or

100

that it even moved through his veins.

"...you're alive?" he asked in disbelief as he stared up to the source of the words.

"In a way, yes I am. We all are," the woman plainly stated as she swept her eyes across the common fustigation of her sisters.

She wore the signatures of middle age and of difficult years. Her frame was thin, and her drab blonde hair hung before her face as she spoke. It looked as though she were once dressed in heavy layers of a gray material, but all that remained were dry strips of ragged cloth. Amil could see no mortal wound on her form, and she didn't appear to house any of the telltale signs of a virulent disease. In fact, she almost looked healthy.

"Wh...what happened to...you?" asked Amil.

"I didn't make it inside, same as the others. I can't imagine it matters. I doubt a fate any better than this would have awaited me had I made it through the orchard."

"How long...have...you been here?"

"There's no way to measure time here. The sun never arrives and it never sets. The seasons do not change and the wind doesn't blow. I truly do not know."

"This can't be...real," he whispered.

"No! Stop, stay away from me!" she frantically screamed, as Amil rose from the ground and advanced toward her. "Don't come any closer. He's watching. If he thinks that I've asked you for help, he'll kill me."

"I...I don't understand."

"I've seen what it means to die here. Please, just don't come any closer. I would rather hang from this tree for eternity than be put to death here."

As he backed away, Amil shuddered. What could

possibly be so wretched that in order to avoid it, one would voluntarily subject themselves to perpetuity as a crucified revenant? He was utterly vexed, and then he recalled her warning: the Spirit Ripper was watching.

In the light offered by the vacancy of the crows, Amil witnessed a being as it darted between the trees like a sewing needle that disappears and then resurfaces in rapid succession. Whatever it was, it certainly was not of the earth. More surprising, it was also not the imposing beast that he had expected. As it drew closer to him and his frightened acquaintance, the creature slowed its zigzag advance, and Amil was able to discern the finer points of its curious features.

Behind a tree it hid, hesitant, shy, almost. It was short in stature and weighed no more than one hundred pounds. The Spirit Ripper's body had a complexion of soiled yellow. It was a hairless beast, and naked at that, although its strange anatomy bore confusion over which parts could be considered obscene. It stood upon two legs, which appeared to have duel sets of knee joints that allowed the appendages to bend in multiple directions. Tentacles sprouted from its thighs, and they felt around the ground and swam through the air, as though searching for something as the creature remained still. At its groin, where some description of genitals should have been housed, nothing more than three narrow slits were found, which ran parallel to each other in a horizontal direction. The skin upon its chest seemed to be under the assault of some manner of wicked pestilence, as puckered lesions were scattered across the flesh. They were raised and reddened around the rims, with the residue of dried pus smeared over their mouths. But for as hideous as the chest was, the condition of the Spirit Ripper's stomach was a far worse sight to comprehend.

A cavity was crudely cut out of the beast's mid-section, and this wound provided a view to the land which lay behind it. The skin around the carving was wet with some variety of blood, as if the hole had lost the ability to heal itself. If the Spirit Ripper did possess some manner of innards, they were absent from the injury. Nothing but the stagnant flavor of the air passed through the hollow. The tortured specifics of the creature's torso should have garnered the most stares from Amil's eyes, but it was the arms of the Spirit Ripper that drew the bulk of his attention.

They were long, possibly ten feet in length, if not more. They wrapped themselves twice around the tree and were fixed tightly into the wood by means of the fingernails. Each hand held the normal distribution of five fingers, but countless jagged nails grew in all directions from the tips, the knuckles, and the bases alike. These chipped knives clacked off one another and added a poisoned medley of sound to the aether with every small movement of their master. As the coarse nails collided, the dull sounds produced reassured Amil with every ominous scrape that he could be filleted like the helpless piece of meat that he was.

For as perversely complex as the body of this beast was, its head was unsettling in its simple construction. Bald, like the rest of the creature, its shape was common, but almost totally starved of features. It was without a mouth. The nose and ears were absent. There weren't even any bumps or wrinkles upon the face. There was one massive eye placed at the direct center of the jaundiced sphere. It was horribly bloodshot, and the black ball at the center never seemed to tire as the Spirit Ripper constantly scanned his surroundings.

Amil couldn't remove his gaze from the shy being as it peered at him from behind the safety of rotted wood. It wasn't until Amil inched backward, and broke the mutual stillness of their common stare, that the Spirit Ripper again resumed its spastic gait. Quicker than Amil could properly witness, the beast lashed its arms around one tree and then the next as it sped away, until nothing more was left of it than the commotion stirred among the branches.

Amil exhaled deeply and looked again to the woman with whom he had been speaking. She sighed at him and turned her face away. She knew he wanted answers, even if they were unpleasant, for the explanation of troubles always seems to bring about a sense of comfort, but for the questions in his eyes, there were no answers. He respected her plea for solitude, and as Aphelianna instructed, he continued toward the mansion in the distance.

He passed woman after woman, each spiked up and bound to an unimaginable misery. Some groaned as he walked by, others attempted to engage him, and a few even heckled him with showers of obscenity and spittle. But Amil paid no attention to them, as a swelling guilt was his to bear as he solemnly pulled his crippled body through the grove. With the prospect of seeing another crucified little girl, he tried not to look up as he pressed further into the orchard. This was quite a difficult task to accomplish, for there is an intangible intrigue that rests alongside abject horror that draws the human eye.

Amil would never know why, but in a fateful instant, he allowed his body to stop, and he again raised his eyes to the Spirit Ripper's trophies. It was an act that served to give him a new understanding of the definition of pain.

Tied to a thin tree by a mass of knotted rags was the body of the love of Amil's earthly life. Ali was rawboned, much skinnier than he remembered, and, other than the rags, she was naked. Her face had been creased by deep lines of age and her skin was dotted by goose bumps. A dull glaze coated her blue eyes. Lethargic in their movements, they stared to the sky above. The thick brown hair that once framed her face in a shroud of enchantment hung limp and thin.

Amil screamed, a howl of madness into the air, until his lungs depleted themselves and failed to offer to his mouth the bare necessities for speech. Like an animal that begs for the mercy of a death that refuses to come, he walked sullenly over to Ali's tree. As her feet dangled before his face, his arms wrapped around the rotted trunk and his head rested against the bony pillow of Ali's shins. His mouth dropped incoherent pleas for forgiveness, as he continued to clutch at the most beautiful part of the wonderful life he had so foolishly squandered.

"Please, stop touching me," Ali meekly voiced.

"Ali, I'm...so...sorry," sighed Amil as he looked up to her in disbelief.

"Who are you?" she asked.

"Wh...what? It's me...Amil."

"Just leave me alone, please."

Amil could feel her skin as it trembled, and he heard the fright in her voice. As she continued to gaze into the sky, he sensed her panic. The fact that he was unable to chase her fears away, or to bring her any amount of comfort, hurt him the way no weapon could, but what cut him the deepest was Ali's refusal to look upon him.

"Ali, please...look at...me."

"I don't know who you are. Please, I'm so scared. Just let me go."

"Ha! The new ones are always so timid," a gruff voice cackled.

Amil twisted his head around and glared into the direction of the words. Cloaked in a red nightgown, and pinned into the highest branches of a tree, was an old woman. She barely had any hair, and all but a few crooked teeth had fallen out of her mouth. She looked at Amil and sneered at the sight of a young man as he held on tightly to the slender legs of his love.

"What did...you say?" he commanded of her.

"Y...y...y...you don't talk so well, do ya?" she teased.

"Fu...fuck...you."

"It was probably just days ago. He chased her down and strung 'er up! It was real quick like, she didn't even fight too much as he fondled around with 'er. You wanna know how he did it? First, dem tentacles got up under her clothes and stripped 'em off. Whoosh! Then, dem feelers got all over her skin and those nails started a cuttin'-"

"Shut up!"

"Fine, I'll stop," the woman stated indifferently, with a shrug. "Was pretty interesting if you ask me, though. Anyway, she ain't said but two words before you come along."

"Wh...why doesn't she...recognize me?"

"The hell should I know, boy?"

His eyes lifted back up to Ali. She looked so sad, so hopeless and distant. She didn't return his stare, and she didn't appear to have any interest in the exchange between

Amil and the old woman. Ali just blankly stared off into nothing.

"I...wo...won't let...you stay here. I promise," he whispered, and kissed her feet.

As Amil recalled the warning given to him from the woman in the tattered gray clothing, he elected to leave Ali upon the tree. As he looked upon her, and then found the strength to turn away, his face twisted in pain. He clenched his teeth and sunk his fingers into the acidic soil below him. Rising to his feet, with eyes downturned, he staggered away, in search of answers, of any solution that might properly reunite him with Ali.

As he trolled though the orchard, Amil was made to realize that Ali had died. It was an impossible occurrence for him to contemplate. She looked significantly older, but for how long had he been in this wretched place? Did the hours turn to days? Had he wandered the fields and this accursed grove for years? Or had it taken Aphelianna this long to tear him from the material bindings of the earth? Perhaps when eternity is the measure of existence, time loses all importance and urgency.

"Please...help me," he begged to the base of the tree that held the woman who had attempted to comfort him earlier.

"Was that you I heard screaming? The voices of men aren't heard here very often."

Amil just nodded.

"Did you find something terrible?"

"Yes, my...Ali. She didn't even kn...know me."

"I've seen this happen before. It is very painful to witness."

"Wh...what is?"

"You see, when we pass from the earth, most of us do so without the retention of our memories. Many have little scraps, while others are just blank slates. I'm sorry, it can't be helped."

"But I...kn...know her. Her name is...Ali, and she's very-"

"Not anymore, now she's just a shell. You should be grateful that she didn't bring her memories to this place. It only makes it more difficult," she whispered.

"Then why...do I know her?...I remember everything."

"You're a Ghost, and so am I."

"A Ghost?" asked Amil.

"That's what we're called, the ones who carry all their memories into this place."

"Can I save...her?"

"No, she is lost," the woman assured quietly, but with conviction.

"Where are...you?" screamed Amil, his eyes in search of the Spirit Ripper. "Where are...you...you wretched...where are you? Show yourself!"

"Please stop! He won't come, and you won't find him. There's nothing to be done, just leave this place and pray that your memories fade with time," she calmly stated, with a quality in her voice that resembled love, if only love were permitted to exist in such a place.

"Have...your memories faded? Ho...how long have...you been here?" demanded Amil.

"I was drowned, in Europe, for practicing witchcraft. I honestly don't remember the exact year," she admitted.

"God...the witch hunts," muttered Amil.

"Hmm, God, I was killed in his name."

"Have...you really been here that...long?"

"In what year did you die?" she asked, with a tremble of hesitation in her voice.

"It was the 21st century," Amil said. He was unwilling to give the exact year. Uttering such a fact aloud seemed too cruel, although, he couldn't be sure who exactly his vague answer was designed to shelter.

The woman closed her eyes, and Amil knew that she was made to reflect upon all that she could still remember as he devastated her with the news of all the time that had passed. Tears slipped from under her closed lids and her mouth formed words, although their sound was muted, and, like the rest of her prayers, they were meaningless.

"Please, leave this place. You can't help Ali, and you can't help me. Just go, find your own way in this nightmarish world."

Amil nodded again. He knew that he reminded her too much of a life long gone. His presence was upsetting to her, and, in a way, the most comforting gesture that he could offer was to leave her alone again to hang from the tree. As he turned away, he watched as a few of the crows returned and landed upon the branches and the prizes that they held. A few of the birds settled down upon the outstretched arms of his acquaintance. One of the birds pricked her skin with its beak, an act that made her flinch, but most rested quietly upon her body. She had been there for so long, that after such a vast expanse of time, it appeared as if the woman and the crows had actually formed a sort of kinship. It was a monstrous reality, and, as Amil thought of Ali, and all the birds which surely bit into her naked skin, he walked back toward Aphelianna and the fountain.

Part 4. The challenge of Aphelianna

"Help her! Help h...her!" begged Amil in a scream, as he approached Aphelianna as she again rested next to the water of her sickened fount.

As she watched him laboriously advance upon faulty legs, she rose from the stone. She saw him emerge from the orchard, and in the grief that contorted his face, Aphelianna saw another chance for salvation. No doubt his task would end with the same result as all the others, but if he was brazen enough to beg for her challenge, she would oblige him.

"Cut her d...down. Hel...help her, save her," he commanded meekly, as he came within a few steps of her.

"Your concerns are not mine, and even if I desired to grant whatever insignificant whim that you have, I am powerless to do so."

With no reservation, Amil drew back and attempted to strike Aphelianna. His fist froze in flight, inches before her face, and he felt as his entire body was rendered immobile and held in suspension by an impenetrable nothingness. Held captive by forces unknown to him, Amil watched in a terrified helplessness as Aphelianna leaned in toward him. She rested her forehead against his, and with this act, the feckless corpse of a man was treated to another patch of frostbite.

"Please, let...me go. I must...he...help Ali," he begged.

Aphelianna turned away, and, in concert, Amil's

body was dropped to the ground. As he lay next to the cracked stone of her fountain, he stared again into the fields and the mass of the reanimated dead as they awaited Aphelianna's guidance. He focused on a girl, maybe no more than 16, who wore a green t-shirt that read, Atlanta! - 2050. She had a gruesome gash in her neck, and the left side of her face was smashed in, but it was not her damage that troubled Amil. The year printed on her shirt, and the man beside her who wore a powered wig, confirmed that the dead of the past and of the future yet to come stood before him.

Amil thought of Ali. How long did she wallow among their ranks before being seized by the Spirit Ripper? Weeks? A millennia? For that matter, how long had he stood there within that sorrowed mass before wandering off and then back again, only to awaken alone? Time made no sense to him. Up was down and quick turned to slow, as everything he had known before was relegated to the description of inconsequential. All that remained was pain.

"Please, help...me," he again said.

"Why?" asked Aphelianna as she turned, returning her audience to him.

"I need to...help Ali. She...doesn't...deserve this."

"I suppose she is now one of the Spirit Ripper's pets, yes?"

"Wh...what is that thing?"

"He got what he deserved," she offered coldly.

As Aphelianna relayed this information to Amil, as cryptic as it was, it made him shudder. For he now knew that the Spirit Ripper wasn't some mindless beast acting upon the nature of its kind. It was something else, something perverted that was under the curse of a divine punishment. He wondered if the condition of the Spirit Ripper was Aphelianna's doing, and, if so, what could she do to him?

"Don't...let her...don't let this be...her fate."

"What would you do to free her?" asked Aphelianna with a stroke of sorrow in her voice.

"Any...anything. Just make her...sa...safe. Let me...let me hold her again."

"I will secure her release, but there is something you must first do for me," Aphelianna explained.

"Wh...what is it?"

"Somewhere in that house, there is a key. It hangs from the neck of my sister, Isadora. She sleeps while I suffer, out here alone to bear this curse. Bring me that key, free me of this curse, and I will free your Ali."

"...you were sentenced to...this?" asked Amil, in bewilderment.

"Yes. That house was once mine and those fields were once lush. But now I am unable to return, that is part of my arrangement. I have sat here alone, tending to these things, since the Earth began its travel around the Sun. I tire of this duty, I long to go home."

The end of Aphelianna's speech was whispered, and for the first time, Amil saw her as a living creature with the same wishes and hopes of all beings.

"How do I...find her?" he asked.

"With this."

Aphelianna drug her hand through the muck of the fountain's water, and, when her thin fingers again surfaced, she produced an archaic-looking key. It was large, and looked to have been formed from a dull metal. The edges were brittle, and it was beaten into a crude shape. The key hung from a length of scrawny metallic rope, which Aphelianna then lowered over Amil's head.

As the charm came to rest against his body, a violent sensation rushed forth. He fell to the ground, as all the blood in his veins turned hard and sharp. It resumed its travel with a furious rapture, and, in doing so, it delivered a torturous agony to him. After intense minutes of this maddening feeling, the fluid again turned soft and warm below his skin. His heart awakened and beat once more. Amil felt as the injured muscles and bones of his legs repaired themselves, and the hole through the roof of his mouth sealed itself over. His skull was healed, the blur left his eyes, the sense of hearing returned to his deafened ear, and his speech was freed of its handicap.

As he continued to wallow on the cool stone of the ground, Amil found this reawakening of his bodies' systems to be a temporary sensation. He felt his heart stop again, and though his lungs still heaved, they processed nothing. But it was the pain that had died away. His body actually felt good, physically strong, and somehow rejuvenated.

"Get up," she whispered. "I have given you the means to find her, and I have erased the frailty of your being. Now, to your purpose," Aphelianna instructed as Amil still lay in a ball, panting like a dog.

"Where do I even begin to look?"

"There are many rooms in the mansion, most of them are locked. That key will allow you to pass to where others cannot tread. It will open one door for every year of your human life."

"How many rooms are there?"

"No one really knows. But there is one room for

every year of age for every human that has ever lived," she admitted with a smirk. The small smile that found her lips curved into a sliver of wickedness, like a chiseled slice of a new moon as it hangs among the empty sky. Amil felt her malevolence, but there was something more in her expression, something hidden. It told of defeat and hopelessness. It was a smile that one makes when confronted with a long task already failed.

"You tricked me! This is impossible! I'm only thirty-seven," he said, in saddened disbelief.

"Then that is your obstacle to overcome, and your task is not impossible. Choose your rooms wisely, and find Isadora. You will know her room, it is unlike any other. When you find her, take the key. Do not hesitate, and bring it back to me," Aphelianna said.

"What does it open?"

"What it opens doesn't concern you. Just bring it back, and I will grant your wish."

"It doesn't matter. I'll never find the fucking thing anyway," muttered Amil, below his breath.

"Oh, you better. Think of Ali if you like, but I will give you a much greater incentive against failure."

They were there the whole time, this was certain, the most abysmal and vicious creations of all hell and ill-conception. They silently crept through the fields and the grounds of Aphelianna's mansion. They skulked through the orchard of the crucified, too monstrous for even the Spirit Ripper to pay them any mind, and they surely roamed the halls and rooms that Amil was asked to navigate.

Gangly and of only the most perverse human description, these beasts were cloaked in a skin that was terribly burnt over the majority of the body. What hair they had grew wild and matted, while the nails of the fingers and toes were vacant, leaving only platforms of diseased flesh in their absence. The eyes were gone, but the openings of the mouth and the nostrils were all too occupied. Streams of vile slime, mostly black in hue, fell from the orifices and further decorated the bodies in a miserable sheen.

Some stood tall and erect, while most were hunched and bent into a pained submission by the unforgiving assault of arthritis. There were those who crawled upon the ground, as just the task of existing seemed sufficient enough a labor to call down the punishment of one thousand hells. All groaned, some seemed to cry and emanate other mournful squeals, but the most insufferable noises of all were the dry screams that tore at the throats of these wretched things. They bit at each other and swiped like wounded dogs if another of their kind strayed too close, and, as he watched them snarl, Amil knew that they were creatures bereft of any kindness or restraint.

"What the fuck are they?" asked Amil, as he watched them jerk around in terrifying motions.

"They are called Wastes. They are what's left after a human being truly dies."

Amil closed his eyes and bit back his panic as he refused to accept Aphelianna's explanation.

"Will I, will we all become those things?" he asked, with the thinnest of voices, almost too afraid of the answer that might come.

"No. Some may wander this land for eternity and escape the fate you see before you, but most will find their way to this end. It is the nature of your kind. But do not fear, for after the sum of one hundred human lifetimes, these creatures will die completely and evaporate into time.

Do you see the ones upon the ground? They're the oldest, their suffering is nearly ended. However, there are a few exceptions, the ones whose agonies will never be lifted. Would you like to know them?"

In silence, Amil trembled.

"They are the ones that have failed my challenge," she plainly stated as she stared into one of the beasts.

"No, take it back, take this fucking key back!"

"Discard it now and you will hasten your descent into their ranks!" she warned. "You wished for the ability to cheat fate, but did you assume your failure would not come at a cost? What cost is too high? Bring me my sister's key, and I will honor my promise to you."

As he felt a fresh vitality in his body, Amil clutched at his key and turned away from Aphelianna. He heard the Wastes scream as he stepped away. The howling grew in intensity, and it told of their desire to devour all that they once were. But, at least for a time, he was safe, as not one of the beasts dared to cross before Aphelianna's feet. They may have been monsters, but they still held the capacity to fear, and, before Aphelianna, they were terrified.

His mind was crushed under the weight of what had been asked of him. An incalculable number of rooms might house Isadora, but he was given only a paltry 37 opportunities to find her. Had he lived for a thousand years, Amil would have felt no better about his odds of escaping what was assuredly the most torturous fate any one being could be forced to endure.

As devastated as he was, his focus was newly narrowed. For as he passed into the orchard once more, Amil could sense that he was being shadowed by a Waste. He looked around with widened eyes and tried not to let the images of strung females distract his vision as he scanned the grove. Under the gloom of the sky and the blackness of the crows, he witnessed the Waste as it staggered out from behind a tree, mere yards from his position. As Amil looked into its absence of eyes, he knew the savage hated him. His existence represented all that it would never be, and possibly, all that it had failed to be. It wanted him dead. With all the fury of the last shreds of consciousness that it held, it wanted him to feel the anguish that it was made to suffer.

Amil performed the only action that felt right in that moment; he ran. He tore through the orchard and allowed the low-slung branches, and all their coiled fingers, to lacerate his skin. He tripped on a root and split his chin open on a rock, but shot back to his feet, as physical pain had been eclipsed by dread. He tried to maintain a straight path, but the screams at his back muddled his mind, and the deceitful ways of fear sent him off course. He thought of the Spirit Ripper and where it might be hidden, but he barreled ahead, fully unsure if any amount of running could carry him to salvation. In a moment of unsteady relief, Amil saw the mansion with increased clarity as it peeked above the tops of the trees, but as his flight though this menagerie of agony was nearing its conclusion, his stride slowed.

Though he knew the better of it, he stopped his flight altogether and looked around for any sight of Ali. She dangled a few rows over from him, and, with nothing more than a brisk and nervous walk, Amil made his way over to her. He kept a respectful distance, as he couldn't bring himself to bother her any more than she had already been troubled. But he had to see her again. To look upon her face one more time and lose himself in her eyes, for this could be the last time that he would ever do so.

She never looked his way, but Amil stared at her all the same, and, as he did, the strident brutality of the world around him slipped away until it was nearly gone. He thought of her laugh, and he remembered all the wonderment of their life together that he had so ignorantly taken for granted. And then, in the most woeful of all settings, he felt oddly protected. To look upon her face gave him a small measure of comfort, but Ali knew no such protection or joy. She only retained the ability to suffer. It was a sensation which served to strip all dignity and self-regard from him, and as he closed his eyes, Amil almost welcomed an eternity of punishment.

"I swear to you, Ali. I will save you, I promise," he whispered between his teeth, a river of tears dammed behind his eyes.

As Amil made his plea to Ali, the curious Waste that had pursued him leapt from behind the shelter of a withered tree. Its flight through the air was unimpeded, and the force with which it left the ground was violent enough to start Amil on a path to a new and horrid death. But in a moment of profane intervention, the Spirit Ripper made its presence felt and caught the wretched beast in a net of its twisted nails.

With the strength of its long arms, the Spirit Ripper threw the Waste down onto the ground and shattered its spinal cord upon the lumpy surface. It sent its nails to work and tore Amil's stalker asunder, as though it were comprised of nothing more substantial than a loaf of warm bread. The Waste was cleaved with shocking ease, and lay limp upon the soil in two savaged halves. Pieces of the being still twitched in pools of its own septic blood, and a moan faintly echoed through its hollow throat, but it lacked the means and desire to track Amil any further.

As Amil watched the Waste shift upon the ground, he knew that it would not die. Not even the Spirit Ripper could fully relieve it of its suffering. That's when it became chillingly clear. The master of the orchard had not punished the Waste, but, rather, it had saved Amil's new life. He turned his vision to the Spirit Ripper. Mere feet away, it hung in the air like a piece of clothing left to twist on a drying line and stared back at Amil with its one infected eye. In silence, it seemed to beg for release. After interminable seconds, it abruptly disappeared into the thicket with nary a sound. Once relieved of the Spirit Ripper's unsettling presence, his bewildered vision settled upon one of captured women.

"Perhaps he desires to see you succeed as well," she ominously said.

Chapter 3 - In the house of Aphelianna

Part 1. The Hall of Worship

The mansion rose before him, mightier and larger than the vast expanse of human imagination. Aphelianna's house welcomed Amil with a cold indifferent silence. The structure looked to have been built out of heavy brick, although the true composition of the stone undoubtedly owed its resiliency to forces far less common than sand and mortar. The sky above was bleak, and littered with smears of clouds that hung in the air in a dark undulation. Enough light was shed, however, to give him a fair view of most of the house before its uppermost details were swallowed up by the atmosphere. The mansion's figure had been formed from strident angles of brick that ran in sharp lines around the edifice. The curve of rounded rooms added definition, and balconies held in restraint by railings of iron hung from the outer walls. They drooped like tired mouths, opened, and hung slack by the weight of sharpened teeth.

  The whole of the ground level revealed itself to be windowless. However, the floors above boasted a wide assortment of crafted glass and iron. As high as his vision could reach, Amil stared into darkened panes, as the edifice towered in the gloomy sky. Some of the windows were rendered banal by the dull shape of a square, while others would have made a spider blush given all the intricacy put into their construction. Metal veins decorated the larger windows, while a wide palette of color brightened the more involved panes, although these hues had faded with time. Some of the casements held back dusty curtains, and others were laced by woodwork, arched by design and warped by weather. Sculptures of foreign beasts with skins of rust, and renditions of elaborately dressed people, bled from the stone walls. In silence and stillness, they reached out into the air, as though they were the guardians of the mansion's many eyes.

There was one oddity that troubled Amil the way no sinister creature of iron ever could. Not one window, nor any corner or fragment of glass, was cracked, broken, or opened to the air outside. It seemed an innocuous observance, but given the age of such a structure, and with the years of neglect that it had surely endured, it was this small curiosity that knotted his stomach. As unease tussled at his gut, Amil came to surmise that the fortified seals of each window did not simply keep the weather at bay and shut out unwanted light, but, rather, the perfect glass and the stones that surrounded the panes were made to ensure that nothing ever escaped.

Though there was more to be discovered about the hardened flesh of this palace of the dead, a repetitive task of daunting proportions was Amil's to master before he would be able to glean the finer details. A set of steps, near one mile in width, ascended to the mouth of the mansion. They were of a substance that noticeably shared it lineage with marble, and, as they rose from the ground in a sharp incline, their numbers easily topped one thousand.

Amil set his foot upon the first step, and, as he did so, the ingredients of his memories separated and then reassembled themselves. It was a sensation that his conscious mind could not quite comprehend or properly capture, but as he climbed, his life was relived one step at a time. Due to forces unknown, but heavily felt, he was unable to tarry upon any one portion of the staircase for too long, though he wished that he could have, in some instances.

In rapid succession, his time on earth was thrown back at him with the subtlety and reverence of a strobe light's flash. He was given a second look at Fog Lake, and all the nights spent with the company of high school dropouts, cheap beer, and easy girls. He revisited the roasted fields of Sarasota, and could taste the salty air of the beaches of the Carolinas. Amil heard the cheers of a crowd as they packed a Major League stadium, and he could taste the food from every Thanksgiving dinner that he had eaten. He delighted in the trivial joys of everyday life's little miracles, and hurt with the reanimation of all his bad days, bike accidents, and personal mistakes.

But his march through the memories of Ali became a fresh hell that Amil was not prepared to traverse. Every step was like a spear thrown his way. He saw all her smiles, heard the sugary ringing of her laugh, and looked again into the blue of her eyes. He felt her touch and sensed the weight of her body as she lay next to him.

Like an old movie, the end arrived with all the pain and fury Amil knew would come. This encore of mutual failure and tragic consequence hurt as much as the original act once had. He witnessed all their arguments and fights, and he watched himself strike Ali's face. He stared down the bus that nearly ended his life, and saw as Ali mournfully sat at his bedside with unconditional devotion. Under the oppression of such memories, he cried during his ascent and longed to be free of these painful reminders. But as he wished for this swell of agony to stop, the taste of metal swelled in his mouth, and his ears absorbed a deafening blast. For a fleeting second, the heaviest blackness imaginable fell over him, but with one last step, he was hastened back to his senses. Before the mansion's entrance, he stood.

Though the building that loomed before him was awesome in its grand scope and menacing in its purpose, Amil turned his back to the mansion. From the summit of the great staircase, he looked out upon the new world he was forced to accept. His stare swept out over the pestiferous orchard. All the trees seemed to run in perfect lines, the prisoners they held lost to the limitations of the naked eye. The mass of crows and the twitching of their wings gave the tops of the trees a proper look, as they fooled the observer into believing that the branches were flush with leaves.

Past the scene of Ali's torment, Amil looked upon the tiny speck that doubled as Aphelianna's fountain, and stared at the long road beyond. From this vantage point, it looked smooth, but this illusion was a passing wonderment, as Amil became befuddled by its true size. It twisted and coursed its way over the land for so long that the fence and the barren fields beyond were placed too far away for common vision to absorb. Upon the horizon, all that his eyes were permitted to see was the omnipresence of the sky as it coiled around the world in a never-changing cloak of despair.

With nothing left to do but move on, Amil turned to the challenge before him. Double doors sealed the entrance to the house, and they stared down at him like a suspicious pair of twin divinities. They each stood one hundred feet tall, and worked in harmony to form a point at the top of the threshold's center. Their skins were wooden, but each door was ornately dressed with an assortment of silver hardware.

Though the decorations had tarnished, so much of the precious material was used that they still garnered admiration. For as beautiful as the metalwork was, the hinges that supported the doors were as formidable. Cast from the heaviest iron, they were all twice the size of a man and held in place by bolts whose weight clearly eclipsed that of the blocks that comprised the great pyramids of Egypt.

A handle, which boasted an inlay of archaic characters that Amil was unable to read, curved out toward him like the figurehead of an ancient ship. He wrapped his clammy fingers around the object, and, with little effort required, the door opened. It swung out slowly and with a fluidic ease that made not a whisper. Nothing more than an enveloping darkness seeped out, but with no options left, he stepped inside.

Though its source was unclear, a dim light that permitted limited vision eventually cast the entrance hall in an amber aura. At first, nothing more was illuminated by the light other than the dull stone of the walls and the surface of the floor below. The planks were milled out of a reddened wood that stretched the breadth of the hall in an uninterrupted dominance, and as Amil's shoes continued their clack over the dusty boards, he wondered how long it truly was. The ceiling might as well have been constructed out of pure blackness itself, for the room was so high that his eyes were denied a gaze at its true proportion. As he started to fear that the hall could be as long and desolate as the road outside, a vision of the mansion's enigmatic nature presented itself to him.

Like a gallery torn from the nightmares of a madman, an unsettling display of artwork greeted Amil.

Each wall held a row of portraits, and while none displayed overt malice, there was an undeniable chill that bled from their frozen and ghostly stares. These paintings, which caused his heart to flutter, were spaced evenly apart about every ten feet or so, and each rendition was softly illuminated by candlelight. It was a curious light. The paintings were all paired with just one candle, which rested in curved bronze fixtures at their bases, but the flames knew no expiration. The waxen sticks were short, but they never seemed to shrink. There were no pools or drips of wax to be found, and the light itself never flickered. It continued to burn, unconcerned for the laws of science and reason.

With an outstretched hand, he was about to test the reality of the flames until he recalled his experience with the water of Aphelianna's spring. His fingers hung before the minute fire, and he could feel its familiar warmth, but Amil knew better than to trust his senses in such a place. With a tremble, he withdrew his hand. Leaving the mystery of the candles to the realm of the unimportant, he put his sights to the subjects of the cured oils, whose recreations were shackled within thick frames of ornately bejeweled wood.

He set his eyes upon a dapperly dressed young man who leisurely leaned against a stagecoach. He wore a top hat, and the shine of his shoes could only be compared with the brilliantly smooth complexion of his face. A sly smile peeked out from the side of his mouth, and an unlit cigarette dangled from his hand. Across the hall from this worldly gentleman, a painting of another man stood in quiet defiance to the cosmopolitan nature of the first portrait Amil studied.

125

This second fellow had obviously cleaned up a bit for the mysterious painter. But for all the artistry that went into the recreation, his usually disheveled appearance could not be completely obscured. His face was shaved, his clothes were straight, but there was something about this sharp image that didn't fit the serious face. He sat in a wooden chair whose comforts were noticeably few. As his freshly combed auburn hair caressed his cheek, the subject intently studied an odd assortment of mechanical parts that lay upon the desk before him. He had a small gear in one hand, and he looked to be researching its origin within the volume of a massive book that lay open across his lap.

Amil continued down the hall, and he witnessed more and more of the strange paintings. There was a man that had crafted a great bell, and a woman with a warm smile who knelt among a bed of flowers. Another young female subject was held inside a lush and beautiful atrium, her body framed by the moonlight at her back. An older man stood erect with a book tucked under his arm and a pair of scratched glasses upon his nose. There was a woman in the next frame over who stared off into the darkness of a dusk-filled forest of evergreens. Another representation was of a man whose wide eyes appeared capable of reading the thoughts of an observer. He held a large silver coin between two fingers. It was as though he were dangling the promise of an impossible proposition, as the silver of the coin shined from the oils like the brilliant glow of a full moon.

So many portraits lined the walls that after some time, Amil simply paid them no mind. After all, he did have a task at hand, and if he took the time to study every painting, he might never reach the end of the hall. He walked on, and the rhythmic light of the candles continued to streak his advance. It became a hypnotizing sensation, but this trance would eventually be broken the way glass surrenders under the punishment of a hammer, as one painting in particular gave off a deathly chill.

There was a woman dressed in a lovely evening gown, her light hair fixed into curls, and her nails painted the same delicate green as her eyes. She sat upon the stone bench of a fountain that flowed with the cool, sparkling water of life. She twirled a stem of ivy between her fingers, as it grew in abundance around the spring. She hooked one ankle over the other as she sat in an easy calm. The water below her seat was as blue as the Pacific Ocean, and the sky above was flush with sunlight.

Amil couldn't remove his eyes from Aphelianna. She looked so beautiful and innocent, so far removed from the beast she had become. Life and nature surrounded her. Now only death and decay were her company. As he looked upon her as she used to be, he actually felt sympathy. What had she done to be charged with the torment that she endures? For what ignoble reason had she been condemned to shepherd the dead? As he looked into a time that passed away eons ago, Amil's mind swelled with a myriad of questions. But he couldn't ignore the most noticeable difference between Aphelianna's recreation and that of the others.

The candle at the base of her portrait had been snuffed out. The wick was cold, and the outer skin of the wax was flaked and cracked. Of the dozens of paintings that he had passed, Amil was sure that every last one of them had held a lit candle. All save for Aphelianna's. He knew not the significance of this, and it was a mystery unlikely to unravel, but still it troubled him. This absence

of light spoke of her damnation, and, in a way, Amil took it
as a warning and as a promise, for he had made a deal with
the goddess of all things black. He shuddered at the
implications of the key that hung from his neck, and, with a
deep sigh, he moved along and left the portrait of
Aphelianna to the darkness behind him.

      As he walked further away from his earthly life and
deeper into the abyss of death, Amil was again handed an
image whose enigmatic nature he was unable to discern.
The hall in which he trod opened up and widened into a
large ballroom. A thick carpet the color of dried blood
washed out over the floor, and a large stage that spanned
the breadth of the room sat at the far edge of the red tide. A
massive dining table, which could have sat perhaps fifty
guests, split the center of the room like a smoothly planed
island. It cowered in fear under the watch of a mighty
chandelier that hung ominously from the blackness above.

      Amil slowly approached the naked table. Like the
many chairs that sat tucked underneath it, this furnishing
was crafted out of wood and stained a deep crimson. Gems
dotted the border, and metal accents streaked the legs.
Nearly the entire surface of the tabletop was recessed, and a
polished slab of dark stone had been laid within its grasp.
Amil stared back at his reflection, and from the look of the
eyes that he studied, he knew the true meaning of regret.

      He continued to cross the ocean of carpet, toward
the stage. There wasn't much to be found. No piano or
other musical instruments. No bar or podium, either. There
were no curtains, candles, or lanterns. Only one object
permitted the stage to skirt the emptiness of the barren
fields outside: an ornate chair sat at the direct center. It was
a throne really, with a back taller than the most massive of

giants, and it held enough gold adornment to purchase the allegiance of whole nations. A material that resembled the plush carpet formed the cushion. The legs bowed out in an exaggerated sweep, as they were sentenced to bear the weight of this monstrous creation. The legs themselves were fixed upon globes at the bottom, and as Amil studied the detailed spheres, he imagined that whoever sat in this chair freely dictated their will to a swath of worlds.

He ascended the steps of the stage to further gaze at the chair and the layers of royal dust that sat upon it. As he stood within inches of the bestial throne, a heavy breath left his lungs and blew a powdery cloud of dust into the air. As the particles took flight, a mysterious flicker of light surged through the crystalline body of the chandelier. Its brilliance colored the room in light. This pale ambiance gave Amil a peek at the arched ceiling above, and the stained glass windows that surrounded the heavy support beams.

Though the upper portions of the room were awesome in their scope and construction, it was the statues that had previously lain hidden that captivated his mind. They lined the walls, and rose from the floor like porcelain stalagmites. Each was easily three hundred feet in height, and, as he craned his neck to observe them, Amil was unable to see the finer definition of their faces. Though their expressions were lost to him, all of the sculptures were draped in some form of prayer garment, and stood with their arms outstretched as though in praise of a divinity forgotten. He swept his eyes down the white stone robes of the figures, and, once the long descent was at last accomplished, the next step in this nightmarish task was made obvious.

Along the walls, between the statues, were doors.

They looked no bigger than peepholes, as they sat beside the enormous parishioners and the silent hosannas they offered. But for as minuscule as they seemed, the doors were there. As real as the fear in Amil's heart. He plotted a course across the scarlet mire. Standing before one of the plain doors, which looked no different than any of the others, he stared at it as though waiting for a reply to an impossible question. His hand shook as he reached out for the knob, and, with a mild jostle, he knew the door was locked. He closed his eyes, and, with a lump in his throat, his grip was released.

He walked down to the next door and tried it. This one was unlocked. He allowed this door to remain closed as well, as he was not yet ready to choose a path. Amil looked around and frantically tried to glean any clue from his surroundings. He counted the chairs around the table and the statues that stood around him. He tried to count the crystals of the chandelier, and racked his brain for answers, as he hoped to recall some fact about the paintings he passed that might hint at what to do next, but nothing was made clear.

As he walked along this row of the porcelain faithful, Amil looked across the room and at the set of doors across the way. They beckoned like a riddle, and tormented him with their variant opportunities. Perhaps something was written on the wall behind him that he could only uncover from a great distance away. But before another thought could be formed, the light that shimmered inside the fixture above began to peter out, much the same as visible gas escapes from a tube. Darkness started to crawl over the room as each crystal grew cold, and this retreat of light served to quicken Amil's heart. However, what came on the heels of the swelling black would force him into a decision.

As the light dissipated, a menacing cacophony nestled inside his ears. It began as a scuttle, a scraping, but soon this discord swelled into a din that extinguished all other sound. It emanated from the hall, and, as Amil stared into the darkening artery, a vision that matched the sound soon emerged. A flood of Wastes poured in, all enraged and determined to aggressively enlist another soul into their damned ranks. Some charged like Olympic sprinters, others lumbered forward on all fours. Howling like feral beasts, the broken sluggishly dragged the failed remains of their decaying bodies, while more still were trampled down under the weight of their fellow cursed.

As this wave of death washed toward him, he tried the knob of the door that stood before his rigid body. It was locked. He was wholly unprepared to waste a turn of his finite key, but there were no more options. As the Wastes drew closer the mouth of all hells seemed to have opened, and its teeth dripped with the desire to consume absolutely. With a robotic rigidity, and a wide eye fixed on the onslaught of savagery that raged his way, he slid the metal weight into the keyhole, turned the knob, and cracked the door open.

Part 2. The Ancient Forest

Only darkness greeted Amil. Not the way a room looks when all of the lights have been turned out, but rather, a true nothingness welcomed him. He stepped into this utter lack of existence and pulled the door shut behind him. In an instant, all the wails of his pursuers were muted into extinction, and a new setting revealed itself.

In total amazement, he found himself not among brick or stone, or in the confinement of four walls, but outside in the open air. The land around him was yellow and sun-scorched. It was a great plain, fitted with only the swirl of dusty winds and the oppressive glare of sunlight as it seared through the stale air. A dirt road snaked out in front of him, and, off in the bright distance, piles of assorted wreckage spotted the path like the carcasses of dead mechanical titans.

Amil looked over his shoulder and to the door. It was again locked, and its base carved out an imprint in the dry soil, but it connected to absolutely nothing. He could see around it, and he even walked in circles around the mysterious barrier. Each side held a keyhole and a knob, and a set of heavily tarnished brass hinges. He pressed his ear to the wood, but heard not a sound. He wasn't simply one room removed from the terrible Wastes. He had ventured somewhere else entirely. It taunted and perplexed him. He contemplated whether or not to spend another turn of his key and head back the way he came. With a thought to the Wastes and all their screams, Amil started on down the road.

He was shocked at the familiarity he found. The road appeared to have been plucked from the desert lanes of the American West. He noticed burnt shrubbery, and when the wind settled long enough to free his eyes of the swirling dust, the sporadic placement of cacti was made visible in the distance. A single sun hung above, and its cruel, accusatory stare forced sweat out of his pores, while the cry of hungry buzzards cut through the air. As he neared the heaps of sandblasted scrap that rose from the ground, the images became clear, and Amil was able to uncover their nature. As he pressed forth, it became clear that he was walking into the heart of a forsaken town.

Abandoned skeletons of cars flanked him as he advanced closer to the village, and, as Amil passed his sight over their rusty skins, he was again stung by the resemblance that he felt to the life he once knew. He was able to uncover the make of most of the automobiles. There was a Chevy that had apparently died just off the side of the road, and so there it remained. It had been repainted by dirt, and sunk into the dry ground. The wheels had shed their former chrome and surrendered to the fate of unprotected steel. The seats inside were torn open and stained stuffing bled through the wounds like gelled blood on the surface of a cadaver.

Amil set his vision on a concentration of Hondas. They seemed to have been systematically broken down, torn to pieces in an industrial gulag long gone. There was a burnt-out old Lincoln that looked as though it had comically exhausted itself while making love to a crumpled Mazda. As he walked past the cars, and on into the heart of the forgotten town, he thought of black holes and the Bermuda Triangle. Maybe this was where the truly lost found themselves.

Most of the buildings had fallen down, and the ones that still stood looked to be pieced together with matchsticks. An old barn leaned over, and a rotted silo lay sprawled out across the body of the main road. Most of the side streets had been washed over by dirt as it blew in from the arid landscape, and nearly every window in this theater of dilapidation was missing. The panes housed only the wind, and hung open like dried-up wounds unable to heal.

There were a few lampposts that stood in arthritic poses, although most lay crumpled on the ground. Dead soldiers left at the site of battles lost. The touch of paint was as forgotten a memory as the rust was dominating, leaving the old village devoid of color.

Amil glanced over at a playground. The metal amusements were frozen in their places, as each had felt the theft of time. Seats were missing from the swings, and the bars that built the structures were rotted away and jagged. It looked more like an obstacle course for the souls of wicked children. A death trap of loose chains, decomposed iron, and exposed nails.

A splintered wooden fence encircled the playground like a discarded snake skin, and, as Amil passed by, his eyes were drawn to a row of shops. They were pressed tightly together, and although impudent sunlight and dirtied wind had become their only customers, the nature of most of the establishments could be discerned. Most were practical. A ramshackle hardware store, a grocer's market, and a butcher shop. A row of knives hung from the wall and gleamed ominously in the sunlight. He peered into a clothing store, and studied the blank faces and incomplete bodies of mannequins. He was given a start, as some of the cotton articles were made to dance suddenly by a rush of wind. To view the displays, they looked to be the ghosts of those gone away, and as he hurried by, the complete erasure of a town abandoned was his alone to absorb.

Or so it did seem. But there are always those who lurk in the dark, behind wreckage, under curtains of filth, and enwrapped in blankets of places despaired. From a space unseen, a gunshot pierced the air, and Amil instinctively darted behind the corpse of an old pickup truck. He saw his pale reflection in the cracked side mirror of the truck as his heart beat wildly. Without purpose, but from habit alone, it thundered, and sweat slicked his hair to his face as the threat of being turned into a Waste was felt.

"Come out, boy! I won't kill you, at least I don't think so," a gruff voice commanded, as it carried out from a place Amil was unable to detect.

Frightened, but relieved to hear another human voice, he lifted up his arms and slowly emerged from behind the rotted truck. Out from between the bones of a two-story shack, whose lead-based outer skin peeled under the affliction of a nasty psoriasis, a gray-bearded man with a shotgun, and a 2 x 4 for a leg, hobbled out. He stared at Amil through a mighty squint and kept a bead drawn on the shaken traveler.

"Well, who are you? Did you bring them with you?" the man asked.

"I don't know," said Amil, totally confused. "Who?"

"Who? What the fuck you mean, who? The Wastes, did they tail ya?"

"I don't think so. What the hell is this place?"

"Hell? That would assuredly be a mighty nice set of environs in comparison to this. This is just a lookout. We take turns picking off Wastes. We make sure they don't follow us home."

"Home?" asked Amil.

"Follow the road a ways and go through the pine. We've set up a small village there. It's a temporary settlement of sorts, until we can find The Eternal City."

"I'm sorry, I don't understand a fucking thing you're saying," admitted Amil from across the barren street, completely overwhelmed, with his arms still raised to the sky.

"So, you're new. Come over here boy, and Uncle Cal will tell you a story."

"Uncle Cal?" Amil muttered aloud.

"As in caliber, boy. Bullets!" he shouted, with a southern drawl.

"Okay, okay, just relax that thing, please," Amil begged as he stepped toward the dilapidated porch that supported Cal and his crude excuse for a leg.

"All you had to do was ask," said Cal though a wide smile of decaying teeth, as he laid the gun down.

"Can you tell me what's going on?"

"What's going on? As in the meanings of things? The hows and whys? The aether and the nether? Hell no, boy. I died, and now here I am, shooting at zombies in a burnt-out ghost town while minds greater than mine search for The Eternal City."

"What is that, The Eternal City?" asked Amil.

"It's a vast city, located somewhere in this goddamn mansion, and make no mistake about it, you're still in that bitch's house. Anyway, it's a safe place for the dead. No Wastes there. There's order, and marketplaces, and theaters. It's a place to have a life again," Cal offered, between purges of chew spit.

"How do you know?"

"There are those that have left. They live in town, and are trying to guide more of us back. Although no dice yet. My shift's over soon, you should hurry on back with me and Letta."

"Letta?"

"She's a shy little German thing. Hiding in the

house back there. I've been teaching her how to shoot."

"Why won't she come out?" asked Amil.

"Do you speak German?"

"No."

"Well she don't speak no English, so I guess you don't have much to say to her. Besides, I need someone to have a gun on your head while I decide if you're alright."

Again Amil shivered. He was one pull of an adolescent's finger away from becoming a Waste, and in order to survive, he had to work himself into whatever definition of *alright* most satisfied old Cal.

"How did you die?" he asked Cal, quietly, hoping to form some sort of bond with the old man.

"Combine," Cal said, with a laugh.

"A combine?"

"Yes, boy, a harvester. I may not be a Ghost, as they say, but I sure as hell remember that. Took my leg off, and left me to bleed out and die among the crop. Quaint little tale, ain't it? What about you? You look healthy as can be."

"It's complicated."

"No, it ain't. You died, just like everyone else here. Hey, I ain't in the business of judging people, boy."

"I committed suicide, shot myself," he admitted, with a deep shame, but also with an odd indifference in his tone.

"In the head?" asked Cal, alarmed.

"Yeah. Through here," offered Amil, as he pointed solemnly toward his open mouth.

"Well your face looks pretty fucking good to me, what happened?" Cal demanded.

Amil pulled his key out from under his shirt and showed it to Cal.

"Get the fuck out of here," Cal ordered sternly with a vicious twang.

"Please, can you just..."

"I say the word, and little Letta takes your head off for the second time. I don't associate with those who have made deals with death. You got five seconds before I find my better senses and give that adorable little *Fraulein* back there the go-ahead. Now, get the fuck out of here."

Bereft of options and understanding, Amil again raised his hands in surrender, and backed away from Cal and the splintered wood of the porch. Once the dirt of the dehydrated road was felt under his feet, he turned away and rigidly walked down the forgotten boulevard. As he cautiously stepped past weathered wreckage and crumbling shacks, he was forced to reconcile with the undeniable truth of his situation: the dead were all around him.

To Amil, the most intimidating feature of his task was that he was going to have to suffer this burden alone. Now, it seemed that loneliness would have been a blessing. He wasn't the only one lost and wandering about within the enigmatic confines of Aphelianna's house. He was just another traveler. He gave a thought to the countless others that shared his plight, and began to accept the gravity of this foreign existence. This was a foreign world, one in which all were made equal by the fear of joining the ranks of the Wastes. Those with a bounty of memories and those without all floated through this land in the search for something that resembled life.

Amil trembled as he imagined all those that had fallen to the Wastes, and the countless others who would assuredly spend the rest of measurable time running from those cursed beasts. He wondered how many others felt the

138

weight of keys around their necks, and felt the lingering twinge of hope as he contemplated the likelihood of The Eternal City. Could it really be a place among all this ruin where the dead could again find life?

As he carried on into the scorched wasteland, he hadn't given much thought to *The Pine* that Cal had spoken about, but as it rose before him, Amil was humbled by its presence. Up from the spent soil grew a mighty forest. It stood in defiant opposition to the laws of nature, and, as it stretched from one side of his vision to the other, it left him with no choice but to accept its embrace.

He stepped inside, and left the unpleasant rays of the sun behind him. It didn't take long before Amil came to notice that this forest was unlike any spotted upon the surface of the earth. The floor of his path was as hard as cold iron, and not a stretch of root or a gathering of leaves dirtied it any longer. In fact, the ground was as smooth as planed wood. Were it not for the dull covering of dirt, his reflection could probably have been viewed upon the forest floor. It puzzled him momentarily, the uniform flatness that spread out underneath his step, but the more he thought of it, the older the forest revealed itself to be. It had existed for so long, and was left undisturbed by any description of life for so great a time, that its surface had spread out and settled, the way glass appears to eventually drain from out of a windowpane.

The trees, massive pines that towered high into the air, did so upon petrified trunks. The bases, and even the thinnest of branches, were one in the same with the composition of stone. His fingers tapped against the brittle bark, and with the dull sound produced by his nails, the ancient rock hinted at its true age. As he gave a closer inspection to the needles, Amil realized that they, too, had lost their nature and yielded to the pressures of an unconquerable expiration. Each narrow, acerate leaf looked to have been molded from glass, and as they shimmered with the remnants of the sunlight above, they cast a green ambiance over the forest.

As Amil walked through the stillness of the frozen forest, he remembered the town that was rumored to exist somewhere among the cool emerald shimmer. He couldn't grasp what they possibly could have fashioned a village out of, until he remembered the dilapidation of the town out on the road. Clearly it owed its dismantling to the cannibalistic necessities of relocation. What a truly miserable place this hidden village must be. He thought of all the different people that might be there, and all the nasty injuries that they brandished. It was a chilling thought. Were they all like Cal, mad and irrational? Or were they more like him? Amil stared through the paralyzed thicket, and, as the green light washed over his skin, he silently prayed to avoid the hamlet.

As the minutes passed, the glow of the needles began to darken, a sure sign that the sun above was about to retire for the day. As daylight began to flee the woods, Amil nearly choked on the anxiety brought about by the prospect of nightfall. But when it seemed that this elaborate arrangement of stone might carry on forever, he found himself on the other side of the forest, and faced with a new puzzlement.

With a line of petrified evergreens behind him, Amil stood upon the tan surface of an empty beach. Sand squished below his step and waves of frothy clear water rolled in from an ocean unknown. The air tasted of salt, and as an ambitious wave washed up over his feet, the touch of the water felt cool and familiar. He turned an eye to the forest at his back, and then returned his vision to the massive size of the aquatic entity. In that moment, he felt truly lost, but was not without a means to find his way.

Placed in the shallows, where the water often kissed the sand, was a door. Much like the one that brought him here, it connected to nothing, or at least nothing that his limited senses could detect. He stared at the dull coloring of the surreal object and slowly advanced toward it. His shoes carved their imprints in the sand, and, as his hand was placed on the knob, he closed his eyes and gave a fleeting thought to the simplistic beauty of life as it once was.

To his relief, the barrier was unlocked. Again, what was held behind the door was cloaked in blackness, but as he stepped forth, the dark soon revealed its secrets. As if spat back from a mouth ill-pleasured by his taste, Amil found himself still firmly planted with his feet in the sand and faced once more with the sinuous roll of the waves. He rubbed his face in consternation, as his eyes absorbed the most startling fact about this reprise. Where there was once only one door, now there were hundreds. They dotted the beach, spaced evenly apart, and postured straighter than the truest line.

The first handle that he jostled was locked, as were the second and the third. Amil ran down the beach, twisting every knob as he went by, but they all demanded the same offering: a cherished turn of his key. He continued over the sand for what felt miles, until he could no longer refuse the inevitable purpose of the tool which hung from his neck. As he turned the steely key, he could feel as it eroded within the sweaty grip of his fingers. All the implications of failure rang louder inside his mind.

An entire vat of misfortune and dire circumstance was upended on Amil, for as he crossed over another threshold, he found himself placed mere steps further down the beach. He stared into the crystalline forest as he leaned against the door at his back and allowed the lick of the waves to dampen his clothes. With nothing more than a discouraged sigh, the lost man chose another door, and slid his key into place. An encore of his previous action was played out, and, again, Amil was forced to choose another path along this maddening beach.

In his frantic attempt to flee the insidious riddle of the shore, a series of unlocked doors was found. However, this boon didn't last for long, and he was forced to expend turn after turn of his deteriorating key. In the grip of panic, focus was abandoned, and logic was barred from his decision making. He burned a total of eleven finite chances to save Ali, but still, he remained upon that wretched beach.

Defeated by the weight of his hopelessness, he crashed to his knees in the sand. He mourned for the loss of his life and for the fragility of the common existence he once knew. As his salty tears added drops to the ocean around him, thoughts of which door to next choose filtered out of his mind. He no longer cared. He already had tired of fighting the undefeatable. Amil fell to his side in the cool embrace of the shallow water and permitted the sand to crawl over his skin.

As he lay partially enveloped by the grains, Amil took in a sideways observation of the woods with half-lidded eyes. Its image sunk into his vision no different than it had before, a monstrous amalgamation of rocky trees and jagged needles. But as he continued to gaze into the frontier that had become his prison, a curious vision was uncovered. Something had changed. Something that was not there previously had materialized. Recalling his stroll past the portraits that hung in The Hall of Worship, Amil thought back to the memory of a woman he had noticed, and how she looked off into the distance of a great forest. The definition of the figure before him was raw, the way an apparition appears inside the eyes of the insane, but, undeniably, she was there all the same.

With caution woven into his every fiber, Amil rose slowly from the swampy embrace of his gritty bed, and walked as quietly as possible over toward the woman. She stood with her back to him, and her blonde hair spilled out across her back in heavy spirals. She was dressed quite plainly, and the gaze that she fixed upon the forest told of a solemn mood, of a longing for a loved one to return.

"Hello?" whispered Amil, as he neared within a few feet of her.

"I wait, every day, for his return," she responded, without a turn to Amil's direction.

"Can you please help me?" he asked.

"He set off to win the affections of a girl. Through the orchard and to the fountain is where he strayed, but he never came home. And now she is a beast. Oh, Goddess Aphelianna, what have you done with my son?"

"Goddess Aphelianna," stammered Amil, as he overheard the woman's lament.

"Do you know of her?" the strange woman questioned, as she turned to him.

"Yes, yes I do. Please, I need help, can you-"

"Have you seen my son?" the tired-looking woman tenderly asked.

143

"I'm sorry, I don't know who-"

"He was always shy. He liked to hide in the orchard and tease the girls that he fancied. He was a mischievous boy, but very sweet. I do believe he truly loved her," she explained.

Amil felt his stomach rot as he pieced together the cryptic ramblings of the mournful woman. He couldn't know how it happened, nor did he care to uncover the truth, but as he thought of the torturous orchard, and as he recalled Aphelianna's explanation of its master, Amil knew that he was in the presence of the Spirit Ripper's mother. He was a young man, perhaps even a boy by some estimations. What could he possibly have done to warrant such a fate? The questions that swirled inside taunted Amil. They flooded him with the waters of unease over the pact that he had made with Goddess Aphelianna.

"I'm sorry, Miss, I didn't see anyone," Amil muttered.

"He should have come home by now. It's getting dark," she stated, with a fresh collection of water in her eyes.

"Miss, can you please help me?" he asked again.

"I wait, every day, for his return," was the only reply he received.

He grew silent, and resigned himself to the notion that he would be unable to draw any assistance from the woman who barely acknowledged his presence beside her. As he stepped back, Amil came to view the living subject of the painting that hung in the gallery. It was an eerie resemblance, as though nothing had changed from that day to this. It was then that he took in the totality of the scene before him. This poor woman, who had lost her son eons

144

before, returns to the sight of his disappearance each day in the hope that hers may be the first face he sees when he emerges from the forest. It was a minute cycle of unimaginable pain that repeated each day, and as Amil looked to the stoic figure, he realized that she had waited for so long that the world around her had turned to stone.

As he left her side, Amil wondered if his journey could last as long as hers. What had she done to deserve such a punishment? He approached another door and gave not a thought to what might lay on the other side. Like a cruel taunt orchestrated from powers unseen, this door was unlocked. Amil shook his head in aggravation. Before he gave the knob a full turn, he looked back to the young mother as she mumbled incoherently about the whereabouts of her baby. As he worked the knob and cracked the door open, hope vexed his thoughts. It was a poisoned hope that for the sake of the woman, she would never find her son.

Part 3. The Wishing Well

Finally, he found himself held within something that resembled a proper room. Even the door that had permitted him entry was commonly framed. Just the ordinary placement of a ceiling and walls seemed a small miracle, and their presence offered mild hope. A floor of smooth stone the color of a summer's sunset flowed out under his feet. The white mortar that fused the rocks together swam in irregular lines, and as Amil stepped over the veins, he felt that a transitory sensation of life was held within the space. He trod slowly, with this inexplicable feeling as his only companion, as his eyes scanned back and forth over the curious shape of the room.

As it took the shape of a hexagon, six walls held six doors. After a substantial reach into the air, the walls all bent inward and continued their ascent until a common point was met at the center of the ceiling. The appearance of the overhead lining was nothing more impressive than pale sweeps of plaster, but at the center was the room's lone window. It was oval and clear, with iron bars crisscrossing the glass, and in between their weave, light cascaded into the area.

Directly below the stream of light was a well. The rounded body was short but robust, and it was constructed out of dull bricks that had lost their shade to the passing of the ages. A wooden framework topped by a pitched roof rose mere feet above the hole and supported an axle and crank. Each corner of the rotted little topper held a bucket, which was tethered in place by a short length of frayed rope.

As Amil walked closer to the well, he observed the walls around him and the odd decorations that they held. Although the walls were dull, built from the same stones that comprised the well, elaborate images had been painted onto the brick. The depictions arrived in random arrangements, and the skill level of each piece varied wildly. Most of the representations were of people who appeared to be praying. Beside them were images of all sorts of things, children, money, and animals. It was almost as though the subjects in the pictures were attempting to recreate what they most desired.

Amil viewed the unskilled and crude illustration of a woman as she lay at the feet of a praying man. He glimpsed images of boats, plentiful fields, and what had to be the victim of a brutal murder. The painting spoke of vengeance desired, to set right the infliction of unspeakable wrongs. Or perhaps the illustrator was just a common madman, a lost soul wallowing in his own lunacy.

Amil ran his fingers along the stone as he passed. It felt cold, and the faded paints flaked off with the delicate stroke of his fingers. This place must have been a temple of sorts, Amil surmised as he gazed upon curious glyphs. They circled the upper portions of the walls, an incised border of enigmatic decoration. In his wonderment, he looked again to the well, and having advanced further into the room, Amil noticed an unsettling sight that his eyes had not been privy to before.

Behind the well, the body of a man was lain out upon a bench of splintered wood. Placed on his back, the man was dressed in a black suit that looked every bit as crisp as the day that it had been tailored. A plume of auburn hair was slicked back over his head and fixed into a long braid that crawled over the figure's left shoulder. A thin beard balanced itself upon the sharp lines of his jaw, and two silver coins rested over the dead man's eyes.

As Amil studied the figure, he soon came to realize that he had seen the man before. Just as with the mother of the Spirit Ripper, this inscrutable vision was also presented within the candlelit gallery. Although they were closed, they were a pair of eyes that Amil could not forget. Even with them sheltered below their lids and the weight of metal, he could feel their pierce. This was undeniably the fleshed-out figure of the man displayed in the portrait hall. In the oils, he squeezed a coin between two fingers, now he lay dead and blind under the press of silver. For as uneasy as finding another subject of the unknown artist made him feel, Amil couldn't be pried away from the man's side. The hands were folded across his chest, and between the nourished, tan flesh of his fingers, a note was held. The creased paper stared up at Amil and practically begged of him to read its cryptic message. With a tremble that nearly shook him out of his shoes, he plucked the note from its trap and carefully unfolded the clean white paper.

> *Lift these coins from off my eyes*
> *Cast them into the well*
> *And wish for my return*

The command was quite plain, but the action itself proved hard to take. Amil looked into the well and saw as the rope that once twisted around the axle had rotted away. Whatever it once held had been cast down the hole into the nevermore. He tried to peer further down the chasm, but only blackness came to his vision. He returned his attention to the coins that rested upon the dead man's face, and, with a fluttered sigh, Amil scooped up the silver and threw them down the well.

He jumped back and turned away, too afraid to view what may happen next. As he stood in a corner like a frightened animal, nothing was moved to difference by the persuasions of change. He heard not a splash or clang, and the man from whom Amil had stolen remained cold and silent. He placed his palms flat against the wall and solemnly contemplated which door to step through next.

"They're quite interesting, aren't they?"

The smooth voice that offered the question carried with it a distinguished accent that Amil was unable to place, however, the origin of the man's speech was trivial. Just the presence of words was enough of a shock to twirl

148

Amil around in fear, and, as he did, he stared into that ominous set of eyes. For there the mysterious man stood, looking rested and energetic as though he had just risen from an afternoon nap.

"Who are you?" whispered Amil, almost too afraid to engage the slender figure.

"Who am I? Who are you? Who are we? Who are they? What is that? What is this? And so on and so forth," he spat, in rapid succession. "All questions that really aren't as important as you might think."

"Can you help me?" asked Amil.

"Well that depends, I know not what you ask. However, I do suppose I owe you a debt of gratitude. Do you know, you're not the first to pass through here and toss those coins down the well? But you are the first who has managed to revive me. For that, you have my thanks."

"How did it happen? I didn't do anything."

"It is very plain, you wished me back to life," he stated with vigor.

"No, I didn't. I didn't wish for anything," said Amil.

"Ah, but you did. I heard your prayer, and it cried out from the most tortured depths of your being. It was a terrible thing to hear, I must say."

"Who were they, these people on the walls?" asked Amil.

"Fools, mostly. Here they would come, and with them they brought offerings of gold and silver. Down the well their money went, along with their hopes and prayers. They scribbled their wants and needs upon the walls, all in an effort to impress and assure me of their sincerity. Although, to be quite honest, I cared not for their vandalism," the man said.

"You're a god?"

"Oh no, certainly not. I was, and believe me, there is quite a difference. I was called Duke Vinzenz, the God of Fortune! This room was a part of my holy property here in The House of the Divine. It was one of the very few that was open to the common person, and here they would come to ask me for things. Oh, the requests I got were many. Some were most trivial, while others were predictably extravagant, and more still were so grand that not even a god could fulfill such a demand."

"Did you ever answer their prayers?" asked Amil with trepidation, as he sensed a malevolent nature emanate from Duke Vinzenz.

"I certainly did, and not for the pictures they painted or for the money they cast into my well, but for the conviction that they displayed. And at other times, I enjoyed granting the meekest of prayers and ignoring the ones that mattered most. Perhaps that was a bit wicked of me. But to use divine power in a predictable manner or pattern wouldn't be very much fun, now would it?"

"I guess not," Amil offered, with heavy breath.

"Do not attempt to humor me, you cannot know of these things."

Amil stiffened. He felt abject vulnerability, as though he were nothing more than the muddy ground as it lays trampled under the hooves of raging beasts.

"But," continued the Duke, with a load clap of his hands, and a change in direction finding his speech, "For as divine as I may have been, and for as insignificant as you now are, I must say, I have missed the exchange of a proper conversation."

Being called insignificant stung, and ordinarily, he

probably would have countered the remark with a shower of expletives, but there was something about the way in which Duke Vinzenz said it that stopped Amil. It wasn't so much of an insult as it was the truth, and although he didn't understand the real implications of the remark, he felt that he could learn a great deal from the resurrected god.

"How did you get here?" asked Amil.

"Ah, now there is a question worth answering! You see, this house was once the home of all the gods in the known world. Long before the fall, we lived here and presided over the common people. We each had our own roles and powers, and certain behaviors were expected of us from the other gods. We worked in conjunction, and formed a symbiotic circle that forever preserved our way of life. But there is always greed and unrest, yes? Someone always wants a little more, harbors a jealousy so heavy it could drag the whole world into oblivion. You look like a bright man, and so I'll continue this little exchange for a price. I'll give you one guess to tell me who is responsible for all the ruin you have found thus far," he taunted, with one finger pointed directly at Amil.

"Aphelianna," was the whispered response.

"Aphelianna! Correct you are. Of course, the Goddess of the Dead. I imagine she has grown more and more unpleasant as time has slipped away. She put me here, you know? Cursed me to lie forever still under the weight of my own silver. Bereft of the one thing that I always cherished most, the excitement of verbal exchange."

"I met a woman. She stared into this forest of stone and asked me if I had seen her son. I saw her likeness in an art gallery, I saw yours too. Was she a god?"

"Oh wonderful! You can string together more than

four or five words, and here, I was growing concerned for the health of our conversation. But, to your question. Yes, she was a god. Her name was Katrina, and she was the Goddess of Nature. Her son held quite the fancy for Aphelianna. A pity for us all, his feelings would prove to be," said Vinzenz.

"Who was he, before he changed?"

"Changed? Now that sounds exciting! I suppose Aphelianna has done something terrible to him? Something that probably makes my own curse appear pleasant by comparison, no doubt?"

"Yeah, he's become-"

"No! Don't tell me, not yet. First allow me to tell you of Saint Calvino. He was the God of Love. He could form a union so strong between any two people that not even another god could break their blessing. But imagine his distress when the object of his affections showed little interest in suave Saint Calvino. He was angered, oh so bitterly angered, and all his rage spilled out and onto Aphelianna one day."

"Was he in the gallery too?" asked Amil.

"We all were. Our dignified likenesses were hung proudly above eternal candles as a reminder to the common person of our supremacy. His was a fine rendition. The artist accurately captured his boyish handsomeness, and properly conveyed the debonair nature that Saint Calvino carried so well."

Amil thought of the dapper young man who leaned easily against a stagecoach. He felt his knees tremble, and suffered a sensation of nausea as he thought of the Spirit Ripper. They were one in the same. There was no use in attempting to confirm this fact with Duke Vinzenz, Amil's gut told him the ugly truth.

"He's a monster," muttered Amil.

"A monster you say? Well what may be a monster to you could very well be kin of another. By what definition do you call him a monster?" challenged Vinzenz.

"He's hideous. He's diseased and deformed. He captures women as they flee through the orchard and he ties them to the trees. I saw them. Some are nailed up, too, and most of them are naked. He tortures them, and the crows..." Amil's words tailed off, as he couldn't hold back his anguish as he thought of Ali.

"Torture you say. Hmm, by what means? Does he touch them, force intercourse, that sort of thing?"

"I don't think so," said Amil, through a cough. "I don't think he can. He's genderless, it seems. Just his being there is torture enough. I met a woman who had been hanging there for hundreds of years."

"Oh, what a pity. Do you know how long I've slept upon that bench?"

"What did he do, to Aphelianna, I mean?" asked Amil.

"He raped her. Ah, now there's a snappy little attention getter, no? You see, as he matured, our dear Calvino had quite an appetite for the ladies. But there was something about Aphelianna that captivated him so. He did indeed love her truly, as his now ripely insane mother surely disclosed to you, but Aphelianna didn't share his affection. It vexed him, ate at him, that as the God of Love, he could not charm the one he truly desired."

"Is he the cause of all this? All this suffering?" asked Amil, as he struggled to properly articulate the miserable severity of the new world that he had found.

"Oh, certainly not. Aphelianna had already committed herself to treason. I like to believe that the act of Saint Calvino just served to hasten the emergence of her fury. And now, as you have cast a dull light on his curse, I find it hysterically ironic."

"What?" Amil asked, with a pinch of impatience.

"Well, isn't it obvious? He feasted on women, and now he is condemned to simply look, but never to touch. He may collect as many presents as he can, but not one does he have the power to open. Aphelianna really outdid herself when she cursed Calvino."

"What do you mean, cursed him? And cursed you?"

"You can't really kill a god. Even Aphelianna doesn't possess such power, but you can silence them forever. A war with one was a war with all, and so the Goddess of Death rained down a litany of curses over the lot of us," explained Vinzenz.

"Aphelianna, she told me that she was cursed, that she longed to be free of it."

The mild amusement that Duke Vinzenz wore across his face turned to absolute ecstasy with this last revelation. For he looked upon Amil as not merely a man lost and wandering about the land of the dead, but a soul bound to the impossible conditions of Aphelianna's charge.

"She gave you a key, didn't she?" Vinzenz asked slowly, with a wide smile.

"She told me that if I freed her from her curse, that I could save Ali."

"Oh, how utterly delightful! A love that transcends the grave has compelled you to make a pact with the most monstrous creation ever to traverse this or any other world. She wants you to find Isadora, and you may, but I must attempt to dissuade you," Vinzenz warned, with a wag of his finger.

"Why? So I can leave Ali as a pet for that fucking thing? So I can wither into one of those fucking Wastes?"

"Spunk! Fire! This is getting most interesting."

"Alright, enough! You said you owed me, now tell me what is going on, and tell me where to find Isadora!" said Amil, as he grew tired of Vinzenz's cryptic explanations.

"Perhaps I have already repaid your charity. I have informed you of more than most mortals will ever know. What more do you suggest that I do for you?"

"Just tell me where to find Isadora!"

"You have already asked so many questions, and I have answered them all. Like all the rest, you should have thought more clearly, chosen your words more carefully, and then maybe you would already have what you desire," scolded Vinzenz.

"Please, just answer me one more question," Amil begged.

"Well, alright," Vinzenz agreed, with a grin. "Ask away."

"Where can I find Isadora?"

"Behind that door," he stated plainly, and pointed at the door behind him.

The Duke revealed the location of Isadora's chamber, and Amil rushed to the other side of the room and thrust his key into place. He gave the knob a twist, but it remained locked, and the door offered no give to his fevered tugs.

"It won't open!" he shouted.

"Just give it another try, it's a rusty old thing, you

understand. Just give that magical little key another twist and I'm sure the presence of Isadora will be open to you."

"Still nothing. It still won't fucking open!" said Amil in a panic as he spent another use of his key.

"Yes it will, try again," Vinzenz commanded.

For the third time, his instrument was guided into the socket, and once again, the door remained locked. He withdrew it and slipped the object back under his shirt. With a rage in his eyes that could rival the wretchedness of a thousand nightmares, Amil turned to Vinzenz, and stared down the disingenuous God of Fortune.

"It won't fucking open," he barked, between clenched teeth.

"Oh yes, terribly sorry, I forgot to mention that. Oh, of course! I'm a bit embarrassed really. I usually have a memory like an iron trap, as they say."

"What? What is it?"

"That door will open, as easy as any other, but it requires no less than one hundred turns to break its locks."

"You tricked me, bastard!"

"Of course I tricked you, you gullible fool. I don't want you to find Isadora. You may believe that this is a most wretched world, and by all estimations you would be quite correct. However, give Aphelianna what she wants, and you will gain the true meaning of hell. You're on your own, now," Vinzenz offered in an uncharacteristic whisper as he slipped away through a door.

Amil banged his fists upon the door and kicked wildly at the ancient wood with the ferocity of a wild mustang, but all his efforts were in vain. It wasn't going to open, that was a plain reality to absorb, although the acceptance of such a fact was a trial that nearly shattered

Amil. Isadora waited on the other side, but he was forced to step away and place his depleted faith in another path.

For a moment, he collapsed into a pile of human defeat and ran his hands over his face. Disheartened, he tried to make sense of all that had happened. It was a torturous exercise. For as he thought of Vinzenz, Calvino, and all of the other tiny fragments of a long saga that he had been given, Amil suffered a sensation of absolute confusion. It was as though he were wrapped up within a riddle so vast that to escape it was only to die.

Upon rising from the floor, he dragged his body across the room and tried every door. All but the one that supposedly led to the chamber of Isadora remained unlocked, even the one which had brought him to The Wishing Well in the first place. But rather than explore another sinister portion of Aphelianna's house, Amil walked back to the well and knelt before its base.

As his arms wrapped around the brick, he did something that he had scarcely done as a resident of the earth, he prayed. His prayer was not offered to an earthly god, or to any divinity that he had crossed so far. No, his plea was whispered only to Ali. He begged her forgiveness and wished for life as it once had been. He pledged his eternal love, and vowed to free her of her torments. He would spring this insipid trap, and he and Ali would forgo the tethers of death.

Born from the depths of his pain, Amil screamed into the void, and not until the echoes of his perverse amen had dissipated, did he leave the well. As he stepped away from the dead cavity, Amil spat upon the ground, chose the closest door to his position, and crossed over.

157

Part 4. The Dead Atrium

In keeping with the order of chaos within Aphelianna's mansion, another elaborate arrangement of decay and hopelessness greeted Amil. He found himself walking into the heart of a massive atrium, and the chill of silence that filled the room caused him to shiver. With his neck craned, he saw that glazed glass curved around the perimeter of the ceiling. This translucent ocean shifted around the decoration of fine metalwork, which aided in the support of a central section of windows. High above, and up against this convex sea of glass and painted steel, three oval windows were recessed. They were as holes, three vacant eyes that stared down upon the emaciated and ravaged remains of the room's forgotten glory.

Born from a spiral stairway that crawled up a far wall like ivy, a balcony wrapped its way around the upper portion of the chamber. In sorrowful disrepair, it sagged under the advanced crumble of the pillars which supported it. Damage was prevalent upon the tired walkway. Whatever railing the balcony once sported, an assuredly splendid ornamentation indeed, had long ago rotted away and was lost. The columns themselves, elaborate newels that were once draped in an arrangement of crafted iron and silks, all stood chipped, and in great need of restoration. The skeletal steel, which gave the pillars their strength, lay exposed from the many cracks and lack of masonry. The metal bones of the pillars were heavily rusted, and in crimson trails, the dried paths of their tears streaked what little stone was left around them.

On each side of Amil, wide stone archways had been built into the walls. The arcades were placed evenly

158

apart, and extended along each side of the atrium. Around their borders, ornate reliefs of woodwork were affixed. These decorations, once employed to welcome a traveler in, hung like warnings, and told of the malice which hides in the black beyond. Like the balcony elevated overhead, the brickwork of the passages fared no better in their present state. The stained wood, which before was so elegant a decoration, hung in rot. Within the vacant mouths of each shallow arcade, along with spider webs and a generous film of grime, one door each was housed. But this was a discovery that was not immediately clear to Amil, due to the remains of a growth once unbridled.

It seemed that before an abundance of nothingness strangled the life out of the atrium, a burst of unchecked and malignant growth had taken place. The browned and brittle remnants of a colossal vine could be seen everywhere within the large hall, and the stench of its advanced decomposition filled the dusty air. The vine entwined itself with nearly everything in sight. The many stems and shoots, which once had so brazenly clung to the intricate steel adornments, lay meek and feckless upon the rusted surfaces.

As Amil walked among the carcass of the vine, he was taken aback at the resemblance that the plant shared with Virginia creeper. He could still make out the definition of the tendrils, and most of the jagged leaflets were grouped in the common assortment of five. Little thought was dedicated to his familiarity with the vine. Surprise was something that was becoming harder to come by, and this felt like a cruel coincidence. It made him think briefly of home, and what home had come to mean. But there was no joy in his recollections, for all his earthly memories felt like pins.

      Amil cut a wide orbit around the room as he walked over the floor. It appeared to be made of shale, horribly cracked and buckled upwards from strain. He stopped to observe a statue. Loosely draped by the arms of the ever-present vine, it rested upon a bench that lay tucked in a corner of the room. The dull gray sculpture was of a woman, and as Amil began to peel the layers of dead flora from her, a sickening realization was his to swallow. Strange though it felt, he gleaned a sensation of life from inside the statue as he stroked her concrete skin. With this act, he was made to remember another portrait. He had only seen her once, in a picture, framed by moonlight and placed within an enchanted scene of lushness and beauty.

      Only a mild quiver of existence was left to jerk inside the stony figure, but its presence was undeniable. It was of the faintest nature. The rhythm in which it flowed was pained and labored, but it pervaded, and assured Amil that this woman was once much more than chiseled rock. He looked into her gray eyes and viewed her curse. She was alive, as much alive as he, and fully aware, of this he was sure. For all this time, she had been made to watch the slow ruin of the atrium and devolve into a cold inanimateness along with it.

      Amil truly didn't understand his own motions in that moment, but he picked up a piece of torn silk that lay nearby, and draped it over her shoulders. Almost as though to relieve her of the cold that permanently dwelled in her cement skin. He then leaned in toward the girl and rested his head against hers. He wasn't sure what purpose this might serve, but he sensed that she may take a small comfort from his gesture. And in a moment of naked honesty, Amil felt as though he, too, needed a warm embrace. No matter how diluted this version of sensitivity would prove to be, it was something he had to feel.

For as real as the life within her motionless body felt, Amil expected to sense her compassion, or at least her reaction to his touch. Instead, he only absorbed a certain feeling of dread. She made her warning felt, but it was taken slowly and with foolish curiosity. It was all that she offered to him, and it was as clear as her body was rigid. She was speaking to him, not in words, but with sensation. For proper language hadn't the tongue to describe the horrors she felt. It was a scream, a blaring shriek that made no sound, but it pummeled through Amil all the same, commanding him to flee.

With his arms still loosely draped around the woman's stony shoulders, Amil peered down the row of corroded benches that lined the back wall. They were sewn together by the vine and crippled by the cancerous effects of oxidation. Piles of dust and powdery metal residue dirtied the floor around their feet, and, at the end of this exhausted and spent line, something stirred.

Amil felt his heart quicken as he focused his eyes upon the charred skin of a Waste. It peeked out from the shadows of an arcade, and the virulent beast met his stare. After a few tense moments, the creature darted out of sight, and Amil was launched from the bench by the fear which hammered inside him. Adopting a sideways gait, he shuffled toward the center of the room, and, with a robotic scan, he directed his vision into each darkened archway. He caught sight of the Waste as it hid in the absence of light, and never removing his eyes from the monstrous being, he plucked a jagged bit of stone from off the ground.

To his surprise, the creature slowly crawled out of its hole and pulled itself into the periphery of the light that flowed in through the broken windows above. It lay upon its side and twitched in agony amid a torrent of dry squeals that grated the inside of its throat into a pillar of scabs. The black fluid that oozed from the orifices of the Wastes poured in abundance from this unfortunate being. The toxic discharge spread out over the floor and formed a pool around its body.

Amil thought to run. There were doors at his back. He should pick one and flee the atrium as his silent companion had suggested, but he lingered. He wasn't sure why he stayed, but Amil couldn't remove his eyes from the Waste. With morbid fascination, he studied the creature as though glimpsing one of the most enigmatic mysteries of the universe. He remained still as the chaotic sight laboriously dragged itself closer, and, as it neared, the blind rage that he had felt from the other Wastes seemed to be absent.

With about twenty feet of empty air between them, the beast stopped its crawl, and a heavy rain of sweat dropped off Amil's skin. In a lethargic process that was spastic and heavy with twitched movements, the Waste pulled itself onto two feet. It stood nearly erect, and as its savaged body hung before Amil, he was able to discern its former gender. The Waste was a woman, or at least she used to be, for there was very little left behind that hinted at her feminine nature.

She was terribly thin, and other than two wrinkled lumps, her breasts had all but disappeared. A shock of matted blonde hair flipped off the side of her flaked scalp, and her left hand looked as though it had its fingers recently

162

chewed off. This gnarled mass of carnage nauseatingly dangled from her wrist, and the bottoms of her feet were mercilessly fitted with an assortment of broken glass. Her wails retreated as she fought to steady herself, the only sounds being made by the rotting female were the sharp pops that were spat out from between her worn joints.

Amil continued to stare in a state of horrified fixation. He came to understand, from the condition of her being, that this Waste was a recent victim of the disease she carried. She still possessed the ability to stand, and not all the aspects of her human description had fallen under the perverse erasure of her affliction. It was in that moment that Amil lifted his sight from her bowed limbs and seared flesh. He looked, not at the opaque pus that stuck to her cheeks and leaked from her nose, but instead, he glanced into her absence of eyes. In the abyss of her sockets, the most excruciatingly painful symptom of her curse was revealed. At least for a while longer, she could still think.

"Oh god," he said aloud, with an almost involuntary reflex.

She stared back at him without the use of her eyes, and continued to bleed the floor black and fill the air with the failings of her joints. Amil gave a thought to who she was before this sickness. Had he known her? Was she the president of a nation or a chart-topping songwriter? Whatever she may have been, it didn't matter anymore. Then he gave a thought to the possibility that she once accepted a key from Aphelianna. It was a likelihood he could barely entertain. Be that as it may, this wretched abomination could have been nothing more than a mirror. A reflection of Amil Young in a future not yet realized.

He choked on the spit in his throat and felt a

genuine sympathy for the girl. He took a step toward her, but as he did, the Waste displayed the one and true nature of her condition. She dropped onto her knees and flung her withered arms out wide as a blistering yell erupted from her throat. Globs of the acidic fluid were forced out of her nose, and, as she screamed, her toes curled and drove slivers of glass deeper into her feet. Her jagged call scraped off the walls and tore down the hallways. Its shrill din leapt through the broken windows, and further saddened the lugubrious statue, who had tried in vain to warn of the Waste's presence.

He knew the time to depart the atrium had come, and then passed him by. For Amil had already tarried too long, and before he could craft a proper thought, his pursuers caught up to him en masse. Wastes stormed the atrium from every cavity and crack, and set their murderous thirst upon him. They crashed through the doors, were purged from the darkened arcades, and they dropped without hesitation from the wounds in the ceiling above. A cacophony of discordant rage filled the space, and soon the whole of the ground would be slicked in their virulent emission.

Near the center of the room, Amil was found exposed and vulnerable, with the visions of every plague and menace set to all sides of him. He cast his eyes overhead, and, as he witnessed the smeared silhouettes of the Wastes as they crawled upon the outer surface of the glass, his instincts took over.

Amil rushed forward and into a crowd of the beasts. His arms flanked his head as he ran, while the sensation of injury was his to absorb with a relentless regularity. Although bereft of proper nails, the Wastes dug rough

164

canals over his skin with their jagged fingertips. As his flesh was divided, Amil's body burned intensely as a hot sensation of distress found his nerves. With a ferocity that could rival the clamp of a pitbull's jaw, the Wastes slashed their prey with rotted teeth. The damage caused from these impressions became evident all across his form. His punishments were constant and cruel, but still, he pressed forward, ever closer to an opening. The only salvation left to him, the splintered remnants of a broken door.

He tossed the creatures aside, and flayed his knuckles upon their mouths as they bit and snarled. But during his desperate flight to preserve the farcical existence that he knew, Amil was tripped, and sent to the wetted ground below. He lay on his back, and the sight of more Wastes swelled into view as they poured through the wounds in the roof. He put that rough piece of rock in his hand to work. As the creatures descended over him, his weapon was thrust with wild abandon.

His crude knife sunk itself into the faces and flesh of the Wastes, but the afflictions they suffered did little to deter their bestial desires. Amil pushed his body backwards as he kicked and slashed, all the while inching closer to the sanctuary of a broken door's threshold. Fatigue momentarily forced Amil's head to contact the soiled ground. His skin recoiled from the acidic touch of the fluid, and his hair stuck to the floor. Ensnared by the pus, a clump of hair was ripped out of his scalp as his head frantically tossed about. In his fevered attempts to spare his lips and nose from the jaws of those that assaulted him, Amil's eyes delivered a sight of bounty and release to his mind. The enigmatic exit was mere paces from his besieged position, and with the hope that this offered, the strength required to continue was found.

He rolled onto his hands and knees, and although the most profane descriptions of humankind tore the skin from his back, Amil scurried for the passageway. He felt the muscles of his back ripped asunder by teeth, and he felt the cold beauty of broken wood as it lay scattered about him. But as he reached the divine barrier of blackness that the threshold held, the mouth of a Waste clamped onto his ankle. The compression of its bite cleaved the material of Amil's shoe, and he felt as the fractured bones inside its mouth sunk deep into his skin. He spread his arms wide, and the desperate grip that he applied to each side of the doorway chased away the blood inside his fingers. Aided by the slick condition of the stone under him, and expending the last of his strength, he vaulted his body fully across the spectral border.

Ribbons of flesh were left behind in the mouth of the Waste. The sounds of ligaments as they snapped were hurled into the air like bellowed vulgarities, but still, Amil was free. He felt as his foot was nearly torn from his leg during his thrust. The pain threatened to send Amil into unconsciousness, but in the instant that his body left the atrium, a fresh door materialized behind his flight, solid and locked tight. Its emergence sealed off the Wastes from his sight, leaving Amil in darkness and perilously near to his own extinction. He allowed himself to go limp upon the ground, and his skin began to burn and twist with all the damage that it had taken. Rivulets of the black discharge dropped from his hair, and as it ran about his face, the fluid stung his eyes and ruptured blood vessels with its kiss.

As he lay on his stomach, Amil's face was rearranged by pain, and as his agony swelled, his form contorted and writhed. Blood spurted and seeped from the many wounds that had been carved, and rivers of the red fluid cascaded off his ravaged back. The escape of blood dulled his mind, and as this warm flow of life rushed away, his face was drained of its color.

After the onslaught of this suffering began to subside, his body started to cool. His anguished twitches softened to a mild tremor, and a fresh outpouring of sweat glazed his skin. The water soothed his fiery body, but as the liquid left him, Amil was robbed of his focus. The ground below the stare of his eyes began to blur, and his tiny world of one started to swirl and shake. A feeling of nausea bubbled up in his gut, and with no inclination to move his face, he vomited a halo of acidic slime around his head. His lids were heavy, and as his mouth slid back into the pool of filth that it had created, he felt powerless to stop whatever may come next.

With only a rudimentary sense of thought left to him, Amil dwelled on the true meaning of death. He felt as it raced toward him. He wondered wearily, through which of his many injuries would expiration elect to enter and collect what remained? He couldn't escape the pestiferous implications of his failures, and as he thought of Ali as she hung cold and naked from that tree of eternal torture, he fell away into unconsciousness.

Part 5. The Great Carillon

Chewed and scratched within an inch of his new and repugnant existence, Amil awoke among a blanket of dried blood and vomit. The amount of congealed liquid that surrounded him was alarming, but most surprising was that

he felt relatively well. Sitting up, he inspected the many
holes in his tattered clothing and the injuries that lay
beneath. It felt impossible to accept, but nearly all of his
wounds had closed up. There were even some that looked
to be scarred over, as though the wounds they described
were suffered many years before. He undid his shoe and
witnessed the ghosts of the teeth that nearly severed his
foot, but other than this faded reminder, little damage was
there to be found. He swiveled his ankle around and felt not
the slightest hint of pain. As he tied his shoe, Amil noticed
that his knuckles bore no signature or scrape of the
punishments they received seemingly moments ago.

It was in this innocuous act of knotting his laces that
Amil was made to wonder about how long he had been
asleep. Had his body healed this rapidly, or had he lain
upon the ground for days or weeks untold? No explanation
was too absurd to believe in this place, and yet, he could
not place the smallest amount of trust in his own senses. If
he had discovered one truth from his journey deeper into
Aphelianna's house, it was that the impossible had become
the common and ordinary.

Minutes after his waking, Amil came to realize that
this was the first time that he had slept since his arrival in
the afterlife. He wasn't sure if what he had experienced
could actually be classified as proper sleep. It was more or
less an involuntary surrender to pain. Then he thought of
food and other such things that fuel life, and how he had
nearly forgotten them. He wasn't sure why no sense of
longing for things once essential could be found. Maybe
this lack of desires could be linked to the relative
insignificance that time now held. He had no means to
crudely mark the passage of time, if, in fact, time could still

be measured. Perhaps, then, it failed to exist, and all that was left were a series of dismal events chained together in an ever-repeating cycle of hopelessness.

Nonetheless, he found it odd that the need for sustenance or rest seemed to have evaporated entirely. The idea of annihilating a steak or just plowing through a bowl of ramen noodles sounded euphoric, but the need to do so simply did not exist. As he felt his chest heave, Amil doubted that his lungs were actually processing oxygen. Rather, they flexed out of habit. He felt truly dead, nothing more than an entity of routine. Doomed to wander the evermore and practice inconsequential and meaningless behaviors.

With nothing more than minor muscle aches that begged for the relief of Tylenol, Amil rose to his feet. He found himself inside an enormous courtyard. The open air was above him, and, in a welcome change of environment, the sky above was blue and decorated with a healthy assortment of fluffy white clouds. The grass under his feet was short, and a bit thin, as the dirt below peeked through, but it was green. Even the trees that spotted the land had leaves, and they shifted with the persuasion of a gentle breeze. Benches of painted iron and weathered wood slept under the many branches, while pillars of stone supported ornate arched roofs that offered a shady cove for a mid-afternoon's nap.

Paths of brick were laid out in a staggered grid that flowed out over the land and curved with the soft undulation of the hills. Amil set a slow pace over the narrow road, and passed decorative archways and stone monuments that were set within landscaped areas of mulch and ground shrubs. He approached a large circular area fashioned out of tan paving stones, and from this surface, a cozy gazebo rose. A few of the shingles upon the roof had begun to peel, and the wood of the railings was mildly warped, but the partial enclosure was too charming to resist.

As he slouched upon a bench, Amil took a respite from his troubling venture and looked out across the land. He closed his eyes and breathed in the freshness of the air. It tasted as cool and pure as a foggy Virginia morning. And that's when he heard it, the delicate sound of a bell as it peppered the air with its song. Amil sat up and concentrated. He waited for the sound to come again, and made not a motion. Every other area of this cursed place had been so deathly silent that he was certain of what was heard. It stood out and grabbed his attention. Desperate to hear it again, to know that he wasn't suffering from madness, Amil barely breathed as he waited for what felt like hours, just to hear that mild knelling another time. As he watched the roll of the clouds and diligently listened, he began to question if this place was real. Maybe it was a cruel illusion, an oasis of sorts, constructed to lull him into a false sense of security, but then the sound came again.

Like a pistol shot to begin a race, the second time that he heard the bell, Amil leapt to his feet and started back down the path. He followed the delicate ringing in whichever direction seemed to bring him closer to the source. As he raced along, the tune became much more than the tolling of a single bell. True music was being played, as a finely tuned melody was produced from many bells. He pictured them to be the size of thimbles, but soon, a low throb echoed over the land. It vibrated in his body, and as it did, he was left with the impression that the bells

170

responsible for the lower tones were the size of grown men. Notes of every variety came to his ears as he advanced, and soon, entire chords were formed and woven together to craft a proper song.

He slowed his pace, and began to delight in the interminable epic that accompanied his walk, but as his eyes were set upon one of the little music makers, he stopped suddenly. Dangling from a tree branch, and strung with a thin pink thread, was a bell. It lay still, and it rattled right on cue, but as Amil's eyes followed the path of the string, he could not locate its source. The material must have traveled for miles. Through the sky and over the trees it went, connecting to other bells, as it flowed in a precise journey to the trained hands of its master.

Amil followed the increased volume of the music, and as he did, he spotted more and more of the bells. Thousands were hung from the trees, while more still were made to swing from the archways and other sculptures that gave definition to the great courtyard. Bells that greatly outweighed his previous estimation were suspended inches off the ground, and from a considerable distance away, he was made to feel near breathless from their reverberations.

It looked as though the pink thread that bound the bells was one impossibly long rope. The thread begat tentacles, fingers reaching into the horizon, that all worked together in awesome harmony. Their sprawl formed elaborate designs overhead, and, as the strings continued to lace the sky, bizarre angular shadows striped the ground. A heavy stitching hung above him, and as he ventured further into the swell of the music, the sky was made to resemble an intricately woven quilt.

The landscape he trod over curved upward, and as

Amil ascended the mild grade, the song's volume rose with his progression. Once the summit of the long hill was reached, he was able to glance down at the origin of the captivating music. Far below him was a massive stadium. It was carved right out of the land, and an immense auditorium of stone seats coiled three quarters around the arena. It looked a bit decrepit and largely forgotten, as most of the stone was dulled by weather and housed a fine glaze of moss. It appeared as though not a soul filled the area reserved for spectators, and probably hadn't for some time, but at the center of the venue sat the carillon player.

As he sat behind the monstrous example of musical craft, the player rapped his knuckles off the keys and stomped the pedals at his feet. All of the veinous threads that spread across the sky had, at last, found their heart. In the web of their concentration, they nearly obscured the man who tugged at their strings. Bells of all sizes hung in the sky like metallic clouds. They were suspended high above the stadium field, and rang in concert with one another. The metal framework of the massive instrument dominated the center of the arena, and it towered into the air. The master of the bells was held in the center like a slave, forever tethered to an unconquerable task of composition.

Amil slowly approached the auditorium with apprehension in his mind. He was certain that he would soon come to face another victim of Aphelianna's curses. But before he would have the opportunity, an unexpected situation was set before him. With a few hundred feet separating him from the stone gallery, he could see that a pair of spectators did indeed gaze upon the tortured musician. They sat in the last row of seats and made small motions as they interacted with one another. The image filled him with uncertainty, but before he could continue his march or flee back whence he came, his trespass was spotted.

A man turned around in his seat and fixed his gaze upon Amil. Soon, his female companion shared his posture. Scared by nothing in particular, but frightened all the same, Amil looked away. Finally, he raised one hand and gave an unsure wave to his audience. The man offered a mild nod of his head and then turned back around. He seemed content in the knowledge that Amil was not a foe, and yet utterly unconcerned for who he actually was.

With shoes of lead, Amil walked toward the couple, and quietly closed the gap between them. He stopped a step or two behind their position and hung in the air like a sheet forsaken on a drying line. He stared straight ahead, bereft, and without comprehension of what next to do.

"If you're not gonna say anything, save us some time then and bugger off," the man said in an accent that hinted to British origin.

Amil looked over. In a testament to how wary he had been to set his gaze on the strangers, lest they turn to monsters before his eyes, he only then noticed that the couple was black. Death revealed itself as the final and absolute equalizer. Only three races were left to exist: the Wastes, cursed deities, and all the rest of the poor, unfortunate flesh bags who were damned to toil and twist among all the ruin.

The man was slender, bald, and, most likely, dressed in the suit that had accompanied him to the grave. His form exhibited the telltale signs of a battle lost to cancer, while the alligator shoes that he wore hinted at his earthly sense of sleek fashion. Surely he had picked his own funeral attire, as no expense had been spared for the last hurrah. The suit was pinstriped, with the pocket square perfectly complementing his tie. As he loosely draped an arm over the stout frame of his companion, Amil was almost humorously struck by their differences.

Although the man was no more than a year or two older than Amil, the girl was clearly a good decade and a half his junior. Even their color varied considerably. While his skin was as dark as nighttime itself, she held that beautiful caramel complexion that Amil had so often dreamt about as a boy. He was probably fifteen before he had actually met someone who wasn't white. Prior to that, his only experiences with black women were from the bitches of hip-hop videos that graced his erotic teenage fantasies.

Their skin tones aside, their outward appearance and choice of dress was comically mismatched. She was squeezed into a pair of jeans, and gold hoop earrings that rivaled the circumference of dinner plates, hung from her ears. Her dark hair was straightened and highlighted with blonde streaks. Her nails were chipped, but polished, and as she held hands with her rakish beau, Amil felt his heart ache out of jealousy.

It was then that his attention was drawn to the tight, midriff-revealing top that the girl wore, and all the bullet holes that dotted the upper curves of her breasts. He must have set his eyes upon her chest for some time, and although thoughts of her bronze cleavage were absent from his mind, he was harshly called out for his lingering gaze.

"Muthafucka, what are you lookin' at?" she barked at him.

"Sorry, I guess I'm still not used to this," muttered Amil.

"Well, getcha eyes up off my titties."

"I was looking at the holes. It was just sort of shocking, that's all."

"Aight, just hadda put you in ya place," she said as she slid a cigarette between her lips.

"That's a Newport," Amil said, puzzled.

"It's not just us that comes over, you know?" the man said. "All kinds of shit makes its way here. Kinda like the earth was a cup that got kicked over. That's how I look at it, anyway."

"How long have you guys been here?" Amil asked, over the constant ringing of bells.

"I tried to measure time for a while, but it doesn't work. Let's just say that I've probably spent a night or two in nearly every room in this place. I met her in the 86th room I visited, after that, I stopped counting," he admitted.

"We're gonna find that Eternal City," the girl added.

"Yeah, I've heard of it," said Amil.

"It exists."

"Man, how do you know?" asked Amil, in irritation.

"Because if it doesn't, what do we have? Nothing. It gives us hope. It's a place where the dead can live. We can be safe and have a real life. Or something close to it, anyway," the man calmly said.

"I guess so."

"So, what's your story, white boy? You're lookin' a little rough, you know?"

"I ran into some stuff. I'd rather not talk about it."

"Okay, so how'd ya die?" she asked, as this change of topic oddly merged into the realm of matters less complicated.

"Killed myself," he plainly stated.

"Damn, crackers do the strangest shit. Black folks die young all the time. Should've just been black, you might have made it here sooner."

Amil actually cracked a smile. There was something in her urban American accent that delighted him. She was jagged and her tone was sharp, but she wasn't judgmental. In some bizarre way, her words comforted Amil. If for nothing else, she had managed to make him laugh. It was surreal and disquieting, being made to chuckle at the memory of one's own suicide.

"I don't remember the last time I laughed," he admitted.

"See? Now that's what I'm talking about," the man said. "It's hope. When I got here, I didn't have any hope, then, I met her. I had a little hope, and then we heard about The Eternal City. Now I have more hope."

"I got this," Amil said, as he produced his key.

"You betta have a whole ass load of hope," the girl said, quiet sympathy in her voice.

He laughed again, only this time it was to stop from crying.

"I've heard about people like you," said the man.

"Yeah? So what did you hear?" asked Amil.

"That you all end up the same way."

"I might forever become one of those things, I can't change that now."

"If it's all the same, that's where we're all headed. I'm just trying to put it off for as long as I can." said the man quietly and, oddly enough, without any hope in his voice.

"But I still have to try. I fucked up in life so many times that I'm due to get something right. I will save Ali," he defiantly stated. "Hope, right?"

"Hope."

"Good luck finding your city, I gotta keep moving," Amil said, stepping away.

"Hey, where are you off to?" shouted the man.

"He might know something," Amil said, as he pointed to the carillon player.

"Just leave that shit alone."

"She's right. Enjoy the music, and be about your way, but leave him alone."

"Why? I know the worst that can happen. Tell ya what, I'll save Ali, and one day we'll meet again in The Eternal City. I gotta go."

He walked away and the couple at his back embraced. They found in death all that Amil had wasted in life, and, as he faded from their vision, the man prayed silently.

"False hope," he whispered.

Amil cautiously navigated the broken stone steps of the gallery as he descended closer to the musician. His shoes tore up hunks of moss, and loose bits of concrete softly tumbled from the brittle steps, adding percussion to the chime of the bells. As he reached the start of the stadium field, he stopped and looked back toward the couple. They were already gone, uninterested in what might happen next.

He stood upon the same surface as the carillon player, although the bell master still remained a considerable distance away. Amil found himself staring directly into the center of the field, and, with a chest full of nervous palpitations, he advanced. Whatever the field surface once was, it had grown barren. The ground was soft below his feet, like clay, but a heavy coat of dirt had accumulated over time, and offered dust to the air with every mild disturbance of a step. With his eyes to the sky in an effort to elevate them above the whirl of dirt, a new respect for the bells was gained as they swung overhead. He thought of the inescapable rain of metal that would wash down upon him if just one of the ropes were to fail. It made him quiver, as he was held in constant shadows by the massive concentration of bronze that dangled above his head.

As his eyes followed the threads, Amil was unaware of how close he had advanced to the mysterious player, when at once he was made a witness to the musician's curse. As the thin pink lines flowed downward and attached themselves to the source of their action, Amil was sickened by what was seen. Like any proper carillon, the wires affixed themselves to clappers and pedals that were used to sound the bells, but much like everything else which had been perverted by Aphelianna's touch, this instrument was a machine of torment.

Countless ropes were fastened directly into the body of the musician. Some were sewn right into his skin, while most of the others were attached by means of curled metal hooks. The barbs sunk themselves deep into the flesh, and, all around the site of their impalement, the skin was reddened with irritation. The wires left no part of his harrowed anatomy unused. They sprang from his arms and legs, and tugged mercilessly at the tender meat between his fingers and toes. His chest and upper back were polluted by the strings, and even his face wasn't spared the pierce of polished steel.

The malnourished and pale frame of the musician was partially obscured by a brown robe, a fact the Amil was thankful for, as every rib of the ensnared man certainly poked at the skin. His face was long, and carved by deep wrinkles and frown lines. A geyser of gray hair sprouted from the top of his head, and, as it cascaded down his face, the thin locks obscured his tired eyes. As Amil moved closer to the bench that this entertainer was forever strapped to, he noticed that the musician was asleep. He wasn't playing at all. It was with every breath and tiny movement of his body that the bells were struck.

"Hello," he stammered, as he looked up at this strung victim of Aphelianna.

In a discordant calamity that could have shattered the earth into brittle fragments of microscopic shards, the musician awoke. Once he steadied his body upon the bench, the bells cooled their rage, and the shadows that were made to sprint all around came to be still again. The sky darkened and the white clouds vanished, almost as though they had been chased away by the discordant scream of the bells. A gentle rain began to fall, and, as it muddied the ground, the carillon player slowly opened his eyes and set his down-turned gaze toward his visitor.

"I'm sorry, I didn't mean to disturb you," Amil blurted out, upon a wave of heavy sighs.

"Look at me," he quietly responded. "How could the words of a man disturb me?"

"I'm looking for Isadora."

"Hmm, I suppose you have a good reason to find her?"

"Yes, I'm trying to save someone very special to

me."

"And yourself?" the musician asked through a cough.

"I'm starting to care less and less about what happens to me. I don't even know if I can be saved. I just want to help Ali."

"That sounds rather selfless."

"I was never very selfless before. I took a lot of things for granted," admitted Amil.

"Guilt, perhaps the greatest curse of all, and a self-inflicted one at that," he grumbled.

"Did Aphelianna do this to you?"

"You know her name? That is truly unfortunate," the musician whispered with thin and labored breath.

Amil felt what he used to call a heart as it sunk ever deeper into his chest. The further he progressed into his journey, the more he was made to regret his deal with Aphelianna. It felt like a damned quest. Even if he succeeded, doubt enveloped all her promises.

"I took a key from her. We made an arrangement," Amil said.

"You would be very wise to find yourself a safe place to hide, and remain there until the end of all existence."

"And then what? I'm just supposed to forget about Ali?"

"Yes. Whoever she is, forget her."

"I can't!"

"You have been given a gift, a rare opportunity that you need to seize," said the musician.

"Which is what exactly?"

"You do not bear the marks of your death, nor will

you ever carry a wound again. You will feel healthy and strong for all time. Some would say that you have become eternal. You have Aphelianna to thank for that. As long as she endures, she will shelter you from the fate of a Waste, and all because her salvation hangs from the thin promise of your success. So run from her, and cast that key away from your mind. Forsake this fool's deal, and keep yourself from the murderous clutches of the Wastes. Remember, you may be eternal, you may not fear death, but you must fear pain. Suffering, it seems, it also without end," stated the enfeebled god, with a glance to his strings.

"I still feel sick. I fucking puked when I arrived here!" Amil shouted.

"That is the human side of you, dying off. It will fade with time."

"I don't want an eternity without Ali. Can you help me or not?" asked Amil, impatiently.

"I suppose, but hear this first. When Aphelianna waged war upon the rest of us, she eliminated any opposition by shackling us all to curses. This is mine. You see, I was the God of Music, and I was very well liked because of it. Aphelianna resented me for that fact, because, as you might imagine, not many people offer prayers to the Goddess of Death."

"I don't understand. She waged war on the other gods because she was lonely?"

"It's not that simple," the spent musician said.

"So an entire legion of gods couldn't stop her?" asked Amil, befuddled and pissed off.

"Death always wins. Didn't you know that?"

"Jesus Christ," whispered Amil.

"Jesus Christ. Who is that? You humans speak of

him often. Who was he?"

"Never mind, they're just stories. Can you ever escape?"

"Only Isadora can free me. However, that would be the end of me," the musician said.

"So, I guess you don't want me to find her either?"

"I tried to discourage you for your own wellbeing, but I hope that you indeed find her."

"I thought dying here was what everyone feared?" asked Amil.

"It's what humans fear, and rightly so. Gods disappear. We cease to be. I am ready for that. You see, the strings of my bells were fashioned from the skins of my family. And so every chime sounds like a scream to me. Every day, I listen to the cries of my parents, my brothers and sisters, and my children. Nothingness would be paradise compared to this curse," explained the bell master with sadness in his voice.

Amil closed his eyes and placed his hands over his face. In every room, he was assaulted by another example of Aphelianna's brutality, but this was monstrous even by her standards. As he felt the rain soak through his tattered clothing, Amil began to weep. He was nearing the edge of sanity, and felt much the same as he did on the day that he took his own life. Only now, he wasn't given the option to give up.

"Will all the curses be lifted if I find Isadora?"

"Yes, and a lot of gods will disappear."

"What about Aphelianna? She told me that she longed to be free of her curse."

"She is cursed too, that's true. It was the unforeseen event of her treachery, but I believe that she will remain," the musician said.

"Who cursed Aphelianna?"

"Please, I am very weak. I can direct you to a friend of mine who may be able to answer your questions, but please, leave me be."

"Okay," Amil said, as he nodded slightly, still straining to understand the unimaginable pain that the carillon player was forced to endure.

"Alright, pay very close attention now. I want you to walk. Walk this yard until you see a door. It will be the only door you can see. Once you have found it, go in. I know not if it is locked, but I can assure you, most every door you find hereafter will likely be locked," he strained out with a wheeze.

"I don't care, just go on."

"From there, you will find yourself in a long hall. It will be very narrow, and lined with doors. Walk to your right, and keep a sharp count as you go. Take the 3947th door, but don't lose count. You'll never be able to start over, as all the doors look identical."

Amil turned around and walked in a rigid circle. He ground his teeth and kicked the mud as he went. His fists balled into anvils of flesh, and all the blood that remained in his veins ignited, and boiled itself into a stream of distilled fury.

"Fuck!" Amil shouted, as he beat his fists into the side of his head.

"Please, try not to despair."

Amil stood with his back to that elaborate device of harmonious punishment for a moment, and stared into the distance. He sucked in a deep breath, and, with a mind full of pestiferous thoughts, he contemplated his own sacrifice at the mercy of the Wastes. At least torture would be easier than this.

"Alright, go on," whispered Amil.

No response came, and soon it was quite clear that Amil's exhausted companion had passed out.

"Hey! Wake up, wake the fuck up!" Amil commanded as he grabbed a handful of the strings and jerked them violently.

"Why? Why do you hurt me?" the musician meekly asked.

"Please, tell me what to do next," Amil begged.

"Okay, yes. Very well. Forgive me, I strain to remember most things these days. Now where was I? The door, of course. Take that door, you will find yourself in another hall, much the same as the last. All you must do to locate the proper door here, is to listen to my bells. In the very instant that you can no longer hear my children scream, you will know which door to take."

For the first time, the carillon player lifted his dry eyes to Amil. Among the call of high-pitched bells, he straightened one of the bony fingers that hung from a hand beset with pins, and pointed it sharply at the deceased human before him.

"Now," the musician began. "You must run. It will be immediately clear as to why. Never hesitate, not for a second, even though it is all you will want to do. Ignore all your emotions, and run."

"What am I running from?"

"That is for you to discover, but as I said before, you must never stop. If you pause for one moment, your key will be lost, and Aphelianna's influence over you will be lifted. A Waste's fate you will have. If you can refuse your inner voice, and you manage to reach the last door left to take, simply use your key again and you will find my friend."

"Who is he?" Amil asked, with a fresh slick of sweat on his face.

"He's an artist of sorts, although his masterpiece has long since been broken. He will help you, he...he will help."

A mild offering of drool collected inside the mouth of the feckless god, and, as he faded from consciousness, a band of the heavy saliva fell from his cracked lips. His eyes closed, and into a restless sleep he fell, as the mourning cry of the bells continued to sound. As the musician hung still among that framework of iron and stitching of sinew, Amil was witness to a vision of absolute agony and unrelenting pain. It was a sentence that no being, divine or common, should ever be made to serve.

Much like the young couple that he had met in the auditorium, Amil simply turned and walked away. Once he had cleared the boundary of the arena, the familiar landscape of the courtyard resumed. The rain persisted as he traversed the undulation of the sleepy hills, but among the rather pleasant environment of artistic sculpture and tended coves, he barely minded the cold licks of the rain. It didn't take long before a door was spotted, but, off in the far distance, was another. He remembered the words of his weary friend, and continued further into the unknown.

As he stepped past a door that stood strident and connected to nothing that human senses could detect, Amil cast not a thought to its impossible nature. Rather, he simply wondered where it went. Even if he never found Isadora, it was certain that he would fail to see what lay on the other side of every door encountered. Could that door hold the secrets of the fabled Eternal City, or would it greedily take a turn of his key, and then coldly place him on the opposite side of its threshold? Maybe it held a treasure so splendid he would be made to forsake his quest to spare Ali from the Spirit Ripper. It was a notion he was pained to entertain, but it was plausible all the same. For nothing seemed beyond the reach of cruel possibility within Aphelianna's house. Amil's mind was stalked by the reality that Isadora herself was waiting on the other side of the door. Perhaps the carillon player was seeking to send him astray, and he was voluntarily passing by his one chance to meet the only being that could save Ali. These were thoughts that would only serve to undo him, and, so, with a refocused determination, he put his faith in the words of the musician, and kept walking.

Amil walked, the rain fell, and doors arrived. In sets of twos, threes, and bunches, they were all put behind him. He started to think that he may never find a lone door, but all at once, the rain remained nestled in the clouds and the sky cleared to allow fresh rays of light to illuminate the way forward. One door, removed from the sight of all the others, had been placed on a hill. Its outline sparkled with a slick of rain that reflected the new light of an eternal day.

Amil set his hand on the knob and grew thankful that a use of his key would be spared. But before he flung the door open and stepped within its shadowy embrace, he scanned the world about him. He strained his eyes to the limit of their function, and diligently searched for another door. Close to half an hour was spent with his sweaty palm upon that rounded piece of glass before he was content to give it a full turn. Once convinced that he had, indeed, found the correct path, he drew a deep breath, and opened the door.

As promised, a dismal and poorly lit hallway greeted him with the compassionate kiss of a sledgehammer's blow. The hall itself supported a low ceiling, and was no more than five feet wide. The pathway was lined with doors on one side of the stretch for as far as the eye could see. To his left ran an unending stream of repetition, and to his right, a perfect reprise. Amil turned to his right, as instructed, and set about the daunting task of finding the 3947th passage.

"One...two...three..." he muttered, as he pressed his fingers to each door that he passed.

Once he arrived at the 100th door, Amil tore a small scrap of material from his pant leg and stuffed it into the one back pocket that he still had. He repeated this action, with some measure of ease, nine more times, and then paused to count his ribbons.

To his relief, he had ten strips of fabric and their sum equaled one thousand. As he kept his legs firmly planted, Amil looked down the hall and realized that if he were to lose count, all hope would be lost. Each door didn't merely resemble its mates. They were exact replicas. He tried to chase from his mind the thoughts of what may lurk behind or what he might come to face, as he knew that such distractions would only cause him to lose count. Once he had given a moment to these terrifying realities, and then another to set them down for the time being, he carefully slipped the scraps back into his pocket and set off in the pursuit of another thousand doors.

One...two...three, as he went.

Although his skin held the gleam of a nervous sweat, Amil felt good about his progress, and didn't stop for rest once he had cleared the 3000 mark. With a mild joy, he tapped his fingers as he went along, with the knowledge that the first leg of his strange saunter was almost complete. Then he heard something, the unmistakable voice of a door as it swings upon the rusted body of a hinge long dried.

"3178, 3178, 3178," he repeated, over and over to himself, as his heart thundered in his chest.

He heard footsteps, and in a motion that he felt damned in doing, he turned around. A hooded figure, some distance away, stood as still as Amil. He continued to utter the clumsy number under his breath, watching in fright as the being slowly began to advance toward him. It appeared vulnerable, and every bit as apprehensive as he, but this fact did little to ease his tensions, for any amount of disturbance would certainly dash his chance at finding the proper door.

"Stay away from me!" he shouted, frantically.

The figure stopped, and then shouted something back in a language that Amil was unable to pin down. A sliver of light washed over the stranger and revealed the being as a young woman. Ringlets of scarlet hair danced from the hood she wore, and her green eyes became enraged as she continued to harshly chide Amil. In a desperate move, he pressed his index finger to his lips and then pointed at the doors. She seemed to decode his message, as she stopped her rant, but resumed her march toward him.

As she drew closer, Amil noticed that she, too, was tapping her fingers against the dull wood of the doors. She was counting, too, and he had nearly broken her concentration. He silently acknowledged his outburst as an act worth cussing out, and then turned away from the girl.

He caught a glimpse of her eyes as he removed his attention from her, and gave a thought as to where she came from and to where she was headed. He started to wonder if she had a key, as well, or if this fiery woman was simply looking for a safe place to rest. He thought of how long she might have been lost inside Aphelianna's house, or, for that matter, inside the very hallway that they shared.

As difficult as it was to do, he reminded himself of his number and resumed his walk down the passage. The hard footsteps behind him and the clack of her long nails were unnerving, but Amil did his best to ignore her and the elaborate monsters that his imagination fashioned from the sounds at his back.

Sweat dripped from his fingers as he poked them against the peeled paint of the wood, and his hair had been slicked to his face from the outpouring of perspiration. His nerves were rubbed raw and his dead heart felt poised to rupture with every violent beat. He could barely contain the fears that tore at him, the possibilities of what truly lingered behind. His eyes began to cloud and his brain was losing its capacity for simple math. As he smacked his fist off door 3947, he spun around to again greet his pursuer.

Salty water was tossed off his head and his eyes were wild and red. His limbs shook and his chest heaved with the power of an earthly fault line. His teeth chattered together and his fists balled into weapons so tight that his nails dug fresh wounds into his palms, but the beasts his mind had conjured up were not to be found. The angered girl with striking features had not morphed into some amalgamation of feverish scourge or a hell-flung servant of wickedness. In fact, she was not there at all.

She must have wandered off some time ago. In his

terror, Amil had simply failed to notice. He stood with his palms to the door for a moment, and allowed the sweat to fall from his body. He devoured the stale air of the hall and calmed his tremors to the best of his ability. Amil allowed his head to softly collide with the outside of the barrier he had so doggedly sought, and gave in to his suffering. His face became twisted by pain, the marks of a man defeated stretched across his look. He permitted the sounds of his distress to fill the hallway, and, with only the faculty of blurry sight, he slid his key into the door's slot and pushed onward.

On the other side, absolutely nothing had fallen under the axe of change. This hall was as dark and lined with as many doors as the last. It owned the same stale stink, and a low ceiling of cracked plaster. As he cast his eyes fore and aft within the long hall, Amil realized that the carillon player had never extended him the courtesy of a direction in which to go. He felt the first ticks of a panic attack grip his being at this remembrance, but, as he started to shake, the weeping of the bells could be heard.

He had placed so much concentration on counting that in the last hall, his ears had failed to absorb a single note of the carillon's song. But in here, he heard it all too clearly, and with a perfection that called a fresh offering of water into his eyes. The sounding of the bells came slowly, like a dirge, and their anguished vibrations could be sensed for far longer than Amil felt equipped to handle. But he acutely listened. He was without choice, if he were to ever locate the proper path.

In the chimes, Amil heard the ghostly voices of deceased beings as they had been grotesquely recycled into a cacophony of grief. He was made to listen to the cries of the carillon master's family, and suffered along with their eternal plight. He walked among the tolling sounds of genocide, and distinctly heard the mournful sobbing that only children can produce. Their cries were impossible to ignore, so much so that he knew the cursed musician did more than relay the annihilation of his family. He was forced to forever relive it. Trapped within the battered bronze of the bells were the razed souls of those once alive, left only to weep for their own extinction.

As he stepped softly in time with the bells, Amil began to notice that the further he trod, the meeker the call of the instruments. He kept his ears tuned to the fade of each knell, and with a few hundred doors set behind him, the strikes came with greater irregularity. As the song slowly crawled toward its death, its cries were hushed into a whisper so faint it caused Amil to question the reliability of his senses. He mistook the dull ring that occupied the inner spaces of his ears for that of a sound produced from one of the shyer bells as their voices became entwined with the thin air. But for all the tricks that his mind dealt him, there was always that deep groan of cast bronze that reassured him that the long walk was not yet at an end.

It became a truly maddening task, a torturous exercise that was ludicrous in its simplicity. All he had to do was to listen and wait. But this felt like an order much too tall to fill, as just when he thought it was over, another toll would sound. After each quiet note, he would stand in silence and stillness with a growing impatience, as the duration between each lick widened from minutes to nearly an hour. But still, Amil waited and he walked. He marched on and began to wish for the fate of Sisyphus, as the ancient Greek's punishment would seem a reward of reprieve from this hopeless stroll.

Lesser men, and those not beset with a terrible stubbornness, would have given up. Most would have exited the hall after an hour or two had elapsed without the wretched accompaniment of one of those bells, but not Amil. He remained, and waited in a racked state of lethargic insanity for the sound that he knew would come. And every time it did, a piece of his spirit was wrung out, left to die upon the air with the dissipation of each phantom call.

But then it happened, when he had no more left to give and all that was required to hold him upright was nearly gone, the absence of sound that he sought finally arrived. It was a silence colder than death, as all things associated with noise shut their mouths and fled from the hallway. Amil could hear not a sound, the rustling of his clothes, his knuckles as they cracked, nor the voice of one single bell. Only nothingness remained, and it hugged him tightly.

He swayed before the door that he knew was his with his mouth agape and an exhausted look stretched across his face. His eyes wandered between cloudy and glazed, and every muscle in his body felt like it was constructed out of a crude concoction of gravel and slush. He formed his fingers around the knob and slid his key into place. That's when Amil remembered his next command. Run.

RUN! RUN! RUN! RUN?

If there was one act that Amil felt wholly incapable of performing, it was the act of running. He was sapped of all strength and stripped of any chance to reach the next door by way of the miserable task that he had sluggishly

192

bested. As saliva collected inside his lower lip, he acknowledged the death of hope, but grieved not a moment for its passing. He pressed his foot up against the door, and flung it wide.

A second had been dissected and split into one billion equal fragments. The paltry sum of one of these nano-ticks was all the time that was necessary for Amil to realize that he indeed must make great haste.

He stood upon the first rickety plank of a narrow bridge, formed from rotted wood and dried rope. It swayed in a tired unease, and the center owned a sickly dip, like that of a distended stomach. At one end, it was supported by the threshold of the door at Amil's back, and at the other was his destination and only means of escape. As the bridge hung thousands of feet above a mighty chasm, a world of fire and utter desolation fell to pieces around its moribund form.

It was stridently clear that Amil had arrived in time to witness the violent apocalypse of a foreign land. The mountains around him exploded and rained rock down upon the burning forest below. Birds dropped from the acidic sky like winged anvils, and the clouds pissed icicles that sliced at the ropes of the bridge as they fell. The river under him swelled and raged. It frothed with sticky black waves, and rose rapidly toward the decayed span.

In a full sprint, he could barely hear as the boards cracked and fell away under the assault of his gait, for the discordant song of destruction was so loud and omnipresent. He kept his focus upon that far-off door, and shielded his head from the falling debris and rocky shrapnel. Fresh expanses were opened in the floor of the bridge as the stone that shot from the sky removed entire chunks of the wooden surface. He jumped the gaps, which bred like savages beset with a wild nymphomania, and tried his best to maintain his balance as the bridge trembled and shed strands of the rope that sewed it together. Lightning joined in the race, and as its fingers touched the wood, they ignited the brittle structure and pressured Amil to quicken his pace.

He descended toward the center, and as he approached the sag and the rapid increase of the river below, his will was bolstered by the fact that he had nearly reached the middle. But once his nervous feet scuttled over the lowest point of the bridge, he was poisonously treated to the true misery that the fury around him had thus far obscured.

The water lapped at the undersides of the boards, and Amil's skin was made wet as the waves crashed around him and peppered him with their spit. In the embrace of the river were those he once knew. Hundreds of people, everyone he had ever come in contact with, now struggled to keep themselves above the rise of the water. He heard their screams, and winced as their gurgles choked out any empty air that remained.

Amil squeezed his eyes shut tight and kept on running. As he started to ascend the second half of the withered span, his calves began to burn. An inferno of guilt was aroused within him as he ignored the many pleas for help. He knew it was all an illusion, a trick to enslave him. But as he clearly heard the voices of those he used to know so well it tore at Amil not to give them a moment's recognition. He listened to the frantic voice of his grandmother, and then he absorbed the silence of her demise. All of those who shaped every memory, pleasant or painful, that he once had, drowned below the bridge. As he fled, he tried to convince himself that those below would not become Wastes. He reasoned that some of them still walked the earth. But he never succeeded in accepting this notion wholly, and, in a testament to his selfishness, he continued to stomp over his fellow man and the outstretched arms of the forsaken.

The god who was strapped into that disgusting instrument had once warned Amil that he would want to stop, that it was all that he would want to do, and the afflicted musician was cruelly correct. As Ali's voice came through the din, she begged him to save her. He had prepared himself for this torturous moment, but it made the disregarding of her voice no easier. He told himself that this was all in a greater effort to save Ali, but as water filled her mouth and muffled her screams, Amil nearly cracked. He wanted to cast himself into the water. At least then he could embrace her. He could feel the touch of her skin once more, and look into her eyes. They could exchange their vows of love, and, though it would be the end, they would drown together, and sink hand in hand into the nevermore.

Perhaps a dusting of Duke Vinzenz's fortune had fallen upon Amil, for as he was about to forsake his quest and dive in after Ali, he collided with the other door. The impact snapped his eyes open. Without a look back, and with an involuntary response that prolonged his existence, Amil thrust his key into its receptacle.

As the door swung open, the bridge fell completely away, and left Amil to dangle from the knob of the wooden barrier. The opening floated high in the dark sky, and, as the door flapped back and forth with the wind, he held on tightly to its hardware. The river had become an insatiable whirlpool, and it sucked everything away. The mountains were gone. So too was the charred forest, and all the people who had begged for assistance. All that was left to devour was a desperate man, whose life was held entirely within the constitution of his own fingers.

As he hung from a door that tried violently to shake him into oblivion, Amil existed in a world of one. Suspended an unfathomable distance into the air, he heard the violent splitting of the wooden bridge as it was smashed to pieces by the grip of the waves. In terror, he saw as the sky itself was sucked downward and into the abyss. He was truly the only thing left for that omnipotent swirl of death to ingest, yet he resolved to again deny the edict of forces higher than he. As he clung to the barrier that sat suspended within the center of a great nothingness, he carefully slithered one hand after the next onto the knob on the opposite side of the door. The mighty wind blew his hair across his face, and his legs were tossed about as all efforts of his muscles were forced into his fingers. He hung from the inside of the door, and it continued to flap with rage and the all-encompassing desire to annihilate, but Amil had already won. The next wild slap of the wood would be a boon. As it made one final attempt to cast him into the swirl of obliteration below, the door unwillingly thrust him beyond the threshold, shutting out that theater of extinction.

Part 6. Tyme's Machine

Shot like a bowling ball hurled down a crooked alley, Amil slid upon his back over a cement floor before a violent collision halted his short journey. His left shoulder and elbow made distinct imprints into the metal storage

locker that put an abrupt end to his skid, while the
disturbance his body created called down a rain from
above. Placed atop the cabinet were glass jars and metal
tins that contained all manner of nuts and bolts. Iron gears,
and an eternity's worth of dust were among their company,
and fell around the site of Amil's chaotic arrival. Most of
the items clanged harmlessly around him, but one of the
heavier jars knocked Amil on the crown of his head. Its
impact called a hazy, prismatic wash of color into his
vision.

Once the focus was rubbed back into his eyes, he
attempted to look around, but saw only the common black
of Aphelianna's house. Wherever he was, it was very dark,
and other than the misplaced parts that lay in a close
proximity to his slumped position, his sight was privy to
little else. As he sat up and leaned his face deeper into the
darkened space, a caress of cheap metal and string washed
over his cheek. This sudden touch caused Amil to jerk, an
action that earned him another kiss from the cabinet at his
back, but he quickly composed himself. Leading with his
hand, he felt around for the thin rope, and as that beaded
string shivered into his grip, Amil gave it a mild tug.

A solemn aura of amber bled across the room as the
light from a tired and heavily yellowed 40-watt bulb
sparked to life. It hung, shadeless, and from a socket that
appeared primed to short out at any moment. The pull-
string pinged off the side of the old glass, and a sound as
melancholy as the light was dull cast a dingy ambiance over
Amil's environment.

It looked as though he were held within the confines
of a storage room. It was cold and cramped, as the thick
concrete walls were lined with steel shelves. Each shelf had

its own unique state of disrepair, as every possible angle at which metal can be bent seemed to have been indulged. All sported a collection of rust, and some were collapsed entirely, but all were also charged with the retention of parts that seemed to have no relation to one another.

Splayed out over the shelves and spilled onto the floor were gears, clasps, rubber gaskets, gauges, electrical components, and pins of all sizes and purpose. Thick encyclopedias and tattered manuals swam among the confusion, as did cans of dried-up paint, along with spools of wire and various descriptions of tape. A myriad of pipe fittings could be found almost everywhere the eye could wander, and tools that looked wildly archaic and obsolete slept under the weight of dust. Brooms and tall scraps of discarded metal slumped in the corners with equally ignored cardboard boxes as their eternal companions.

Amil rose to his feet and cautiously stepped between the frozen rivers of junk that lay around him. His exit from the narrow space felt oddly shorter than his quick and rude introduction had been, and, as the path was retraced, he was made to chuckle at the course that his ass had carved through the disorder. Once he reached the end of the corridor, Amil set his eyes upon the door that had shat him. With no want to linger before it, he stepped away and then parted the dirtied plastic flaps that sealed off the storage room, to explore whatever lay beyond.

Hauntingly dark, as usual, he realized that he had stepped into a room that possibly occupied the square footage of a small country. Even his soft steps created an echo. To his right there was an enormous instrument panel affixed to the wall. Its door was absent, and the distinctions given to each switch and lever were faded, and of a language that the human brain was pained to try to understand. He reached out and flicked the first switch. It turned over like a sick, lethargic animal roused from sleep, but other than the sharp echo that it created, nothing happened. Switch after switch was tried, but change failed to arrive. There were large levers and knobs that he twisted, and others that were frozen so tight, it would require the grip of an ogre to undo them. But like the first that he tried, all remained functionless, as the room held fast to the constant black.

Although the panel was as tall as Amil and nearly as wide as a car, he was halfway through its puzzle with no reward for his hasty efforts. He stepped back, and then it occurred to him that there was most likely a precise pattern required to unlock its secrets. For a moment he debated the merits of forsaking the task of unraveling this riddle. Perhaps whatever it commanded was better left alone, unmolested by the hands of clumsy men. But then Amil peered into the rolling black. The want of light was felt supreme inside his quivering mind, as a venture into the dark was a task he felt ill-suited to best. Between palpitations of his weary heart, the light from that old 40-watt suddenly flickered and drew his eyes away from the unknown. Just off to the side of that massive network of levers and valves, there sat a previously undiscovered and lone button. It seemed unnecessarily big, and placed below it was a symbol that was comically auspicious in its simplicity.

A metal plate had been riveted into the wall with the carving of a perfect circle at its center. All around this object, short straight lines were spaced evenly apart, and as they ventured further away from their source, the lines began to thin. Amil ran his fingers over the recesses, and felt the callous touch of rust as it stained his tips in a crimson residue. His hand ascended up the plaque, and with the delicate nature of a hummingbird as it feeds upon a flower, his index finger came to rest upon the dull button. He ran his fingers around the circumference of the object and heard the tale of its interminable existence as every fine chip and scrape introduced itself to his skin. He closed his eyes and balled his fist. With a deep breath sucked into his lungs, Amil drew back his arm and then forced the side of his tense hand against the button.

So very far above him, held aloft to dizzying heights, filaments and tubes burst to life. Bulbs that were set in rows and bulbs made to resemble small planets all became flush with energy. Some failed to join their brothers in this mass awakening, but with the absence of some, the room had still found itself flooded with light. As Amil gazed up to the thousand suns that burned above, he saw the frailty of life displayed in the form of minute insect carcasses that lay dried and brittle under the glare of their gods. He also was witness to the might of industry, as the great fixtures were hung from heavy chains and platforms of iron. All were suspended from a ceiling insulated with yellow foam, a substance that promised to make the effects of asbestos feel pleasant by comparison.

Once his gaze descended from the world of illumination above, Amil tried, in vain, to gather the enormity and purpose of the room. The floor was a gray and nondescript concrete that had been blanketed by dust, but the reason for which it had been poured was a fascinating one. Plastic tubes and metal piping of all conceivable sizes rose from the floor and ran through the gigantic room in

elaborate patterns. Some were smooth, and looked to have
felt the touch of fresh paint a short while ago, while most
others were dull, the sweat of moisture and oil caked
around their connecting points. Nearly all of the pipes
looked to have had repair or inspection at some point in the
past, as they wore patches of differently hued but similar
materials. The majority of the metal tubes were decorated
and fastened by the likes of iron bolts or rivets, but their
plastic kin were held together by all manner of hose clamps,
tape, and putty.

As Amil slowly walked among this perplexing
creation, he noticed that gauges sprouted from the pipes
like coarse flowers. In triangular and circular shapes, the
meters grew from all directions out of the tubes that they
were meant to monitor. Though few were found, the most
puzzling instruments that he had come across were gauges
that had a crescent-shaped body. Rimmed in a dull glow,
they floated mere inches above the pipes on nothing more
substantial than the constitution of thin air. He placed his
palm between the empty space of a pipe and its little moon,
and as he did so, the strange gauge dropped from the air and
clacked off the ground. Once the curious object came to
rest, its light flickered out and extinguished itself by way of
a small effusion of violet smoke.

Startled, Amil looked around to see if his trespass
had been noticed, and, once he had been comforted by the
uninterrupted march of silence, he bent down to examine
the odd tool. The markings meant absolutely nothing to
him, as he couldn't glean any understanding of what the
bizarre symbols were intended to represent. He had noticed
these foreign characters on some of the other gauges, and in
a condition that was perhaps the strangest of all, he also

looked upon some that numbered a common one through ten. However, every last one of the dials, no matter how cracked, clean, or dirtied they were, all failed to register the presence of anything with their needles.

Directionless in his advance, Amil set his eyes upon cables of wire both bare and insulated. He traced their paths as they ran into and out of transformers, switchboards, and, in some cases, directly into the pipes themselves. He passed puzzling amalgamations of valves, brick stacks that were made to purge who knows what, and massive coils that looked capable of passing all the energy of one world directly into the next. Built into a far wall was an enormous column of fans that sat cold and motionless, a netting of cobwebs on their blades. Spoked turbines of iron, as silent as the fans and the size of modest houses, peeked through gaps in the thick floor. In more unsettling cases, others dangled from the ceiling on ancient cables of braided steel.

He drifted his eyes over countless stairways of extruded metal. Rickety in appearance, they rose into the air and birthed catwalks of the same mesh. The narrow walkways were without railings, and most likely had been used to work on the upper portions of this mammoth machine. Strings of loosely tethered lights streaked the platforms like the rigid nervous system of a great beast. As the elevated paths traveled in complex patterns throughout the room, to traverse them would seem tantamount to suicide.

The disrepair and dirt that clung to everything, like the overbearing mother of filth, gave this monstrosity the feel of pre-World War II industrialization. It was dangerous, heavy with a dense variety of cast metal, and cramped. The components were old and neglected, and most of the parts that looked capable of motion were without guards or other shields. Furnaces, long disused, sat perilously close to objects that should never be in the vicinity of fire, while hastily spliced wires often bathed in the same sweat as the pipes. But as Amil carried on, he realized that all the decay masked the true order of the place, and the undeniable majesty that it presented. He began to think that the most technologically sophisticated power plants of modern America would be ashamed to consider themselves advanced if ever placed beside this maddening collection of scientific understanding.

Amil continued to move about this industrial labyrinth, and soon his mind entertained the iron Minotaur that diligently stalked him. It was only a matter of time, he figured, before his curious stroll through this quieted wonder of mechanics turned into a frantic flight for his life. Or, rather, were the entire workings of this creation merely the tortured insides of a sleeping animal that had already swallowed him? That summation seemed all the more plausible, for sure enough, as he explored deeper into the guts of this beast, Amil came to face its monstrous heart. Before him lay the very soul of the room's existence, its reason for being. But like the failed gauges and frozen turbines that he had passed by before, it revealed itself to be as still and dead as the rest of its overgrown body.

From the floor, and all the way to the cancerous touch of the ceiling, was a framework of polished silver. The gleaming skeleton shimmered like a galaxy when juxtaposed with all the ruin around it, and looked to have been formed from one monumental piece of material, as not one fastener or weld graced the structure. There were no breaks or creases. Its entire flow and form was an uninterrupted series of carefully molded curves and twists. Artistic sweeps of the shiny metal bulged from the outer areas of the creation, giving it a robust look, while a complex assortment of hammered bands and thin silver netting crafted a great globe at the center.

Held within this reflective world was a dense collection of gears, all as equally splendid and cared for as the silver. They were bound and held snugly in place by the likes of rubber belts. Made to run true with the aid of bearings and pulleys, the gears all sparkled with a slick of fresh oil. Massive chains, whose blackened links most likely outweighed the heft of a herd of oxen, wrapped themselves around the larger gears, and slept delicately between the iron teeth. As Amil stepped around this divine beast in order to fully appreciate its magnitude, he peered deep within the machine. He spied gears that were no larger than nickels, and as thin as a slip of paper. He examined their placement, and was humbled by the mad precision of this device, as even the tiniest of cogs swam in complete harmony with the mightiest of their brethren. They interlocked with one another in a massive and interminable display of gracious intercourse.

In a task that demanded Amil to step backward a considerable distance, he finally set his eyes upon the top of the machine. One gear, larger than all the rest, and the breadth of a Fog Lake baseball diamond, stood still. Frozen in place, it was enwrapped in that dark chain and frosted with a glow that language was ill-equipped to describe. The way in which beauty lovingly gazes upon something even more beautiful than itself, the gear radiated a brilliance that awakened a guilt in Amil as he looked upon it.

Above that magnificent example of metallic

supremacy, a brick column descended from the ceiling and obscured the top of the gear. That hollow cylinder of stone, which seemed to kiss the jewel of this marvelous apparatus, hung open, patiently awaiting the day when the machine would run again and deliver forth its divine breath.

As Amil thought of to where the rise of the bricks might extend, he felt as his eyes fell down the creation until they drifted onto its base, and the awesome nature of its being. He hadn't thought of it before, as it seemed a foregone conclusion that this elaborate mechanism would be supported by titanic means. But, as he had been made to accept many times before, the impossible was the new common.

A few feet from the floor, the silver boning twisted around itself like a mirrored whirlpool, and formed the structure's only point. With a base no broader than that of a pinpoint, the metal tip rested upon the ground and supported the entire workings of this gorgeous monstrosity. In perfect balance and rapturous synchronicity, the enigmatic machine sat sturdy, sound as a mountain. However, it did so on only the pinnacle of minute craftsmanship and the wild genius of its creator.

"It's magnificent, isn't it?" a voice offered, in a brogue flush with grandfatherly affection.

Though spoken with no malevolence, the question caused Amil to nearly jump out of his skin. As he spun around with a heart full of flutters, his eyes set upon the proud caretaker of the stilled device.

A short man stood a considerable distance away. Dressed in wrinkled clothing that was a few sizes too large, he polished a pair of scratched glasses with the bottom of his shirt. His hair was thin and mostly gray, although streaks of his former crimson shone through, with a matching cooperation of stubble forming the shadow of a beard. He had a pot belly, the only portion of him that held excess meat, and stood with a posture that told of the distress nestled within his back.

"Well? What do you think?" he kindly asked of Amil.

"It's...I'm at a total loss for words," whispered Amil, as he gazed back at the machine. "I've never seen anything like it. What is it?"

"My greatest creation," the man relayed, in the way that a parent laments the accomplishments of a child who has passed away.

"What does it do?"

"It directed and maintained the flow of time itself. Now, it does nothing. My name's Arcanus Tyme," the man said, with an offering of his hand.

In an act that felt wonderfully familiar, Amil introduced himself as he briskly walked over to Arcanus to shake his hand.

"I don't mean any offense, but you're in desperate need of some new clothes," said Arcanus, with a smile as he swept his eyes over the shabby condition of Amil's rags.

"I'd just settle for an explanation of things."

"Fair enough. But may we continue this conversation somewhere a bit more comfortable?"

"Lead the way."

Amil followed Arcanus with a sense of awe as they slowly plodded through the massive room. The wonders that he saw previously were matched, and in some cases surpassed by the things he was given the privilege of seeing. Machines of impossible construction and elusive purpose stood quiet in various states of neglect. Small and trivial items, much akin to the brainteasers that usually grace the tops of office desks, could be found hiding in corners and slumped over the larger creations. But for as mesmerizing as all these inventions were, they all shared a common bond: rot and decay. Rust was the color of their skins, and all the metals were weak with corrosion. The plastics were warped, and the instruments were dead, their needles long ago frozen in place. Yes, everything in the room looked to be long past servicing, or even salvaging. Everything, that is, except the impeccably clean and polished object that made Arcanus most proud.

A light of soft amber drifted from a corridor that looked no cozier than a warehouse lunchroom ripped from the time of America's industrial revolution. There was a chipped desk, stacks of yellowed books that knew no proper order, and a few pieces of furniture that obscenely exposed their springs. A dirty sink with patinated pipes of copper protruded from the cracked block of the wall. A small, wobbly table was placed nearby, and upon its scratched face, an ancient percolator sat, practically tethered to the surface by streaks of dried coffee.

With a squeal almost as wretched as the screams of a Waste, Arcanus pulled out his chair. As he plunked down, he motioned for Amil to sit. He poured them both a cup of the burnt liquid without any prompting, and picked up a dented lunch pail that slept under the table. He cracked open the metal box and offered a stiff roll to his new friend.

"Sorry, I know they're dry," he said, as he ripped the hard bread asunder. "So, young man, what is it you want to know?"

"You're a god, aren't you?" asked Amil slowly,

with the eyes of a wondering boy.

"I never really cared for that title. A bit arrogant, don't you think? I always thought of myself as a mechanic, more or less. A creator of things, I suppose."

"Did you build that thing, the thing with the gears?"

"There's something you need to understand, it is not a thing. Things are simple and insignificant. That is so much more than just a thing. It is time itself, and yes, I built it, just as I constructed everything else in this room."

"By yourself?" Amil asked, perplexed.

"Me and no other."

Amil's mind was beset with confusion. But he didn't move or even exhale. He was simply stunned by the enormity of Arcanus's words. It might have been the logical path of thought, but he didn't consider of how, or even why, Arcanus had built the things he had seen. Rather, he thought of the immense amount of time that must have been used to create such a vast network of machines. It gave him a vague understanding of the old man's age, and as Amil thought of it, he felt that eternity was probably young in comparison.

"What do you mean that it's time itself?"

"Forgot what you know of the earth. Hours, minutes, and so on. They're not accurate, barely real, even. Anyway, my machine has been the catalyst for all change. It created the very fabric of time, and was designed to ever preserve its flow," he explained while gnawing through the bread.

"What happened?" asked Amil as he rubbed the key that peeked out from the holes in his shirt.

"I'm sure you know that answer," stated Arcanus solemnly, as he noticed Amil's fingers.

"Aphelianna."

"This is my curse, son. She ruined my machine. And although I know it's beyond repair, every day I attempt to revive it."

"Why?"

"You have a key, that tells me there's something that you haven't given up on. I don't know what that thing is, but even you can surely admit, it is an endeavor far less important than my labor."

The words stung, but there was no use in trying to deny that hard truth of the lesson. Arcanus was right. Amil's pursuit was relatively meaningless, and only held value for one soul. Mr. Tyme's work however, affected the entirety of existence.

"Since her hexes, the days fell apart, the world grew stagnant. The flow of time was set adrift, and the beast that I once tamed has grown feral again. The measurement and meaning of time was lost. It troubles me to talk of it, and yet I find it comically ironic, that human beings are the one creature largely unaffected by the cruelties of time, and the ultimate failure of my work."

"How do you mean? I don't understand. How are we unaffected?" asked Amil.

"Beyond the ones like yourself, who have felt Aphelianna's touch, the condition in which humans arrive here will never heal, nor will it ever naturally deteriorate further. Humankind is, for all practical means, locked in a state of suspended animation. The Spirit ages and yes, it will die one day. The life of a Waste then awaits, but it takes a very long time. It is a change that even I don't fully understand. And so I, like many others have already assuredly done, will attempt to convince you to abandon your quest."

"I won't do it, and I'm tired of hearing that. I don't care about your curses," Amil said, harshly.

"The lifting of my curse has the potential to restore order to the world. I pray for that day to come, and, in a way, I dread its arrival. I dream of the day when my machine will roar back to life. But I accept that no human will ever find Isadora. The challenge is much too vast. That is why I selflessly beg of you to stop."

Amil said nothing, as he stared down at the cracked veneer and picked the scabs that had formed on the table's face.

"Let me tell you something, Amil," Arcanus said softly, before the introduction of a long and melancholy pause. "When Aphelianna gave you that key, she also gave you a gift. Unlike the rest of your kind, your health was restored, your vitality, and your vanity. Furthermore, any injury you suffer will heal rapidly. You are not made perfect however, as I have seen your condition before. Be careful. If you suffer traumatic injuries repeatedly, a massive loss of blood, maybe, with no time to heal, the Spirit will wither, and you will die again. You will become a Waste. If you manage to avoid these things, you will live forever. Find a place to call home, forget about what hides behind the many doors, find that Eternal City, and be at peace. You have a gift that so few enjoy, don't allow it to become your curse."

The argument was spoken with quiet conviction, and its words were so strong that they could not be disputed. Arcanus mildly contradicted the words of the musician, and of Aphelianna herself, when he spoke of a new death. Amil knew not who to believe, but there was

210

something in the old man's speech that rang of truth. He then contemplated the notion that his questions would forever endure without the companionship of answer. Maybe so much time had ebbed away that even the minds of gods had grown murky and unsure. Perhaps it didn't matter who was wholly correct. After all, only suffering awaited Amil's failure. He then thought of it, finally, the prospect of eternal health. For a moment, Amil felt a renewed feeling of safety that he forgot existed. Beyond the salvation of Ali, Aphelianna offered him little, and, with a long, hard thought of himself, Amil contemplated taking the old man's advice.

"Blood," whispered Amil. "Why blood?"

"I don't know," replied the old man. "Maybe the loss of enough blood tricks the mind, or, better stated, the Spirit, into thinking that the body is about to die, and therefore it does. Maybe it is your essence. Maybe it is actually your soul."

The words stuck in Amil's mind the way moss slowly spreads over an old gravestone, as he thought of the chilly and thick fluid that rested in his veins. He wondered if blood had always been something more than science was able to detect, or had it been recently changed, mutated like everything else that entered into the house of Aphelianna?

"There is something else that you should know," said Arcanus softly.

By the tone of voice used by the ancient engineer, Amil knew to fear the words to come. They were going to bring only sorrow, and he contemplated the usefulness of hearing them spoken aloud. With a deep breath in his lungs, he nodded at the old man, foolishly thinking that he was adequately prepared for the revelation.

"There are those who will suggest that the dead human will endure forever here. This is wholly untrue, as they lack knowledge of the Spirit. Other than those like yourself, who have been granted exception from decay by either Aphelianna or Isadora, every human will one day become a Waste. All of you. This is not a new death, but the final form, the last and most torturous stage. It may take thousands of years, to put it in a time frame that you understand, but it will happen, as all the blood within the body slowly dissolves. It seems harsh, and indeed it is, but I believe that humanity was never meant to enter here. I have a theory that Aphelianna was never meant to escort humans here. There has been some mistake, a transgression, and there is a consequence for this failure of time."

"Stop. Stop, enough," said Amil, exasperated, as he raised his hands in front of his face as though to shield himself from the spears of Arcanus's words.
"Maybe...maybe if I succeed, I can take Ali to Isadora," he said to himself, in desperation.

"Amil," begged Arcanus. "You cannot save her. Remember what I said, take my advice."

"Arcanus, I truly can't tell you what I'll do," he admitted as a tear broke from his eye. "But can you do something for me?"

"Of course, my boy, just ask," he replied gleefully, happy to be moving on from such a sorrowful subject.

"How did this happen? The gods, the curses. Please, help me to understand."

"It's a painful history that hurts me to repeat," Arcanus paused, contemplating the ending of this discussion. "But, I suppose that you're just as much a part of it now as I am. Perhaps you are entitled to hear of it.

Hmm, for that matter, you're the first person I've talked to in a long time. Who knows how long it will be before someone else trips through my home...disturbing my gauges," he said, with a grin of disapproval.

"Sorry," Amil said with a smile.

"So, where would you like me to begin?"

"With Aphelianna. Why did she do this?"

"This was once called The House of the Divine, and in it, all the deities of the world did reside. From our grand home, we worked together to maintain order and the existence of all things. We each had our own charge and responsibilities, as you have no doubt gathered by now. Once a Mortal had passed away, they were ushered into different areas of the house, based on their actions in life. Here, they could mingle with the gods they once prayed to, and in some cases, they could attain godhood as well. It was a truly beautiful way of life." Arcanus stopped and looked into the bleak distance of the world he knew, and in his tired eyes, Amil could see a reflection of a paradise lost.

"After an interminable amount of time, Aphelianna grew jealous of the other gods. The Mortals never prayed to her in life, they feared her in death, and once they were here, they avoided her completely. She was a beautiful woman, truly kind, but hers was a dark task that could undo any of us, I am most certain of that. She longed to be free of her duties, and I voted in support of her."

"Voted?" Amil asked, quite surprised.

"Yes. The council of gods had a meeting, and after much deliberation and a speech by Aphelianna that still calls water into my eyes, we decided her fate. By three voices, she lost her bid to leave her morbid occupation. It was ruled that she should remain the Goddess of Death for

1000 more aeons, at which point she could apply for dismissal again. But Aphelianna didn't take to the news very well."

"Arcanus, did you pity her?"

"Yes. By some measure, I still do," he admitted, after a long and pained absence of speech.

"Anyway, on with this, I suppose. She was furious with her sister, Isadora, the Goddess of Life, who did not support her plea to be relieved of her post. She blamed Isadora for nearly everything, and turned her back on the other gods, even the ones who spoke in favor of her. From that day on, she relinquished her duties without sanction."

"What happened to the people who died?"

"They wallowed in the fields. Starved of sunlight and swollen with the weight of the dead, the grass died and the soil became poisoned with their waste. And all the while, Aphelianna sat upon her fountain and stared into the darkening water."

"That water, or whatever that sludge is, what is it exactly?" asked Amil.

"The essence of life. It was once clean and pure, and of the mightiest blue. When the dead arrived, they would wash themselves in it and prepare for a cleansed rebirth in the afterlife. But as Aphelianna grew negligent, the water turned sour. I can only think of how black and acidic it must be now. It very accurately tells of how sick life has become and just how close we are to absolute nonexistence." For the first time, the cadence of Arcanus's voice had changed. The warmth of his brogue died away, and the strength of his words faltered.

"Then one day, the whole fucking world fell apart. Pardon my language. It was decided that Saint Calvino go and speak with Aphelianna. He loved her so deeply, and once, so very long ago, she loved him as well. It was felt that she might listen to him. But he never got the opportunity to make his pitch for the other gods. Instead, he first tried to rekindle the love they once shared."

"They were together? I thought he was barely a man?"

"He was the eternal boy," said Arcanus, with a fake exuberance and a sweep of his hand. "He was the God of Love. The perfect mix of adolescent passion and boyish innocence. But do not be fooled, he was no child. Anyway, Aphelianna rejected his advances. He was a god, after all, and she had grown to despise him. She slapped his face and dirtied his shoes with her spit. With her cheeks wet with tears, Aphelianna hurled insults at him and renounced any affection for him that she had once held."

Amil thought of Ali, and the last fight they ever had. He remembered the terrible things that they said to one another, and felt an eerie similarity to this epic example of the imperfection of life and of the irrational behavior born from savaged feelings. He shed a tear for Ali, and, in what felt like a continuation of his punishment, he allowed another to fall for Aphelianna.

"Arcanus, I was told that this Saint Calvino raped her. Is that true?"

Old Father Tyme rubbed his closed eyes, and as he did, tears wetted the dried tips of his fingers. His face exposed more wrinkles in its saddened state, and his chin trembled as Arcanus fought valiantly to suppress a breakdown.

"Yes, it is," he said finally, with a nod. "He held her face under the water of her fountain and beat her body until she had no will to resist. He then took his time in the desecration of her, and then he left her there. Naked! Cold! In front of all those Mortals...why do you make me do this!?" shouted Arcanus as he rose from the table. A spark of sadness ignited a fury within the old man. In his grief, Arcanus dashed random items to the floor and bloodied his knuckles upon the coarse stone of the walls.

"Okay! Alright, I'm sorry! Just please stop!" pleaded Amil.

"No, no, no, I'm sorry, my young friend," whispered Arcanus, once he had moderately composed himself. "It is not your fault."

Slicked with sweat and wheezing on the foul composition of the stale air, Arcanus stood with his back to Amil as he caught his breath. He rubbed his face and flattened his hair back down with the application of a greasy palm, and once again motioned for Amil to sit as he resituated his chair.

"Would you like me to continue?" Arcanus asked.

"I just want to understand all this, as best I can."

"Very well then, moving on. That night, Aphelianna put curses onto us all. She shackled every one of us to tasks or conditions that we could never break on our own. This was all done in an effort to silence Isadora."

"Why her? Why didn't she just curse Calvino?"

"In the great order of things, he's quite unimportant. But still, I'm sure Aphelianna reserved a particularly nasty curse for him."

Amil said nothing, and, in his telling silence, Arcanus took solace.

"In order to escape her godly task, her torment, as it had become, Aphelianna knew that she had to silence

216

Isadora. Her sister is the Goddess of Life, and if she can no longer create, then eventually all life will expire, and there will be no more dead to shepherd."

"And then Aphelianna will be free."

"Exactly. Aphelianna knew the other gods would try to save Isadora, and so that is why she cursed the rest of us. Do you remember that great throne you surely noticed in The Hall of Worship?"

"Yeah, I don't think I could forget it," said Amil.

"That is the seat reserved for the god of gods, and no one has ever sat in it. It was constructed of invincible materials, regrettably, it now seems, and was meant to remain empty as a reminder to us all that no one god was all powerful, that we all depended on each other for our own survival. Aphelianna knew that without interference from the other gods, she would be free to claim that power."

"Why couldn't she have just sat in it before the curses? I could have," said Amil in astonishment.

"No, my boy, you couldn't have," said Arcanus with an irritated laugh. "Had you placed yourself in that chair, a Waste's body you would now have, maybe worse. During the better times, no god could take the throne, either, as a unanimous vote of approval from the other gods was required before any one of us could claim almighty power. This, of course, was something that was never going to happen, and so we were all forever protected from treason. But now the other gods are rendered impotent, and Aphelianna is all that remains. So, now as to why she could not have taken the throne for herself. You see, once someone becomes the God or Goddess of Death, as it is in Aphelianna's case, they are prohibited reentry into The

House of the Divine until they are succeeded."

"Why? They're still gods."

"Would you invite death into your home? No deity of death before her had ever reigned for more than 5000 aeons, and on the day of Aphelianna's ruling, she was closing in on her 7000th aeon. She just wanted to go home, Amil," said Arcanus, woefully. "So, with the other gods snugly imprisoned within her curses and Isadora silenced, all Aphelianna had to do was wait. And once the day arrived that the last Mortal fell from life and was plucked from existence, she would be unfettered of her duties. Then, she could return to her home and claim that seat of unspeakable power."

"But she's still outside," Amil said.

"Yes, a quite curious thing happened on the last day of Mortal life, you appeared."

"Me?"

"No! Please don't make yourself out to be that foolish. Human beings appeared! There was a fresh flock that needed Aphelianna's tending, and to this day, your kind remains the barrier between her and ultimate reign. It seems that Isadora had a curse of her own in store for Aphelianna. That, I'm sure, she did not expect. It is why she hates humans so much. You represent her inability to rule, to rest, to sleep."

"How did we get here, Arcanus? Humans, I mean," asked Amil with a quiver in his voice.

"I don't know for sure, although I have heard rumors to the origin of your being, none of which I will repeat," he stated, in a defiant tone.

Amil was about to demand to hear of the birth of mankind, but then he thought better of it. Arcanus wasn't

going to crack, and he had already been of so much help
that Amil simply respected his wish to allow this tale to end
prematurely.

"I want to help Aphelianna. I can't imagine anyone
deserves what she's been through."

"You're probably right, but you mustn't think in
terms of individuals and of years. You must think in terms
of aeons, and of the overall health of life itself. Aphelianna
is beyond salvation. Leave her there, Amil, leave her there,"
begged Arcanus as he poured himself another cup of coffee.

"Arcanus, do gods die?" asked Amil, unsure as to
why.

"We age, and so I suppose the answer is yes, but
none of us have yet," he explained, and then exited the little
corridor.

Under the dirtied glow of fluorescent light, Amil
was left alone to comprehend all that he had heard. He
thought of eternal life, or an approximation of such, for
those who wandered The House of the Divine, and he
thought of how he couldn't truly die by the means of
disease or time. Many of those that he had seen had entered
the afterlife in bodies racked with distress, and of a
condition that didn't distinguish itself far from that of a
Waste. But he was different, somehow. Amil would never
know sickness or prolonged pain. If he took the advice of
gods, it appeared that he could live life as it was meant to
be lived, and he could do so evermore. Or, he could risk the
punishment of the ultimate damnation.

It was a decision, obvious and easy, that tugged
upon his mind, but it was too much to absorb. In that
moment, he couldn't picture Ali's face without feeling
shame, and so to relieve himself of this ghost, he turned his

attention to grander matters that seemed so much simpler to understand.

He was struck by Aphelianna's descent into furious treason, but as Arcanus had suggested, spending that much time with death and loss would ultimately corrupt even the noblest of souls. He wondered if inside her there was still a canal carved out where sympathy could reside, or if all compassion had deserted her form. He thought of all the gods she had betrayed, and contemplated what she would do if he were to succeed. Would Aphelianna focus all her rage upon the surviving gods again? Would she desire to exterminate all traces of human life, Waste or otherwise, or would her loneliness send her down a path that even Aphelianna could not see?

Amil had once yearned to know all he could about the world he now knew, but as he gathered more knowledge, the more pleasurable ignorance had become. He had learned of a mysterious Spirit, a race of forgotten Mortals, a pantheon of gods undone by one of their own, and a scourge that loomed over the expiration of every human life. He was pained to accept that his own flesh, and all the people that he had once loved, were apparently conceived by accident, or, at the very least, as an act of revenge. His mind was full of questions, all of which were shackled to a brutal gravity. Amil stepped out of the room, and travelled back into Arcanus's workspace in search of the kind old man.

With absolute predictability, Amil found Arcanus tending to his time machine. He stood deep inside its silver belly, and was in the processing of resetting a gear. His ancient fingers carefully spun a naked bearing, and as he tightened a stud that protruded through the wheel, he dispensed even drops of oil onto its surface. Once he was satisfied with the faithfulness of its travel, Arcanus slid the little cog back into place and wiped it clean of his greasy fingerprints.

"I'm not even gonna ask how you got in there," Amil said, as he stared at Arcanus through an abstract arrangement of metal.

"You'd be surprised at the dexterity that still resides in these old bones," exclaimed Arcanus joyfully, as his work, impossible as it might be, still brought him a sense of peace.

"What happened to the Mortals? You know, the people before human beings came along?" foolishly curious, Amil couldn't believe his need to pry further into a troubled past.

"They are just gone," said Arcanus, with a small screwdriver held between his teeth.

"I think I'm gonna move on."

"As you should, but Amil, remember what I said about your gift."

"I kinda wish I didn't know. Hey, how do I get out of here?"

"Continue east for a while, you'll find a wall of doors. I don't know where any of them go and I don't know which ones are locked."

"Which way's east?" asked Amil, as a proper sense of direction eluded him in this place.

"That way," pointed Arcanus, with a smile. "Farewell, Amil Young."

Already with his back turned, Amil waved and plodded along, and as he did, it became clear that this wing of Arcanus's domain was largely forgotten. It was poorly lit, as most of the bulbs overhead had died out or were in the last throes of a flickered life soon to cease. The floor was utterly polluted with spare parts and forsaken manuals, and was booby-trapped by spills of oil and other slick liquids. Broken chunks of metal were kicked aside by his shoes, as were worn-out tools and other indefinable scraps of failed mechanisms.

As he wandered on and the darkness that stalked him continued to swell, Amil was forced to slow his pace and strain his eyes. With little attention being paid to the floor below, he tripped over the chewed-up leftovers of what most likely was once a 2 x 4. Down upon the cold concrete, he found himself slicked by grime that clung to him like an adhesive. Once righted, he wiped the heaviest filth from his skin and clothes. But as he did, a certain object caught his eye, one that had been discarded long ago.

It was a picture, or at least what remained of one. Amil plucked it from the floor, and as he wiped the dusty years of neglect from its surface, he was sure that one of Arcanus's machines was responsible for its existence. Under the layers of caked grit, the image of a woman was uncovered. Undeniably, this was Aphelianna, but in a time far less violent and woeful. She looked happy, enchanting even, and as Amil studied the torn edge of the photo, he couldn't help but wonder whose arm it was that wrapped itself around the Goddess of Death.

As he allowed the paper to drift downward back to the realm of the abandoned, Amil set his vision on the wall and all the doors it possessed. Standing upon the floor like any proper passageway, a door stared directly back at him. It was one of many, as the entire breadth of the wall was one giant stretch of doors. Placed above them was another row of the weathered barriers. This pattern of sorrowed columns repeated until the ceiling put an end to their bloated bloodline.

Amil tried a few, and, with no discernable logic, some were locked, while others lacked even the presence of a keyhole. Making use of a ladder that slept in a corner under a blanket of cobwebs and dirt, Amil climbed up to inspect some of the higher doors. Under his paltry weight, the aged wood groaned and loudly threatened to drop him. Ignoring its complaints, Amil took his time and gave a jostle to most every knob that he could reach. It was an exercise that he soon came to accept as nothing more than pointless, and so, with little thought and less reason, he chose one of the secured barriers and broke its locks.

Part 7. The Eternal City

Like he had done so many times before, Amil eased shut the door at his back and watched as a new arena colored itself around him. But before he had a thought to run, or to raise violent defiance against his assailants, he was tackled by three men. With frantic haste, he was bound. His mobility was stolen away as restraints were slapped over his limbs. They were crude devices, deformed throwbacks to the sadistic and dark years of Europe's Middle Ages.

Trapped within the cavity of a small tunnel that stank of wet earth, Amil was dragged away amid a fit of profane verbal opposition. He was tossed into a cell, a makeshift cage, and watched as the door was slammed shut and sealed with a padlock. Ensnared on all sides by fortifications of decayed rebar, the trap was short, mere inches taller than he, and bereft of a bottom. His body lay upon the cold stone of the dank tunnel, and Amil felt as his freedom and will were left to bleed out, crushed under the weight of steel.

With no time to sort out the rash of dizzying stimuli that flooded his mind, Amil's attention was quickly snapped onto a singular focus. Through bleary eyes, he stared directly at the murderous end of a revolver. Slid between the bars, and resting upon the center hinge of the crooked door, was a gun. It was a fearsome instrument. A cannon scaled to fit comfortably in the human hand. The bullet inside was brutal, crafted by destiny to splatter his head all about the cell. Amil knew this as cold truth, but what was worse: his enemies knew it as well. This weapon had a specific purpose, to fling the enigmatic Spirit from its host. Its master, a man probably ten years older than Amil and whiter than bleached chalk, held it firmly, and locked its fatal stare onto the shaken Ghost.

"Judging from your little tirade, I'm guessing you speak English?" the gunman questioned.

"Yeah," whispered Amil, with his face in the dirt.

"Are you alone?"

"Did you see anyone else come through after me?" he snapped.

"We have to be sure. We have to take precautions."

"Yes, I'm alone. Now would you tell me what the fuck you're doing?"

"I'm gonna take you to see Mr. J. He's one of the mayors of The Eternal City."

"This isn't quite what I expected," Amil said quietly, as he gazed out of the dark artery that played host to this harsh encounter.

"There's two ways we can do this," the pasty man offered, as he tapped the gun against the bars. "You can put this sack over your head and we'll take ya to Mr. J. I promise, you'll be fine. Or, you can refuse, and we throw you back through the first unlocked door we find."

Amil weighed his options, and to choose either felt equally foolish. He certainly had no mind to allow these men, whoever they were, to select his path for him, but on the other side of this damned coin lay the request of his complete surrender. It took him a while to decide, and, strangely, no one seemed to grow impatient, almost as though they completely appreciated the gravity of the situation. With his faith loosely placed in the man who pointed a gun at his face,
Amil agreed to the appointment with Mr. J.

"Okay," the man replied, as though either answer would have elicited the same reaction.

The door to his cage was opened, and, once Amil had been set up upon his knees, he had a bag of dry-rotted fabric slipped over his head. His leg irons were unbound, and, carefully guided by the hands of strangers, he was led out of the tunnel.

During this tense little stroll, no one said much, and other than the plop of water as it dripped from the curve of the stone overhead, sound was a scarce sensation. Within the expiration of short minutes, Amil was suddenly made aware of the open air, and of his escape from that rocky wound, as a flood of light beat against his covering and warmed his face. Was it the pleasure of sunlight, or the fierce glare of a deity that he felt? There was no way of truly knowing, but before he could deduce the finer points of the land around him, a touch of things common and

225

curiously familiar was his to absorb.

Gently placed into the backseat of a car, Amil was scooted into the middle and made to ride bitch between two men. He could only assume they were plucked from the earth. This explanation seemed quite implausible to him, as his captors seemed to share their genetics with small titans. He heard the engine start, and felt as the automatic transmission was forced into gear. He listened to the gravel as it spit at the wheel wells of the sizeable automobile, and felt every rough jostle extended his way by a rather hearty sample of potholes. To his amazement, he heard the telltale clicking of a cassette player's buttons, and his ears were soon at the mercy of fuzzy Euro-pop. The driver quickly earned complaints from the backseat, and from the protests of his massive companions, Amil was made to laugh.

"Yuck it up, bag boy," the driver taunted, as he increased the volume and sang along with the absurd tunes.

Set to a soundtrack torn from the gay bars of 1980s New York City, interspersed with huffs and grumbles, the journey was closing in on the one hour mark. Even though the air conditioner was on, a glaze of sweat formed on Amil's face. He was growing restless, agitated, as the heft of the unknown bore down upon him. He felt the weight of his key as it shifted with the palpitations of his chest, and shuddered so loudly that his action caught the attention of the driver.

"Hey, you alright?" he asked as he lowered the volume.

"Yeah, I guess. I'm just nervous."

"I told you, you'll be alright. This is just procedure. We're not about harming people here."

"What are you about?" asked Amil through the

scratchy fabric.

"Mr. J's gonna offer you a life here in the city," he explained, while twisting the volume knob back up.

The roll of the wheels slowed, and the light that bled through Amil's mask disappeared. Once the cumbersome vehicle came to a stop, the shroud was removed and his eyes gazed upon one of annoyance's proudest achievements; a parking garage. He was helped out of the rusty Lincoln, and as the group stepped toward an elevator decorated with chromatic graffiti, Amil allowed himself to exhale.

"What's your name?" he asked the slender fellow with the lunar complexion.

"Well, those two are both named David, oddly enough. As for me, I don't know. I'm a Nothing. So call me what you like," he replied, with somberness.

"A Nothing?" asked Amil.

"Look, man, we're just couriers, so to speak. Mr. J will fill ya in. What about you, you got a name?"

"Amil."

"Amil? That's a weird one. What else you got?" one of the Davids questioned.

"I was born in Virginia, almost played pro baseball, and died at 37. That should about cover it," he sarcastically answered.

"You remember it all, don't you?" asked the Nothing.

"Yeah."

"You're a Ghost. You're one of the lucky ones."

"I've been led to believe otherwise," Amil whispered as he thought of Ali.

"Guess that depends on your memories," the

Nothing said, as the elevator doors sealed shut.

Whoever this Mr. J was, he must have been a busy guy, because Amil's meeting with him was a long time coming. It was a wait that bothered him little, though, for the newest resident of The Eternal City had been put up in a room that resembled that of an extended stay hotel. He was provided with new clothes, took a shower, and relished the touch of warm water like never before. He brushed his teeth, shaved, and curled up atop the crisp sheets of a twin bed. There was a TV in front of him, and, as he gave a thought as to what programming might be like in the afterlife, he dozed off.

A knock came at the door and it roused Amil from the clutches of the sleep imposter that held him. Before he could rise, a stout Latino man with a receding hairline and no left arm stood in the threshold and smiled at his newest guest.

"Hello," he said warmly. "I'm Rick Jimenez, but everybody calls me Mr. J," he explained, through a heavy Spanish accent.

"I was told that you're the mayor?"

"I'm one of ten mayors of The Eternal City. You're in my jurisdiction, so you get me. I'll get right to the matter of things. I don't know what you've heard of our city, but it is a haven for the dead. A long time ago, we laid claim to what is surely one of the largest rooms in the mansion. We cleared it of Wastes and built a city. As you might imagine, we have souls from all backgrounds and from all periods of time. Our architecture reflects that, but most of all, this collection of minds has greatly aided the development of our home."

"One of the men who led me here, he called himself

a Nothing. What did he mean by that?"

"Ah! Our caste system. At the top are the Ghosts, people like you and me. You see, since we have carried with us all our earthly knowledge, we have the greatest opportunities here. Then there's the Halfways. Their memories are in pieces. They need some assistance with things, but for the most part, there are tasks that they remember wholly, and so they can be productive very quickly. After them come the Nothings. They arrived in the afterlife like blank slates. They're overgrown babies who need to relearn even the simplest of tasks. They require a lot of attention and resources, and tend to make up most of our labor force. Sadly, because of their ignorance, most never even make it here. They usually become victims of the lowest class, the Wastes, who are the only class completely devoid of rights," explained Mr. J with an odd enthusiasm.

Amil tried to suppress his anxiety, but he was made to squirm, as Mr. J was so matter of fact about the rigid classification of people. He was bound and chained upon his arrival, and then, he was told exactly where he stood. It might be safe, but he was growing suspicious of the utopian fantasy of The Eternal City.

"Hey, we take care of our own. You will not find a fairer society," the mayor calmly said.

"I just need some help," Amil admitted.

"I'll have one of my assistants help you with whatever you need. They're experts in helping the dead to acclimate themselves to our way of life. But first, I need to know your intentions. Would you like to stay here, in The Eternal City?"

"Maybe, I don't know. At least a while, I suppose."

"Okay. If you want to stay, you will be documented. The process doesn't take very long. You will have to abide by all our laws, and, in doing so, we will provide you with everything you need. You may leave at any time. Now, if you wish to go, please let the authorities know, and you will be escorted to the nearest exit. So, what do you say?" asked Mr. J.

"I can go whenever I want?"

"Yes, declare you want to leave, we strike you from the registry, and it's goodbye," he said with a wave of his fingers.

"Alright, yeah. I want to stay, at least for a bit."

"Maravilloso," he chirped while flipping open a battered cell phone.

Mr. J cursed the bad reception under his breath and was forced to redial the number a few times. He shook the shabby device a time or two, as though this could accomplish anything, and strained to communicate with the person on the other end of the line. Once he had finished, Mayor Jimenez gave a smile to Amil and urged him to sit tight.

Another vast expanse of time, if time still continued to roll, would be put behind Amil before he would meet Mr. J's assistant. He was left alone to the distractions of his room again, but, strangely enough, he did little. In fact, he scarcely moved. The enigmatic TV remained silent, the assorted books and magazines that intermingled upon a shelf were ignored, and the twin closets that sat to each side of the bathroom went unexplored. Amil did nothing other than look deep within himself. He sat on the edge of the bed and thought endlessly of this life that refused to expire. He had been given paltry few opportunities to reflect up until this point, that engaging in the act of introspection felt foreign. It became overwhelming, as his mind devolved into a mush of unanswered questions and regrets, so chaotic that no divine intervention could emancipate him from their barbaric assault. Under the suffocating weight of his own mental anguish, he again fell into sleep.

He awoke, and only by the grace of a lantern that burned fragrant oil was Amil spared the company of total darkness. As the presence of shadows grew to disturb him, he quickly rolled from the bed and rushed to the nearest light switch. He flooded the room in light, and placed his mouth under the faucet in the bathroom. Amil rubbed the cool water over his eyes and drew the liquid through his hair. Gazing upon his reflection in the mirror, he couldn't remove his eyes from those of the dead man that stared back at him. With heavy breath that coated the glass with a fog, the staring contest was at once called off. The small sounds produced from knuckles as they tap upon wood could be heard, and they pulled away his rapt attention.

Amil nervously twisted the knob in his hand and cracked the door open. It was a pleasant experience, opening a door and finding nothing more than the banality of the hallway on the other side. There was no vortex or alternate plane of being, just a continuation of the hotel, and a short girl with amber pigtails, a nose ring, and mildly bloodshot eyes. She burst in and introduced herself as Rave, in as bubbly a fashion as possible. She wore baggy jeans and a white tank top, and urged Amil to follow her down to the registry department.

"You look pretty good, not all mangled up and sick and stuff like most of the dead can be," she said, with a crack of chewing gum.

"All thanks to this," Amil admitted, while drawing attention to the key which hung from his neck like an anvil.

"Wow! Oh, this is trippy," she said, staring at Amil's key. "I've never met one of you before."

"I don't care. Where are we going?"

"To the registry. Weren't you paying attention?" she chirped, smacking one of her multicolored nails against an elevator button that read G1.

"No, no, I was. I'm just still really confused."

"Yeah, everybody is when they first arrive here. Just be glad you're not a Nothing. Those poor bastards don't have a clue!" Rave said.

On the way down, Amil was struck by the effervescent attitude of Rave. She was undoubtedly ecstatic to be dead. She bounced on her feet as the elevator descended and hummed loudly, bobbing her head in concert with the phantom song.

"How did you die?" he questioned quietly, frightened to find himself in a world were such a question could be asked.

"At a rave, that's how I got my name. I took a shitload of Ecstasy, and that was all for me."

"Don't you have a real name?"

"I'm sure I did once, but I'm a Halfway. I forgot that part."

"What do you remember?" asked Amil in a tone so dismal it sounded ready to wage war on Rave's perky nature.

"Let's see..." she thought, while tapping a finger against her head. "I remember music, TV, 90s television was awesome! And the taste of fast food. Mostly a lot of pop culture stuff."

"No people?"

"Nope, no people."

"Not even like family? No friends or anything?" asked Amil, a bit saddened but also shamefully jealous.

"Nobody," she admitted slowly. "Hey, no memories, no regrets, right? I'm happy as shit here."

When they arrived at the registry, it proved to hold all the charms and charisma of an office building. Amil was guided into a cubicle where his picture was taken and all the pertinent information that he could recall was recorded. He described his skill set and answered general knowledge questions. He divulged likes and dislikes, and took a brief, and rather silly, personality quiz. During his earthly life, he'd had little patience for such trivial matters, but there was something in pretending to be alive that made him feel better, almost whole.

"Okay," said Rave, after the last series of questions were asked. "This is how it basically works, you'll be assigned a job. We don't have a monetary system yet, so if you work, everything is free! Well, kinda, we have vouchers."

"So, money."

"No dum-dum, these are different. Contributing is what's important here. Work, prove you're contributing, earn vouchers, get stuff. It's like this, a candy bar and a car might cost about the same price. It just depends on the seller. The guy with the car might not need many vouchers to get by at the moment, so you might get it cheap. The guy with the candy bar might need a job done that you're good at, do it for him, document the work, and get a snack. Trust me, it's simple, you'll figure it out."

"Sounds brilliant to me," said Amil, with sarcasm.

"Pipe down, I'm not done. We have laws and fair punishments. You can review them here," she offered, with the exchange of a small book. "But we have two that you can't ignore. No rape, no murder."

"Murder? We're all dead," said Amil, dryly.

"Don't be difficult," scolded Rave. "Call it what you want, if you're responsible for causing another resident to turn into a Waste, we call it murder. So, if I can continue, no rape, no murder. The punishment for either is immediate banishment."

"Immediate banishment," he echoed.

"We don't have time to sort out that shit. More dead come in every day, and, other than the Ghosts, they require a lot of time and attention. Banishment simplifies things, because anyone who has ever left the city, willingly or not, has never found their way back. It's a punishment that will deter almost anyone. So, you ready?"

"For what?"

"Well, you can't stay here, silly. C'mon, I'm gonna take you to your new place."

Amil thought a moment and looked around. He saw as a dozen or so other workers like Rave, and studied them as they attempted to classify the dead. Some of the interviews looked to be replications of the exchange between he and his perky guide, while many others were painful to view. People, some maimed and horribly deformed, cried at the reality of their new setting, and had to be assisted and comforted by numerous employees of The Eternal City. Others were coldly silent, some loud and uncooperative. The more boisterous types were restrained by guards, as they could not come to terms with the conditions of Aphelianna's house. But as Amil set his eyes upon a girl no older than ten, he was made to look away. She seemed sweet, and not totally aware of the finality of death. Even with wounds scattered about her face that told of a vicious animal attack, she behaved as though relatively unaffected by the sorrow that gripped the room. Then he figured it out, what acutely bothered him about the girl. She was just behaving like a child, innocent and ignorant to the wretchedness of reality, and it broke his heart.

"So, let me get this straight, you decide where I live, too?" asked Amil quickly.

"No, Mr. Grumpy," Rave began as she grabbed his trembling hand. "We provide you with a place to live, and once you get settled, you can relocate on your own. We can't do everything for you!"

"Alright then, take me to my shitty new apartment. Just get me out of here."

Predictably, Rave smoked clove cigarettes and drove a cheap compact that masqueraded as a sports car. Although the techno she played was juvenile and annoying, Amil paid it little mind once he was permitted to set his vision over the true wonders of The Eternal City.

As they drove over asphalt roads that begged for repair, he became enthralled by the different districts they passed. There was the Antiquity District, which catered to those who had lived out the back pages of history. They tended to prefer the company of their own, as the industrialized world and all its tiny devices were frightening and odd. The architecture of this district seemed to be formed from the melding of many villages and timeworn cities. Ripped from differing points in time, and across all the cultures of ancient man, the Antiquity District sprawled out over the land. It came to Amil's eyes like all

235

the beginnings of man's inventiveness had been sloshed
together and let to spill out in random arrangements.

The splendid construction of ancient Greece was
prevalent, as was the influence of the Middle East, when it
reigned supreme in the days that predated Christendom.
Glimmering under the sun, Aztec temples spotted the
streets, and Asian craftsmanship could be seen everywhere
the eye could wander. Small castles, obvious nods to the
heavy brick edifices of medieval Europe, rose from random
locations, and forced Amil to cast a thought to the
residents. Perhaps King Henry III and Faisal I were
neighbors, or maybe the kings of the earth never made it
this far. He almost smirked as he imagined the common
dead occupying structures they could only once marvel
upon in life. As Rave drove on, Amil witnessed a
kaleidoscope's worth of races intermix and commune while
they shopped in the markets and went about the day's work.
Death had erased all their differences, and the hole left
behind after life's vacancy had been filled by a miraculous
combining of knowledge.

They slowed their pace, and Rave quieted the music
as they progressed over the bumpy roads of the Lush
District. This was a land ruled by the fury of nature, and
stood as a testament to man's mastery over it. Rave mainly
stuck to the main roads as the pair crossed this land.
Flanked by massive farmlands and interminable rows of
crops, the Lush District appeared orderly and groomed. But,
in the distance, Amil could glean a vision of the true
wildness of the area. Dense jungles closed in all around
them like a tapestry woven from every thread of green that
had ever once existed. The landscape of the jungles held a
partiality to the look of a rainforest, but among this orgy of

feral growth, flora from every corner of earth carved out places for themselves. Stretched over the canopy was a blanket of Japanese kudzu, and hanging like apparitions from the limbs of the trees was Spanish moss. The brilliant blue chicory of Amil's Virginia was in bloom, and among the shadows of giant baobabs, were clusters of white pines, the very trees who dare to stand in flushed defiance to the scourge of winter.

On they traveled, and, as the tires of Rave's car kissed the outskirts of the Industrial District, a place where the majority of The Eternal City's technology and energy was produced, Amil noticed something a bit curious. Over the towering stacks and busy factories hung the sun, or something purported to be a star. Its blaze had cooled, and the light was noticeably less intense than when they departed, but as they carried on over the concrete of the highway, he was certain that the orb had never moved.

"Rave, what's up with the sun?"

"You're perceptive, just like a Ghost! It took me ages to realize that our sun doesn't move."

"Okay, why? What is it?" asked Amil.

"Well, when you died, you entered into a great mansion, right? So, this is just another room. Fly high enough and you'll find a ceiling, run far enough and you'll hit a wall. Crazy, right? Anyway, somebody got the idea to replicate an ordinary day on earth. They built a huge sun," explained Rave, as she removed her hands from off the steering wheel and spread them wide.

"But it's dimming," said Amil, as he studied the phony star.

"Yep, we dim the fucking thing! Every day, it's somebody's job to set the sun to slowly brighten, and then slowly fade out until it's dark, just like a real day. We've even developed clocks that are fairly representative of what a 24 hour cycle feels like. It comes in handy having some of the greatest minds in science all here. Hey, you wanna hear something weird?"

"I just did, Rave."

"This is cool. There was this Greek philosopher guy named Aristotle, who was supposedly super smart..."

"I know who he is, Rave," griped Amil, as he grew weary of her schoolgirl cadence.

"Yeah, he's here, but he's a Nothing. He has been unable to learn, so now he sits in one of our asylums and mumbles."

"Alright, stop! Please, just be quiet."

With no offence taken, Rave turned up the music and continued to drive without another look in Amil's direction. During this welcome absence of exchange, the dead pair plunged into the heart of the city's center. It resembled a proper town, complete with apartment buildings, shopping plazas, and grocery stores. They passed a prison, and, as his vision washed over the gray stone of its formidable body, he squeezed the book in his hands. There was an eatery on the corner of a busy street, and as a group of patrons dined on a patio, it resembled lunch hour on the set of a zombie flick. Amil almost laughed, but he felt too disturbed to exhibit proper enjoyment. They turned down a side street, lined with row houses, and it appeared that their journey had come to an end as Rave whipped the car into a space and killed the engine.

"We're here," she squeaked. "Apartment 3," Rave said, as she handed Amil the most ordinary of keys.

"That's my place?" asked Amil, as he glanced up at

238

a large brick house that, predictably, had seen its insides
ravaged by the need for subdivisions.

"Sure is. Most everybody in this neighborhood
speaks English, and lived within about a 300 year window,
so you should adapt quickly. You'll find a phonebook and a
map of the city inside. There's a part in the beginning of
our law book that explains things a bit more clearly, and,
although we haven't been able to reproduce the internet just
yet, channel 1 on the TV gives constant updates on things
going on around town."

"Okay," whispered Amil, as he grabbed the key
from Rave.

"Hey, I could stick around for a bit. I won't get in
trouble. I fuck off on these assignments all the time,
especially when I have to escort a cute boy around town!"
she said with a smile.

Rave was downright adorable, and, although she
could be annoying, her sweetness in a world of gloom was
a blessing. She wasn't deformed, cut all to hell, or old and
sickly like most of the dead were. If anything, she promised
to be the perfect distraction from the coldest of realities.
But Amil denied her company. He had become so
accustomed to sorrow that to abandon its embrace would
have felt foreign and uncomfortable. He didn't say a word,
and stepped out of the car and walked toward his new
residence. With his back turned to her, he gave a mild
wave, and studied the street sign that hung above his
residence. In an ordinary arrangement of green and white,
the sign read *mercy*. Mercy Street. Amil couldn't decide if
this was a monstrous hilarity played at his expense or just a
failed attempt at humor. He pondered the notion that the
street was named in an effort to comfort those like him. No

faith was found in this idea, and he discounted the charity offered from the streets moniker. To him, it seemed like another monstrous lie. A jagged riddle that one day would unfurl, to turn its teeth upon him.

Amil walked about the interior of his new home. He felt out of place, like a prowler nervously skittering around a stranger's house. He peered into every room and behind the doors of every cabinet and closet. Slowly, Amil calmed himself, and took a seat in a worn armchair. Unable to relax, he sat up straight and thumbed through the laws of The Eternal City.

Most were predictable and made sense to him. The penalties were understandably light, loss of vouchers and privileges, as to live within Aphelianna's house was punishment enough. And, in lieu of fines, extra work was assigned to those who committed minor infractions. He traced his fingers over the lines of a massive map that he bothered to only partially unfold, and was struck by how many different faiths were represented. The sites of churches seemed to be everywhere, and almost every religion conceivable had at least a modest smattering of temples. As Amil set aside the map, he appreciated the true power of denial, and almost longed to suffer from its delusions. For in a world of irrefutable evidence that boldly colored the sickest of pictures, there were those who still held fast to their beliefs, no matter how absurd they obviously had become.

A small envelope, horribly beige and bound by string, was stuffed into the pages of his new book. He had ignored it thus far, but stamped in block letters with a smeared blue ink was a print that he could no longer deny: AMIL YOUNG.

240

He undid the tie and studied the contents held within the dull folds. There was an appointment book and a calendar, which suggested that it was February. Given the pleasant nature of the day, this felt quite empty as Amil recalled the cold winds and snow that tend to pound Fog Lake in late winter. Throughout the rest of the month, the blocks of the calendar were left blank. A note was affixed to the page that encouraged him to use this free time in order to familiarize himself with the city. But the two weeks that followed were already filled out. It was ordained that due to his relatively good health, he had been assigned the job of a courier. Amil knew what that meant and dreaded the occupation. He imagined that there were more important, more skilled, jobs that he could do. But then he thought of the true meaning of the occupation. He had experience inside Aphelianna's house, and he had retained his knowledge of life. Again, it seemed, the conditions of a Ghost would serve to torment him further.

He hoped that Rave had been sincere when she suggested that after an initial break-in period, Amil would have the opportunity to make his own way. Out from the embrace of a few more information cards and an assortment of flyers, which looked to have been ripped directly from a Val-pak coupon book, there slid a plastic identification card. Much like a driver's license, it had his picture and apparent address. It listed his height and other banal things, along with his country of origin and preferred language. As cold as the blood in his silent veins, Amil read the date of his birth, and then the date of his death. He set his eyes upon his classification: Ghost. It shattered him, his earthly existence disregarded with such easy indifference.

That evening, or what disguised itself as the latter

part of the day, saw him do nothing more than stare into his television set. He watched, with tired eyes, the programming of channel 1 that described life in The Eternal City. When he could bear no more evidence that he was, in fact, very much dead, Amil flipped through the rest of the channels with restless fingers, and without any care for what he might actually find. Sometime after 2am, he grew weary of the torturous needles of conscious thought, and gave in to boredom and old habits of the body. Still in that heavily used chair, he sealed off his vision, and mercifully drifted off to sleep.

In defiance of recommendation, Amil barely left his apartment for the first two weeks. He seldom ate, and paid little attention to the books that were provided for his entertainment, and treated his neighbors like the phantoms that they were. But like any animal that hides from a beast more monstrous than itself, he eventually grew bored, curious, even, and poked his head out of his hole.

As that faux sun overhead started to quell its glare, Amil stepped outside and decided to take an aimless stroll. According to his map, National Street ran through the heart of his neighborhood, and hosted the densest concentration of businesses. Although this promenade was wide, and graciously accommodated plenty of car and foot traffic, it was unreasonably steep. He knew his lungs no longer performed their intended purpose, but he could feel them burn, and, as he stepped over the chunky sewer lids that were sunk into the concrete of the sidewalk, he cursed the man who built National Street.

During his walk, he was again treated to the power of denial, and of the need to feel human. All around him were restaurants and pubs that offered products that the body had ceased to need, along with other establishments that allowed the dead to play life. He passed tattoo parlors, arcades, a hair salon, and a clothier, surely one of the busiest careers in The Eternal City. He watched as couples walked hand in hand, and viewed a decrepit old man as he relaxed on a bench with a ragged dog. He noticed the stares that swept over his unscathed form, and, as he passed all manner of the mutilated and diseased, Amil felt like the freak.

He stepped into a bar that was comically named The Dead Zone, and ordered a beer. The man behind the counter, a genuinely friendly soul with a large gouge in the side of his face, poured the drink and offered him a cigarette. Amil didn't smoke, but the temptation to join the cult of denial was too much to resist. He lit the stick, and sucked the mightiest drag he could muster into his hollow chest. He sipped his brew and stared up at the muted TV, which was tuned to a sports network.

A good time played out around him, as most of the people in The Dead Zone were clearly regulars who had all lived in the city for some time. A jukebox played, and the atmosphere felt friendly and ready to accept a new arrival into its circle, but Amil kept to himself. He wasn't sure what he was doing, or what he should do next, and as he sipped a relatively cold glass of beer, he thought of Ali. He could almost feel the bark of the tree as it bit at her naked skin, and he could swear to the taste of the Spirit Ripper's breath. With images that battered him with guilt, Amil slid the half-empty mug away from him, and walked back outside.

A journey of a few city blocks and the procurement of one beer hardly sounded like a full evening, but by the time he had returned to his apartment and flopped on the bed, he felt exhausted. It was as though the memories that should have died with his corporeal self would prove to be his undoing. As he had wandered alone, he harbored a brutal sense of despair. Hopelessness, as wide as his anguish was deep, was born within him. The only force that served to push him on was the absolute fear of standing still. But, with safety all around him and the prospect of a second chance that most could scarcely imagine, Amil wanted nothing more than to keep running. Into the teeth of a Waste he might fall, or in the divine presence of Isadora he would stand. In a fresh world of opportunity, these seemed to be the only options left to him. With agony as his attentive lover, into sleep he once again fell, and, for the next two weeks, entwined in the grip of his bed he would stay.

A new morning came, and its bright rays brought a lessening of Amil's pain. It wasn't something he could detect, for it was so minute it bordered on the epitome of insignificance, but it was there all the same. The friction of time and a sense of security had started to rub away at his sorrow and shame.

Into the third week on the job of collecting those who tripped their way into the city, Amil remained a silent being, with eyes drained of vigor and of purpose. He reported for duty, did his tasks with a total absence of enthusiasm, and slumped home without as much as a whispered goodbye to his coworkers. But this drudgery was approaching the level of tolerable, and on an ordinary Wednesday night that promised to be as empty as its name, a radical change shook inside Amil.

All to himself one evening, Amil laughed as he

watched a comedy revue on his grainy television set. He felt a bubble in his chest, and the tickle of enjoyment was his to appreciate once again. It was a strange sensation, one that put him off, initially, as the experiencing of mild pleasure aroused his guilt. But this small prick of joy acted like a drug far superior in potency to any narcotic. He needed it as sustenance. It dulled the spears in his mind and made the act of simply existing a bit easier.

As Amil slipped into a routine of a morning coffee stop, and as he developed a rapport with those he worked with, he began to assign rationales to the inner demons that screamed at him. This reliving of life was necessary to prepare him to continue his search for Isadora. It would rejuvenate him, and give to him the strength required to stand in the face of impossible odds. But as the weeks vomited across the calendar and spread themselves into months, Amil began to lose faith in his own excuses.

The iron truth of the situation was that the further he segregated himself from Aphelianna and all her wretches, the more fearful of them he became. He honestly desired to free Ali, but he was stopped by the weight of the fact that he was an inconsequential man who wallowed among forces far greater than he. In his repose, Amil dreamt of Ali, and was made to endure vivid nightmares brought about by his inaction. But these nocturnal stalkers failed to push him out and back onto the darkened paths that spread themselves throughout Aphelianna's impossible quest. Amil acknowledged that he had been beaten. He became a scared man and, relieved of determination, he began to wonder if he would ever leave The Eternal City.

As the grains of the hourglass continued their tumble, Amil ventured further and further up and down

National Street and the concrete veins it sprouted. His tongue, or, rather, old habits of his mind, fashioned a liking for the barbeque served at the corner of Miracle Lane, and a dusty record store that he frequented would often see him leave with the weekly maximum of 5 LPs. As most of the cafes reminded him too much of life as it once was, he took to hanging around a bar situated partway down America Alley. He liked most of the music in the jukebox, and formed a genuine friendship with a war vet named Curtis, a man who saw his earthly life extinguished by a roadside bomb on the outskirts of Baghdad.

Amil danced with a few of the girls, and secretly nourished a crush for Jill, a pale twenty-something from Nova Scotia. She was friendly, and known for her wild collection of colored wigs, as cancer once robbed her of hair and complexion alike. But for the twisted feelings that strangled his heart, he never left the pub with anything more than a few beers in his gut and a gentle hug from thin Jill. Amil knew that the more time he spent with Jill the less likely he would be to resume the task he promised to complete. But, all the same, he desired to abandon his resolve, and welcomed the day when he would give in to the temptations of a fresh beginning with Jill.

The endless sun shone, and, most predictably, this day was clear and absent of clouds or rain. Although the wrappings were pretty, the day that they contained was quite far from the description of its pleasant box. It was ugly and violent. It oozed with all the vulgarity of the underworld, and introduced Amil to the rarely spoken about Waste District.

Stationed near a door only recently discovered among the maze-like and overgrown condition of the Tribal

District was where Amil and a couple of his coworkers found themselves. A land of narrow paths and modest villages constructed from materials harvested from the ground was where many peoples of Earth's tribal societies felt most comfortable. Clans from Africa, the Aborigines of the Australian outback, and many Native American tribes shared space and called this place home. One of the city's earliest settlements, it was a refuge for those who shunned, or were intimidated by, other cultures. It allowed dead chiefs and their deceased people to continue unabated in the practice of their old ways. In-fighting was rare, as most of the clans developed a higher understanding of harmony that many had failed to attain during life. Unbothered by self-righteous conquerors, left alone by the government of The Eternal City, their state of being was barely caressed by death's interruptions.

Ordinarily, those descended from one of the tribes would stand sentry over all the known passages in this sector. But this day was different. With major religious ceremonies taking place that saw the district understaffed, Amil and a couple other men were assigned to monitor a recently discovered pathway. To them, it was a humbling honor. On earth, white men on native land usually meant genocide and betrayal. Here in The Eternal City, it was cooperation and respect.

Unloaded from out of the back of a Jeep Cherokee, which was nearly beaten into ruin, were three milk crates that served as stools for Amil and his mates. A folding table with a top of plywood was spread between them, and it played host to a spirited game of blackjack.

Greg, a retired NFL player who had dropped dead of a heart attack at 47, had won the first four hands. He was boisterous and engaging, and, with every victory, he alerted all to his prowess. The spirits of the men were high, and the pleasant day promised hours of ease and leisure. Amil had grown to enjoy the company of Greg and Seamus, an Irishman who'd had the sour luck of succumbing to the afflictions of food poisoning. The men were friendly and kind. He felt mildly blessed to share their company. They preferred a gentle approach to greeting those that entered into the city, and employed none of the mad zeal that Amil had been forced to endure when he had arrived.

They were positioned mere feet from the door they were charged to watch, with not a worry in their minds. The barrier appeared to be part of the background. It barely seemed real. The door rested over the dusty ground, with nothing more than silence and a water-starved thicket as its support.

They were on the plains, and, with only mild vegetation and the relative accessibility of the area, it was a wonder that this entry point had gone unnoticed for so long. It made Amil think of the room that lay beyond. It must be quite vast, or extremely hostile, to have produced almost no one from its mouth. It made him quiver with anxiety as he imagined the horrors that irritably stirred on the other side, but as the minutes slipped away, his tension melted with every new hand dealt.

The hours of a dull day ticked by, and the men, who often rode together and had formed a tight bond, shared laughs and tiny snippets of the pain formed from the memories they still carried. But conversation only kills so much time, and so above the dirty ground and under the watch of a clear sky, they began to check their watches with increased regularity. The boredom mounted, and the desire to see this mundane shift end intensified within them. On most days, Amil was without complaint over the dull nature of his occupation. It was a banality that he welcomed, as the task of a courier typically involved little more than babysitting a door that might never open. On this day however, he appeared distracted, distant to the company of his friends.

"How you been holding up, Amil?" Seamus asked.

It was a vague question, but all present knew its implications well. A week before, Amil had been behind the wheel, directing the three of them back to the city, when he spilled his guts to Seamus and Greg. He wasn't sure why, but he couldn't stop blubbering about his walk through the orchard, and the guilt that pressed upon him over his leaving of Ali. His sobbing became so intense that Greg was forced to muscle his way over to the controls and stop the vehicle. On the side of the road, Amil cried into the arms of the former defensive lineman.

In life, Greg had fancied himself the most macho of men, and was rather homophobic, but as a friend fell to pieces in his embrace, Greg comforted him with a well of compassion. With Amil absorbed into Greg's massive body, Seamus had attempted to lighten the mood. He cracked a joke about how he had died a virgin, but what did he know? Seamus was a Halfway. In that moment, his ignorance worked well and relieved Amil of a scrap of anguish, but on this day, it felt cruel.

"Seamus, now ain't the time," scolded Greg, as he, too, was shackled to the full weight of his earthly memories.

"No, it's okay," said Amil quietly, mustering the courage to speak aloud the thoughts that he had begun to harbor. "Honestly, I'm getting over it. Remember when your first girlfriend broke up with you?"

"End of the world, right?" asked Greg.

"Yeah, it's kinda like that. But the further away you get, the less it hurts," admitted Amil.

"How long you figure you've been dead?" Seamus asked.

"How should I know, leprechaun?"

Greg and Seamus both laughed at the joke they recognized as a shield, but there was something about this little discussion that felt therapeutic. Prior to this, Amil had only spoken about the past. Here, on the desolate plains, he was confronting the present. Out loud, he was being honest with himself.

"It feels like forever," Amil began. "Ali just feels like a part of someone else's past that I'm forced to relive. I know this is gonna sound fucked up, but I know I can't save her. I'm done trying. I guess that's what I'm trying to say." He turned away from the others and stared off into the distance. In his own way, he was saying goodbye to Ali.

"There's no shame in telling the truth. Hey, I'll never win the Superbowl," said Greg, with a sheepish smile.

"That was never gonna happen anyway. You rode the bench your whole career. We came from the same era, remember?" said Amil.

"Hey, shh. Shut up," whispered Seamus, sharply.

A scratching, wild and desperate and of an animalistic fashion, could be heard. The knob jostled, and a beating was applied to the other side of the door, as the creature struggled to work the simple mechanism. A screech that Amil knew too well tore through the air, and as the men readied themselves, each silently hoped that the Waste beyond would give in to frustration and move on with its torturous day. But it was a stubborn beast. It could smell the stench of the others, and the Waste hungered to spill the cold blood of those that possessed conscious thought.

"It'll pass, they always do," said Greg, with a finger pressed to his lips and his eyes on the door.

During the time that Amil had worked as a courier, he was yet to encounter a Waste. Most days passed as nothing of consequence, as a visitor to The Eternal City was actually a rare occurrence. When a door would open, it usually only produced a startled traveler. Events unfolded rather predictably, and only once were Amil and his mates forced to throw someone back. The discarding of a conscious soul was a troubling experience. The man they were forced to cast back into the mercy of Aphelianna's house came at them erratic and crazed. He bit and snarled, overwhelmed by his new condition, much the same as an animal gone rabid. In his mind, Amil could still see the man's eyes. They were wild, like those of a horse, bullied and lassoed. Amil saw no understanding in the eyes, but still, he felt as the pins of shame sunk themselves into his conscience. On that day, he had felt like an executioner.

He imagined that the disposing of a Waste could feel no worse. It would be a difficult order, yes, and frightening, but Amil assumed the task would be easier to carry out. Wastes were simple creatures, unbridled by the complexities of intelligent man. But these were the assumptions of a man without proper experience and knowledge, as he was yet to be asked to perform his duty to the fullest.

The remnants of a broken Spirit burst through the door with a rage that made a volcanic eruption seem calm by contrast. It wailed and spit, gnashed its teeth, and perversely tore at its own flesh, as though readying itself for combat. No amount of preparation could have steadied Amil's mind against this vision, but, thanks to extensive training drills, the monster was quickly quelled. Greg snapped the neck of the charging Waste by means of a thick forearm to the head, and, as the soulless fiend crumpled to the ground, the three men thrashed it without any vapor of compassion. It was kicked, stabbed, and hammered with the corners of the crates, until only a pained tremble moved its form. Once the Waste shivered into unconsciousness, its assailants, all slicked in sweat and surged with adrenaline, bound the creature with rope and chain. The Waste was tossed into the back of the Jeep like old luggage, and before Amil slammed the gate shut, he spun a few wraps of duct tape around its mouth. The oily black discharge would loosen the adhesive eventually, and once the beast returned from unconsciousness, it would fight like all the devils in all the hells to undo its tethers. Without a thought to collect their things, the couriers piled into the Jeep and sped away.

The truck bounced fervently over the rough terrain, while a cloud of dust and stone was put behind its flight. The siren on the roof screamed at full volume, and once they reached the semi-smooth touch of the highway, Seamus pegged the speedometer needle. Although the Jeep pleaded frantically for a reprieve, its whipping continued at this pace for another hour, until the sight of a deleterious place that Amil had been only quietly briefed about came into view.

Far from any inhabited region, and with only the

sight of a brittle mountain range for a backdrop, the couriers crossed into the limits of the Waste District. It was a simple and barren place, for the nightmares that festered there had no need for complexity or aesthetic construction. A road of buckled asphalt, flush with weeds, carried them in, and all along the borders of this broken stretch sat the asylums.

The first buildings that Amil saw looked quite familiar and unthreatening. Some amount of artistry was put into their design, and a generous collection of bushy trees lent a comforting blanket of shade to the many courtyards. Much akin to the mental institutions of modern society, many boasted fresh coats of paint, and sat upon lawns of a modest green. Though fenced in, many of the patients were free to roam the yards, but their continued safety depended mightily on the aid and goodwill of their caretakers. This was where the most helpless of the Nothings were held. They were fed, bathed, and, though it was painfully arduous, this was where they received an education and the ability to perform the simplest of tasks.

It felt cruelly inhuman to separate them from the rest of society, but it was necessary. During the earliest days of The Eternal City, the Nothings were cared for in private residences and boarding houses. This process went on smoothly for a time, but it soon became clear that Nothings are quite unpredictable. Some take to education well and systematically relearn things forgotten, while others, for reasons unknown, take to violence. Maybe it is fear that twists their Spirits, maybe it is simply random chance that causes them to behave in such a way. Or could it be something else? Something trickier, of a morbidity too tangled to be unraveled. The toxic influence of Aphelianna

253

perhaps? The true face of mankind?

****

      Long before Amil arrived in the city, a riot had broken out at one of the boarding houses. A group of Nothings attacked the small staff and wrenched the Spirits from the mutilated bodies of three orderlies before the authorities could arrive. The Nothings were detained and bound. Hastily, they were rushed to the nearest door that bore Aphelianna's influence, and, without discussion or compassion, they were cast out of The Eternal City. But the damage had been done, and the transformation of a human Spirit into a Waste had been put on display.

      The survivors of this attack wailed in agony and despair. Their cries swam out through the open door at the front of the boarding house, and the din pulled a crowd close. A group of spectators gathered around the wounded, as the imposter sun began to dull its glare. An elderly man who had survived three separate wars during his earthly life before giving in to old age held one of the staff members close within his bony embrace. She was barely a woman when syphilis ate her brain to pieces. A selfish harlot when she had walked the earth during the 19th Century, Elizabeth found meaning in her existence in The Eternal City, as she cared for those viewed as throwaways.

      As an ever-thickening fog had rolled into her vision, Elizabeth had seen the writhing bodies of her friends, and the puddles of gelled blood that seeped out from their wounds. She heard the old man whisper comforting words to her in a language that she couldn't comprehend, as she watched her patients being hauled away like garbage. In the last moments of her un-life, Elizabeth revisited the sight of the Nothings as they were beaten into rubble. This occupation was her path to atonement, and, as she lay in the arms of a stranger, she felt failure settle over her. As this sensation soaked into her mind, Elizabeth had felt as her Spirit unfettered itself from her earthly representation. Like loosed balloon strings as they unwind themselves from each other, her Spirit uncoiled itself from true existence, and floated off into the nevermore.

The frail war veteran had felt as the body of Elizabeth fell limp and colder than before. Fatefully bound to her by fatal compassion, the old man continued to hold the doubly dead girl, unaware of how quickly the turn would come.

All across her skin, small creases had formed like lines on a page that has been improperly fed into a printer. The slices widened slowly, but not from the influence of something underneath, instead, it seemed as if the skin was separating from itself. Out from these slim tears came the flames, burning low and black. The heat inside her body had risen rapidly, and, as the instincts of the old man told him that it was time to let go, the body of Elizabeth erupted.

Like shadows cast from the whole of hades, the flames had burst from her with such intensity that they dissolved the old man, and the wall behind him, into one ashen pile. In a flash of infernal darkness, Elizabeth was erased, and in her place stood a newborn Waste. It stood rigid and tall, powerful, and wreathed in coils of smoke that stunk of obscenities far more foul than scorched flesh. As the telltale acidic discharge of a Waste began to escape from its orifices, the nails of the beast dropped off and the eyes dissolved like butter into a hot pan.

The onlookers before her were frozen with fear. It was a fear of the creature that Elizabeth had become, and it was a fear of the stilled bodies of her slain coworkers. The reality was clear. More of her kind would be quick to come. As the gallery absorbed this terror, they all knew that it was already too late for them.

That night had been bloody and filled with the presence of absolute death. From Elizabeth and the two others with her who were killed by the rogue Nothings an epidemic was born. In just over an hour, more than a dozen Wastes had been unleashed upon The Eternal City, and before the mock sun would again open its infernal eye, their numbers were legion.

****

Amil knew this story well. It was a poisoned legend, a warning that every resident of the city knew to heed. He knew what just one Waste let loose inside The Eternal City could mean. It was a cautionary tale that justified the unflinching class system of the city, and it instilled in him the sentiment that Wastes carry not a shred of Humana. They were indeed something else, something virulent that warranted only the attention needed for disposal. As the creature in the storage compartment behind him mildly stirred, Amil voiced his fevered request for Seamus to drive faster.

Further on down the rocky stretch, the buildings continued to rise, and as they did, corpulent shadows were cast over the grounds. Looking much like the Nothing houses, albeit with skins of chipped paint and patchy lawns of unkempt growth, were the infirmaries. Though some attention was paid to the appearance of each building, aesthetic pleasantries were an afterthought. Those who can no longer think no longer care for cosmetics, or most anything at all.

The infirmaries were mercy centers to some, barbaric gulags to others. But, undeniably, they were places of an ominous silence that kept the most brutalized dead in a state of sedated ignorance. People who were little more than shredded hunks of humanity were kept there, as where those who had been stripped of every defining feature of a living person. Under the influence of a monstrous amount of sedatives and anesthetics, the patients slept beneath waves of low light and layers of fire-proof sheets. They were chained to the stainless steel framework of the beds, a measure taken in the event of a Spiritual expiration. Abandoned and forsaken, the patients were sealed away behind doors that remained locked at all times.

The narrow and dimly lit hallways were nearly devoid of activity. The presence of a nursing staff was all but nonexistent, as there was nothing to be done for those that slept. A small contingent of guards patrolled the halls and inspected each cell on a weekly basis. They peered in through barred windows, apathetic to the plight of the shackled as they checked for the emergence of Wastes. It was a rare occurrence, as the Spirit endured almost interminably, but once a Waste was detected, they were dealt with quickly. Armored in riot gear, the guards removed the deleterious beings from the infirmary and prepared them for the burn pits.

Understandably, these buildings were few, as those who resided in the infirmaries had no other means to reach

The Eternal City than to be escorted there by loved ones or
the kindness of strangers. This spoke of the unwillingness
to shed the past, and it made Amil contemplate the wicked
nature of each fate that he was presented. Those in the
infirmaries were nothing more than glorified Wastes. They
would never recover, and, seemingly until the end of all
time, there they would slumber under the weight of treated
polymer and drugs. It made Amil wonder as to why these
beings weren't euthanized and spared the anguish that they
were made to endure. Of course they would become
Wastes, but a Waste was a sick being that would eventually
and truly die, freed to finally evaporate into oblivion. And
that's when it occurred to him, that this is precisely, and
mercifully, what should be permitted to happen to those
who could never care for themselves. It was the families of
the incapacitated that had intervened, who crafted this
torturous version of purgatory in the name of life. It was a
realization that called acidic fluid up from his gut and into
his throat. But for as sick as he may have felt, the pure
revulsion that the Waste District inspired was yet to come.

The row of Nothing houses and infirmaries had
ended, and only empty space was again in view through the
dirty windows of the Jeep. According to the clock, which
strained to relay its message through the cracked lens of the
stereo deck, they carried on for another half an hour. Amil
grew nervous as the Waste tied up behind him turned its stir
into a slight thrash, but before he could turn to inspect the
beast, a wide swathe of ugliness was cut into his vision.

The road underneath the vehicle disappeared, as
only the beaten vision of tire tracks coursed over the land.
An iron gate lay ahead, chained shut and decorated with a
myriad of faded signs that aggressively advised a wayward

traveler to turn away. A line of soldiers stood at the ready, all covered in layers of armor that made them appear like warriors from another, more feral, plane of existence. They held thick shields and brandished long spears that sprouted coiled barbs at the tips. Each guard donned a helmet, a blanket of anonymity that obscured every detail of the face. The lenses of the masks were smoked-out black, and from the lower portions of this protective gear, a breathing apparatus grew. Like the tentacles of a beast long lost to the bottom of the sea, the large coils swayed with the persuasion of the wind.

Seamus rocketed dangerously close to the gate. He spiked the brakes in time to avoid a collision with the guards, none of whom so much as flinched at the sight of the speeding Jeep. Amil knew the drill. He and the others were to remain inside the car. Their role in this woeful task had reached its end. The time had come to hand over the garbage to the incinerators.

The soldiers surrounded the Jeep and tore open the back gate without care or a thought to its future use. The catch was dragged to the ground and another layer of rusty chain was wrapped tightly around it. The restraint was secured with a bolt, and the beast was dragged away. Two guards had remained by the gate, and, as their brethren dragged forth the condemned, they undid the locks and jarred the barrier open. The heavy iron parted enough to permit the Waste to be escorted beyond its threshold, while inside the car, Amil and his companions tensed noticeably. On the other side of the fortification, the guards worked to lift the beast above their heads, and, with nary a moment spared for prayer or compassionate thought, the Waste was hurled from the bluff. It tumbled hundreds of feet to the pit below, partially freed of its chains during the descent, but before it could escape, the burn was upon it.

Against every good sense inside him, Amil exited the vehicle amid loud protests from his friends. He walked to the mouth of the gate and directed his vision down into the guts of an insatiable abyss. Far below him, an expansive chasm had been carved out of the land. It resembled a massive landfill, but its only aggregate were the bodies of entrapped Wastes, bodies of those once alive and filled with the human spirit. Most had been burned to piles of ash that shifted with the will of toxic breeze, but there were those that crawled under the embers, yet to meet their final extinction. Up from the ash, and the partially immolated corpses of their kind, the surviving Wastes shifted. Helpless, in an agony greater than their affliction was capable of dealing out, the entombed remnants of humanity screamed.

From behind the dilapidated fence, Amil sunk his eyes into the mass grave and its chaotic arrangement of the last vestiges of human disfigurement. As he looked on into that soulless mass of erasure and insatiable genocide, panic spread over him. He noticed the thin corpse of a female. Only partially burnt, she retained shreds of the human being she used to be. In a way, this condition made her appear all the more hideous. Exhausted and broken, she lay draped over the charred bodies of a few others. They were smaller than she, at least they appeared to be, and, as her spindly arms flowed over those beneath, Amil saw a true embrace hidden among all the decomposition.

The forsaken family was intertwined by a common disintegration, as the bones of one swam among the bones of another. Hollow faces rested in pained expressions, and

260

dried flesh rolled out of the vacant mouths to become one with the skin of so many others. Into the mother's eyeless face Amil did stare, until he found himself lost, immersed in the horror of the deathly leftovers. He was drowned in a sea of mutilated faces and an entanglement of body parts, stitched together by rot and exhausted flame. The stink that rose from the pile clung to him like a filth destined to refuse any soap or scrubbing. Sweat pushed its way out of his pores and his vision failed him. His body took to the suffering of tremors, and nausea strangled his gut.

In this state of extreme fragility, Amil head the roar of a rickety pump truck as it shook to life, and, before he could discern its purpose, the metallic beast purged a thick fluid down to the pit below. Some manner of sticky accelerant was sprayed down upon the pit and its filth, and with one shot from a flare gun, the mass was lit ablaze. A wall of fire rose from the pile and it added further ruin to the tapestry of decay held under its infernal assault. The newest Waste to this collection of gore was trampled by the combustion, and Amil watched as it sank under a swamp of flammable liquid and runny bodily remains.

Brighter than the sun overhead, the flames soared from the pit, as they seemed destined to lick at the ceiling of this strange room that Amil and the others had the audacity to call a city. Rank stench and a deafening chorus of wails filled the air as the blinding nature of the fire swept before Amil's sight. He was stunned into rigidity, like a statue frozen by the punishment of the harshest winter. All he could do was stare in horror and utter disbelief as he witnessed The Eternal City's solution for ridding itself of the unwanted.

The Eternal City was a lie. This place was neither

sanitized nor safe. Amil learned that as stone truth. It was barely civilized. As his eyes absorbed the disintegration below, he heard screams and the sounds of flesh as it bubbles from bone, but there was something more. In the sky, and through the smoke, he heard the cries of those that had been reduced to ash long ago. It was a ghostly song, a swirl of spectral agony. Not even the insatiable hunger of fire could free the Wastes from their persecution. After the burn, whatever remained of their Spirits became somehow trapped within the aether above the pit. They were invisible, but undeniable, harmless, and horrible. Countless souls had been launched into the sky, and there they would wail laments to the uncaring and unnatural sun above. Amil had heard stories about the poisoned air over the pit, but he never believed them. How could he?

Like a madman pushed by forces he cannot see nor control, Amil beat his fists into the side of his head in a futile attempt at knocking the visions and all the noise back out. He desperately needed to be free of this place. His very sanity, or what remained of his already flayed mind, depended upon his flight from the Waste District. He never could have imagined a region so vile. Perhaps this room was the worst that Aphelianna's house had to offer. Was it all nothing more than the most massive of curses? The entire room, a vexation designed to further needle out the last goodness in man. In a gesture of divine mercy, as Seamus and Greg rushed to the side of their overcome companion, Amil fell to the dirt, and passed from consciousness.

As was customary, he was given a week off after his little journey into the Waste District. He was assured that Waste runs were infrequent, but all the same, Amil put in his resignation, and applied for any other job that he was qualified to perform. No amount of incentives could dissuade him from quitting, and for nearly the entire duration of his forced time off, he stayed in bed with the lights on, and thought heavily of Ali. The fate that she suffered began to look less and less malignant to him as the days passed. As long as she hung from that tree and stared wearily down at the image of the Spirit Ripper, she might never come to experience the condition of a Waste. She was a Nothing, and, as much as it hurt him to admit, Amil came to terms with her classification. In a way, it made things better. She didn't have her memories, her sense of joy or sadness, or even her name. As he counted all the things that Ali was made to go without, he resolved that to leave her there, forever, was better than to cast her into a future that would assuredly be more barbarous than her present sets of sorrows.

He could not bear to think of her as a Waste, but as Amil continued to dream of Ali, he was haunted by this nocturnal Nothing. For just the same as his earthly love, this specter had a pair of blue eyes that he could not forget. She had been placed so very far away from him, but it was as if she always crept quietly behind, unseen and untouchable. Unable to be attained or saved, she wallowed in betrayal, her lone acquaintance.

Amil was eventually placed into a new occupation, and took to the demands of a truck driver's work. His able body and his familiarity with interstate highway systems, which had carried over from his days on earth, made him dually equipped for the job. The distribution of goods all across The Eternal City was crucial, and always in a demand near impossible to sate. The differing terrain of the city made this a challenging task, and the days were often long, but it awarded Amil an unexpected therapy. He thrived on being alone, as most interactions with others served to remind him of the cruelty of death and of all that he had been made to leave behind. The incomplete maps and roadways that he was asked to navigate offered to him a feat that distracted his mind from the ghosts that always hung heavy across his back.

Two months into the job, his nightmares, born from the torturous visions seen on his last day as a courier, began to recede. His mood lightened, and during the longest of trips, Amil again succeeded at justifying his abandonment of his sworn mission to save Ali. Thundering down a forgotten road that was bare of markers or a centerline, he tapped his foot to the tunes of the stereo as they screamed over the roar of the Freightliner. With sunglasses on to shield his eyes from one of man's oddest creations, Amil set the cruise, and thought of going out later that evening. He hadn't seen much of anyone lately, and, as the feeling of being alive bubbled up in him again, he gave a seconds' entertainment to the memory of Jill.

Night fell, or, rather, it was set to come down, and Amil sauntered into that cozy bar on America Alley. Curtis was there, full of shrapnel wounds and beer, and all the pool tables in the back hosted spirited games. The counter was lined with moderately attractive singles, who, in their common deformity, searched for a spark as they partook in the dating game. Amil grabbed a seat next to his inebriated friend and ordered a drink. As he waited for his glass to arrive, he glanced down the row of faces and found the wide smile of Jill.

She was sporting a wig of neon pink that had been

chopped into a punky style, and her pale face was decorated in a lively arrangement of makeup. The tall boots that she wore made her look even thinner, and with the intended effect, they made her skirt appear all the shorter. Her top exposed the cold cleavage of a chest once stilled by cancer, and, as she caught Amil's eyes, Jill skipped over with the usual and comedic sight of cigarette smoke encircling her head like a charcoal halo.

During the course of the hours that followed, the pair flirted and gently pawed at each other, as is typical of a courtship born from anxiety and alcohol. Jill's affections were loosely veiled, and her advances came all the stronger since Amil had made himself a scarce sight as of late. Although the attention flushed him with a tickle of fun rarely indulged, he at last bid goodnight to Jill, and made for the door much the same as he had arrived: alone.

He could see the disappointment on Jill's face as he left. Her bewilderment was not lost on him, as Amil had previously taken other girls home, while leaving Jill and her charms to fade into the background. He only had sex a few times since entering into The Eternal City. The act had become too unsettling to bear. The first woman that he fucked in this vulgar un-life was a fairly attractive redhead that had fallen victim to meningitis. Her name was Marianne, and she was as uncomfortable about the whole process as he. They were equally turned off by the fact that an artificial lubricant was always necessary to keep things moving along, but it was a much more disturbing fact that cut short their affair. Here in Aphelianna's house, the inside of the body is quite cold. Sex had become an act that lost all desirability, and it was not a sensation that Amil was ready to share with someone for whom he cared about. In his melancholy, he advanced mere paces down the sidewalk before Jill rushed up from behind and forced herself into his arms under the suspicious glare of a lamppost.

"Hey, what's the deal?" she asked.

"This ain't right, Jill. None of it is, anymore."

"Quit being so goddamn tight. Let yourself have fun once in a while."

"I doubt this would be any fun," said Amil, flatly.

"Well find out then, fucker."

The wooziness of her state only magnified her cute persona, and, with little coaxing required, Amil finally gave in to her allure, and kissed the drunken Jill. They scurried out from under the light and hid in the darkness of a nearby alley. The sloppy make-out session intensified, and soon Jill relieved herself of her shirt. He had a hand up the back of Jill's skirt, and sucked on her breasts before returning his attention to her lips.

Under a voluntary blindness, the feel of Jill's fingers as they undid his pants, and the touch of her painted lips, surged a myriad of sensations through Amil. He was poisoned on a cocktail of happiness and guilt, and swam among this insipid brew over another quick round of passes from Jill's tongue, until he could bear no more of the conflicting emotions.

He pushed her away and felt his chest flutter. Amil stared deeply into her mildly sunken eyes and knew that a decision that would forever influence him looked back. He could momentarily brush aside his guilt, and add her to the list of late-night distractions, but Jill was somehow different. As he looked upon her face, all aglow with a distant yellow light, Amil knew that if he went home with Jill that night, he would never leave. The choice loomed

266

heavy and abominable. He could open himself to her, a caring figure, salvation from ruin, or he could run into the arms of certain oblivion.

Jill's lips trembled with dismay and her eyes begged for answers. They begged for compassion and common understanding. They speared into him with the promise of happiness. All that was required was for Amil to give in, to give up. The choice to be free hung on her breath, the way to emancipation from his wretched toil. In that moment, he felt Jill's pure offering, the pull of love as it promises to sooth away all the scars of the past. But, like revenge for damage suffered long ago, the face of Ali stared back at him. Agony consumed his mind and pain shattered his soul. He turned and briskly stepped off. Jill shouted for him to come back, but as Amil heard the clack of her boots as she started after him, he took to a sprint, trying in vain to outrun the hurt that shadowed him.

He was in immediate need of a new distraction. A tonic to pummel down the horrors inside him, one that didn't involve the influence of others and one that presented a hole that he might crawl inside to again hide from his shame. As he walked the avenues that carved their way through the neighborhood, Amil gazed upon little else besides his shoes as they scuffed over the cement. But in a flash of fluorescent light, his interest was stolen from the ground and set upon the marquee of a movie theater. It brightly offered the escape he sought, and so Amil left behind the condemning air of the evening and disappeared into the mouth of the film house.

He caught a light-hearted flick about alien invasion. Sci-fi was a favored topic among those who made their homes within the limits of The Eternal City. Predictably, gloomy movies which told of the end of the world fell out of fashion. The feature wasn't terribly well put together, but the theater was barely populated and the air inside the darkened room was as clean and fresh as the breeze that blew outside. Comfortably reclined and temporarily lulled into numbness, Amil sipped the last of his soda and worked the candy out of his teeth as he watched the credits roll.

"Did you enjoy that little slice of mediocrity?" a voice questioned.

Amil didn't have to turn around. He wasn't even startled, as the unmistakable tone of the mischievous Duke Vinzenz blasted away the ambient music that accompanied the movie's expiration. He sat silent and stared ahead. He didn't know the reason for the Duke's appearance, but he was certain that is was not for love of the cinema.

"What do you want?" asked Amil, as he grew nervous.

"You seem to have adapted quite well to life here in The Eternal City," Vinzenz exclaimed. "Congratulations, most people never even make it this far. Oh yes, you must be quite extraordinary indeed to have crafted a life here and forgotten all about what drove you to twist your little key over and over again in the first place."

"I'll never forget about Ali," said Amil, through clenched teeth.

"Then why are you here, basking in the glow of the silver screen and cavorting with zombies at the local taverns? Oh what lecherous fun it must be, to drink ale and sing songs. Perhaps you could bed an easy girl, or purchase a new album for tomorrow's travels. I hear the swine is quite good around here. Tell me, is the honey glaze served down on Resurrection Road really as delectable as everyone claims it to be?" asked Vinzenz, with no interest in the answer.

"What the fuck do you want from me?"

"How so very human of you. To suggest that I came here to deprive you of something dear. No, on the contrary to your suspicious beliefs, I wish to give you an item that you might find quite useful."

"I'm not interested," whispered Amil, as he stood up and sidestepped his way down the row.

"If you may indulge me, why did you quit? Why did you just give up?" shouted the Duke, his voice echoing through the empty theater.

"I know it's bigger than me," admitted Amil. "I would do anything to help Ali, but there's nothing I can do."

"Maybe this could be of some assistance," replied Vinzenz, as he tossed a small round medallion over to Amil.

Much like the coins once used to free the former god, this charm held a high polish, and was absolutely littered with strange inscriptions. On the reverse, the ornate decorations were absent, and, in their vacancy, there was etched a number: 1373. In the center of this unearthly piece, there was an oval hole, but rather than nothingness, an enigmatic haze of violet restlessly swam.

"What is it?" asked Amil, terrified of the revelation.

"Just a simple tool. It comes with no ramifications or ill effects. Most unlike that little gift that our dearest Aphelianna gave to you. No, this wondrous device will simply show you the way. Hold it up to a door, who knows what may happen next," said Vinzenz as he grinned widely and stroked the braid which crawled down his breast.

"I thought you never wanted me to find Isadora?" asked Amil, confused of the Duke's intentions.

"Oh, make no mistake. That still remains true. And, Amil, I possess no faith in you. I just wanted to see what you might choose to do if presented with all that you've wanted while positioned snugly amongst all that you really need."

With his eyes closed, Amil tightened his fingers around the glorified coin and turned away without a word. He had nearly marched to the exit when Vinzenz verbally halted his flight.

"Oh, one more thing," he shouted. "I understand that you had the pleasure of meeting Arcanus Tyme. A lovely old man, I'm sure you would concur. However, did he speak to you of his daughters? Did he lament the torture of one while he spoke longingly of the other?"

"Daughters?"

"Oh, poor old Arcanus, he didn't tell you. Aphelianna and Isadora are his blood. Can you imagine his suffering? One daughter ruined the world, and the other keeps it afloat like a corpse that bobs over the sea. Truly monstrous. Even I pity him." Vinzenz grew quiet, as though he actually was telling the truth when he spoke of sympathy for Arcanus.

Amil was immobilized by the weight of what he had heard. Left with nothing else to do but stare at the God of Fortune, he silently cursed the whole of existence and its furiously morbid nature. The Duke stared back with a curious smile and checked his pocket watch. He looked around the theater and the dim light that it held, as though glancing at what the time to come might hold, and then bid adieu to Amil with a slow nod of his head.

"Good luck, Amil. The choice is yours," Vinzenz maliciously uttered as he casually stepped away.

Alone in the theater, but immersed in a well of sadness within, Amil gripped his new possession. He thought of Jill, and how the burn pits seemed a proper storage space for Vinzenz's present. He had sense enough to know that to cast this object away would definitively put an end to his quest to find Isadora. He then thought of Ali, and cursed the unrelenting design of memory. Feeling damned to unmake all he knew and all that existed outside his understanding, he slipped the charm into his pocket.

Much like the key that hung from Amil's neck, his gift from Vinzenz accompanied his every step. But it was just a weight in his pocket, as Aphelianna's charm was a shackle around his neck. They were chains that tethered him to the memories that he could never shed, but in these days that saw him reconcile all that he had forsaken, the tokens slept neglected, left to wallow among the company of their master's afterthoughts.

Painfully, and arduously slow, but victim to the will of the almighty calendar, the months turned and died away. The seasons didn't come behind this expiration of days, nor did the scenery yield to the suggestions of change. The sun shone every day, even when it mysteriously rained, and every night was of the blackest black, barring only the influence of manmade neon and artificial light. As it usually failed to fluctuate inside the main limits of The Eternal City, temperature was a near forgotten concept, and the repetition of all that would ever be continued on quite unimpeded.

It was by freak chance, an accident, and a conspiracy of faulty maps and a distracted mind, that set

Amil before a decision which would forever change his version of the evermore. He was supposed to take Highway 91 past the Ice District. The land of this area lay crippled under the assault of freezing conditions, and was the least inhabited portion of the mammoth room that held The Eternal City. He had already traveled the thirty-odd miles that had been mapped, but he still failed to reach the next turn onto Separation Road. The curiously named avenue that he sought never appeared. Old 91 just flowed on in an ever-increasing state of ill repair and abandon. About the time that the asphalt under his wheels gave way to dirt and lumpy patches of congealed stone, Amil realized that he had missed his turn. It wasn't with reasoning that he could deduce, but he elected to put his responsibilities on hold as he bore straight ahead into a colorless expanse.

Called by the dullest of Sirens, his pace was limited to a healthy crawl due to the poor conditions of the road. But the utter desolation that spilled out as Amil chugged along bore a fascination within him and deprived his mind of the faculty of independent will. It was as though the dissolving of any and all description spoke to him in a voice as empty as his own. After hours of staring into that icy plane of white and the pale blue horizon which rested upon it, the path under him suddenly vanished. It bled into a uniform gray with the rest of the land, and all the trees, markers, and even the smallest undulation of a hill was lost. The sky beyond began to lose it hue, until all the land had shed its affections for color. It was as if a plug at the bottom of the world had been pulled, and all the color in all things was left to drain out.

Amil allowed the Freightliner to sleep as he killed the engine, and relieved his tandem of mechanical beasts of the air pressure which hammered its way through their brake valves. He stepped out and set his feet upon the bloodless gray. Everything had grown so vapid that Amil could barely distinguish the sky from the ground under his step, but still, he walked. Even the air around him elicited no reaction from his body. It was no longer cold, nor was it warm, dry or humid. Perhaps it, too, had run off with the color. About 100 paces away, he turned to view his truck. Though caked under months of dust, and with a color that had been baked into a soft fade, the rig looked like a brilliant palace as it shimmers under a desert sun. The colors that it possessed appeared magnificent placed among the conquering gloom, and, though it honestly beckoned to him like a paradise of kaleidoscopic beauty, he ignored its pleas and continued a methodical plow into the vast absence.

Fully among the gray, and with so little to set his bearings by, Amil became disoriented. Were it not for the glances that he shot to the creases in his jeans and the sharp maroon of his button-down shirt, he would have tumbled to the ground below. This task was so dull and devoid of any stimuli whatsoever, that he came to view it as a punishment. It was his to endure for all the enjoyment that he allowed himself to share in while Ali still hung naked within that orchard of misery. At least this seemed plausible and remotely fair, but it was something else that drove him further on into the gray. Yes, it was a fool's curiosity. It was the odd sensation of repeatedly passing beyond the touch of any and all creation that permitted him to place one foot before the next. And, in a strange way, Amil felt totally safe in this most godless of places, for it was as though he was beyond the reach of anything at all.

As he started to think about The Eternal City and the comforts of his apartment, and how in the hell he was going to find his way back to the truck, a small feature introduced itself to him. Placed a bit further on, was a door. It was as gray as everything else had become, and the frame that held it was no more impressive than the complete desolation of the world all around. Amil approached with caution, as though the door were an illusion, a mask that obscured a voracious monster solely responsible for the meticulous murder of all that was prismatic.

He never told it to do so, but his left hand descended, and, once it emerged, the appendage held the medallion of Vinzenz. Amil turned it over in his palm and stared into the violet swirl of its center. He looked to it, and then his eyes flowed to the door, and then back to the ornate disk once more. He read the number which was imprinted, 1373, and, then with a rigid ascendance of his arm, the mysterious coin was held up against the colorless barrier. Like an essence of purity entangled in violent resistance to an intercourse it was ill-equipped to refuse, the purple fog twisted and bent within the hollow. Slowly, it was contorted into a proper form, and, once its body had been fully mutilated, all that remained was a ghostly figure of indigo whose ephemeral shape revealed the door's identity of 1373.

Amil dropped the piece, and the suffering child of its belly was cast out, as the shapeless swirl returned, but he had already learned a truth never to be dashed from his mind. The token was a map. Its number revealed the source of the correct path to Isadora, and, thanks to Aphelianna and her wretched gift, Amil also had the key necessary to follow the map's direction. He knew not if Isadora herself waited just beyond, but was certain that he had the means to reach her.

There were no guards to stop whatever action he might fancy, as this door was undiscovered. Amil knew he should take responsible action and report his find. He should be wary to trust Duke Vinzenz, and disregard the temptations which stood before him. He should, at the very least, say goodbye to his friends and thank all those that had been so kind to him during his time in The Eternal City. There were a myriad of things that he should have done, but all that he could really do in that moment was to think of Ali. It was fleeting, but his mind then cast a thought to Jill. Conflict enveloped Amil as he stood before the door. He knew that his truck was waiting for him, as was Jill, just a bit further away. That was the way to go, the right path to take, but he knew that Ali was waiting as well. She was waiting for him, her only chance of salvation.

He thought of her in the orchard and he thought of her on earth. Fully awake, he dreamt of her skin and of the lips that produced the brightest of smiles. He remembered their early days, and all the innocence that they each failed to see. He watched her as she tended to his every crippled need, and was humbled and weakened by the presence of her inexhaustible patience, which he could still feel. He felt her love, a love from perhaps the only soul who truly and deeply had ever loved him for all that he was, and all he was not. It was an emotion that transcended existence and all the barren planes of the afterlife. It was love, for Ali's love, that Amil had stopped searching. Plucking his map from the gray soil around his shoes and sliding his key into place, he bid farewell to The Eternal City.

275

Part 8. The End of Time

Amil emerged into a land transformed. Moments before it might have held life and all sorts of activity, but forevermore, it could lay claim to nothing of substance. A red dusk colored the atmosphere, as whatever once existed had been reduced to smoldering piles of embers. The stumps of trees rose mere inches off the ground and were pointed at their tips, as the lick of fire had burnt them to near nothingness. The structures that had once dotted the land were baked into collapsed heaps of brittle matchsticks. The ground itself was warm, steaming with the smoke of exhausted fires, and even through his shoes, Amil could feel the radiant heat left behind from the infernal decimation.

The scents of burnt wood and ignited earth filled his nose, and this scorched land was viewable in wavy segments, as the hot air coiled and rippled away. Crackles and pops were the only sounds, and other than the occasional blast of fire that emanated from a piece of charred wood, all motion had either fled this place or was incinerated. Flakes of black peppered the sky like diseased snow, and as they polluted the air, this macabre confetti found its way down Amil's throat and into his lungs.

He choked on the air and quickly concluded that whatever boon or assistance there may have been in this room, it was long gone. He stared ahead, into this wasteland of interminable ash, and grew weary of setting his eyes upon fresh depictions of ruin. If the singed air hadn't already robbed him of moisture, he would have cried. He could bear no more of Aphelianna's atrocities, and, as his eyes were forced to absorb all which had been burnt away to nothing, Amil gazed into a succinct example of his own soul.

Without a step into this eradicated world, he turned and faced the door that had sent him to this somber space. He gave a feral stare to the barrier, and each eye displayed hatred for the two faces of the Janus who conceived the malevolent passage. As he spat on the wood, Amil didn't hesitate to shove his key into its receptacle or to twist the knob open, but he did pause before crossing its threshold. He was gripped, frozen like a millennia-old mastodon trapped in ice and denied even the mildest respect from the laws of time. Like that great beast, he was not permitted decay. He was not extended the inalienable right of all things to simply disappear. He feared the revelation that awaited him on the other side, and for the first time, Amil came to fear the true magnitude of eternity.

It was expected, but his heart sank all the same as Amil stepped not back into The Eternal City, but into a different room altogether. He knew it then; the truth was confirmed for him. He would never find his way back to the city. It was a part of his life now past, nevermore to be revisited, and like his earthly days with Ali, he had willingly forsaken safety and comfort yet again. It was all or nothing, Isadora or damnation, Ali or the jagged embrace of perpetual emptiness.

Held within a circular room, Amil was numbed, but he came to terms with his decision and surveyed the environment. The room wasn't very large, no bigger than a hotel lobby, but what it lacked in size, it greatly compensated for in substance. It was built almost entirely from marble. The variant colors were rich and bold, dark in their nature, and in the possession of a crystalline sheen which reflected from the swirls of stone. Sconces of intricate metallic creation hung from the walls in abundance. With shapes inspired by femininity, shades of stained glass covered the lights. A prismatic wash of color, like bands of a scattered rainbow, swam around the room and coated the marble in a brilliant glow.

As Amil stepped into the room, he actually gave a thought to the dirt that rested in the treads of his shoes. He took to a delicate pace as he trod across the floor with a respectful consciousness. Everything was perfectly clean, impeccably polished, and buffed to a luster that he thought impossible to achieve by mortal hands. The brass fixtures beamed with magnificence more regal than gold, and to refer to the glass globes as stained felt tantamount to blasphemy. To use such a word seemed a disgrace. No, the colors in the glass were more like essences of purity unseen. It occurred to him that they likely were not constructed of simple glass at all. It appeared that the panes were in fact the differently hued sources from which all color is carved.

Fixated upon the sconces above, Amil was made to stare at abstract versions of his reflection, as the sharp pitch of the ceiling had contorted his image. With a thousand unique expressions, these transitory doppelgangers gazed down at Amil and asked of him which path he would next take.

Like an inverse carousel of unknown destinies, the room was lined with doors. They were much unlike many of those that Amil had passed though before. All were different, and all were splendid in their presentation. Some were circular, while only a select few took the shape of an ordinary door. One was tall and thin, but its nearest neighbor harbored the resemblance of an upturned triangle that was made to rest upon its point. The hardware of each was ornate and crafted from precious metals. Materials so assuredly rare that all that could be harvested had been exhausted in the building of the hinges and knobs. Jewels of glittering passion were beaten into the metals, and spectacular patterns of intricate lines and weaves were carved into the wood. In the center of each door curiously shaped windows had been placed, whose variant colors were solid, and of the same constitution as the lampshades overhead.

Amil stared into an enchanting purple pane. As he studied the glass, which resembled a question mark in reverse, he fumbled through his pocket and withdrew the map coin. He brought the object up to his eyes. On its backside where the 1373 had been, a simple inscription of 0 had taken its place. He immediately knew the meaning: door 0 was where he next needed to be, and one of these illustrious barriers was the pathway to his next destination.

The shapes of the windows were as cryptic as the doors that held them and were equally enthralling. Like hieroglyphics penned from the hand of the divine, the arrangements of the windows, and the gorgeous complexions they possessed, enraptured him. He took time to admire each door and the radiant hues they offered, but this was purely for pleasure, as he didn't check any of their identities with his charm. Amil already knew which path to take. He would have bet the whole of the afterlife upon it.

Passing beyond splendid red, azure, and yellow, he walked the circumference of the room, whose absence of a baseboard yielded to a woven ring of metal leaf. He admired, and then ignored, noble green, orange, and hazel as he floated within this sacred temple. He maintained this joyful orbit until he approached a door whose window was black. It was a color so deep that as Amil looked upon it, he felt a tug, as though the glass wanted more than just his weightless reflection. The shape was a simple circle, a hole, most unlike the voluptuous nature of its peers, and it told of the expiration that lay beyond. Slowly, and only in a matter of procedure, did he press his medallion up to the surface of the door. Predictably, the victimized cloud formed the symbol of 0, and as he stood before the only door in the room that instilled in him a mighty fear, he reached for his key.

Amil was not blind. His eyes functioned perfectly well, and with some intangible sensation, he saw all things clearly, and yet, nothing at all. Beyond the door, there was simply nothing more to see. All was black. All aspects of description had not been painted, stained or faded into darkness. And they were not even absent, but rather, everything, anything, was never there at all.

Amil looked about himself, and he, too, owned a uniform black. His clothes, his shoes, and even his skin were awash with the complexion of night. Upon his flesh, these changes were not the result of the skin-deep persuasions of melanin, but something much deeper and far more complex. Whatever it was that befell him, this force took Amil apart piece by piece, down to the very basic and infinitesimal stages of his creation. He was left to float weightless among the empty air like a specter. Only now, he was far less substantial than a phantom. He was the dissolved embodiment of nothingness. And as he swam among that which never was, he was still cursed with the weight of his own thoughts.

Without heft or definition, he drifted through space on merely the constitution of his mind alone. He saw as the dreamer sees. Abstract concoctions of memory and fantasy, all jumbled together, but beyond the faculty of recollection all the same. Sound came to him through the filter of a coma. And, as Amil lingered perilously near to the precipice of absolute oblivion, he was made keenly aware of the distance stretched between him and everything else. The greatest joy, the most abysmal crime, they were held at equal length from him. The unassuming description of a suburban street and the most fantastic nascence to be found within Aphelianna's house were all removed, and placed as far away as galaxies only rumored to have once existed. Perhaps he had escaped the influence of Aphelianna and of death after all, but in doing so, Amil uncovered a greater curse. He was among the vast impossible, the literal Nowhere.

If time had ever failed to impart its friction upon him, it had done so then. Amil felt not its drag, and he could sense no rapidity. He experienced no boredom, panic, or dread. He only continued to be, a fragile, barely-there entity of the truly lost. But, like any traveler, he inevitably came upon a destination. Perhaps it was not what he expected or even what he sought, but at the end of Amil's wade through extinction, his eyes were made privy to what lay after forever.

His reanimation went unfelt. He didn't watch as his body returned to a tangible object, nor did he view specks of matter as they assembled themselves into something greater. A world did not spring up about him one piece at a time, rather, it just appeared. In one moment, Amil was a tiny part of a large brocade of absence. In the next, his feet were firmly planted upon stone.

Blocks of twilight blue clung to one another and formed the wrung spiral of a staircase that began from nothing, and was tethered to more of the same. It descended into the invincible black, and once its coil dipped below the depths of eternity's void, Amil was set upon a narrow walk of mahogany. The timbers were true in their flow, and as they lay flat-out like a plank off the edge of the world, they were escorted by railings of rope that bled starlight from the fibers. Into the dark unknown, he walked with trepidation. The floor below held a gloss, but it reflected nothing, for Amil didn't really exist. He ran his hands over the luminescent ropes and traced their dips and swells, but he felt not the touch of thread or the blunt bodies of the posts that created the union, for they, too, weren't really there. He walked on through the antithesis of creation, and knew this precisely and with a poignancy that made him weep invisible and tasteless tears.

"That's far enough," a tired voice suggested.

Amil's body locked, like his feet were sunk in week-old concrete. He gazed ahead, down the boardwalk to Neverland, and there upon the edge sat a man of paltry stature. He held his back to Amil, and dangled his skinny legs over the side of the mahogany's end. As he slumped into the unnatural posture of a shrimp, the rigid bones of his spine pushed at the cloth of his shirt, and a mat of gray hair weighed down his head like the crown of oblivion's king. The flesh of his hands had collapsed, and their brittle shells perversely exposed every coarse vein as the fingers lay splayed out over the wood. He lurched forward, an act which noticeably brought him a considerable measure of pain, and then back again, as though bullied by some unfelt breeze. Even from a few paces behind, Amil could hear as the man wheezed. In silence, Amil gave thanks that the stranger hadn't turned to look his way. He had no desire to look into the eyes of the one who was forever cursed to stare into eternal darkness.

In a break from his normal operating procedure, Amil didn't question the man as to who, or what, he was. He could only assume that this creature was once a god, but to confirm this fact was something that he had little interest in undertaking. He didn't care to learn the man's name, or of what series of worldly tasks were once his responsibility to oversee. The nature of his being, whether wicked or of the kindest benevolence, was something that Amil was content to leave unfounded. He dreaded the man's face, and hesitated to engage him in conversation, but as Amil stared into that spined back of bone, cotton, and asthmatic strain, he felt the vibration of words as they escaped his throat.

"How do I get out of here?" he asked, with quiet demand.

"How did you get here?"

"I died," responded Amil, solemnly.

"And so has everything else," the voice explained, as the source of the words continued to gaze into the blackness. "This is The End of Time, the unavoidable future, and I'm all that's left."

"Did Aphelianna cause this?"

"Aphelianna? Hmm, it's been so long since I heard her name. I can barely even remember the last time I saw her. I held her in my arms as she died. It came sometime after-"

"Stop! Please, don't go on," Amil begged, as he felt wholly unequipped to handle the explanation to come.

He had tripped into the last day, a day which had nearly forgotten the monstrous name of Aphelianna, and though this meant that Amil was too long gone, he had no fear of it. All things have an end, and this was the end of ends. But it remained so distant that it felt completely unreal, like a tragic accident in slow motion that he was never meant to see. He sensed that no version of life, death, or anything else of a trickier description had any right to stand where he did. And so, as he trespassed into the last eye-blink of existence, Amil knew that he must make haste away.

"Then what is it that you want?"

"Just tell me how to leave. I don't belong here," Amil said.

"No, you most certainly do not. Nothing does, so make your exit," the man directed, curtly.

"How? I haven't seen a door."

"Every door, every passage in every hall in every room, is at your back."

Amil had grown weary of what happened beyond the gaze of his eyes during his stay as Aphelianna's guest. Things were never what they seemed, and, in keeping with this insipid riddle, another collection of puzzles had snuck up on him. As Amil slowly turned, he could almost hear the pestiferous laughter of Duke Vinzenz, but it was not the God of Fortune who was to blame. He had taken that medallion from Vinzenz of his own volition, and as he stared into endless rows of doors that hung neatly arranged among a backdrop of pure black, Amil realized that he didn't need Aphelianna or her kind to suffer curses. He was plenty good at cursing himself.

As he stood before the gateways to every moment in

measured time, he withdrew his map stone and glanced at his next objective, door number 18514. With a fluttered sigh, he moved, and his feet left the boardwalk and found themselves planted upon the same empty space over which every door sat. He approached the first barrier in the first row and checked its name, 9009. Its neighbor read 76, the next was 67033347, and the door that floated next to it was numbered 32114. The random assortment revealed to Amil that the placement of the doors was just that, random. Door 18514 hide among the countless billions, and to find it, would require him to check each that he passed. He would have to walk back though time, ignorant of his place therein, but knowing full well all the while, that to traverse every last second of existence might be the price of getting one step closer to Isadora.

Down the first few rows, Amil methodically plodded and double checked the identity of each door. His fists were curled with anger and his face twisted fore and aft between visages of outrage and disgust. He kicked the doors, which all remained indifferent to his assault, and shouted his displeasure to the empty heavens above. As he thought about the task before him, one that was of the cruelest vulgarity in its utter simplicity, he felt cheated, and allowed a tumor of self-pity to develop. It trailed behind him like a medicine ball of regrets, and slowly, from the evolution of this cancerous grief, was Amil's rage made to crack.

The wounds opened upon his psyche were small at first, tiny fissures that only glinted at the devastation that lay beneath. But they grew, were forced open and bred new faults with every thunderous beat of his furious heart. Eventually, the incendiary cloak of ferocity that he wore began to split at its seams. Like an insect purged from a spent cocoon, Amil's own facade fell from him in slivers and was lost upon the nothingness. His strength and his will, a will that was only supported by his rage, were gone, and all that remained was the broken and vulnerable remnants of a man.

This new condition festered for much longer a time than the initial burst of madness had flamed. It clung tightly to him, and soaked his skin in a lugubrious film that made all movement, and just the notion of perseverance, seem too lethargic a weight to drag behind. Like a mechanized beast that developed only the intelligence necessary to contemplate the taking of its own life, Amil lifted his little stone up to each barrier that he faced. His head would then solemnly bow in defeat, as he was made to acknowledge their predictable answers.

At last, centuries into his troll, he had found something solid and very much alive among all of Aphelianna's deathly leftovers and ruin; the root of true hopelessness. It had become his lone and most loyal companion. It dogged Amil's every step and constantly whispered reminders to him of the unforgettable facts of his bleak and interminable situation. He couldn't stay, but to pick the wrong door was to stray from the path to Isadora. A path that would evaporate like breath into wind were he to forsake the mission he once so passionately begged to be awarded.

Deep into the rows he traveled, until only a narrow world of perfect repetition surrounded him. Put behind Amil were a million lines of like doors, and to his face was an arrangement of many more. No matter the direction in which he stared, his eyes viewed innumerable passages, doors that gradually devolved into smaller and smaller objects as they floated out to the nevermore. He had become a lost little rat, trapped within a maze of straight lines that rose from the most abandoned sector of the black abyss. He wanted to run. He wanted to flee this damned cause and suffer the consequences that awaited his failure. He even experienced a souring of his memories for Ali, for it was her unforgettable face that was responsible for his being here. But it was too late to indulge the slothful pleasures of quitting. Giving up wouldn't free him from this task. Neither would a marathon sprint that endured for centuries serve to liberate Amil from this path of his own choosing. He had ventured too deep into the back catalog of time to escape. He was ensnared, a whimsical plaything for the ages.

At some indefinable moment into his walk, he started to shed the basic characteristics of his humanity. Sleep forgot who he was, and the desire for food, the action of chewing, became entirely foreign to Amil. Speech died from his tongue and his mouth dried into a hollow desert that was home to nothing more than discontented grunts and the occasional scream. The sharpness of his vision softened to a rudimentary function, as no stimuli higher than the dull doors and the stone in his palm were present to keep his eyes keen. A mental genocide was brought down upon him from the virulent tentacles of a far-reaching insanity. Madness was the only essence held within his skull, but this too died away with time, and was replaced by something even more punishing.

After his inner meltdown, Amil's body became a shell that held the dusty fragmented reminders of a life deserted eons before. He could still remember earth and the places upon its face, but they came to him in fuzzy collections of dream-like flashes. Reality had become a failed experiment, as he scarcely recalled his own name and heavily doubted the validity of loved ones and the events which once shaped his life. He could still see Ali's face if he squeezed his eyes shut tight enough, but the memory of her, too, precariously bobbed over the ever-widening sea of uncertainty that had washed over Amil's mind.

Like a face that looks up from a photograph of faded paper was how Ali looked to him. He could see her, but it was without a clear definition. The color of her eyes came into question and the curve of her smile was a shipwrecked treasure, sunken and gone. Her hair was brown, possibly it was, or maybe this was just a reasonably good guess given the lack of chromatic variety that sprouts from the human head. Like the still image that tarried in Amil's mind, Ali no longer had a voice, and her movements went unremembered. It was as though the notion of individual personality was ludicrous, and the love, joy, and tears which she once so intimately shared with him were all forgotten. As the last scraps of her generosity, kindness, and of her very being unwound their hooks from his soul, Amil strained to remember why he was looking for door 18514 in the first place. The urgency to find Isadora ebbed away, and as he was stripped of all he once was, his fingers closed over the chain around his neck.

His pale hand, ripe with veins and fragile bones, tugged at his key. Amil wanted so much to tear the key away from his flesh and cast it into the enveloping black, but not even the smallest flare of defiance was left to him. His fingers instead hung meekly from the fine links of the rope, and dreamt woefully of the days when they possessed the constitution of vigorous action. Bent over by the gravity of guilt, Amil rattled on like a slave being whipped by an invisible entity who never tired of sadism.

It looked like all the others, and with no fanfare or prick of excitement did Amil pass his medallion over the door called 18514. What he had suffered so habitually for the last eternity or so had become a routine so unbroken, that his numbed mind, or what remained of that pile of mush inside his skull, had failed to recognize his destination. Like a farm bird that is slow to view its own doom as it stares up at the axe still crimson-slicked with the blood of its family, Amil kept on going. He walked on slowly in his defeated gait for miles, centuries, and down untold rows. He still checked his stone, but barely saw the numbers that surfaced as anything of significance. It wasn't until much later that the grand discovery did finally settle inside the dulled areas of his mind.

Once the full impact was felt, Amil sensed a return of thought. Imagination crept back inside him, and nervousness jerked through his skin which awakened deadened sensations. Like a clock of perpetual motion which at last feels the sting of failure, his body stopped. He turned and sent his eyes down the rows, and deep into the dark fabric of space and of times never to be written. It was back there somewhere. Far away, but not lost, the gateway to emancipation. He thought not of Ali or Isadora; Amil only thought of himself, and of a release that finally felt attainable. It was enough to set his feet in motion again, and with a renewed sense of hope, bitter and sickly as it was, he retraced his steps.

The pathetically small jubilation which percolated through his heart was quickly extinguished. It was a fluke really, the happiness he felt. It came like a hiccup, and left with all the mourning which follows the end of winters' cold. The long trek back to the door he had so foolishly ignored earlier was the final ingredient needed to achieve self-disintegration. There was no more Amil Young. All the same, the hollow man who endured finally stood before door 18514, and walked out of The End of Time.

Part 9. The Endless Library

From an incalculable number of moments, and from the maw of infinity itself, Amil emerged from the abyss. He lay exhausted and empty, crumpled into a heap upon a floor of hardwood. It flowed outward, like the ocean as it recedes from the shore. Though faded and scraped by the multitudes which once stepped over them, the boards still fit neatly together and were thoughtfully decorated with a generous assortment of rugs. Their fibers held dust, but they also still retained their colorful designs, which gave each a unique flair. Most of the stitched creations were woven with nothing more than a common circle for inspiration. Upon the rugs, small tables, rocking chairs, and writing desks, complete with wetted ink wells, rested quietly.

Placed upon the many desks and other pieces of ornate furniture were oil lamps. They burned low, and gave the enormous room a comfortable light. To view such a display from high above would return to the eyes, not a warmly lit room, but rather, an elaborate constellation. The walls, which seemed to delicately breathe with the wavering light, were dressed in stretched layers of heavy paper. Stained the color of blood after it has been left to dry upon cotton, this craftsman's parchment was given fantastic detail by trails of black ink that never exceeded the width of a human hair. Laid down by some genius brush, the strokes arrived in dizzying swirl patterns and line work, so intricate, that to stare at them for too long would call about the disorienting effects of vertigo.

The ceiling above, moderately high in its rise, was formed entirely of hammered copper plates. In various spots, the metal panels separated from one another, open to the air, like the promise of a welcoming embrace. The hollows they formed allowed for the growth of staircases, straight and spiraled, which led to places unknown. As the copper shapes hung in the cold air above, much too distant to receive warmth from the fire of the lamps, they gazed down at collections of shelves that seemed to know no extinction.

Fortified by the ancient union of wood, nails, and stain, thick shelves streaked the floor in arrangements of perfect lines, diagonal settings, and crossing patterns that sharply cut through the room. More of their kind lined the walls. Grouped in differing formations that appeared quite odd, the placement of each collection of shelves undeniably knew a true order. Bizarre symbols of arcane origin, which appeared meaningless to modern eyes, were carved into the wooden spines of the shelves. The curious glyphs had been devised to direct an inquisitive reader down the aisles and inside the pages of the many books held therein.

Every inch of each shelf was called upon to support the many tomes. Some were quite thick, while others were so pitifully thin, that to print and sort them seemed wholly extraneous. Most volumes were of a respectable size, and all looked to pridefully carry cosmetic changes that hinted at their age and told of their usage. The bindings were plain and of subdued coloration. The corners of many had frayed, while nothing more than a few printed words graced the covers. But there was something in their collective banality that spoke to an elevated purpose. The covers had no need to lure a reader over with intriguing images, for what they held inside was so fascinating that to further trumpet the subject matter would have been an exercise in the superfluous.

        This labyrinth of knowledge sprawled out for years untold. The shelves carved their paths like rivers through mountain ranges, and much akin to the nature of water, they spawned smaller, stranger versions of themselves. Some shelves were placed so tightly together that to squeeze between them would require an intimate familiarity with the emaciating effects of anorexia. Even more still were so tall that to reach their uppermost portions would demand the assistance of a Titan. In a truly perplexing situation, a band of rogue shelves conspired to curve together and form a ring. The inner circumference was that of a small house, one which possessed no means for entry, and extended almost to the copper above. The books placed on the outside gave themselves freely to a voracious reader, but to access the titles that slept within the ring was a riddle as thick as the pages were many.

        Further on into the room, the walls continued to reflect the greatness that detailed them as the light from the ignited oils continued to bleed in a soft glow. Artistic visions of landscapes, and portraits, of individuals whose names had been forgotten by time, were rendered on canvas and hung from the walls. There they clung, in a complementary fashion, beautiful and utterly devoid of the malice that slept under the paintings that decorated The

Hall of Worship.

Staircases of tight spirals, and ones that widened into cascades of carpeted steps, rose to floors above and sunk to darker levels below. Charming alcoves could be spotted with an observant eye and furniture designed to accommodate a thinker and his thoughts no longer depended on the construction of wood alone. Deep sofas that practically oozed sleep rested over the rugs, as did complete beds. Massive pillows, which sat whimsically like low-slung clouds, catered to the sensibilities of the playful.

But Amil was yet to view anything that sat on display within Aphelianna's library. He remained on the floor, passed out at the foot of the door that had spat him out. He saw nothing more exciting than the insides of his own eyelids, and, as his mind lay nearly devoid of activity, reason suggested that he might finally die away from humanity altogether. Not from bodily trauma, and not even at the murderous clutches of a Waste, but rather it appeared likely that Amil's being would pass away just to have something to do.

Deathly silent, but peaceful in its lack of sound, the air of the library finally became the home of a quaint noise. As pleasing as warm honey over fruit, chattering tones arrived to displace the former silence. The air was brushed aside by the flapping of wings, and soon a melody was formed as a pair of fanciful little creatures came to inspect the unconscious man. Two figures, notably female given the abundance of silky curls which sprouted from their heads, stood no more than three feet in height. Lazily, they floated above Amil on the support of fleshy wings. The skin of these appendages was dark, an elusive variant of purple, and tightly stretched over minute bones below.

Darkness swept over Amil as one of the women fluttered down and knelt beside his head. She brushed her golden hair aside with a hand of pale green fingers, and stared at the comparatively giant man. Her companion reached into the folds of her thin dress and withdrew a small vial. Whatever it contained, the substance was lighter than air, for when the bottle was uncorked, the fluid inside rose up and threatened to drift away like a balloon carelessly let loose by a child. The one that gazed upon Amil with a pair of unblemished white eyes collected the escaped potion with her spined fingernails and delicately rubbed it onto his face. It stuck to him in a thin film, but disappeared with immediacy, as though terrified of the world outside of the glass. As they waited for whatever was next to come, the creatures garrulously communicated with one another. In a language of clacks, their conversation was orchestrated by the sounds of teeth as they slap against one another.

Their treatment served to unfetter Amil from the chains of abyssal sleep, and as his eyes slowly opened, he hazily gathered the description of his saviors. Seeing him flirt with consciousness, the chatter stopped and the fairies held still, as though allowing Amil time to study them.

Although they both had blonde hair, one was colored in a complexion of green, while the skin of her friend was of a burnt red. The vibrancy of her red flesh appeared to glow with a fire held just beneath the surface, a conflagration barely contained. Their lips were fat, their short bodies voluptuous, and they seemed to both share an affinity for light dresses that any earthly man could admire. But for this collection of pleasantries, the women certainly didn't share a bloodline with the gentle fairies of children's lore.

Beyond the hesitations brought about by the rigid wings and vacantly white eyes, the beings held a plethora of features usually reserved for malevolent creatures. Horns grew out from the sides of their faces and swept backwards behind the head. These hardened slivers of keratin continued their run until they coiled around the small necks of their masters like barbaric necklaces. The teeth responsible for the fairies' speech were long, and many took the appearance of fangs. They were black, not from filth, but rather they shined like water as it lay still under the weight of midnight. Their tiny feet had only four toes each, and, curled like talons, they harbored claws that looked fully capable of shredding the thickest of hides.

As Amil's vision returned to him in full, he nervously absorbed the finer points of the fairies' forms. Small pins protruded from the skin upon their backs, and the short barbs twinkled with a liquid that acutely alerted any curious fool to the virulency of the venom contained within. This field of spikes swam over the shoulders, and crawled across the chest, until it finally ceased along the arches of the breasts. Down the outsides of each thigh were rows of scales. Though harmless at rest, it seemed likely that the sharpened flaps could spring up at any moment and bloody the source of an unwelcome touch. Amil studied their mouths as the females resumed their cryptic conversation. Between the gauntlets of teeth, he witnessed a dual set of tongues. Each was forked, and behind the clicks and clacks of their language, Amil watched the muscles as they twitched in spastic motion, to taste the air of the world around them.

He was about to speak. He felt the urge to resist

295

their ominous touch, but the morbid nymphs decided otherwise. One under each of his shoulders they flew, and with a strength that Amil could have never imagined, the fairies elevated him from off the floor. Floated like a feather by wind, he was guided deeper into the library, toward a destination unknown. At first he struggled, meekly as it was, but it was still enough for Amil to earn a kiss from the poisoned pins. He complied under pain's suggestion, and allowed his body to settle, but apparently not fast enough for the mercurial pair. Quickly, his sides were given an intimate brush from the jagged scales, and Amil fell into disorientation as fog shrouded his mind.

He felt as a foreign substance was released into his dead body, but whatever its purpose was, it was not designed to cause discomfort. Amil didn't feel a burn at the site of his many punctures, nor did nausea wiggle into his gut. He sensed no sweating or misfiring of his nerves. Everything was made serene and unreal. The scenes around him melted away in runs of color, as if everything had been carved from candle wax. The floor below twisted into a swirl, as though the material upon which the whole library drifted was made liquid and left to drain away. He could hear the voices of the lights, and felt as their vibrations passed through the pores in his skin. Every vocal clack of his escorts shot along the paths of his veins and ran in pulsations of euphoric adrenaline. Though he still knew to fear the possibility of truly dying, Amil was ready to accept it, for if that is where his destiny awaited, at least the journey there would be a beautiful one.

"All right, that's enough," a smooth, male voice announced.

Placed into the soft envelopment of a recliner, Amil

was loomed over by an intimidating centaur. The mythical beast waved away the fairies that had taken to lounging upon Amil's form. He then placed a glass of ordinary water atop a round table. It rested beside the chair, over a rug of azure and gold. The centaur had gray hair and lines over his skin that looked to be the trenches dug out over a land that hosted a tiny war. He raised the wick of a nearby lamp and gave a mild jostle to Amil's knee.

"Come on now, you can awaken. They didn't take that much," he reassured.

Amil didn't have the energy to move, but a trickle of fear pummeled through him all the same as his senses convinced him of the reality that stared him down. Although with little focus, his eyes eventually found those of the centaur. It was unexpected, but Amil discerned no malice from the creature that towered over him. In fact, he was somewhat relieved to be free of the fairies' company.

"Who...who are you?" Amil asked, slowly.

"I wish I knew, but we have time for that later. Can you remember anything?"

"Not really. I...the name Ali comes to me," admitted Amil.

"Your name?"

"No. No, it's someone else's, I think."

"What about yours? Can you remember that? Think hard now, concentrate. Your name," the baritone voice instructed.

Amil thought of what a name meant. He found it odd that a string of letters could be shouted in his direction to gather his attention. He wasn't sure of how to respond, or even if he fully understood the question. His mind wandered, lost in contemplation for minutes that felt to him like hours, but at last, a collection of letters came to the fore of his memory.

"Amil...I think my name's Amil," he said clumsily.

"Hmm, a bit odd. That is good. How about a last name, or place of origin?"

"Fog Lake," Amil said, his eyes closing. He didn't really know what meaning it held. The words came out like an impulse, a reflex to a stimulus forgotten.

"Okay, sounds like a village. North American perhaps, possibly European," muttered the centaur to himself. "To the last name again. What followed your name *Amil? Amil what?*"

"You...young. I think it's Young."

"Terribly common," said the centaur, with a grimace.

The impossible combination of man and equine slapped his hands together and rapidly gathered the attention of the green fairy that was perched on a shelf close by. She didn't move, but she raised her eyes to his thunderous clap and gave him her full audience, with a sneer that plainly told of her annoyance.

"Amil Young, human, probably American. Fog Lake, most likely a village. Search all entries from seventeenth century Earth to what we understand as their present time. Go on now, don't give me that look," he bellowed.

With a chattering of teeth that seemed to hammer off one another with a bit more ferocity, the teratoid little creature buzzed away.

"It won't be long now. They're ornery beasts, but masterfully efficient all the same."

"What are they?" asked Amil wearily as he watched

298

her disappear between a row of bookshelves.

"Please, have some water, wet your throat. Your body may no longer require such things, but it will be helpful. Please, I insist," urged the centaur.

With no mind or means to resist, Amil brought the glass to his mouth with a quivering motion, and eased down the clear liquid. The centaur was right. The feeling that a seemingly banal glass of water delivered to him was indeed a blissful one. Amil felt as the cool stream soothed his dry insides, but it was the significance of the act that served to inject Amil with a small amount of resurrection. There he was, in a comfortable library, sharing a drink with friendly company. Sure, his companion was a fable, and the room around him was populated by devilish nymphs, but this was, at least, a version of solace.

"What are they?" repeated Amil after he downed the last of his drink.

"They are called Draymataya...dream nymphs," said the centaur, while pouring his guest a fresh glass from a bottle tied around his neck.

"Thanks, that cleared everything up."

"A sense of humor! In this place, a sense of humor is an essential weapon. Draymataya are the only creatures, other than Aphelianna, that have access to the world of humans. But where Aphelianna can only harvest the dead, Draymataya come to visit while you are sleeping. Lost in that scant void that resides between life and death...dreams," explained the centaur, with a dramatic sweep of his hand.

"Dreams?"

"Yes. You see, the Draymataya are vampiric. To sustain themselves, they take a minute fraction of the living human as it sleeps. It is so inconsequential that without the unfelt touch of the Draymataya, human life expectancy would be lengthened by only three days. Even the most ravenous of their kind will only deprive the host of about one week's time. But they are not wholly wicked. In return for the life that they extract, the Draymataya tell you stories as you sleep. They are what provide you with dreams."

Amil thought for a moment. He was given a chill as he thought back to all his nights on earth and how, as he slept, he was visited by forces unknown. Unconscious, he was fed upon, murdered on the most diminutive of scales, all while snuggled in his bed. He tried to recall the strangest of dreams that he had experienced, and, oddly enough, they were his most vivid memories. He sucked in a deep breath, as the explanation offered to him was almost too much to process, and looked around the library. He hoped to spy a Draymataya, as though to locate one would help him to understand their nature.

"What did they inject into me?" asked Amil finally, as he rubbed the tiny hives that peppered his skin.

"Inject? No, no, no. I told you before, they're vampiric. They take from you."

"Alright then, what did they take?" asked Amil, with alarm.

"Just a small fraction of the life you are yet to have."

"A Waste's life?"

"You're human, it is unavoidable," said the centaur, with pity. "You should be grateful to have met the Draymataya. They can shorten the suffering you will eventually experience."

"What about this?" Amil asked, as he withdrew his

300

key, a foggy recollection of its terrible conditions swirling through his scattered mind.

"Even with that, they can help. Nothing endures forever. Even a cursed Waste will die one day. If you allow them to feed long enough, you might relieve yourself of a year or two of the fate you will come to face. I know it is paltry, placed up against an existence that seems interminable, but if it is yours to suffer, you will be grateful for their theft."

Amil offered nothing in return. He took small and regular sips of his water in order to busy himself and to maintain a fragile quiet between him and the centaur. He sent his eyes across the sea of bookshelves, and was awed at how many volumes were within his field of vision. Filled with the illumination of the lamps, and under the glow reflected off the copper above, the room promised to extend out to forever, or so it seemed that it could, making the true number of books held in the library close to a figure that mathematics was yet to name.

"Have you read all these?" asked Amil, without looking to his companion.

"Ah! It's arrived," said the centaur heartily as he ignored Amil's query. Instead, he thanked the Draymataya, who set a book onto the table next to her earthly visitor.

It was bound in black leather, unremarkable and plain, with pages of an eggshell hue. Down the spine, Amil's name was printed, and as he gathered the humbling gravity of what the book truly was, he was saddened by the small size of the document. It was thinner than most that he saw, and with no need to turn a page or sweep his eyes over a single word, Amil was reminded of how short his existence had been. He ran his fingers over the cover, and, as he set the book into his lap, Amil crumpled under the weight of shame.

"There is a reason why your book is so little, Amil," said the centaur, sympathetically. "I will understand if you choose to leave your memories lost. But if you decide to rediscover yourself, all that you have forgotten can be found upon those pages."

"Everything I've done?" asked Amil.

"All that you are."

"Why is this happening?" Amil asked, desperately.

"The condition of the present is the sum of the actions of the past."

Amil got up. He didn't look to the centaur nor did he extend an appreciative glance to the Draymataya who had recovered his record. He tucked the book under his arm and staggered away. Amil wandered through the library, down rows of labyrinthine design and around the curves of the more artfully crafted shelves. He sent his fingers through random sets and read the names that were pressed into every spine over which his nails clacked. His mind wondered about the lives of those whose volumes were impossibly thick, and was dogged by a brutal melancholy as the thinnest of books, sometimes no more than a single page, surely relayed the painful tales of sickly children and those stillborn.

To his astonishment, he was not alone in this paper museum of the dead. There were many others like him. He was startled by an old man. Fully absorbed into a book, he stood in a corner like an apparition as he thumbed through a saga, never bothering to raise a bespectacled eye to Amil. There was a woman who sat at a small table, with grief as her only company. It spread onto her from the pages, as she revisited the violent deaths of her sons in wartime. Amil came across a stout fellow. Charming in his ease, he gleefully amused himself with a refresher of the deeds committed during his obviously happy stay on earth. Amil then noticed a teenage girl. She looked the proper part of bookworm, but with stab wounds in her neck. She sat partially obscured behind a stack of other people's achievements and shortcomings, and paid no mind to the lingering eyes of a stranger.

Unaware of what lay directly before his distracted stare, Amil nearly tripped up the first step of a staircase, whose handrail poked him in the ribs. He knew not where it went, but with no destination or sense of immediate purpose, Amil ascended the skeletal iron coil and advanced upwards on vertebrae of semi-clear stone.

He emerged into a tiny room, a mere pothole upon the road of outer space, and settled himself onto a wingback sofa. It sat under the watch of a crystalline fixture, which held an array of extinguished candles, its many points smoothed over by runs of dried wax. The few sticks that still burned poured a soft ambiance over the surroundings. A dusty lectern, the blackened planks of the floor below, and a tapestry of archaic symbols were all warmed by the light. The blocks that gave the room its octagonal shape stood exposed. They slept between lines of chipped mortar, hardened masonic blood once picked at by the likes of the morose and the bored.

Constructed for solitude and introspection, the room beckoned for Amil to open the book which rested beside him. The tight confines promised to withhold judgment and offer Amil the embrace of comfort, were the words held between the leather too much to bear. As the cushion at his back hugged him like a kindred spirit, Amil wondered how many others had been reintroduced to themselves in this very room. And so, with heavy eyes, and a mind that cautioned him against going forward to seek the truth, Amil opened to page one.

As with any refresher course, the minutia that clogged the hours of everyday life was left out, but the pivotal moments were all clearly described. Every high and low, all the decisions which had shaped Amil's life, lay there for him to read. Events that had once seemed insignificant had their true identities and implications revealed as Amil sunk deeper into the book.

The mystic author reminded Amil of the brief stardom he had once enjoyed, and returned to him the sensations brought about by the warmth of a southern evening. Amil could smell the stale air of the bus station in Ashland, and he felt the chill of a winter in Pittsburgh as he nervously awaited a proper date with Ali. He walked the warehouse of the paper plant, and paced back and forth across the darkened space of The Back Shelf Bookstore. As Amil watched the dead and unreachable likeness of himself as he spent each day with Ali, he was made fully aware of the beautiful enormity of ordinary existence. It was a wondrous treasure, one which during the course of his life, Amil had never given a second's consideration.

The chapters which chronicled the early days spent with Ali were read time and again by Amil. Wallowing in the purity he had failed to feel at the time, his eyes passed over the words slowly, as he joyously relived the carefree days of their young union. He happily dwelled upon every idiosyncrasy of Ali's being, and not until he had memorized the passages, did Amil move on to the next segment of the book.

Sadly, but with cruel predictability, the book began to read like a tragic play, one in which the audience quickly realizes that the main protagonist will inevitably suffer great torments. The only solace offered from such a production is that when the lights go up, everyone is permitted to return to their comparatively better lives. But not Amil. He saw the disheartening end as it crept up on his literary self, and though he desperately wanted to warn the Amil of the past, he was nothing more influential than a bound slave. One who is forced to watch the erasure of life as it once was.

During this descent back into time, the lights went out, and a furious darkness settled over everything that came next. Amil's eyes identified the signs of his unraveling, and his desire to read further evaporated. Words, terrible words like *ACCIDENT, SURGERY,* and *VIOLENCE,* came to his vision. There were clues, like harbingers of misery that haunted him: *POOR, SADNESS, HANDICAPPED, BETRAYAL,* and *PUNCH!* He was made to remember what they implied, and, as they harshly judged all of Amil's earthly failures, the words chased Amil's stare away from the pages, until he stood before a road that he could not take. Unable to bear the reminders of what he had put Ali through before he so selfishly invited a bullet into his own skull, Amil skipped ahead.

As he read on, past the surreal descriptions of his expiration, Amil had to remind himself of the safety that currently enveloped him. He was made to shiver as he again stood among the dead as they wallowed beyond Aphelianna's fountain, and as he felt the gaze of the deformed Saint Calvino. He snickered at the memory of

Uncle Cal, and felt his heart swell with pity as the stone maiden of the atrium came back to his memory with cold clarity. He walked the avenues of The Eternal City again, and, much like before, the decision to leave seemed a foolish one. Amil was made to smile as he again heard the voice of old Arcanus, but regretted the decision to read of the God of Music and the horrible curse that he carried.

It came to Amil at once, like a trick of the mind or a trick of the cosmos. He hadn't sensed the last page as it rested between his thumb and pointer finger, but he turned it over and stared into the most bizarre of all mirrors. As he learned of the exploits of his life and then his afterlife, Amil watched as the words of the present scrawled themselves over previously blank paper. The dark little characters detailed the room that held him, and they told of his bemused visage, as though the book had eyes of its own that had looked back upon Amil the entire time.

He slammed the volume closed, and it clamped shut like a snare designed to subdue an animal. Amil flung it into the corner of the room and shot up from the couch. He tightened his fingers around the handrail, and, with feet that threatened to disobey Amil's call for balance, he descended the stairs.

When he emerged back into the main area of the library, Amil was a changed man, different, as he had a knowledge that should have remained as far off as the earth itself. Like the zombie that he was, Amil plodded lethargically around, as it seemed he could never tire of absent wandering.

There was activity, and the day appeared busy, as many witnesses to the weakness of flesh passed by Amil. It was startling at first, how populated the library seemed to be, and as more examples of death crossed paths with Amil, he longed for solitude. He had no want for company, and so all greetings that were offered his way went ignored, his eyes shyly hiding from the looks of others.

With a growing irritation, Amil noticed as a Draymataya took to following him. Her skin was yellow, a hue akin to mucus, and this unsavory pigmentation only served to make her pale eyes all the more sinister. Her hair was as black as her teeth, and the beat of her wings so unnecessarily strong that the vibrations could be felt by Amil. She may have just been curious as to the identity of this wandering stranger, and true harm was something that she seemed incapable of inflicting, as she nervously darted out of sight anytime Amil turned her way, but her presence greatly perturbed him. He needed to be alone, the way a plant longs for water. The distant company of the diminutive nymph was enough to make Amil feel crowded. With no warning, he swiped a book from off a shelf and flung it at the little creature. He didn't turn to look and see whether or not he had struck her, and, unashamedly, Amil cared not for her wellbeing.

He drifted down between rows of shelves that towered high into the air. The opening of this dry mouth, created by the massive bookshelves, was so wide that a parade could have passed through the gap. But as Amil progressed, the aisle narrowed and closed in on him with yellowed rows of verbose teeth. The dust mounted in layers, like ancient rock as it tells of the past eras of time, and the tidiness that touched nearly everything in the library started to ebb away. Books were toppled over one another, and large spaces where tomes should have rested were empty, as though the previous readers had concluded that it would be better to burn the wicked books rather than return them to their brethren.

Perfectly suited for sorrow, and of the need to bathe in one's own misery, a chair was set at the end of the aisle. It offered little in the way of comfort, and kissed the stained wall behind it with its splintered lips. Just wide enough for that rickety excuse of craftsmanship to assume a crooked posture, the row had become so tight that all sources of illumination strained to bleed through. Only small slivers of light crawled between the cracks of the books, but this brightness, too, was dirtied by airborne dust and microscopic filth. It seemed a forgotten place, like a lot in a cemetery whose stones have been washed clean by centuries of rain, those that lay beneath rendered as faceless as their weathered markers by the passing of the ages.

Amil closed his eyes and faced the wall. As Aphelianna's key pulled on his neck, it became the only feeling left in his skin, as though it tugged upon his very soul. He silently wished for the jaws of the corridor to close tightly around him. He wished to be swallowed, to be digested by oblivion, for he had already been broken down to near nothing. Like an exhausted creature as it folds and dies among its family and upon the fields that it once used to graze, Amil fell into the chair. Clobbered by sleep, he sank into the underneath of the mind.

He truly dreamt for the first time since his earthly passing. Yes, he had been visited by the ghosts of his memories, and tormented many times by the unwillingness of the mind to rest since his arrival in the afterlife, but this was different. It was a proper dream in its nonsense, its blissful disorder and whimsical arrangement. Characters from his life, and from his death, made appearances, but they rarely played themselves in this nocturnal sonata. The thoughts of any tribulation did not follow Amil to where he had gone, and the cursed gravity which incessantly sought to drag him into obscurity finally unwound itself from his troubled mind. He floated among this illusion for a time too short. The fragile dream cracked and shattered, leaving Amil with only the sharp shards of the reality he could not escape.

He awoke, not fully, but he was freed from the clutches of unconsciousness all the same. His perception of what existed around him was foggy, as the walls of the dream were slow to melt away. He felt the pressure of a Draymataya as she nuzzled her head onto his chest and mercifully stole away infinitesimal amounts of the torturous future that awaited the death of his Spirit. He could taste the dusty air, and the spears of light that netted his body helped to crack open his eyes. Amil began to discern the outline of a figure that stood over him, but not until the Draymataya vaulted herself from his lap like a cat spooked by the roar of thunder did he recognize it as a Waste.

Wastes were normally quite similar to one another in their construction, but this beast wore the marks of excessive punishment. Its bubbled flesh was scorched so deeply that in places the charred bones below were made visible. What little hair it still possessed grew from the scabrous skin in raised clumps that seemed to harbor a will all their own. The matted patches pulled away from the pus fields that birthed them, almost as though they, too, feared the very sight of the Waste. The black discharge, which seeps so endlessly from every fissure of these abominable creatures, dropped in fevered abundance from the hollow eye sockets of the monster. The sight called vomit to rise in

Amil's throat, but all bodily action was frozen once he witnessed as a mass of something unknown shifted behind the vacancy of the eyes.

Perhaps the most pestiferous example of bestial nature had made a burrow within the ruined skull, or maybe, Amil watched as the Waste's brain broke down and melted away. But he sensed that this unusually tall Waste was just a shell, a diseased incubator employed by hell to hatch an untamable evil. The cocoon was nearly spent. It shook before him, and soon it would split asunder and purge the abysmal demon beneath, warm with bile and hungry to commit acts that a common Waste would deem deplorable. The Waste began to moan. Its teeth smacked off one another until they cracked, and the sounds of its tormented insides boiled from its wetted mouth. Amil turned away. Like a child, he hid his head in his arms. Defenseless in a ball, he refused to watch. From the broken womb of a mother empty of affection, this new beast would rupture. It had come to end Amil, and, under the darkness of his eyelids, he would give himself to its teeth.

He heard it emerge, and with his mind's eye, Amil witnessed its birth. With a murderous tenacity, the hellish creation housed within the Waste began to beat its way out. Fists of barbed knuckles battered the inner skin, and they tore wounds from within, that, between expulsions of septic blood, revealed images of the demonic parasite. It furiously kicked and distorted the body of its host, so much so, that Amil was sprinkled with a fresh film of the Waste's venomous blood. It stuck to him like glue and was cold to the touch, although a burning sensation burrowed into his skin as the fluid sunk deeper into his pores.

The Waste had been bent onto its knees, and above

its groans of pain, the sharp snaps of bones as they are forced to split could be heard. The imprisoned killer screamed in impatience, and, in harmonious discord, the Waste wailed a brittle lament that acridly spoke of its assault.

Though squeezed tightly by his hands, Amil's ears detected the dying cries of the Waste as it thrashed upon the floor amid a tornado of violent convulsions. The chest cavity of the defeated creature swelled with a cancerous mass of something foreign, and one by one, the ribs exploded into clouds of bony shrapnel. The matricidal birth was nearly complete, and Amil couldn't help but imagine the ill-conceived child as it rose up from the cavity, slicked in black, and adorned with the carnage of a creature nearly as deleterious as itself.

But then there was only silence. Gasps of heavy breath followed this brief flight of sound, and, from between the gaps of his fingers, Amil peered at the scene before him. Set adrift among the oceans of horror that comprised Aphelianna's house, and lost within the halls of imagination, Amil's mind had been taxed of sanity. Overcome by dread, his eyes had been robbed of clear and accurate vision. There was no teratoid fiend, and the Waste had secreted nothing more than its own fluids. It did, however, lay motionless on the floor, beaten into unconsciousness by a book.

"Thanks for your help," a winded man sarcastically remarked.

Amil didn't say anything in return. He shivered in a cold sweat, but then it occurred to him, he wasn't sweating at all. His mind had called for his skin to release water, but his body no longer listened. In that moment, Amil recalled the carillon player's words when he relayed to Amil that his human side would eventually die off. It was strange, and it felt like a new death. Amil had noticed this about some of his friends in The Eternal City. There were those who could no longer cry, breath didn't leave their lips, and their blood had hardened to putty. Ever stubborn, the mind still experienced all the sensations of being alive, but the body failed to act accordingly. It was a cell in which the ephemeral aura of consciousness was forever trapped.

"Hey? You alright?" the man asked, his sarcasm replaced by concern.

Amil's attention was snapped back to reality, although that was a concept which had long felt loose and rather ridiculous. All the same, Amil set his vision on a slender figure that comically resembled a storybook wizard. He was white, lined with age, and had a graying beard of considerable length. He wore a robe emblazoned with the images of stars and crescent moons, and, in absurd fashion, he was topped by a pointed hat of purple that boasted the same celestial arrangement.

"Who are you?" whispered Amil, as he was unsure of whether or not to thank the wizard.

"I told you before, I don't know," he responded, in the unmistakable baritone of the centaur.

"The centaur?"

"Sure, why not?" he said, solemnly. "You see, I am not just the caretaker of these books, I am *of* these books. I can be anyone or anything I have read, but I can never be me."

"This is your curse," Amil stated, as he remembered the image of the aged librarian that hung in The Hall of Worship.

312

The librarian might have calmly explained his plight to Amil, but with the mention of his curse, he flung the bloodied book to the floor. As it crashed into a shelf and busted the lowest plank, Amil saw that the large tome was bound in iron, the heavy pages riveted together. It was splayed open like a gutted animal, a smattering of dark blood on the pages. The print inside was archaic, and although the characters were nothing more than ink pressed onto paper, there was an undeniable malice that emanated from the still symbols. If for nothing else, it had made a splendid weapon.

"Whose book...whose life is that?" asked Amil.

"It doesn't matter."

"Are we all here?" Amil wondered aloud, as his eyes scanned the rows.

"All the humans, all the Mortals, all the gods. Everyone. I'm in here too, but I just haven't found myself yet. I'm not even sure if I would recognize my own life at this point. But I'm sure *you* feel lost," he said, with a sneer.

"What should I call you?" asked Amil.

"I don't want any name but my own. Until I find it, you don't call me anything."

As the terror brought about by the quelled Waste started to soften, the invincible curiosity that nestled between every aisle eventually sank its hooks into Amil. He continued to look around, not really at anything in particular, but he started to gather the true purpose of the room.

"You know what happened to them, don't you?"

"Pardon?" asked the wizard, as he removed his wrinkled hat.

"All the mysteries. Amelia Earhart, JFK, King Tut,

Jack the Ripper, all of them. You know how they ended."

"Umm hmm," said the librarian with a smile.

"Is Jimmy Hoffa really buried under Giants Stadium?" asked Amil as he chuckled.

"Read the book!"

"Hey, uh...what happened to the Mortals?"

"Come on, I'll show you," the librarian stated as he walked away from the stilled Waste with no care if Amil followed behind.

Through the aisles and down the rows they went. Amil shared company with a winged dwarf, a cyclops, and a man who looked to have once been a successful CEO, as the lord of the library seemed to possess little patience for each new shape that he took. Amil's guide changed form so often that, after some time, Amil barely found interest in the immediacy with which the transformations took place. However, this erosion of awe coincided with their ascent of a wide balcony. It undulated softly, and overlooked a rather busy portion of the library.

Amil peered out over the railing, a structure comprised of arched metallic ribs topped by a banister of bejeweled oak, and observed the activity below. Down upon the floor, Amil witnessed as a colorful assortment of the wandering dead floated up and down the rows. They fed their darkened brains with the tales of others while seated around tables or sunk into comfortable chairs. He was made to smile as a smattering of Draymataya fluttered about and assisted those in need of help. Many more simply gave the gift of companionship to the lonely, while a few of the curious beings formed groups and conversed amongst themselves in that indiscernible language of bone clacks.

The balcony, warmed by a carpet of amber and

soaked with the cozy illumination produced from the fires of lantern light, had finally curved to an end. Before Amil and his mate, who eerily resembled the Egyptian god Anubis, a barrier stood. It was a pair of doors that seemed capable of turning away an army.

The barricades were thick, built of layers of steel, fortified by carbon, and wrapped in skins of the densest wood. They sparkled with a glut of hardware. Precious metals had been shaped, manipulated, and blended with one another until they all worked in harmony to reflect a polish so bright that it brought a squint into Amil's eyes. But this beauteous and elaborate flesh was just a decoration, a mask that shielded the true majesty that lay within. All throughout the doors ran an intricate system of bolts and tumblers. It was a mechanism that took years to contemplate, many more to craft, and for all the pins and levers that aided in the formation of the mechanical skeleton, one truth was certain; a key was required for entry.

"This is where you come in," the dog-faced creature declared.

"I have to use my key?" asked Amil, with a start.

"Only if you want to see what became of them. Even I can't enter without a key. It has been many years since I last visited this room, but I will not ask you to so frivolously spend a turn of your key."

Amil felt as a pull came through the doors. It was undeniable, and perhaps even unable to be resisted. He thought it foolish to consider using a treasured turn of his key on nothing more substantial than the whims of curiosity, yet he entertained the concept. After all, beyond those spectacular doors was the entire history of a race vanished. The beginning of life, as the incalculable multitudes once knew it, was there, as was the finality of their extinction. They were the precursors to humans, or perhaps they were humanity's true origin. Whatever the facts may be, they were all there, waiting for Amil to discover them. He imagined that in learning of the Mortals' end, maybe he could glean the fate of man, or, at the very least, learn of the creation of his own kind. Amil sensed an invaluable knowledge rested just beyond his grasp. It had to be revealed. Amil could not stand before the gate to such enrichment and willingly walk away. His eternity be damned, his quest be lost, and Ali, oh poor Ali, be forsaken, Amil directed his key into the slot.

The doors parted without a squeak or squeal of complaint or strain. A light from sources undiscovered washed out from within and colored the faces of Amil and the false Anubis. The light was brilliant, but not bright. It was soft, but Amil could still feel as definite warmth came to his skin. Across the threshold, the room revealed itself to be circular, but the walls held no shelves, decoration of wood, or any other cosmetic touch. They were pure white, and not simply from the application of paint, but white like milk, stilled in mid-tumble. It seemed as if the room was alive, like it drew breath. The walls shifted like lungs, Amil knew they did, although his eyes were too slow to capture any of the movements.

As he stepped inside this living beast, which held the tales of countless deaths as its only treasure, Amil was overcome by what he saw. A book, unlike any other, was set at the center of the room and opened to a page. The last page likely read by the room's previous visitor. Stretching the breadth of the wide room, and extending for nearly a mile, the massive volume lay splayed out in repose. Freely, it offered up secrets which would certainly require an eternity to exhume.

The print, a beautiful script, was impossibly small, and called for the assistance of an interpreter in order to be read. In a black ink, the words rested fresh and unblemished over pages that surely eclipsed the weight of some of earth's heaviest machines. But this fact was of little concern, as an elaborate device that testified to the genius of Arcanus Tyme was employed.

Using his signature gears, the heart of the mechanism rested beside the book, heavy with an assortment of the interlocking iron wheels. They were fused by rust, along with the levers once used to operate the device. All stilled, and besieged by the metallic cancer. Above this frozen engine rose the more precise pieces used to turn the gigantic pages. Rods, pivots, ball joints, and arms like elongated fingers were suspended above. They were all married together by rubber belts that slept within the grasp of silent pulleys. Two metal plates with rubber sleeves over their tips dropped down from the instrument like a buzzard's claw. Carefully, they pinched the top corner of a page. Starved of oil, they, too, exhibited signs of rust around their movable parts, and as the forgotten machine hovered deathly still overhead, it resembled a specter that is doomed to forever haunt what others have left behind.

Amil slowly walked to the edge of the book with the shadow of a jackal's face at his back. He ran his fingers across the paper and pressed his tips over the unreadable characters. He opened his hands and laid his palms flat upon the inside of the book. With his eyes closed to the words he couldn't understand of a book he could never finish, Amil stood over the Everything and the Oblivion of an entire existence. As he floated in silence, in blindness, and bathed in that mysterious light, Amil absorbed only nothingness from the book.

"I...I need a book," he began. "Ali Jett," said Amil, with the sensation of sorrow wound around him.

In the same room where he rediscovered himself, Amil sat with the book of Ali tucked under his arm. He was still, entirely motionless at times, as he wrestled with the task of opening the chronicle. He heard voices from the floor below, and the flapping of a Draymataya's wings echoed up the stairs. Silence nestled with him for long periods of time and bouts of dreamless sleep came to call for Amil. But his fear of what could not be undone served only to delay the inevitable. He would open the book. He knew that a day would arrive when he could no longer hide from the revelation of Ali's final moments. Amil continued to sit, perhaps for weeks, in that room, sitting upon that couch, unable to open that book of a life now ended.

Then came a time when Amil decided resolutely that he could not bear to read of Ali's death. Even if her end came in the most peaceful of fashions, he cared not to know of it. Her death was done, what did it matter? What was there for him to gain from such a woeful exercise? With a defeated sigh, Amil removed a candle from the fixture above him and delivered its kiss to the tome in his hands. He pressed his lips to the name printed on the leather spine, and said goodbye. The pages ignited, and the contents within were soon swallowed by flames. Once the book was fully ablaze, Amil cast it softly down the stairs, disinterested in the consequences of his actions.

Down the spiral he finally shuffled, and, to his surprise, he was greeted at the bottom. There stood a small boy, his complexion so dark that his birthplace was undeniably rooted in the heart of Africa. He was dressed in clothing no more splendid than spent rags, and wore only one shoe. The muzzle of a dirty gun rested against the skin of his boney shoulder, and, judging from the rest of his frame, the child was dangerously malnourished. Amil knew straight away that the librarian stood before him, but the reason to assume the life of a subject as tragic as that of a child soldier was one that Amil simply could not understand.

"You cannot destroy what has already happened," the deep voice announced.

Amil looked at the small hand, and there among the calloused fingers, sat a fresh binding of the book of Ali Jett. It had reappeared, unconcerned with Amil's wishes, as what it contained was not his to immolate. Amil reached out and took the offering. It felt heavy to him, almost as though a portion of his guilt had been mixed into the ink. He thought to place it back on the shelf, but it would always be there, waiting for him. He had once asked for it, and so he was forever bound to hold up his end of the arrangement. The book would haunt him until its desire to be read had been sated, Amil came to understand. He had pledged to read of Ali, and to appease this spirit, an exorcism of discovery was required. Perhaps the book was the earthly ghost of Ali herself. One condition, however, remained unchanged. The book was not rewritten. That was something which could never be. With a heart heavy, cold from inaction and broken from the absence of love, Amil ascended the stairs behind him.

He knew full well of the earthly life of Ali, and Amil was painfully aware of the existence she presently suffered, strung up among the Spirit Ripper's menagerie of persecution. For this knowledge, the pages that resided at the book's beginning and at its incomplete conclusion were left unread. Instead, he thumbed to the center of the modest volume, where he found, oddly as it may have felt, the end of Ali.

In the years that followed the suicide of her love, Ali withdrew deep within her own lachrymosity, like a flower left to die among the vacant stretch of a barren field. She indulged a pattern of working less and drinking more. In the nascence of her decline, she spent most of her time at home. Alone, she hosted the sullen company of the quiet stillness brought on by the desolation that Amil had left her. But boredom was soon an ingredient found within her cocktails, and as Ali spent less time inside the chill of her own bed, her responsibilities and obligations were cast into the realm of afterthoughts.

Her bills mounted, as jobs were steadily lost and only casually replaced by those which paid progressively less. She shunned the customary behaviors of adulthood, and the tolerance for an individual who struggles with addiction was an ability exhausted by her friends and family alike. Feeling barred from happiness, Ali shut out anyone who had the audacity to offer her help. She was forced to move time and again into apartments of smaller and more squalid description as landlords lost their patience with her disinterest in paying rent. Eventually, she bounced herself out of her comfort zone and drifted away from those who knew her best. The lure of low-income housing dragged Ali away with promises of excess money left over to spend on alcohol.

She moved into a sector of Pittsburgh that proud city dwellers and travel agents hesitate to acknowledge. The neighborhood was a moribund cluster of building that should have been condemned years before. The rows of houses were shanties, patched together with cheap materials and streaked in spray paint. Owing to disrepair, the dwellings became incubators for mold and insect larva. A thin street of cracked asphalt supported her crumbling building, and doubled as the work space for drug peddlers and opportunistic muggers. Her neighbors were comprised of the likes of low-lifes and junkies. Their infectious and virulent diseases permeated the streets and called to the most bereft areas of Ali's soul.

No living creature should be made to pay for hell, for such a place holds no privileges, but that's what Ali had done. Her apartment was a ragged efficiency, which held rooms of yellowed walls and stained carpets. A shower ravaged by mildew crouched down a narrow hall, and a toilet that rattled the pipes with every flush sat above cracked tile. Her cell, as it were, functioned with the same purpose as a hole carved into the ground. It was a space to hide, and to pass out from the battery of chemicals.

She hadn't lived there for long, but quickly, this cavity became polluted with empty bottles, cigarette butts, and the occasional jug of mouthwash, a product only employed when the alcohol ran out. In keeping with the traditions of the sick, Ali routinely failed to pay the meager cost required to keep her from the ranks of the homeless. This dilemma was soon resolved by Ali's realization that her landlord, a disgusting polyp upon the orifice of humanity, was wont to overlook her lack of funds in exchange for a blow job.

She attracted the attention of those who had deserted the possibility of salvation long ago. She made friends with people that most would consider enemies, and it wasn't long before Ali reawakened her fondness for drugs. At times, she had sex out of boredom, especially when her TV misbehaved, but with greater regularity, Ali offered what was left of her body to those who could keep her intoxicated.

Over a period of rank summer months that were colored blacker than any tribulation of her sordid youth, Ali dispatched all shreds of her former self in a cycle of fucking, drugging, and misery. The smell of vomit swam through her teeth, and the trails left behind by tears were coursed over so often that to hide their paths was impossible. She had hit the bottom, but rather than rise and look up from the depths of the abyss that she had dug with Amil's shovel, Ali simply laid there.

She had not planned to end her life. No note was written, and Ali didn't weigh the consequences of what may come of her actions. But even in her bleary state of perpetual inebriation, she knew that what had been done carried the power to be the catalyst for the end of her anguish. Partially unaware of their contents, Ali washed back a plethora of pills with as much alcohol as she could possibly suck down before the invincible hammers of sleep beat her unconscious.

Ali had wanted to die, yet she feared it. She feared the grip of death so stridently that, as she thought of Amil, Ali couldn't fathom the determination required to see such an act through. But as she lay on the floor, nearly naked, and bruised from a lack of nutrients, she felt like the end was already with her. In pain brought about by self-abuse and sickness, she rolled onto her side, and the booze in her otherwise empty stomach sloshed with her lethargic action. Grime and small bits of trash from the floor stuck to the skin of her back as the humid day cooked her apartment. As she sensed the life as it spilled from her, Ali extended a thin arm out away from her, and left it to hover in the air. Mere inches above the carpet that her unfocused eyes could no longer see, Ali keep her arm suspended for as long as she could, and pretended that she was no longer alone. Before death took her, and long before a hot week of undiscovered decomposition ate at her body, she thought of Amil. In death, she stole a small comfort in her final minutes as she pictured him beside her.

With a slam of the book, Amil screamed. It was a scream of distilled madness. A scream only the truly haunted can make, and, although the pain which caused it would never recede, the only thing left for Amil to do was to wail.

In the end, Ali had thought only of Amil. The gravity of her devotion had pulverized Amil, until all that remained was the stain of his former selfishness, and the smear of shame that he had become. No matter his state, all she had ever needed was him. Amil finally realized that by taking his own life, he had not freed Ali, as was his intention. He had damned her. Amil enwrapped her in a curse as mighty as any that he had witnessed within Aphelianna's house. There was no one left to blame, for it was his own hand that had bound Ali as a plaything for what remained of Saint Calvino.

Amil passed through the main hall of the great library, and was bitten by unease as he began to notice the quiet all around him. The towering rows were vacant of those in search of books. The Draymataya were nowhere to be seen. Even the sounds of their wings as they flapped or the chattering of their teeth was totally absent. The furniture was deserted, the tables unoccupied, and all remnants of former activity had gone away. There were no books left out, the desks held no cups or warm lanterns. It was as though the massive room had been scrubbed clean, meticulously organized, and then hastily abandoned.

Amil came to face a wall as it drew near. He followed the intricate patterns on the surface as they swam blackly up toward the cool touch of the copper ceiling. He felt like a speck. Like a drop of the ink once used to decorate the crimson wall. Only then, the ink was all dry, and to locate a single drop was impossible, for they all had blended together and became one. That's how Amil felt, like the most insignificant splash of the darkest color. He was another inconsequential soul, corrupted, and lost among the great tapestry of Aphelianna's masterful annihilation.

"It's time for you to go," suggested a voice that Amil knew as the nameless librarian.

"Yes it is," answered Amil. "Where did everyone go?"

"This is no business of theirs. This was your path to find, and the choice to continue on is yours alone to make."

Amil turned slowly, the way the moon does as it shies away from the earth in apogee. There before him was the image of a Waste. It was ugly, and bathed in a putrid stench. Boils irritated its already ruined skin, and the bones of its feet poked through the singed flesh as though crying out for escape. The mid-section was horribly thin, and as

Amil watched, the ghosts of internal organs churned in failure as the beast scratched scabs from its neck with the bloodied stumps of its gnarled fingers.

"Why a Waste?" asked Amil, bitterly.

"I am you, as you will be, if you are to fail."

Amil almost collapsed. He became instantly dizzy and his gut restlessly bubbled, as though a rash bout of influenza suddenly sprang to life within him.

"Why are you doing this?" questioned Amil, as he looked away in nausea.

"To test you," said the Waste. It produced a book and delicately set it on the table next to him.

It didn't look all that spectacular. Its binding was ordinary, and although the print on the cover was cryptic, it didn't appear fantastic. It was quite plain, and were it not for the rusted metal clamps that banded the book shut, he would never have given its appearance further consideration. But as it lay there in stillness, Amil knew it called to him. Like the last of the sirens, it cried out. It desperately pined for him every bit as much as he had longed for its contents. He listened to its silent voice, and as Amil gazed deep into the dark recesses of the locks, he knew that he stood before the last door to Isadora.

"I want to go on. It's all I have left," Amil said resolutely, as he drew his key.

"Even if it means this?"

"I don't care anymore. I have greater desire just to see Ali smile one more time than I have fear of becoming a Waste. I just want this over with," he admitted.

Amil slid his key into the first slot and turned the lock. With a squeal, it released the thin band from its teeth and left it to dangle in the air, finally sprung from the bondage it had long suffered. His hand nervously passed over the dark line left behind from the clamp, and as his fingers drifted over the faded cover, Amil guided his key into the second lock. He snapped it open, but before moving on to the third of the five restraints, Amil froze with trepidation, as he couldn't recall how many twists his cracked key still possessed.

"She will be guarded. You know that, don't you?" asked the steady Waste during Amil's prolonged hesitation.

He felt endlessly foolish, but the possibility that Isadora would be protected was something that Amil had simply not considered. How could he have been so ignorant? How could he have been so absolutely vacuous to think that Isadora would be left alone, to the whims of the one who would eventually find her?

Amil sunk his key into the cavity of the third lock, but this was an action that only served to rest his hand. His mind had been halted, and, as Amil wandered around inside himself, it was going to require a prolonged stay at the dark intersection of consequence and introspection before he found the will to move forward.

"By what?" Amil asked, finally, as his eyes shook in their sockets as they peered into the locks.

"Krykus, the God of Battle."

"What can I do?"

"I'm not sure. But as I understand it, Krykus avoided being touched by Aphelianna and her curses. It was Isadora herself that enslaved the god. You see, Isadora was never pleased with Krykus, as he destroyed life. He indiscriminately ruined that which she had given life, and although Isadora stood in stark opposition to her sister, Isadora always respected Aphelianna. She understood the duty of her sister, and she felt a bond with her that ran much deeper than blood. But Krykus, on the other hand, was truly despised by both sisters."

"Both of them?" asked Amil, a bit perplexed.

"Yes. I assume that you view Aphelianna as evil, and perhaps now, you are correct. But in times past, Krykus was the one and only god who was purely evil. He took from Isadora and laid the bodies of innocents at the feet of her sister. Maybe that's why Aphelianna left him alone, almost as though she knew that her sister would have the final say in the fate of Krykus."

"What did she do to him?" questioned Amil, as he felt fearful of Isadora for the first time.

"Before Isadora succumbed to her curse of eternal sleep, she imprisoned Krykus in the room with her. He can only escape if the book is opened, so if you decide to proceed, you must do so quickly. But to his curse, it was quite simple. It has been just her and he since the curses took hold. Krykus has spent an eternity with his lust for blood unfulfilled, and, though he did not agree to guard her, I imagine that the first soul to enter into Isadora's chamber will have to contend with his insatiable desire for combat. I tremble to think of how enraged he has become after all this time. A true madman he must now be," explained the rotting Waste.

Amil absorbed the chilling tale, and in the end, it mattered not. During his quest, he had been afraid for so long that to instill a deeper fear within him was near impossible. As his fingers shook and his grip tightened like a vice as it is forced shut, Amil broke the locks of the remaining three bands.

"Do you think she'll forgive me?" asked Amil, with

his head down and his hand upon the cover.

"She? You mean Ali?"

Amil nodded in silence.

"You should sincerely hope that she never recovers her memories. But I can assure you of this, if you are the one who frees Ali from the Spirit Ripper and takes her away from that cursed orchard, she will love you forever."

Amil unfolded the book to page one and the bindings creaked like old bones as they are forced to move after ages of motionlessness. Up from the pages sprang an ephemeral door. It was built of nothing more substantial than vapors of a vibrant coloring, and, true to the nature of such fluids, the door shifted with the soft tumbling of the air within the library. It emanated warmth, and, as the differing hues bled a new complexion onto Amil's face, he was overcome, as he stood upon the threshold to God.

"Hurry! Go through, or close the book!" commanded the librarian.

Amil said nothing in return, but he wrapped his fingers around the spectral knob all the same. As it shifted inside his palm like putty that refuses to set, the object barely spoke to Amil's sense of touch. He placed his fingers upon the surface of the door, and though they sunk partway through the outer skin, the door cracked open. A sliver of light cut its way out, and as the ray widened with the swing of the door, the illumination enveloped and absorbed him, until no reminder of Amil Young remained in the library.

Chapter 4 - Revelations

The door evaporated as it eased shut. But a feeling of being trapped was not created by the barrier's dissipation, nor was any other sensation of dread or anxiety. Amil thought of Krykus, but he declined to fear him or the harm that he might have brought, for in the company of God, there is no room for fright. He undoubtedly stood in the chamber of Isadora, and though he could not see her, Amil knew she was there. It was an intangible enlightenment he felt, as if every piece of the universe were as familiar to him as his own thoughts. He experienced a great euphoria, not a high caused by chemicals, but rather, he was elevated in all respects as he shared space with the creator.

The advancement of life was Isadora's charge, and, here in this room, untouched by the icy fingers of her sister, Isadora had triumphed. The ground below was lush with moss that grew thick and prismatic in its appearance. Small pools dotted the land, and within their blue and watery embraces, plants of a fantastic description were held. Healthy stalks of green supported wide leaves, and as they unfurled themselves from the bosom of the water, flowers did emerge. They came in explosions of color, and like silent fireworks, they offered their beauty to the air. Some were comprised of thin petals, while others took the shape of a cone. Many of the flowers spread themselves wide, like a cocoon which longs to nourish, and more still towered high into the sky, wishing, it seemed, to kiss the stars. Color was a vision that nearly overwhelmed Amil, and as he glanced upon flowers that he could see through, he knew better than to assume that they were simply transparent. They were instead colored by hues that his eyes were not divine enough to observe.

Ivy and ground cover swam among the ocean of flora as it gave abundant birth to the rise of vines. Up from that rolling sea of nature, large vines crawled into the branches of the trees, but their presence therein was pure. They stole nothing of substance from the trees. In elaborate coils, the vines became the home of fresh shoots, which produced an assortment of velvety treasures. Far above him, on these ropes of creation, fruit dangled in the gentle breeze, and Amil watched as the blossoms opened up to drink of the misty air.

The trees, the pillars of this towering masterwork of life, were like gods themselves. They were thick at their trunks, and grew knotted and bumpy, but not from disease or old age, but rather, from all the life held within their wooden skins. With sleek bark that was shaded with every variant of cream, the giants explored the upper reaches of the atmosphere with complex networks of branches. Draped in vines and flush with leaves whose veins sparkled with an iridescence of a slow-moving magnificence, the trees nearly obscured the beautiful paradox above.

As he looked to the sky, Amil witnessed a cooperation of opposite forces. Typically segregated by the commands of time, he saw the darkness and the daylight, bright brilliance and conquering black. The sky was blue, like the ocean at dusk, and decorated by stars. Planets, entire solar systems, were clearly definable, as was the orange sun as it blazed above the natural stitching of the forest. Its wavering light bled through the trees and sent rays of amber into the pools far below. As Amil followed the lines of the sun's extension, he also traced the curve of planetary rings as they wound themselves around their masters like celestial blankets.

The air around him was fragrant and adorned with sound. He could not see the creatures which produced the pleasant melody of chirps and peeps, as they played soundtrack to his step, but Amil was fully content to allow their divinity to remain in the realm of imagination. The air itself was thick, not humid or full of allergens, but bountiful in its concentration of vaporous riches. It felt wonderful in his lungs, almost as though he truly lived again, and the mist which fell upon him returned a forgotten feeling of moisture to his skin.

As he continued to weave through this arrangement of vitality, Amil never gave a thought as to when he might find Isadora. He no longer cared. Not from complacency or heartlessness. He simply wasn't permitted to feel things which caused him distress or alarm. He had been refreshed in the breath of calm, and though he still clearly knew his task, he could sense no urgency or pain. Among the translucent haze of starlight and fog, as it rose from the water-rich soil below, Amil was content to endlessly wander. For if this was a curse, forever he be damned.

Amil came upon a small lake that was enveloped by a hedgerow. This living border was swollen with young growth, and appeared to be frosted in a layer of pollen. The powdery substance shimmered with the same brilliance as the leaves above and delicately moved as one being. All around the tops of the shrubs, the sparkling pollen moved lazily about like a river that cannot decide on a direction of flow. As Amil neared, he was fascinated by its soft undulations, but what truly enraptured him was the quivering voice that rose up from the powder. Like a spirit as it ascends into heaven, the song drifted up into the bounty of the sky.

It was near silent, but in its quiet, he could feel a praise whose magnitude surely reached into the far corners of the cosmos. Words were not offered from the hymn. The aural treasures were not directed toward Amil. Nor was the collective voice altered for the presence of a common man. They were sung for a greater purpose. Like a million voices in a singular worship, the song was a chorus for the grace of Isadora. Amil allowed the sound to fill his being until it was all he could sense. That divine dusting of life, those infinitesimal specks of the purest creation, they wove through his soul like vapor through a screen, and drew him into the embrace of the lake.

The water was cool and slippery, almost like it had been polished until every trace of impurity was removed. As Amil waded into the pool, the azure mirror rippled away and caused the moonbeams upon its surface to dance with the shifting of the liquid. He stared up and watched as all the color of the magical forest slowly rose away from him, as under the surface he sank. Dragged down by the weight of Aphelianna's key, he drifted deeper into a world of wetted blue. With no desire to swim against the touch of Isadora, Amil invited the fluid into his lungs and welcomed the water and the drowning that its company might bring.

Amil next found himself lying upon a sandy trail that was flanked by reeds that grew tall and nodded with the breeze. He opened his eyes, and, there above him, held within a great ring of rock, was the bottom of the lake. It hung, suspended by nothing at all, and shifted as water is wont to do. As he stared up at the liquid and desired to again feel its touch, the thought occurred to him that perhaps he was much too tainted a creature for the pool to retain. Instead then, it had released him, and onto a new path, he was free to walk.

He rose to his feet and trod down the narrow road. It exited the little cove and proceeded to coil its way through hilly terrain. The slender grasses which ran along the curve of Amil's path all shared complexions of purple, and as he wound the sandy pathway further south, the plants grew taller than he. Walled in by the stalks and guided by them, he sent his eyes skyward again, and reached for the key around his neck. He felt the breeze as it kissed him. He watched as the long grasses were swept aside by the wind like waves. He stood within the center of purity, and as he felt cleansed by the harmony of life, Amil knew it was time to relinquish Aphelianna's gift.

That piece of damned jewelry felt jagged to his fingers, as it had been nearly dissolved by the lick of water. As it sat in his palm, brittle and malformed by wide cracks, he stared down at it and was reminded once again of all it had done to him. There was nothing but pain in that metal object, as it had only unlocked further misery. He thought longingly of Ali, and though he desired to free her now more than ever as he walked the fields of paradise, Amil felt no more need to carry such a pestiferous artifact. He slowly removed the rusted rope from his neck and allowed the key to drop to the soil below. He exhaled all the torments that had long pursued him, and suffered no consequences for his discarding of the key. As he watched the metal crumble to nothing, forever lost among the grains of sand, he felt as relief was finally given back to him.

The clouds above, healthy and thick with the hue of white, began to drop rivulets of water onto the reeds beside

Amil. They were enriched by the liquid's delicate touch, and as they were nourished, the plants opened up and offered plumes of colored light back to the sky. As the reeds gave freely of their only possession to the charitable clouds overhead, Amil found himself encircled by the bands of a rainbow. The warm lights sank themselves into him. Expunged of Aphelianna's wicked stain, he was allowed to feel the supreme generosity of Isadora.

He fell to his knees, overcome by divinity and the sensation of life as it exists beyond the influence of any blemish or sin. Amil felt the caress of beauty, humbled by its touch, and by the mere fact that it had paid him any mind. Though surrounded by the majestic, he did not feel like a god, but rather, he felt *with* God, and as that ephemeral voice of the Everything spoke to him, it asked of Amil only one favor: to leave.

Against the wishes of God, he rose to his feet and resumed his walk down the narrow trail, drawn on by the ultimate curiosity, and by the tease that his journey was near completion. After another blessed collection of blissful minutes, Amil came to the end of the sandy path. He parted a thick growth of the stalks, as they hung before him like a living drapery. The shoots were bent aside by his touch, and as they curved, so, too, did the light which emanated from them. There, beyond that arc of vaporous color, slept the Goddess of Life. Isadora lay before him.

The forest around her was as lush and spectacular as the one that had led Amil to the lake, only here, every inch of the woodland seemed to softly breathe in concert with the rising and falling of Isadora's chest. He stepped respectfully toward her, careful not to disturb a tree root or length of vine as he went along. He could feel everything.

Even the soil beneath his feet seemed a conscious being that commanded great reverence. He was advancing upon the source of creation, and, as Amil looked upon the vegetation that surrounded him, he began to wonder if in fact he was in the presence of the oldest tree, the most ancient grass, and the first mosses to crawl over a rock.

Partially obscured behind this immortal weave of nature, and located undoubtedly within the massive center of this interminable forest, was a bed. Curtains of blue hung from the silver bedposts, but they had been drawn back, as Isadora delighted in the feel of light upon her face as she slept. The sheets were of a deeper blue, adorned by gold stitching, and as they rippled down the stillness of her body, they spilled themselves out over the ground. Strange, but somehow appropriate, the linens turned to water as they touched the forest floor and eternally enriched the sacred life that grew next to the resting place of the great goddess.

A ring of blooms, more full and vibrant than any Amil had previously seen, formed a wide border around Isadora's bed. Their community was thick, nearly as tall as the bed frame itself, and the flowers kissed the mattress with their velvety chromatic lips. A pleasing zephyr blew through the petals, and as the tallest ones brushed the skin of Isadora's arms, he heard as she hummed in contentment.

The gentle sound, the sensation, whatever it was, almost brought Amil to tears. He had witnessed what no human had before experienced, and was humbled by the purity of the being before him.

The divine Isadora lay upon her back with the oceanic sheets stretched up to her chest. She wore a simple gown of honeyed amber, and her milky white hands were folded across her stomach. Curled locks of blonde unfurled themselves over her small shoulders, but much more than ordinary hair grew from her head. Roots swam among her ringlets and ran to the ground. Most were slender, however, some were very thick, and grew in intricately woven patterns as they made for the cool comfort of soil. She appeared to be tethered to the forest by her brown and earthen locks, a mother Medusa of life, as all that she touched grew healthy and beautifully wild. She was the heart of it, The Beginning. Perhaps the whole forest, and all that lived therein, could be referred to as Isadora.

As Amil gazed at the massive network that fell from her head, and all its subtle movements, he looked upon her face for the first time. She looked radiant in her repose, calm, and washed over by peace. Oh, how he longed to stare deep into the eyes of God. Lost below her lids, her eyes were surely a treasure too magnificent for any common and tainted man to view. Respectfully, Amil removed his attention from Isadora's face. Slowly, and with great admiration, he followed a strand of springy hair that caressed the side of her neck. Before his eyes, the prize of his interminable journey awaited.

Upon the tender flesh of her chest was a key. It was a bit large, like Amil's used to be, but where his was a heavy, ugly thing, Isadora's treasure was predictably splendid. It looked to have been carved from soap, or another like substance, and was the color of the sea as it washes up on the shore. Its lower portions were meticulously cut for appeal as much as purpose, while the upper ring saw a rope of flower petals run through it which affixed the key around Isadora's neck. Amil felt as his fingers descended. He wasn't sure if he was yet prepared to steal from the Goddess of Life, he just longed to finally touch the object which had eluded him for eons.

"I can only implore you to stop," a strained voice said.

Amil glanced over toward the source of the words, and there, feet from where Isadora slept, was a frail old man. He sat upon the ground, horribly gray and overtaken by wrinkles, with his back against the trunk of a tree. The closer that Amil looked, the more it became clear that he was in the presence of another cursed deity.

Below the knees, the pathetic twig-like legs of the being simply disappeared. Like sacks of grain torn open, the appendages bled into the soil below and crumbled into the consistency of dirt. The back of this forgotten god had been propped against the mighty tree behind him for so long it appeared that he had become engrafted to it. Just where his flesh ended, and the bark began, was a boundary impossible to discern. As Amil was forced to peer deeper into this stranger's affliction, he made another upsetting discovery. The wrinkles that lined the man's skin were not the paragraphs of old age, but rather, his flesh had started to turn into coverings foreign to the body of man. The bark of a tree was slowly stretching itself over his bones, and shoots were already visible as they pushed out from his fingertips. To Amil, it seemed only a matter of millennia before the defeated being at his feet would be no more recognizable than any of the other wooden giants which stood stoically among the forest of Isadora.

"Krykus?" stammered Amil.

"You have heard of me?" he groaned. "I suppose I am not the fearsome beast you must have envisioned."

"How long have you been here?" Amil asked wearily, as he gazed upon the sleeping Isadora and a supposed immortal who looked to be teetering upon the brink of death.

"It is incalculable," said Krykus, as he stared into the trees beyond as though he felt a much stronger kinship with them than with anything else.

"Do you know what her key will unlock?"

"Physically? No, I do not," he answered quietly, with elegance usually absent from the voices of warrior gods. "But I do know that it should forever remain with Isadora."

"Why?" asked Amil. "You don't know what it does any more than I do. I've come this far, maybe it's mine to have. Maybe Aphelianna finally deserves to sleep."

"Aphelianna, the Goddess of Death," Krykus whispered. "That key, she should never hold."

"So she cursed you after all, and you're bitter. Oh, the torments you must have suffered," said Amil sarcastically.

"It is not Aphelianna who is responsible for my...transformation. More than just ensnare me, it is she who cursed me so," he explained, as he raised a finger toward Isadora. "Do not confuse creation with purity. Isadora may not be evil, but she is also not pure. Wickedness is the nature of man, and now where do you suppose your kind came to inherit that trait?"

"Krykus, I'm gonna take that key," Amil said, softly.

"Very well. But may I relay something to you first?"

"Go ahead, try to discourage me," said Amil, with patience in his voice.

"On no, not a plea, just a tale."

"Okay then, let's hear it." Amil was torn. Every

fiber of his being wanted to grab the key and dart away. After all, Krykus could be setting a trap, but curiosity forced him to hesitate. He had to know of Isadora. He had to know of himself. He had to know of the forbidden.

"In a time so very ancient, when I was young, virile, and strong, Isadora lured me here. I followed her charms, as she knew I would, and on the day that her sister cursed her with eternal sleep, I was forever trapped in this massive garden. With no means to escape and no ability to rouse Isadora, I became her unwilling guard. This was my land to endlessly wander in the hope that I might one day find something to slaughter in order to alleviate the boredom. And so I stalked these woods like a true monster, in search of you, the challenger of fate, but you never came.

"Then I grew tired. It was a day much like this that I sat upon the ground and leaned against this very tree for rest. And then I slept, and in my dreams, I, a god myself, was subject to the true magnificence of divinity. When I awoke, I had become a part of the tree, and one day I will become a part of this forest, and eventually, a part of eternity.

"Over the arduous course of broken time, my vitality has been drained, my essence sucked away. It is almost as though Isadora employed this forest as a means to purge all the evil from me, and I suppose it has worked. You may see a dehydrated skin of a life since evaporated, but what I have lost in physicality I have gained a thousand fold in knowledge.

"You see, after my anger receded and my desire to escape was exhausted, a great epiphany was mine to hold as the richest treasure of all. In time, once I am fully absorbed into this forest, I will also be absorbed into Isadora. You cannot flee here without her key. I'm sure you have gathered that by now, but consider the choice simply to stay. It will take aeons for your own absorption, but the serenity that you felt when you first arrived into this garden will accompany your every breath between this and that final moment. To be absorbed into God, now, that wouldn't be so bad, would it? This is how you escape Aphelianna's curses, Amil. This is how you cheat death."

"What about Ali?" Amil asked, skeptical of the heavenly promise offered from Krykus, and shaken as the god called him by name.

"She will be with you. She is waiting now. Isadora can give to you all that you need."

"You're a liar! And so is she!" shouted Amil as he glared at the sleeping goddess. "Ali is waiting for me...in a fucking orchard of torture. She's being eaten by crows, molested by some...diseased relation of yours!"

"Amil, please..."

"She's scared, Krykus. She's lost," he said with resolve. "When I looked into her eyes, I saw more fear than I have ever experienced in all my time in this horrible place. I saw where she is. I know where she is, and I'm going to use that key to free her."

"Amil, if you will permit me to speak once more, I have one more thing to tell you. I promise, if you still wish to take Isadora's key, I will not interfere further."

Amil said nothing in return. Instead, he turned toward Isadora and slipped his fingers under her key. He felt the warmth of her skin, and, as his hand closed tightly around the object, he could feel Isadora's heart as it fluttered.

"Would you like to know the origins of man?"

340

asked Krykus, boldly.

Amil closed his eyes. All he had to do was pull, just a jerk of his arm, and his obligation to Aphelianna would be fulfilled. It was an action he could not take. Frozen like a moth that stares into a bright burning light. He allowed the key to rest once more, and turned back to Krykus, impatient to hear the ultimate explanation.

"I can feel as she feels. I hear her thoughts as clearly as I hear your voice," said Krykus.

It was painfully clear that the affliction that fused Krykus to the tree had also set to work on his insides. His tongue was dry and split, like the wood that it was soon to be, and his throat was thick with sap. His voice was already labored from his previous speech, and as he squinted with greater regularity, Amil knew of how difficult it was becoming for the fallen god to form words. But for as uncomfortable as he was in his deformed immobility, Krykus kept steady, and took extreme care in respectfully lamenting Isadora's condition.

"Trapped under the weight of sleep, Isadora grew lonely, so desperately lonely. The pain she suffered in absolute silence was maddening. It was a sorrow mightier than the sum of all my former misdeeds. You see, Isadora is the Goddess of life, and, punished by her sister's curse, she could not participate in living."

"More riddles. I'm so tired of your explanations," said Amil.

"Please be patient," Krykus pleaded. "With the Mortals gone, she was left all alone, hollowed out and emptied by the death of all of her children. But, in her saddened unconsciousness...she dreams of them," he said, as he raised his ringed eyes to Amil.

Amil froze and he shook. His eyes watered, and what remained of his heart was savaged by the jagged clarity offered from the feeble god.

"To suppress her loneliness, her mind found a way to cope, and so Isadora created the earth and those upon it," continued Krykus.

"The world is a dream," whispered Amil as he fell to his knees among Isadora's flowers. "The world is a dream."

"It was her invincible will, her absolute love for life that brought your kind into being. To be just a dream of Isadora's is an honor."

"None of it was real, was it?" questioned Amil, as he leaned his head back against the mattress behind him.

"Was it real to you?" challenged Krykus.

"What I feel, what I felt, that doesn't matter, does it? My family, my friends...Ali," he said, in disbelief. "Did they even exist?"

"No, and neither did you, until the day came when Aphelianna plucked you from the earth. I'm sorry. I cannot even fathom how difficult this must be."

"But...but I remember them," said Amil.

"You were all imaginary players that shared the same stage. Memories of things that never happened overlap, and in what you understand as death, you were given life. But in this life, you retained the memories formed while only a figment of Isadora's unconscious. It is truly a testament to her majesty."

"So...I never actually met Ali? We never...we never..."

"You never did a thing, Amil," said Krykus. "Your body is just a shell, a lookalike of someone who lived a life

342

of fiction. Those you knew, those you recognize, they are but shadows. Devices your mind conjured up in order to somehow integrate itself into Isadora's dreams. Do you see why the pursuit of her key is purposeless? I know it must hurt, but be sure: Ali never existed. She was just a fancy of Isadora's imagination placed beside you in her dreams. So you see there is no need to try and free her from whatever torture she suffers. The woman you seek to save is an artist's rendering of a character from make believe."

"Then what am I now?" demanded Amil.

"When you arrived in the afterlife, you were born. Arriving into the physical world of Isadora gave you life, a real life. Isadora is that powerful, and it is with that power that she keeps us all safe from Aphelianna. In sleep, she has created humans to save the world from her sister's treachery. You should be proud of your race, however transitory you may be, for you are true saviors. If you value the miracle of life, you will leave Isadora be," said Krykus.

"Do you consider a Waste a miracle?" asked Amil.

"They are the influence of Aphelianna over her sister's miracle."

"I don't see any miracle in this, and I don't think I can value this life. I value my old life, even if it was all a lie. I love Ali, the Ali I remember, and I will keep the promise that I know I made to her," said Amil, as he rose to his feet.

"Think of your actions, think of Ali if you like. What you are about to do will eclipse even the most selfish of acts perpetrated by Aphelianna. Would the woman you desire to save wish for you to do such a thing? Keep your fond memories of Ali. Cherish the fact that all your bad days never occurred, and leave Isadora her key," Krykus

343

pleaded.

"Krykus, what will happen if I take the key?"

"You have won, Amil. You know the secret of life, you can stay here forever with Isadora, and you will never again have to fear Aphelianna."

"Answer me! What will happen?"

"Isadora will awaken, and the dream will end," said Krykus.

"I don't believe you."

"It is not for you to believe. It is truth. I grow so weary..."

Before she was subdued, Isadora had thought of everything. She took every measure to preserve the life that she had created, and had set the ultimate trap for the one enlisted by Aphelianna who would eventually gaze upon her key. If the promise of eternity with God wasn't enough to halt the advances of someone like Amil, then the revelation that all of creation depended on the perpetual slumber of the goddess surely would.

Amil was free to do as he pleased. There were no Wastes to destroy him. Krykus was powerless, and there were no more locked doors that stood in his way, but still, he remained motionless. He could not accept what he had heard. He could also not live with the consequences of waking Isadora, were the tale offered from Krykus proven to be real. But what Amil could no longer bear was the image of Ali as she suffered. He once told Aphelianna that he would do anything to save Ali, and, as everything proved the price of his triumph, Amil knew that he had to make good on his foolish promise.

With a sudden motion, an apocalyptic reflex, he tore the key from Isadora's neck. He jumped back as a trail of

flower petals were tossed asunder in his wake, and heard as
a heavy sigh left the lips of Krykus. Isadora remained still
for a moment, and Amil prayed for her continued stillness
as he looked on from a pose born of tense muscles and rigid
bones. But then it came, a sight that his eyes could not
ignore or pass off as a trick of the mind. Isadora stirred.

It began as a tremor, a rustling in sleep, a harbinger
of the awakening to come. Isadora rolled onto her side, and
her face twisted with the telltale signs of the tears which
would soon emerge to wet her face. She curled into a ball,
as though a deep pain sank pins into her stomach, and a
distressed wail cracked its way out of her throat. The roots
that cascaded off her head were pulled taut as she squirmed,
and, one by one, their fibers began to snap. The thinnest
tethers went first, and, as they were severed, they uncoiled
themselves over the ground like worms put under the
sudden assault of a virulent toxin. Small fissures surfaced
over the skin of Isadora, and the more she writhed, the
longer each of the splits became.

"What's happening? What's happening to her?"
shouted Amil, in a panic.

"She is dying, and so am I," stated Krykus.

"What? Why? How can this be?"

"It is a broken heart that will end her, as you have
taken the lives of her dream children," he whispered.

Isadora shot upright in the bed, and the cracks over
her skin widened like sinister eyes. Out from the wounds
light did radiate, and, as the tears opened further, beams of
white brilliance poured from Isadora. As luminous bands of
energy escaped from her, the goddess finally opened her
eyes.

The dream was over. All that Isadora had created

345

and nurtured, while asleep, for eons, had been undone with the ascendency of her eyelids. Her magical dreamland world was torn asunder by chaos, shattered into slivers of life unmade. Unspeakable rage and violence smashed the wonders conjured up from her imagination, and ushered the end unto all that she had bore. Interminable seconds of cataclysm erased every trace and reminder of the earth. A sweeping black ate the world away in a rampage of stillness that knew no sound. All was eclipsed, extinct, and final, as all that humanity had ever known was blinked from existence.

Isadora screamed and she shook. Her beautiful ocean blue eyes, rimmed with a green penumbra, were wide with fear. The roots had dropped from her head, and as she continued to convulse and shout, she ran her shaking hands through her hair. The feel of the severed roots called water into her eyes. With clumps of hair knotted around her fingers, Isadora lowered her arms and stared into her hands. They, too, were cut deep, and as she stared into the light that bled from her palms, a terrifying realization was Isadora's to accept. She was actually going to die. After an eternity of existence, death was coming for her.

The streams of white shot from her like machine gun fire, until the whole of her body was wreathed in the purged magnificence that had been contained within for so long. Isadora was, at last, enfeebled. The highest action left to her was merely to sit helpless and stare into her palms as disbelief and tears continued to smear across her face. Once her mouth seemed to have depleted its supply of screams, Isadora steadied her erupting body, and raised her eyes over the horizon of her fingertips. They told of the fear and of the loss that gripped her. They trembled in their sockets, and for a moment, her eyes found Amil's stare. As he watched her lips quiver, and tried in vain to hide from her accusatory and sorrowful glare, Amil witnessed the death of God.

A blast of energy, more powerful than the collapsing of the Sun, was the death rattle of the ancient divinity. It conquered everything in a searing white blaze, sweeping out over the ground and rising into the vastness of the sky on a tower of flame. The wash of luminescence rolled upon all that it could reach, and took apart the tiniest of atoms as its purifying onslaught inexhaustibly raged. Its terminal glory filled the whole of existence, and then forcefully blew it away, with all the fury of a thousand heavens betrayed.

Far away, down upon the stone bench of her fountain, Aphelianna knew that Amil had done the impossible. Her gaze left the fields beyond and all the dead thereupon. Her vacant eyes passed over the rancid swamp of her spring as it roiled with every description of sickness, and they flew over the rot of Saint Calvino's grove. Upon the weathered face of the house she once called home was where Aphelianna stared. She looked into it, through it, and her lips quivered with emotion as a menagerie of feelings were reawakened and set loose within her. Like a child who views the return of a pet once lost, she was overcome by forgotten passions. She was shaken by the irrefutable death of her sister, and by the ability to finally return home. But, like the monster that she had become, Aphelianna's mind was soon overrun by what now stood at her command. She rose, the collective of existence cowered, and Aphelianna walked toward the mansion.

Amil awoke, or, perhaps, he merely remained. He

could be sure of nothing, as no sense was to be trusted. The extinction of Isadora, which had seemed to annihilate everything that it had touched, had spared him. His continued presence suggested that the key that lay strangled in his palm had served as a relic of omnipotent protection. But as he looked out upon the ruin that had been left behind, all he could feel was the need to flee the scorched garden.

It haunted him. The fact revealed that he had once viewed the future. This razed land, tinted to a red ambiance and warmed by the furious eradication of the previous minutes, was a place that he had already been. Before he ventured into The End of Time, Amil had set foot upon this ashen wasteland. Among the charred flakes of things once majestic, as they blew through the air, this image of a time prophesied paralyzed his mind. He felt as though he were frozen into the background of this woeful setting. Condemned to forever bear witness to the destruction he had wrought. Soon, however, a more terrifying blend of imaginings came to Amil's consciousness. He became stricken by chills, sensations that stung so cold, they felt powerful enough to shatter bone. He was made to ponder the realization that perhaps he had witnessed other futures as well. What else had he seen? What else did he fail to see as a promise, a warning, of things to be?

Exhausted from twisting in the net of riddles that was The House of the Divine, Amil pulled himself from the ground, and stood before a door. It was the last barrier, the final gateway to extinction. It was unlocked and plain. It appeared new, and though he had not seen it materialize, nor did he know of what awaited on the other side, Amil knew the passageway had just come into being. It was the next step for him, and for everything else that remained. It was the true unknown, the ultimate conclusion, and into its mercurial embrace Amil did offer himself.

He emerged into a place familiar, The Hall of Worship. Out from one of the doors guarded by the massive statues, Amil walked onto the soft cushion of the scarlet carpet. The crystalline fixture overhead radiated with the glow of moonlight as it reflects off of snow, and among the pale blue aura, Amil wandered. His vision was drawn to the massive dining table. It looked as brilliant as he remembered, with its bejeweled wood and silver accents. The stone slab that topped it held a high polish, and looked to be as deep and mysterious as the ocean in repose. But one feature had changed. A lone guest was seated at the far end of the table, and through the dark, the silhouette of Aphelianna was unmistakable.

"You have something for me," she said, softly.

"Where is Ali?" he meekly asked.

"Where you left her."

"But...you promised me," said Amil, as he could not find the will to challenge Aphelianna.

"I promised to secure her release, and I have honored my promise."

Aphelianna rose from the table, and from her lap tumbled the deformed and bloodied head of Saint Calvino. Finally free to do as she pleased, Aphelianna had silenced the Spirit Ripper. The monstrous head had been severed in a manner terribly violent, and overly involved, as evidenced by its grotesque condition. As the pasty orb rolled out into the light, Amil saw the abject horror that was burned into Calvino's lone, bloodshot eye. It forever relayed the agony of his final moments. As his gaze swept over the jagged flesh of the Spirit Ripper's neck, he saw the ghostly imprints of teeth marks. It was a wretched truth. Aphelianna had chewed off the head of a man she once loved, but it was understandable in its perversity. For her, it had to be personal, the undoing of Saint Calvino. He once had stolen from her, and for his lecherous violations, she had, at last, taken everything from him.

"Give me the key, or I shall take it from you," Aphelianna said as she stepped away from the table, the blood of Calvino still visible on her lips and where it had sunk between her teeth to rest along her gum line.

Flatfooted, she appeared quite tall, more intimidating and powerful than before. Her dress shifted around the motion of her body, and, as it did, the cloth resembled an entanglement of specters as they squirm in unease. Her white locks swam over her shoulders as she approached, and once she stood before Amil, Aphelianna placed a hand upon his cheek. The arctic kiss of her skin, and the poisoned tips of her nails, sent a terrible sensation through Amil, and forced him onto his knees. Bowed before her like a feckless servant, he felt the failure of the bones and muscles in his legs. His vision began to blur and his hearing dulled. He felt as a hole opened itself up inside his mouth, and he was rendered powerless to resist whatever atrocities the Goddess of Death had in mind.

"Will you give me the key?" she asked as Amil knelt before her with all the physical disabilities of his earthly life returned to him.

"Ye...ye...yes," he strained out, while offering up Isadora's treasure.

She took the key tenderly, and Aphelianna kissed Amil's forehead. Her gesture impressed upon him a heavy measure of pain, as the cracks upon her lips felt like shards of glass sunk into his flesh. But he knew something more than blind virulence was offered through her action. Under the punishment of her kiss, kindness and appreciation was felt.

She walked quietly to the stage that floated at the end of the crimson lagoon, and washed her empty eyes over the throne before her. She hesitated to assume the seat reserved for the god of gods, almost as though she couldn't believe it was hers to take. Almost as though she feared the conclusion of the fantasy she had long harbored. But like Amil before her, Aphelianna had not come this far to turn away. Everything be the cost, everything be damned, everything be cursed. Aphelianna sat upon the throne.

She had done the forbidden. Every god that had before passed through The Hall of Worship knew never to sit upon the throne. All knew the unraveling that would follow. Even the arrogant Krykus dared not to take that seat for his own. It offered a power too strong for any to control. It stood empty, like a warning of the future to come if any were to seize it for their own. It was a lone seat, one that should have remained vacant for all time as the ultimate testament to symbiosis, and Aphelianna had broken the eternal circle. She had upset the balance of order, and surely even the most benevolent of spirits would eventually lead all into ruin with the feral supremacy unfurled before the wicked Aphelianna.

Amil watched as the Goddess of Death eased herself into the chair. She allowed her slim body to be hugged by the fabric and draped her arms along the rests, leaving her long fingers to dangle over the sides. She learned her head back and closed her eyes, as some perverse relative of

351

serenity snuggled up to her. She seemed to beg for sleep, as a thick collection of hair swept over the side of her face, and, eerie as it felt, all then fell into silence. It was an absence of sound that Amil did not realize as being possible. Everything was not simply muted to his ears, but even the vibrations caused by his heart as it hammered or his lungs as they heaved were sensations that went unfelt. Aphelianna had asked for a moment of total calm, and so all the world did comply, but when her lids ascended to reveal the empty sockets below, a din of evil praise did erupt.

The porcelain statues, those towering parishioners who for all time had stared silently down upon the hall below, awakened. Like milk swirled within a bowl, the white stone of the figures moved with perfect fluidity as the worshipers offered their outstretched arms to the arch of the ceiling above. The stained glass panes affixed to the curve of the ceiling, darkened further by the gloom of the sky as it bled through, were nearly touched by the fingertips of the congregation. Pushed to the limits of their constitution, the glass shapes shook in their frames with the collective boom produced from the voices.

Like a chorus to proclaim the arrival of hell as it returns from the fields of bloody conquest, the voices sang as one. The male members of Aphelianna's new church fed the massive volume, and were responsible for the vibrations that threatened to drive cracks through the mortar of the foundation. But it was the haunting soprano harmony of the women that articulated the finer points of the menace unleashed. Like velvety poison as it courses through veins which beg for a rapturous death, the higher pitched arrangements of this cursed movement filled the chamber with a siren voice that called forth the nature of all things corrupted.

Aphelianna rose from her seat and slowly walked from the stage. She basked in the spectacular aural adulation that was showered down upon her as she seemed to float over the bloody complexion of the carpet. Her arms remained outstretched as she drifted toward Amil, almost as though she absorbed some unseen sorcery from the song being given to her.

Once she stood over Amil, he was given no option but to remain still. Crippled by the limitations of his body and exhausted by what he had done, he cowered in defeat. She peered down upon him, and, as her absent stare burned its way onto his flesh, he found the strength required to squirm. He wanted to flee, to forever leave the sight of Aphelianna, but, like a broken puppy, all he could muster was the ability to inch his body backward by means of his damaged legs.

Aphelianna knelt down beside him, her locks tumbling down her breasts like rain clouds as they obscure snow-whitened hills. The icy fingers of her left hand crawled over his, and they tightened themselves around his flaccid grip like slender constrictors. He looked upon her face and into her empty sockets. Like mysterious rivers as they hide themselves under the weight of fog, the pale green eyes of Aphelianna came into view. To her parted lips his eyes did fall, and, in an instant, the congregation cooled their song to a respectful and beautiful whisper, as their Goddess desired to speak.

"I will not hurt you," she delicately said to him. "But I will ask one more favor of you. Just lie still and accept my hand, painful as its touch may be. I cannot bear

353

to be alone for this. I've always been alone," she whispered.

Aphelianna exposed the key she held, and after a moment set aside to gaze upon it and all the memories which it held, she crashed her sister's treasure into the floor. The soft material broke apart and scattered around her in chunks. From their division, the true nature of Isadora's key was revealed. Below the broken stone encasement, a blade was held. Unlike the menacing example of bestial craft which Aphelianna employed to cut the dead free from the earth, Isadora's little dagger was nearly as beautiful as she had once been. The handle was ivory white, and had been shaped into an exaggerated curve, while the blade sat upon an oval bolster of water. This tiny pool was held in place by nothing tangible, yet it retained its form, and from that glittering well did the blade extend. It was translucent, like crystal, and shimmered as does the sun when it dips into the sea at evening. She twisted it around in her hand a few turns, and allowed small tears to crawl from her eyes as she gazed into its glory.

"This blade," she began, in a voice choked by sorrow. "Was what my sister once used to carve out the first forms of Mortal life. It *is* Creation. And now I can sleep," she whispered.

With the speed and fury of lightning, Aphelianna stabbed that little blade into the side of her neck. Her eyes bulged at its penetration, and, as she pulled it down through her skin, pain deformed the sides of her mouth. Tremors shook her as she sliced, and by the time that she had reached the top of her collarbone, her hand was forced away from the hilt by shudders. Awash in blood, the dagger hung from her damaged neck as her voice cracked and her eyes purged centuries of tears. As Aphelianna was forced to sway from disorientation, the dagger slipped from the fresh wound, and disappeared into a coil of smoke before its short fall toward the floor could be completed.

Horribly red with her own blood, Aphelianna pressed her dirtied hand onto Amil's shoulder as she braced herself up. Her chest heaved with the palpitations of the dying, and blood leaked out from between her teeth as desperate breath was sucked into and out of her lungs. Her fingers bit into his flesh as she suffered, and her nails dug pits that would surely never heal. Though she desired the eternal darkness that raced toward her, the body resists death, and so Aphelianna fought the inevitable as she stared down at Amil.

Of all the times he had envisioned what may happen were he to hand over Isadora's key to the Goddess of Death, perhaps the only outcome never anticipated was what unfolded above him. It was strange to him that the blood of Aphelianna was the usual red, and, even more surprising, was that it was warm. It didn't sting his flesh as it fell, and, as she leaned in closer to him as the end neared, her hair actually felt soft as it tumbled down across him.

The closer she sank, the more visible her eyes became, and, for the first time, Amil truly saw Aphelianna for what she was, a child, a sister, a creature perverted by the task bound to her. Through walls of tears, her eyes spoke to him, as her mouth no longer held a voice above that of gurgles, and as she stared into his wide and frightened gaze, he was witness to a power even greater than Death Herself: fear. Aphelianna was afraid, terrified of the blackness to come, and as she bled out atop him and strangled his skin in her grip, Amil knew that Aphelianna didn't want to die alone.

Once he had been thoroughly drenched in the fluid that once coursed through the veins of Aphelianna, Amil was given the full weight of the drained goddess as she passed out over his chest. He heard the last, indecipherable murmurs of her voice, and felt the final convulsions of her body as it surrendered to the assault. He felt her grip unwind from him, and as her chest failed to rise, and all remained still, Amil felt her die.

There was no great catastrophe that followed her passing. There was just a dead woman upon the floor who was striped in the colors of her own ruin. But it was in the smallness, in the silence of her expiration, that the true result of their combined actions was seen. He discovered the abominable nature of what Aphelianna had so long planned, and had at last achieved. She could never go home again. Nothing would ever be as it was. She could never heal anything, and so, she would kill everything. Her will was supreme. Her command was an order that all would one day obey, and into the cavity of death that Aphelianna had cast herself, everything would eventually follow.

The blade that was responsible for the formation of life had been used to murder, and by this paradox, absolute extinction had been won. All that remained was all that would ever be, and once every living speck had died off, once every Waste had expired, and once every god did disappear, the eternal nothingness would prevail. The End of Time had begun.

Under the bluish glow bleeding down from the chandelier, Amil slid himself out from under Aphelianna, and rose laboriously from the slippery floor. Once he had righted himself, and found the strength to assume a rickety stance, Amil looked again to the daughter of Arcanus

Curse

Tyme. She appeared small, feeble even, as she lay with her face pressed into the carpet.

The red weave, which bore the dead weight of Aphelianna, played a trick on his mind. The sensation he felt while in the presence of Isadora, a feeling of boundless life and serenity, had been inverted. The sodden fibers looked to be an extension of the blood that spilled from the expired goddess. The vision that surrounded him was one of supreme death. It was a conquering erasure of life that promised to extend into the furthest reaches of time.

Amil felt this weight, but gravities more immediate descended over him as he viewed the lifeless deity as she lay in the embrace of her forsaken home. Gazing upon her with genuine and common pity, he felt sympathy for Aphelianna. Though she had condemned the remainder of existence to oblivion, Amil knew that it must have felt like the only option left to her as she had spent aeons there herself. As he momentarily forgot her savagery, and partially identified with the epic journey of torture which she had undertaken, his heart broke for her passing.

Once he turned away, his gaze was drawn to the statues, who just moments before were in the praise of the queen of curses. That seemed ages ago, as the sculptures were riddled with cracks, and stained by the touch of bacterial growth and the unforgiving disfigurement of time. Everything was silent again, and, as Aphelianna commenced her descent into rot and decay, Amil knew that it was time to leave. At last, it was time to find Ali.

As Amil walked back through the gallery, he tried not to look upon the portraits and all the extinguished candles which rested below. He could feel the glares as they shot at him from each set of oily eyes of gods dead or soon to be. As he endured this silent gauntlet of accusation, the stigma that Aphelianna was forced to wear for so long was his to carry. He hated it, the revulsion cast his way. As he hobbled down the hallway with divine reproach draped over him, Amil learned to despise Aphelianna anew. He was nothing like her. He wanted to scream it, to explain to every soul that he had served to ruin that he was only trying to save the one being who had truly loved him. It was a selfless and righteous quest. How could it not be? It had to be. Overmatched, as always, by higher forces, he again found fault and failure in his excuses.

It was a miserable condition, a collapsing of the soul that he suffered, as he still felt the bond formed with Aphelianna. Though their journeys had taken different paths and their desires stood worlds apart, it was Amil who had trusted and lent his aid to the Goddess of Death. Each had won victory, a poisoned version of triumph, and completed their monstrous tasks in the pursuit of different ends, but the final result was one in the same. And for his sin, for this ultimate blasphemy, Amil wondered what his punishment would be.

He parted the doors and stepped back outside, and under the grim look of a saddened sky, a sensation of failure settled over Amil. He stood before the great staircase and looked out over the barren land beyond. From his vantage, the orchard of the crucified looked much the same as he remembered, although now, he could spot activity between the trees as those once enslaved began to escape. His eyes scanned past the fountain, which would remain forever dry and bereft of company, and along the twisted road over which all the dead would one day walk.

Confronted with an image that set him upon his

crippled knees, Amil saw the final cost of his greed and Aphelianna's cruelty. The fields beyond were choked with the deceased. In numbers near incalculable, they trampled every square inch of ground and poured across the boundary of the ancient fence. Spread like ants across a summer feast, they moved as though one organism. Led along by the curve of the road, the dead shuffled on in packs and scattered pairs. All lost, all stranded without direction, all of Earth's dead drifted toward the mansion. It came as a flood of melancholy that practically erased the enormity of the land and the horizon beyond.

As Amil looked to the bitter smear of sky in the distance, and then to all the dead that shifted underneath its watch, it was difficult to fathom that one day, nothingness was all that would remain. The multitudes were so many, it seemed possible that the sea of displaced souls would never reveal its end, but, much like the barbaric task that Amil had bested, this, too, was a ruse. It was the explosion before the ash, the chaotic burst of activity that would precede the eventual and unstoppable wind-down of all things. It some ways, this *was* the end, all fleshed and animated by mournful color.

Dusk, the last twilight of mankind, accompanied Amil as he descended closer to the darkened grove. A cool wind, which whistled only emptiness, swept over him. Rain fell about him in indifferent surges, and the droplets crashed into the ground. There was nothing else that followed his step. No stimuli that hinted at life, no reawakening of his memories, no chronicle of remembrances of times both wicked and lovely, nothing. The power of the stones had been silenced. They were returned to ordinary rock, killed off, like everything else, by the infernal rage of Aphelianna.

As Amil felt his feet come in contact with the soft ground of the orchard before him, he stared into the trees. He watched as women struggled to free themselves, and as the crows greedily picked at those soon to be unbound. Some of those who were freed tried to help emancipate those who were still strung, while a few women who Amil glanced made not a motion. They hung there as though nothing had changed, victimized by eternal habits and frozen in place by the fear of the unknown. This inaction then served to suggest that maybe they had simply elected to remain among the branches of their own volition, as the ground below hosted a fresh set of miseries.

In a state of confusion, many of the women wandered aimlessly around the orchard like former patients of an asylum abruptly flung into the unknown. Some of the newly freed ran frantically in all directions and without purpose. Simply away, far away to destinations unreachable, as the ghosts of the mind cannot be outrun. Most, though, elected to walk. This common action proved difficult and felt wholly foreign after an eternity spent as an ornament. Some had been there for so long that they had simply forgotten the world outside of the trees, and so they knew not even the desire to leave. Others were plagued by phantom images of the Spirit Ripper, and hid like frightened children from every shadow. Under brush and behind tree stumps they silently crouched, suspicious of every movement, with eyes wide and ablaze with the insanity brought about from the hellish nature of the grove. The ground became a place of peril, as those whose minds had grown feral were quick to violence, and among the entanglement of the trees and souls sent adrift, the Wastes did roam.

Cries swam through the trees in voices of both relief and dread, and, for this ominous melody, Amil's step was halted. He hadn't advanced far into the orchard, just deep enough for the shadows to swallow him, when he realized that his damaged body, and all its tired bones, made him defenseless. Profanely blessed with good health during his journey through The House of the Divine, he truly had forgotten what a painful labor it was to get around. His joints screamed for rest. His head pounded. His poor vision blurred the danger around him and cast pins into his temples. His faulty hearing left him vulnerable, and the fractured speech produced by his tongue barely gave him the ability to call for help, though he doubted anyone would rush toward the sounds of screaming.

Amil felt as the false sensation of a nervous sweat left his skin. His nerves twitched with unease, as it occurred to him that he might have come this far to be eaten by a Waste. Nothing had the power to spare him. He had no key or means of escape. Strength was an exhausted gift, and even the Spirit Ripper no longer remained to guard this perverted garden. It became frighteningly likely, inevitable, perhaps, that he would finally meet his end at the jaws of Wastes. As Amil was made to weep for this irony, his focus was newly straightened by the sound of a hollow bite.

A small girl, who scampered over the ground like a beast, had snapped at Amil as he staggered too close to her. Her action nearly sent him into a panic, but as he observed her plight, he was filled with nothing but sorrow. She was thirteen, maybe, old enough to come into his eyes as the ghostly version of the woman she would never become. Built from frail bones, she stared at Amil through an avalanche of knotted blonde curls. Dirtied by death, her yellow locks seemed to enhance the ill pallor of her face. Pathetically, she hid behind a bulbous root that arched itself up from the soil. It was coiled over with vine, and, through stems, leaves, and hair, Amil saw her feral eyes.

She was savage, like a beaten and neglected dog, and here in this wilderness, her young mind had come of age. Though not a Waste, she had already been stripped of humanity. Dirt was packed under her nails as she had used them to dig holes and forage for food like a beast. Her skin had turned rough from a lack of care or shelter, and as she snarled and hissed, she exposed the temperament of a mind gone rabid.

Upon his unsteady legs, Amil stepped a few paces away from her. He bent down and raised a fallen branch from the soil, and as his body straightened back up with complaint, the girl barked a warning. He poked the stick into the ground and wrapped his fingers tightly around the top. With his free hand, he snapped off most of the twigs, and with weary eyes set upon the girl, Amil tested the strength of his cane. Satisfied that it would not snap under his weight, he turned away. He left the territory claimed by the broken child and hobbled farther on into the heart of the orchard.

Along his toil, a few women begged assistance of him. Quietly, he denied each request. Though he had traveled deep into the mansion beyond, Amil gave no guidance to the lost. Shouts for help were hurled upon him from those not able to unfetter themselves from the grip of the trees, but their desperate pleas were ignored as well. He felt like a monster, and maybe he was, but Amil's body was a useless machine, his mind emptied of compassion. He had come to harbor nothing more complex than the stubborn will required to drag him back to Ali.

"Help me, you bastard!" a woman shrieked, as he passed her by.

He stopped and turned slowly. Her plea was no more shrill or desperate than the many others that he had chosen to ignore, and Amil wasn't exactly sure why he had paid her any mind, but it was an act which he quickly regretted. Nails had been pounded through her torso, and, as her thin arms reached out for him, the pins sunk through her gut stretched the skin and tore open old wounds. She yelped and flailed. She beat her fists against the bark and kicked her feet into the air. Amil focused on her eyes. She had been blinded, as two spikes had been driven through her skull and into the tree. He hung his head in shame and felt as vomit bubbled in his throat. It wasn't from physical sickness that this nausea was felt. It came from a place more intangible. This feeling impressed upon him that all that was once redeemable inside him was about to be purged.

"I'm sorry," he whispered. "I can't even help myself."

The activity in the orchard started to wane as Amil pressed deeper into the embrace of the darkness. The dismal clouds overhead remained in place, as though frozen to the background of the sky, and the crows slept upon stilled branches. This area was quiet, deserted, almost, as many of the women had already fled. Perhaps those once wrapped in bondage here had viewed the grisly end of Saint Calvino. It was a horrible thought to entertain, that human eyes could be subjected to such an event. Amil strained to keep the visuals from his mind. However, he could not help but see Aphelianna, overtaken by murderous lust, as she tore to pieces the body of the God of Love.

An unsettling stillness fell over the orchard. The branches didn't shift, and the brush around Amil went undisturbed. This should have comforted him, for where there is no noise, there is not a Waste. But as the voices of other humans faded away, and as the calls of the crows grew softer in the distance, he felt as a chill settled over his skin. This wasn't a place where sound grew weary, it was a place already forgotten. Abandoned, and set aside for only the company of the eternally forsaken. And there, a few empty rows from where he stood, hung Ali, cold and frightened.

Over time, her body had slid down the tree. Almost to the ground she hung, as evidenced by red trails of dried blood that lined her tree. Her small shoulders were rough with the damage caused by the crows' kisses, and the knotted rags that strapped her to the tree were wet with rain. Ali's limp hair clung to her pale skin, and as the water lazily coursed its way down her body, Amil saw as she shivered.

She continued to stare up to the sky, an empty expression in her eyes, as though no time had passed between this moment and the day that Amil crumpled to her feet. She seemed totally unaware of the fact that the others had gone. He was made sick by this realization. That no one else had cared to help Ali. He was then propped up by an idea that felt naïve as it swirled inside him. Maybe she had refused the charity of others. Possibly somewhere in her jumbled mind, she still thought of Amil. Perhaps she had waited for him.

He undid the knots that ensnared her freedom, and,

without a word, Ali remained rigid and still as Amil's wet fingers pulled at the dirtied ribbons of cloth. Like a doll knocked from a shelf, she fell into his arms. Her paltry weight was enough to jar his body from balance, and so onto the cool soil, fitted with tree roots and damp leaves, the pair did fall. Lost like a frightened child among the darkening forest that enveloped her, Ali pulled her body into a ball as she clung to Amil. It was not love or remembrance that drove her action. It was simply fear that forcefully nuzzled her into his chest. He tightened his grip around Ali's marked back and kissed her forehead. He pushed the damp bands of hair from her eyes and gazed down upon her.

Her eyes shook in their sockets, as though her scattered mind frantically tried to assign meaning to the face of the man above her. Her mouth moved as though it desired words, and, as her lips cracked open, Amil heard as the chill nestled in her body commanded her teeth to chatter. He removed his shirt and draped it over her. It clung to her like a shroud carelessly flung over the body of one deemed insignificant. As Amil pressed the brunette hair firmly against his face, he heard a small sound break its way out of Ali's throat.

"Am, am, Amil?" she said, unaware of what the word truly meant.

"Yes, Ali. It's...me, Amil. I love y...you so much, I love you so m...m...much," he sniveled.

"I'm so cold," she cried, as she pulled herself tighter to him.

"It's...okay, it's...o...okay now," he whispered, and rocked her gently.

"What do we do now?" she asked wearily, as her eyes drifted slowly over the dark spaces between the trees and up to the angry sky above.

"I...I...don't know...Ali. I don't know."

- END -

Acknowledgements

As always, thanks to Meghan Miller for her incredible editing work.

Special thanks go out to my friends and family: Mom, Dad, my hilarious sister, Pudge, and my wonderful girlfriend, Rachel. You guys are the best.

About the author

Rich Hayden was born and raised in Pittsburgh, PA, and still resides in the area with Rachel and a couple of ridiculous cats. *Curse* is his second novel.

Other titles by Rich Hayden

CrimeSpree – 2015
> ISBN# 978-0-9963969-1-2 (paperback)
> ISBN# 978-0-9963969-0-5 (E-book)

Website:
http://hayden428.wixsite.com/richhayden

Rich Hayden

Curse

Synopsis:

Amil Young was born into poverty and disadvantage. His hometown, Fog Lake, was gripped deep within the dark shadows of the Appalachian Mountains. The ridges and thick woods encircled the moribund town like a prison built of stone and bark. But a charmed turn of fate saw fit to deliver Amil from the mud and misery of Fog Lake.

Fleeting though it was, success was found in the game of baseball. His fame lasted barely the fifteen minutes all are promised, but it proved enough time to unfetter him from the shackles of Fog Lake. He left the mountains behind, settled down, and started life anew.

Happiness and domestic security showered their gifts over Amil and his girlfriend, Ali. Two individuals, once broken, came together to form one life, a full and vibrant companionship that seemed destined to endure into the reaches of old age.

With the passing of the years, old ghosts resurfaced to haunt the couple. The knives of the past tore at the union of Amil and Ali until their bond was severed. Black days descended over the pair, and the guilt of his many failures grafted itself to Amil. A great many things cast shame over him, but it was his violent betrayal of Ali that he could no longer carry. At thirty-seven years of age, Amil took his life.

Lost among the desolation of the afterlife, Amil encountered horrors he could have never imagined while alive. He learned of a new world cut to ribbons by treason, and a pantheon of gods, now feckless, undone by one of their own. However, it was the myriad arrows of time that would serve to most torment him. He found Ali there among the ruin. It seemed cruelly impossible. When Amil elected to take his leave of mortality, Ali was young, decades of life ahead of her.

Suicide was an exercise designed to rid his mind of vexation. Instead, it had dropped Amil into a challenge, so vast that none before had ever known victory. To free Ali from her suffering, for the chance to set right all he had destroyed, Amil made a deal with the Goddess of death, Aphelianna. With fragile promises of a second chance, she offered Amil a quest.

Her challenge would send him deep into the land of the dead and back through the fragmented halls of a history nearly forgotten. His target was a key, the sole treasure of Aphelianna's sister, Isadora, the Goddess of life. Amil knew better than to trust the words of Death, but, for Ali, he was willing to forsake anything. However, if he were to succeed and place the key of life into the hands of wicked Aphelianna, everything would prove to be the price. And Amil, a mere man, would come to learn the truth of what everything and evermore come to mean when viewed through the eyes of an immortal.

www.ingramcontent.com/pod-product-compliance
Lightning Source LLC
Chambersburg PA
CBHW061310170626
46817CB00001B/124